ISAAC ASIMOV INTRODUCES A FRIEND. . . ROBERT SILVERBERG

"If there is one thing I like to do, it is to beam condescendingly down upon bright young authors who enter my field; that is, science fiction. There is something delightful about unbending from my awesome height as established master in the genre (I am Isaac Asimov, by the way, if you haven't already guessed) to encourage some eager young person who has set his shaky foot upon the path I have myself trod so sure-footedly and so far.

I was all set to do this to young Robert Silverberg when he began to publish science fiction stories in the middle 1950's. I prepared my little speech, one that was not too awe-inspiring, of course, but yet with just a touch of necessary dignity, and was set.

And then what do you suppose the miserable ungrateful creature went and did? He zoomed upward at rocket velocities!

I was just bending down to pat him on the head when he whizzed by and nearly took the skin off my nose. When I leaned back and looked upward, there was Robert Silverberg—a first-magnitude star in the science fiction heavens. He went from mere fan to bigtime writer in exactly zero time."

INVADERS FROM EARTH
AND TO WORLDS BEYOND

ROBERT SILVERBERG

SF
ace books
A Division of Charter Communications Inc.
A GROSSET & DUNLAP COMPANY
360 Park Avenue South
New York, New York 10010

INVADERS FROM EARTH
Copyright © 1958 by Ace Books, Inc.
TO WORLDS BEYOND
Copyright © 1965 by Robert Silverberg

An ACE Book
First Ace printing: April 1980

2 4 6 8 0 9 7 5 3 1
Manufactured in the United States of America

INVADERS FROM EARTH

1

TED KENNEDY had a premonition the night before. It came, as so many premonitions do, in the form of a dream. Guns blazed, innocent people died, fire spread over the land. Looming thermonuclear mushrooms hung in the skies. He stirred fitfully, sighed, nearly awoke, and sank back into sleep. But when morning came he felt pale and weary; he ended the insistent buzz of the alarm with an impatient wrist-snap and dangled his legs over the edge of the bed, rubbing his eyes. The sound of splashing water told him that his wife was already awake and in the shower.

He had never awakened easily. Still groggy, he shambled across the bedroom to the cedar chest, groped for his robe, and headed for the kitchen. He punched buttons on the autocook, setting up breakfast. One of these mornings, he thought wryly, he'd be so sleepy he'd order steak sandwiches on toast instead of the usual bacon.

Marge was out of the shower and drying herself with all her awesome early-morning vigor when he returned to the bedroom to dress.

"Breakfast up?" she asked.

Kennedy nodded and fumbled in the closet for his best suit, the dark green one with red lace trim. He would need to look good today; whatever the conference on Floor Nine was, it was bound to be important, and it wasn't every day a third-level public relations man got summoned to Floor Nine.

"You must have had a bad dream last night," Marge said suddenly. "I can tell. You're still brooding over it."

"I know. Did I wake you up?"

She smiled, the bright sudden smile that so astonished him at 5 A.M. They had always been different that way—he the late riser who was still fresh long past midnight; she buoyant and lively from the earliest morning hours till the middle of the evening. "You didn't wake me up, no. But I can see the dream's still with you. Tell me about it—and hurry up. You don't want to miss the car pool."

"I dreamed we were at war," he said.

"War? With whom?"

He hesitated. "I don't know. I mean, I don't remember any of the motivation. But it was a terrible war . . . and I have the nagging feeling *we* started it."

"How could there possibly be a war? Everyone's at peace, darling! It's been that way for years. There aren't going to be any more wars on Earth, Ted."

"Maybe not on Earth," he said darkly.

He tried to laugh it off, and by the time he had finished breakfast some of the irrational fear-tide had begun to recede. They ate quietly. Kennedy was never much of a breakfast-table conversationalist. It was nearly 6 A.M. by the time they finished and Marge had dumped the dishes into the washer; the sun was rising now over the low Connecticut hills. He finished dressing, tugging at his collar to keep his braided throat-cord from throttling him, and gave his epaulets a light dusting of powdered gold. Marge remained in her gown; she worked at home, designing house furnishings and draperies.

At 6:18 sharp he was on the porch of his home, and at 6:20 the shiny yellow '44 Chevrolet-Cadillac drew up outside, Alf Haugen at the wheel. Haugen, a stocky, meaty-faced man with bright sharp eyes, worked at the desk behind Kennedy's in the Steward and Dinoli office, and this was his week to drive the car-pool auto. Of the six of them, Haugen had by far the best car, and he enjoyed flaunting it.

Kennedy half-trotted down the walk to Haugen's car. He glanced back and waved at Marge, noting with some annoyance that she had gone out on the porch wearing only her filmy morning gown. Some of the men in the car were bachelors, and, unlike Haugen, Kennedy didn't believe in flaunting his treasures openly. Marge was a handsome woman, but he felt no urge to demonstrate that fact to Lloyd Presslie or Dave Spalding, or to any of them for that matter.

He slid into the back of the car; Presslie and Mike Cameron moved over to make room for him. Haugen nudged the start-button, the turboelectrics thrummed, and the car headed smoothly off toward the city.

Apparently, Spalding had been in the middle of some joke when they stopped to pick up Kennedy.

Now he reached the punch-line and the five of them, everyone in the car but Kennedy, laughed.

Kennedy disliked Spalding. The slim young fourth-level man lived in the apartment development three miles further along the road; he was unmarried, deeply intense about most subjects, and almost never let anyone know what he might actually be thinking. It was not a trait that endeared him to people, which was probably why he was still only a fourth-level man after three years at Steward and Dinoli. It was no secret that old Dinoli preferred outgoing types, married, in his higher levels.

"Any of you know anything about the big deal brewing today?" Mike Cameron asked suddenly.

Kennedy jerked his head to the left. "What big deal? Did you get invited to Floor Nine, too?"

Cameron nodded. "We all were. Even Spalding. I guess Dinoli sent that memo to the whole third and fourth level yesterday afternoon. Something big's brewing, mark my words, friends!"

"Maybe the agency's dissolving," Lloyd Presslie suggested sourly. "Or maybe Dinoli hired a bunch of top-level men away from Crawford and Burstein and we're all being bounced down three notches."

Haugen shook his head. "It's some big new account the old man landed. I heard Lucille talking about it near closing time. Whenever you're in doubt, ask Dinoli's secretary." He laughed coarsely. "And if she's reluctant to spout, pinch her a little."

The car swung into the main artery of the Thruway. Kennedy peered pensively out the window at the towns flashing by, a hundred feet below the gleaming white ribbon of the main road. He said little. The thunderburst of H-bombs echoed in his ears, souvenir of the past night's dreaming, and in any event he still felt drugged by sleep.

Some big new account. Well, even so, that shouldn't affect him. He had started handling public relations for Federated Bauxite Mines only last week —a long-range project whose ultimate aim was to convince the people of a large Nebraska district that their economy wouldn't be upset and their water supply polluted by the local aluminum-seekers who had newly invaded their district. He had just scarcely begun preliminary research; they wouldn't yank him off the account so soon.

Or would they?

There was no predicting what Dinoli might do. Public relations was a tricky, fast-moving field, and its province of operations was expanding all the time.

Kennedy felt strangely tense, and for once the smooth purr of the throbbing generators beneath him failed to ease his nerves.

It was 6:52 A.M. when Haugen's car rolled off the Thruway and rode down the long slanting ramp that led into upper Manhattan. At 6:54 the car had reached the corner of 123rd and Lenox, in the heart of the business district. The gleaming white tower that housed Steward and Dinoli was before them. They left the car, Haugen turning it over to attendants who would park it on the second floor of the building.

At 6:57 they were in the elevator; by 6:59, they had reached the front door of Steward and Dinoli, and precisely at 7 A.M. Kennedy and his five car-pool companions were at their desks.

Kennedy's working day lasted from 7:00 to 2:30.

This year, by city ordinance, public relations and advertising men worked early shift; come January 1, 2045, they would move up an hour to the 8 A.M. group. Only a stagger-system such as this prevented frightful congestion in the enormous city. To have every worker in the city report to his office and leave at the same hour was unthinkable.

Kennedy's desk was neatly arranged, as he had left it yesterday afternoon. The memo from Mr. Dinoli lay pigeon-holed in the catchall to his right; he unspindled it and read through it again.

Floor Nine
2:12 P.M.

Dear Theodore:
Would you be good enough to come downstairs to my office tomorrow morning, at 9 o'clock or thereabouts? A matter of some urgency is on the docket, and I think you're one of the men who can help.
Thanks—and best to your wife. We ought to get together more often socially.
LD:lk

Lou

Kennedy smiled and dropped the note into his ready file. He was hardly fooled by the cheery tone or by the affable "Lou"; Dinoli amused himself by keeping up a first-name relationship with the second- and third-level men, but Kennedy knew he had as much chance of ever seeing the agency head socially as he did of becoming a star center-fielder for a big-league baseball team. There was a certain gulf, and that gulf was *never* bridged.

The casual "or thereabouts" in the note was to be

ignored, Kennedy knew: he arrived at Floor Nine at 9 A.M. *sharp,* or else he bounced back to fifth-level in a hurry. You learned punctuality around Dinoli.

The morning passed slowly; Kennedy was expecting a telestat report on the situation in Nebraska from one of the agency's field operatives, but this wasn't due to arrive until one. To kill time, he doodled up a few possible opening gambits for the campaign there, centering them around a standard point of reference: What's Good For Big Corporations (in this case, Federated Bauxite) Is Very Good For You.

His mind wasn't fully on his work, though. By 8:15 he realized he wasn't going to get anything done on the current project until he'd had that meeting with Dinoli, and he shut up his folders and filed them away. There was no sense working on a project with his mind clogged by anxiety. Public relations was a difficult job and Kennedy took it seriously, as he took most other things.

At five to nine he shoved back his rollchair, locked his desk, and crossed the floor to Alf Haugen's desk. Haugen had already shut up shop; there was a look of keen expectancy on his heavy-jowled face.

"Going down to see Dinoli?" Haugen asked casually.

Kennedy nodded. "It's pushing 9 A.M. The old man wouldn't want us to be late."

Together they walked down the brightly lit office, past the empty desks of Cameron and Presslie, who apparently had already gone downstairs. They emerged in the less attractive outer office where the fourth-level men worked, and there Spalding joined them.

"I guess I'm the only one on my level going," he whispered confidentially. "None of the others are budging from their desks, and it's two minutes to nine."

They crossed the hall to the elevator bank and snared a downgoing car. Kennedy saw that the four private offices in which the agency's second-level men worked were dim and unlit; that probably meant they had spent the entire morning with Dinoli.

Steward and Dinoli occupied four floors of the building. Dinoli's office (Steward had long since been eased out of control, and indeed out of any connection whatsoever with the firm) was at the bottom of the heap, taking up all of Floor Nine. Floor Ten was the agency's library and storage vault; Kennedy worked on Eleven, and the fifth-, sixth-, and seventh-level underlings labored in the crowded little cubicles on Floor Twelve.

The elevator opened into a luxurious oak-paneled foyer on Floor Nine. A smiling secretary, one of Dinoli's flock of bosomy young females, met them there. "You have an appointment with the chief," she said, not asking but telling. "Won't you come this way?"

She led them, Kennedy first, followed by Haugen and Spalding, through the vast salon which served Dinoli by way of a vestibule and waiting room, then into the narrower corridor where tiny television cameras studied them as they approached. Kennedy heard relays click shut as he went past; the spy-system had passed on him, it seemed.

Dinoli's office door was a thick plank of rich-grained oak, in which a tiny gold plaque reading

L. D. Dinoli was deeply inset. The door swung open as they drew near.

The vista thus revealed had always seemed breath-taking to Kennedy. Dinoli's private office was a room five times as long as it was broad, which seemed to swing away into the reaches of infinity. A giant picture window, always immaculate, gave access to a panoramic view of Manhattan's bustling streets.

Dinoli himself sat at the head of a long, burnished table. He was a small, piercing-eyed man of sixty-six, his face lean and fleshless and surmounted by a massive hook of a nose. Wrinkles spread almost concentrically from that mighty nose, like elevation-lines on a geological contour map. Dinoli radiated energy.

"Ah, gentlemen. Won't you come in and be seated." Again, statements, not questions. His voice was a deep black-sounding one, half croak and half boom.

Immediately at Dinoli's right and left hands sat the agency's four second-level men. Dinoli, of course, occupied the lofty eminence of the first level alone. After the second-level boys came those of the third: Presslie, Cameron, and four others. Kennedy took a seat near Cameron, and Haugen slipped in across the table facing him. Spalding sat to Kennedy's right. He was the only jarring figure in the otherwise neat pyramid, which began with Dinoli, sloped to the four second-level men, and was based on the eight third-level executives.

"We're all here, then," Dinoli said calmly. The clock over his head, just above the upper rim of the picture window, read 9:00:00. It was the only clock Kennedy had ever seen that gave the time in seconds elapsed, as well as minutes and hours. "Gentlemen,

I'd like you to meet our new clients, if you will." His clawlike forefinger nudged a button on the elaborate control panel near his hand.

A rear door opened. Three elegant men in crisp green full-dress executive uniforms entered, stiffly erect, conscious of their rank and bearing. They were cold-eyed, hard-looking men. Poised, mildly contemptuous of their hosts, they stood by the door.

"Our newest clients," Dinoli announced. "These gentlemen are from the Extraterrestrial Development and Exploration Corporation, Ganymede Division."

Despite himself, Kennedy shuddered faintly. The image of crashing cities flickered once again before his eyes, and he wondered if perhaps his premonition had held some truth.

2

Dinoli looked marvelously proud of himself. His beady eyes darted here and there through the room, fixing on each man at least once, as he prepared to deliver himself of the details of his latest coup.

Kennedy had to feel a sharp twinge of admiration for the savage old battler. Dinoli had clawed himself to first rank in public relations by sheer vigorous exertion, coupled with some judicious backstabbing; to be affiliated at all with him, whether on third-level or sixth, was a measure of distinction in the field.

"Executive Second-Level Hubbel of Public Liaison. Executive Second-Level Partridge of Public Liaison. Executive Second-Level Brewster of the Corporation's Space Expeditionary Command." Dinoli indicated each of the men with a quick birdlike hand gesture.

Kennedy studied them. Hubbel and Partridge were obviously desk men, fiftyish, well built and on the stout side, both of them deeply, and probably artificially, tanned. They looked formidably competent.

Brewster was a different item, though. Short and compact, he was a dark-faced little man who stood

ramrod straight, hard, cold eyes peering at the group
out of a lean, angular face. He looked tough, and the
heavy tan on his cheeks was convincing.

Of course! Kennedy thought, with a sudden shock
of wonder. *The space explorer!*

"As members of my staff," Dinoli said, "you all
know well that anything you may be told in the confines of this room is absolutely confidential. I trust
that's understood, gentlemen. Otherwise get out."

Thirteen heads went up-down affirmatively.

"Good. May I say by way of preface that this is
perhaps the biggest and most important job Steward
and Dinoli has ever handled—perhaps the biggest S
and D will *ever* handle. Every PR firm in the nation
was canvassed for this job before we landed the contract. I needn't add that successful handling of this
new account will result in substantial upward alter-
ations in the individual status increments of those
men working on it."

Dinoli paused a long moment. The old man was a
master of the dramatic approach. He said at length,
"To fill you in on the background, first: Executive
Brewster has recently returned from a space journey
sponsored by his Corporation. The Major was connected with the Mars expedition, of course, and with
the less successful Venus mission that preceded it—
and I might add that his heroism was a major factor
in minimizing losses on the unfortunate Venus encounter. Executive Brewster's third and most recent
Corporation-sponsored mission was to Ganymede—
which is, of course, the largest of the moons of our
great planetary neighbor Jupiter."

Kennedy wrinkled his brows in surprise; Dinoli
seemed to catch the expression, and shot a terrifying

glance at him. The old man said smoothly, "The existence of this third interplanetary mission is still secret. The poor publicity aroused by the Venus mission was a factor influencing the Corporation to suppress information on the Ganymede trip until its successful conclusion."

Dinoli made an almost imperceptible gesture and a motion-picture screen unreeled itself in the back of the great room. "Executive Brewster has brought us a film of his activities on Ganymede. I'd like all of us to see this film before we go any further in this meeting."

Two of Dinoli's young undersecretaries appeared, pushing a sliding table on which was mounted a movie projector. One girl deftly set up the projector while another pressed the control that would opaque the picture window. The room grew dim; Dinoli signaled and the remaining lights were extinguished. Kennedy turned in his seat to see the screen.

The projector hummed.

A PRODUCTION OF THE EXTRATER-
RESTRIAL DEVELOPMENT AND EX-
PLORATION CORPORATION, GANYMEDE
DIVISION

said the opening title, against a pulsing background of red, white, and blue. Credit-lines followed. And then, quite suddenly, Kennedy found himself staring at an alien landscape, oddly quiet, oddly disturbing.

Bleak whiteness confronted him: the whiteness of an almost endless snowfield, beneath a pale blue sky. Jagged mountain ranges, rock-bare and snow-topped, loomed in the distance. Clouds of gray-green gas swirled past the eye of the camera.

"This is the surface of Ganymede," came the attractively resonant voice of Brewster. "As you can see, frozen ammoniamethane snow covers the ground in most areas. Ganymede, of course, is virtually planetary in size—its diameter is thirty-two hundred miles, which is slightly more than that of Mercury. We found the gravitation to be fairly close to that of Earth, incidentally. Ganymede's a heavy-core planet, probably torn out of Jupiter's heart at the time the system was formed."

As he spoke, the camera's eye moved on, and Kennedy's with it: on to examine the fine striations in an outcropping of rock, on to peer down at a tiny, determined lichen clinging to the side of an upthrust tongue of basalt.

Suddenly the camera whirled dizzyingly upward for a look at the sky. Kennedy was jolted. Jupiter filled a vast segment of the sky, a great heavy ball hanging like a brooding giant just above.

"Ganymede was about six hundred and fifty thousand miles distant from Jupiter at the time of this film's making," Brewster said dryly. "At this distance Jupiter takes up quite a chunk of the heavens."

Kennedy stared uneasily at the monstrous cloud-wrapped planet, whose velvety pearl-gray surface gave hint of unimaginable turbulence deep beneath the outer band of atmosphere. To his relief, the camera finally left the huge world and returned to the Ganymedean landscape.

For perhaps five minutes more the film drifted on over the lonely, bleak land. Then eight spacesuit-clad figures appeared, faces nearly hidden behind their breathing masks, bodies shrouded by the metal-impregnated suits.

"The members of the expedition," Brewster commented.

The camera panned to a spaceship, standing slim and tall on a bare patch of rock. The ship bore dark green numerals painted on its shining silver flank.

"The expeditionary ship," Brewster said.

After a survey of the outer skin of the ship from various angles, and a few more glimpses of the spacesuit-clad crewmen, the camera shifted to pick up a strangely cold-looking pool of greasy liquid.

"One of the occasional Ganymedean paraffin lakes," said Brewster.

The camera skirted the pool's edge, doubled back through a snowfield, and centered suddenly on four weird figures—four creatures vaguely man-shaped, their faces noseless, their eyes hooded by folds of flesh. They were pale white in color, hairless, virtually naked except for some sort of woven cloth girdle round their middles. They were staring sadly at the camera, faces devoid of any understandable expressions.

"These are the natives of Ganymede," Brewster remarked blandly.

Brewster had certainly underplayed it. It took three or four seconds for the effect of his quiet words to make itself known, and then Kennedy felt as if he'd been bashed in the stomach by a battering ram. He had been watching the film intently enough, but superficially—observing it in a detached manner, since the mere sight of alien landscapes was not enough to involve him deeply. But now, suddenly, to have alien life sprung on him. . . .

The Venus expedition had been a dismal failure, mechanical difficulties making it nearly impossible for the explorers to cope with the formaldehyde soup that was Venus' atmosphere. But in their short stay they had definitely verified the fact that there was no animal life on the second planet.

Mars, too, had proved barren, despite the hopes of many. A few lichens, a few podded weeds that survived in the near vacuum, but nothing else. Humanity, and Ted Kennedy, had begun to decide that man was alone in the Solar System, and possibly in the universe.

And now, suddenly—

"The Ganymedeans are a primitive people living in sprawling villages of a few thousand inhabitants each," Brewster said, in a standard travelogue manner. "They seem to cover the entire land mass of Ganymede, which is distributed over three continents. We estimated their numbers at about twenty-five million."

Moistening his lips, Kennedy stared at the four alien beings against the alien backdrop of methane snow. He still had no idea what possible tie-in Dinoli had with all this, but he was waiting.

"During our stay," Brewster went on, "we learned the rudiments of their language. It's a fairly simple agglutinating tongue, and our linguists are at work on it now. We discovered that the Ganymedeans have a working clan system, with sharp tribal rivalries, and also that they show neither any particular fear nor any liking for us. The expeditionary geologist's report shows that Ganymede is exceptionally rich in radioactive minerals. Thank you."

The film came abruptly to its end with the last

word of Brewster's sentence. The light went on, dazzling Kennedy's eyes; the secretaries appeared from somewhere, deopaqued the big window, and wheeled the projector out. The screen vanished into its recess in the ceiling.

In less than a minute the room was as it had been before. But none of its occupants were quite the same.

Dinoli leaned forward, his eyes glittering brightly. "I think you begin to see the magnitude of what's unfolding before us, men."

Kennedy squirmed uneasily in his contour chair. He saw some of the implications—particularly in that punch-line Brewster had tacked on to his little travelogue. *The expeditionary geologist's report shows that Ganymede is exceptionally rich in radioactive minerals.*

The way he had said it as a *non sequitur* made the fact seem almost irrelevant. Kennedy had a good ear for seeming irrelevancies; ultimately, they often turned out to be of critical importance in the case.

Dinoli glanced at the taller and fatter of the two liaison men and said, "Now, Executive Hubbel, will you fill my men in one some of the implications to be drawn from this situation on Ganymede?"

Hubbel coughed ostentatiously. "You've seen the existence of alien life on this planet-sized moon. You've seen also that Ganymede holds exceptional mineral wealth, which our Corporation proposes to mine in the name of the public good by virtue of our U.N. charter agreement. We've gone to considerable expense developing and outfitting ships to explore space, and naturally we're counting on recouping our expenditures on Ganymede. Partridge?"

The other blinked like a sleepy cougar and said

smoothly, "We feel there may be certain difficulties in obtaining mining rights from the Ganymedeans."

Suddenly Kennedy began to understand. He felt a muscle in his right calf start to quiver.

Dinoli grinned triumphantly. "Here's where *we* come in, boys. There might be conflict—conflict with the obstinate Ganymedeans. Some people might call that a war of aggression. Actually, of course, it's sheer *necessity*. We need what Ganymede has; the Corporation has sunk billions into opening up space for humanity. You understand this. You're all clever men. That's why you work here instead of for a second-rate outfit."

Partridge said, "Naturally, the people might not sympathize with our plea of necessity. They might think we were imperialistic."

"This impression would of course have to be counteracted by careful public relations management," Hubbel said thoughtfully, putting a cap on the whole thing.

"And we've been chosen to handle it," finished Dinoli.

That was it. That was all there was to it.

Kennedy kept his face blank of emotional reaction. The "agency mask," Marge called it privately. What Marge didn't know was that frequently the agency mask hid an equal blankness of inner feeling. Kennedy suspended judgment, waiting to hear more.

"We plan an intensive worldwide blanketing," Dinoli said. "These gentlemen will be working closely with us at all times. Specific target dates have already been set up. There's a date on which first knowledge of the existence of life on Ganymede will be given to the public—almost immediately, I can tell you—and there's a terminal date on which the

3

THE WARM, cheerful, expensive odor of real food filtered through the Kennedy household. Marge bustled about the kitchen, setting the table, while the autochef prepared the meal. They were having shoulder steak, mashed potatoes, garden peas. Nothing on the menu was synthetic; with so many S and D men living clustered in this one Connecticut township, Kennedy could never allow himself the risk of having someone discover he used synthetics. Personally he saw little difference in taste, and an enormous one in price—but prestige was important too, and had to be considered. Third-level men *never* ate synthetics.

"Supper's almost ready," Marge called. She was a brisk, efficient housekeeper.

Kennedy drained the remainder of his pre-dinner cocktail, scratched the cat behind the ears, and flipped a switch on the master control panel of the sound system, cutting out the three living-room speakers and switching the output to the dining area. The playful flutes of Bach's Second Brandenburg came piping out of the other room, accompanied by Marge's lilting, somewhat off-pitch humming.

Kennedy entered the bathroom and jammed his

hands into the handkleen socket. The day's grime peeled away. He caught a glimpse of his face, pale, too thin, wrinkles already beginning to form around the eyes even at thirty-two. He wondered if he had always looked this bad; probably not, he admitted.

The handkleen's gentle purr died away. He shook his hands in the unbreakable drying gesture, pointless but habitual, and crossed over into the dining area. Marge was bringing the plates to the table.

"It's Spalding I don't understand," Kennedy said, abruptly reopening a conversation of an hour before. "Here he is, a fourth-level man jerked up to third just to work on this project, and he's sour as hell on it."

"Maybe Dave isn't interested in the project."

"Maybe—huh? What does *that* have to do with it? Any PR man worth his pay can damn well *get* interested in any sort of project. You think I cared about the good folk of Nebraska when I took on that Bauxite deal?"

"No."

"Exactly. And yet within two weeks," Kennedy said, "I was so wrapped up in that project, so identified with it, that it actually *hurt* to be pulled off it and put onto this. Can you understand that?"

Marge smiled sweetly. "I think I can grasp the general picture. But you say Dave's not anxious to work on the new contract? There must be some good reason for that."

"It's the same reason that keeps him down in fourth-level, when he should be in third." Kennedy attacked his meat fiercely, and after a moment went on. "He doesn't have the right spirit. Talent, yes— but that intangible *extra*, no. And don't think Dinoli doesn't know that. I wouldn't be surprised if Dave was put on this thing just as a test—either he delivers the goods now, with third-level responsibilities, or out he goes."

"I've always thought Dave was too sensitive for PR work," Marge said.

"Implying I'm not a sensitive man?"

She shrugged. "Your potatoes are getting cold, darling. Of course you're sensitive, but in a different way. You know?"

"No. But drop the subject." Kennedy had never appreciated his wife's fondness for Spalding, and regularly tried to avoid the necessity of inviting him to their house.

"I suppose Alf Haugen's wild with enthusiasm over the new contract," Marge said.

"Alf's a company-first man. If they gave him the job of selling humanity on turning cannibal, he'd take it on if they boosted his salary. Naturally he's enthusiastic. He'll do anything Dinoli tells him to do, provided there's a buck in it for him."

Bach ended. The robot arms of the sound system gently lifted the record from the turntable and replaced it with an early Beethoven quartet. Kennedy was old-fashioned that way; he still bought discs, rather than tapes.

"You haven't told me what this contract's about yet, you know," Marge said quietly.

Kennedy paused, fork in hand. "It's classified. Top confidential."

She pouted. "You've done classified work before. Have I ever let it spill?"

"This is different," he said slowly. "This absolutely must not leak. I can't, Marge."

They were both silent for a moment, Kennedy

knowing that the real reason why he refused to tell her was not that it was classified—he had never kept secrets from her before—but that she would think the project was ugly and brutal. He had always tried to shield her from brutality, even though he knew in some respects she was tougher and more resilient than he was.

"All right," Marge said. *"Don't* tell me. Marie Haugen will. That blabbermouth can't keep quiet for—"

"Marie won't know. Alf won't tell her." Even as he said it, he knew how foolish the words sounded. The food in his stomach felt as if it were curdling. He shook his head bitterly. "Marge, can't you take a straight *no?"*

"If I have to," she said, sighing. She began to clear away the dishes. Kennedy could tell from the sudden angularity of her motions that she was angry.

He shut his eyes for a moment, thinking, looking for the strength to tell her. They had been married eight years—were married on the evening of his college graduation, in 2036. He held a Bachelor of Communications from Northwestern, and, finishing first in his graduating class, had eagerly accepted the bid to come East and work for Steward and Dinoli as a fifth-level man.

Eight years, and he had worked up to third-level, with second perhaps just a few years away. He had tried to be perfectly frank with Marge on all matters, and she loved and respected him for it. But now . . .

He was damned either way. There'd be a wedge between them if he refused to tell her, and perhaps a wider gulf if he did. He began to sweat.

"Come here, Marge," he said in a hoarse voice.

"Sit down. I'll tell you about this new contract."

She sat opposite him, watching him with her clear, dark-blue eyes that had never needed optical correction of any kind. She looked very grave ... like a serious eight-year-old, he thought suddenly.

"Well?"

"There's been a space expedition to Ganymede. That's one of the moons of Jupiter, you know. It's almost big enough to be a planet itself. Well, they've found people on Ganymede—intelligent people."

"How wonderful! What are they like? Have you seen pictures yet? Are they—"

"Wait a second," Kennedy said, his voice dull. "They also found radioactive ores there. The place is literally packed with minerals that Earth needs desperately. Only the natives refuse to permit any mining operations whatsoever. Some tribal nonsense, I guess. So the Corporation may have some trouble. If there's armed resistance they may have to ask the U.N. Army to intervene in their behalf. It's a matter of the public good; they're not using their minerals, and our entire economy is based on them. So S and D was called in to handle a publicity campaign. On the surface, you see, it might look pretty nasty—that the Corporation was greedily aggressive, attacking primitive creatures, and so forth. Naturally we can't have that kind of publicity. So here's where we come in, to smooth everything over, to make it clear that it's a matter of simple need, and—"

He stopped suddenly, catching the expression that flew momentarily across Marge's face. And was that the edge of a tear in the corner of her eye?

"You dreamed about this last night," she said in a soft, barely audible voice. "About war. You even dreamed we started it. Funny, I never believed in supernatural things like this. Until now."

"Marge!"

"You said it would be a terrible war. Innocent people slaughtered. Remember?"

"It won't be a war, Marge. They'll just occupy the place. Peacefully. We can't let all those valuable ores just rot away there, you know."

She looked at him strangely. "Suppose they object to this occupation. What then?"

"Why—why, how can they? They're just primitive alien beings. I don't even think they have explosives, let alone atomics."

"Not one of you has a conscience," Marge said. "Except Dave Spalding. He's the only one that seems to be upset by this. None of the rest of you are. You just see bonuses and status increments." Her voice was wild and sharp now. "Alf Haugen's probably planning to trade in his car for a custom model. That's all he thinks of. And you, Ted—do you think at all?"

She rose from the table, broke away from him suddenly, and ran off into the darkened living room. He heard the cat squeal in surprise and come dashing out of the room, complaining vehemently. It was a very old cat, and disliked noise and motion.

Things were getting out of hand, Kennedy decided. He tiptoed into the living room. In the darkness he made out a dim form lying on the couch that converted each night into their bed. Marge was sobbing quietly.

Frowning, Kennedy sat down on the edge of the couch and let his hand lightly caress the firm muscles of her back.

"Marge," he whispered. "Don't carry on this way. It's just a job. That's all—just a job. I'm not going to be killing Ganymedeans. I won't be carrying a gun. No matter what I say or think or do, it's going to happen anyway. Why take it out on me? Why hurt *us?*"

The sobbing stopped. He knew she was staring sightlessly in the darkness, battling within herself. Finally she sat up. "All right, darling. I'm taking this whole thing much too seriously, I guess." She tried to smile.

He leaned over and kissed her. But it was a tense, uncertain kiss. They had not seen the end of this quarrel so soon, he realized unhappily.

It was pretty much of a lame evening. They had tentative plans to visit neighbors down the road, but Marge was puffy-eyed from crying, and Kennedy had fallen into a brooding mood of introversion that made any socializing a dismal prospect for the evening. He phoned and begged off, claiming urgent work that simply had to be done this very evening.

There were some awkward moments while he helped her put away the dinner dishes; twice, his eyes met hers and he flinched. He felt very tired. The Ganymede contract was going to occupy his attentions for more than a year, and it wasn't going to be healthy for their marriage if they spent the next thirteen months bickering over the moral issues involved in his acceptance of the assignment.

He had long been proud of the fact that his wife had a mind of her own. Her independent thinking was one of the things he loved her for. But, he saw now, it could also get somewhat burdensome. *Perhaps if we'd had children,* he speculated. *Maybe she wouldn't be so touchy about Causes and Movements.* But they had never had children, and probably never would.

They listened to music awhile—Kennedy only half-listening to the Boccherini quintet Marge loved so, and the Schubert octet. She was terribly fond of chamber music. Ordinarily, Kennedy was, too—but tonight it all seemed frilly and foolish.

At five to eight he suggested, "Let's watch video, eh, Marge? We haven't done that in ages. Let's watch some comic, the way we used to years ago."

"Anything you like, dear," she said mechanically.

He dimmed the lights and switched the set on. It was a new set, hardly a year old, a forty-eight-inch job Kennedy had had installed in the wall opposite the couch. Again, a social necessity. They hardly watched it, normally.

A vortex of colored light swirled dizzyingly for an instant, and then the screen cleared. They had tuned in at the tail end of some program, and a gay, sprightly commercial was on. Kennedy found the dancing stick-figures offensive. He drew Marge close against him on the couch, but she was still and unresponsive.

The program ended. The time-bleep bleeped and a deep voice said, "Eight P.M., Eastern Standard Time. From coast to coast, Levree Radionic Watches keep you on time, *all* the time. No gears, no springs."

Again the screen showed the color vortex. Another voice said, "The program normally scheduled for this hour has been canceled to bring you a special Government information release program."

"Let me change the station," Kennedy said. "This'll just be dull junk. We need something funny tonight."

She grasped his arm tightly. "No. Let's see what this is, first. It may be important."

An announcer appeared, white-toothed, neatly tanned, his mustache stained red and meticulously clipped. "Good evening," he said. "This is Don Howell from your network newsroom, bringing you a special program covering the big news story of the day, the year, and possibly the century—the discovery of living intelligent beings on another world of this solar system."

Kennedy stiffened. *Already?* he asked himself. *They're releasing it so soon?*

"We must have missed the news bulletins," Marge said.

". . . was revealed by the President at 4:45 this afternoon, at a special press conference. The news electrified a world long fascinated by the possible existence of life in outer space. Details of the expedition are still coming in. However, it's our privilege to present the first public showing of a special film taken by members of the Ganymede expedition!"

The film was the same one Kennedy had seen in Dinoli's office earlier in the day. This time, though, a slick professional commentary had been dubbed in. The newsbreak, Kennedy thought, was apparently the work of a Dinoli second-level man who'd been preparing it for some days. He thought he recognized Ernie Watsinski's touch in the commentary.

When the film reached the point at which the Ganymedean natives appeared, he heard Marge utter a little gasp. "Why, they're like children!" she said. "Defenseless naked creatures! And these are the beings we're going to make war on?"

"We're just going to occupy their territory," Kennedy said stubbornly. "And probably administer it for them. In the long run they'll be a lot better off for it."

"Unless they don't *want* to be better off," she said. "Or administered."

Kennedy shook his head. The public knew, now; come tomorrow, the behind-the-scenes campaign would begin in the offices of S and D. What shall it profit a man, he wondered bleakly, if he gets promoted to second-level, and loses his own wife in the process?

He pulled her tight against him, and after a few moments of hesitation she turned from the screen to him, with what he hoped was unfaked warmth.

4

THE NEXT DAY was the fourth of May, 2044, and the first day of intensive work on what was rapidly becoming known around S and D as the Ganymede Contract.

The dramatic newsbreak of the night before seemed to be the universal topic of discussion; every telefax sheet, every news commentator, every cab driver, had his own set of opinions on the revelation. Kennedy thought of this time as a kind of primordially formless era, before the shrewd minds of Steward and Dinoli went to work shaping a clear-cut and unified public opinion from the present chaos.

They met in the office of Ernie Watsinski, second-level public-relations man, and, incidentally, Dinoli's son-in-law. Watsinski was a tall, stoop-shouldered man of thirty-eight, weak-eyed, with a dome-like skull sparsely covered with sandy hair. Physically he was easy to overlook. But he had a razor-keen mind and an astonishing capacity for quick decisions. He had made second-level at the age of thirty-one, marrying Dinoli's daughter the following year.

He affected twentieth-century functional by way of office furniture, and as a result his private room looked severely ascetic. He perched on the arm of a lemon-colored desk chair and glanced around the room. All eight of the third-level men were present, and Dave Spalding.

"How many of you saw the big newsbreak last night?" he asked. His voice was thin and high-pitched, but still somehow commanding. "All of you? Fine. That's what we like to see here. I worked that program up myself, you know. With aid from Hubbel and Partridge."

He slouched back in the chair, crossing his long spidery legs. "Your colleagues of the sixth- and seventh-level have been running gallups all morning. We've got some of the early results in. Seems almost everyone saw that spot last night, and the early gallups show tremendous interest focused on this Ganymede thing. Okay. The interest exists; it's our job to channel it. That clear and pellucid?"

Without waiting for any response, he continued. "You've all been relieved of your present assignments. You'll be working directly under me; the other three second-level men will be operating peripherally in the same general area, but the key work on this contract is going to come out of this office. I have this straight from Dinoli. Any questions? Good. Now, let's toss this around for half an hour or so. First thing I want is a suggestion for a broad approach. Kennedy?"

Kennedy had been astonished by the sight of his own arm waving in the air. He recovered quickly and said, "I have an idea or two on our general slant, if that hasn't already been determined."

"It hasn't. That's what we're here to do. Go on."

"Well," Kennedy said carefully, "My wife and I

saw the program last night. Her reaction to the sight of the Ganymedeans was one of pity. They aroused her maternal protective instincts. I'd suggest we play to this, Ernie. The poor, childlike, innocent Ganymedeans who have to be taken over by our occupation forces for their own good."

"Shrewd point, Kennedy. Let's kick that around a little. Haugen?"

"I'm dead opposed," Haugen said thickly. He twined his fleshy fingers together. "My wife reacted pretty much the same way Kennedy's did. She even thought they were *cute*. The gallups will probably tell you that it was a universal reaction. Okay. We follow Kennedy's plan and build the Ganymedeans up as babes in the woods. What happens if they decide to fight back? Suppose there's a massacre bloodier than all get-out when we try to occupy Ganymede?"

"Amplify," Watsinski said.

"What I'm getting at is this: it may be necessary to gun those creatures down by droves. We can't hide that completely from the public, Ernie. And the outcry will be fantastic. We may even have a revolution on our hands. The government's certainly going to be in trouble."

Watsinski narrowed his eyes until they were mere slits, and stroked the side of his long, curved nose. At length he said, "Kennedy, you see the flaw in your proposition?"

Shamefaced, Kennedy nodded. Haugen had deflated his idea quickly and sensibly. They would have to prepare the public for the worst.

Watsinski glanced around the table. "Before we move on, is there anyone else who wants to argue for Kennedy's point? I want to make sure."

Slowly Dave Spalding raised his hand. "I do. I think it's wrong to go into this expecting a bloody massacre. The occupation ought to be as peaceful as possible, and if we build up a publicity blanket of love for the Ganymedeans then it damn well *better* be peaceful."

There was an instant of silence. Kennedy distinctly heard Watsinski's sobbing intake of breath, as if he were being very patient. Watsinski said, "Spalding, you're only a fourth-level man, and we can make allowances. But we try to shape public opinion here. We *don't* try to shape the doings of the Corporation to fit the kind of atmosphere we've created. They happen to employ us. This kind of thing has hurt you before, Spalding, and it's likely to hurt you again if you don't get your thinking clarified."

Kennedy glanced quickly down the table at Spalding, and glanced away. The young forth-level man had gone very pale at the rebuke. His nostrils flickered in momentary anger; he said nothing.

Watsinski said, "Well. We can go ahead, then, Kick it around some more, fellows. I'm listening."

Lloyd Presslie got the floor. "We could take the opposite track. Paint the Ganymedeans as monsters. Alien demons from an ice-bound planet. Wipe this damn mother-love out of the picture, just in case we have to come down on them hard."

Watsinski was smiling, showing yellowish, uneven teeth. "I like," he said gently. "I like. Let's kick it around some more, shall we?"

But Kennedy knew that any further talk was going to be superfluous. Watsinski's smile meant that the meeting had arrived at what was going to be the policy; that Presslie had accidentally hit on the plan which Dinoli and his top staff men had already formulated, and which Watsinski had been prepared to shove down the third-level men's throats, if necessary.

Kennedy ate lunch that day, as he had every day of his eight-year employment at Steward and Dinoli, in the agency cafeteria on Floor Ten. He twitched his yellow status-card from the protective folder in his wallet, slapped it against the translucent plastic plate in the dispensary wall, and waited for it to be scanned.

A moment later the standard Thursday third-level lunch issued from a slot further down in the dispensary. Kennedy repocketed his meal-ticket and picked up his tray. Algae steak, synthetic vegemix, a cup of pale but undeniably real coffee. Dinoli had never been very liberal with his lunches. The second-level men ate in their private offices, so Kennedy had no idea of what they were served, but he was willing to wager the menu wasn't one hundred percent natural foods.

Just as he started to head for the third-level table in the front of the cafeteria, someone nudged his elbow, nearly spilling his tray. He turned, annoyed.

Dave Spalding stood behind him, smiling apologetically.

"Sorry, Ted. I didn't mean to knock your tray over. But I called you, and you didn't answer."

Kennedy glanced at the tray Spalding held. The fourth-level menu was something he had already thankfully forgotten, and he was not happy to see it again. Weak soup, chlorella patties, protein sauce. Synthetic caffeine drink. He looked away, embarrassed.

"What is it, Dave? You want to talk to me?"

Spalding nodded. "Unless you've already made plans for lunch. We can take one of the tables at the side."

Shrugging, Kennedy agreed. Perhaps Spalding wanted to ask his advice. As a third-level man, it was his responsibility to help any lower-rated man who sought him out.

There were a few small tables arranged at the far side of the cafeteria for meetings such as this. Ordinarily, one ate with one's own level, but tables were provided to care for inter-level lunches as well. It simply would not have done for Kennedy to have had to eat at the fourth-level table in order to speak with Spalding.

They sat down. Kennedy was happy the second-level men ate elsewhere; he did not want his name linked too tightly to Spalding's in Watsinski's mind.

"Can I speak to you with absolute honesty?" Spalding asked.

"Of course, Dave." Kennedy felt ill at ease. Spalding, at twenty-eight, was Marge's age—four years his junior. When Harris had left the Agency for independent press-agenting work a year ago, Spalding should have entered third-level. But instead, Lloyd Presslie had been jumped over him into third. "What's on your mind?" Kennedy asked.

Spalding paused, a forkful of chlorella patty poised midway between plate and mouth. "The Ganymede contract. I want to know how you feel about it."

"A job," Kennedy said. "Possibly quite a challenging one."

Spalding's dark eyes seemed to bore into him. He was scowling. "Just a job? A challenge?"

"Should it be anything else?"

"It's the biggest sell since the days of Judas, and you know it as—as *pellucidly* as I do," Spalding said, bitterly mocking Ernie Watsinski's favorite word. "The whole thing is simply a naked grab of strategic territory. And we're supposed to peddle the idea to the public."

"Does it matter," Kennedy asked, "which particular commodity we're selling? If you want to start drawing ethical boundaries, you'd have to ring the whole agency. I've had plenty of jobs just as—well, shady—as this one. So have you. That Federated Bauxite thing I was on, just to take one example—"

"So you had to convince some people in Nebraska that they weren't having their water supply polluted. I suppose that's small enough so you can swallow it down. But Ganymede's too big. We're selling two worlds—ours and theirs. Ted, I want out."

"Out of the contract?"

"Out of the agency," Spalding said.

Kennedy chewed quietly for a moment. "Why are you telling me all this?" he asked after a while.

"I have to tell someone, Ted. And I feel I can trust you. I think you're basically on my side. I know Marge is. She can convince you."

"Keep Marge out of this discussion," Kennedy said, forcing back his anger. Spalding was only a wild-eyed kid, despite his twenty-eight years. Some of them never grow up, never learned that life was essentially a lot of compromises within compromises, and you had to do the best you could. "You'd really leave the agency over this contract?"

Spalding looked so pale as to seem ill. "I've been building up to it a long time. We've been handed one sell after another, but this one's too big. It's lousy, Ted. I tried to play along with all the others. But they had to go and yank me out of fourth-level to work on this one. Why?"

"Maybe they wanted to see how you'd react."

"Well, they're going to see," Spalding snapped. "I tried to put in my pitch when we met with Watsinski this morning. It was your point I was defending, too, even if you gave up. But you saw how I got slapped down. Policy on this was set a long time ago, Ted."

Kennedy felt inwardly calm. He mopped up his plate with exaggerated care, thinking that this was no problem of his, that he took a mere intellectual interest in Spalding's qualms of conscience, with no emotional involvement. "You haven't thought this through, Dave. Where would you go? You're not a youngster any more. You're twenty-eight, and still fourth-level. Dinoli's sure to blacklist you. You couldn't get a job anywhere in PR or advertising."

"I wouldn't want one. It would be foolish to jump out of Dinoli into some other place just the same, only not quite as big."

"You couldn't get a job anywhere else, either. Dinoli has influence. And he doesn't like three-year men to quit," Kennedy said.

"You don't understand. I wouldn't get a job. I've always wanted to be a writer, Ted. This is my chance."

"Video? Dinoli has his fingers in that, too. He'll—"

"No. Not video. *Books,* Ted."

For the first time Kennedy realized the glow in Spalding's eyes was as much that of fanaticism as youth. "Books? You can't make a living doing books," Kennedy said. "Could you get along on two or three thousand a year? That's if you're a smash success right away, I mean."

Spalding shrugged. "I'd manage if I had to."

"Don't you want to get married? Isn't there anyone you love, man?"

"There's a girl I love," Spalding said quietly. "But she can wait. She's waited long enough already."

Kennedy studied the younger man's slim, curiously intense face. "Have you mentioned this quitting business to anyone else in the agency yet?"

Spalding shook his head. "I was hoping something might come out of that conference this morning. But nothing did."

"Listen, Dave. Stay here awhile. A week, two, maybe a month. Don't rush into anything." Kennedy wondered why he was going to all this trouble persuading Spalding to stay in a place he obviously hated and was ill-qualified for. "Think about this move for a while. Once you quit Dinoli, you're sunk for good."

Spalding's eyelids drooped broodingly. After a long silence he said, "Maybe you have something there. I'll stick for two weeks more. Just to see if I can bend this contract into a better direction, though. If nothing works out, I'm leaving."

"That's a sensible attitude, kid." The patronizing *kid* annoyed Kennedy as soon as it escaped his mouth, but by then it was too late.

Spalding grinned. "And you're an agency man for life, I suppose? Solidly sold on the virtues of Lou Dinoli?"

"He's no saint," Kennedy said. "Neither am I. It doesn't pay to aim for sainthood these days. But I'll keep my job. And I'll be able to live with my conscience afterward."

"I wonder about that," Spalding murmured.

"What's that?"

"Nothing," Spalding said quickly. "Just shooting my mouth off again. It's an old habit of mine." He grinned pleasantly and said, "Thanks for sparing the time, Ted. You've cleared my mind tremendously. I really appreciate it."

The gong sounded, ending lunch hour. Spalding touched Kennedy's arm in a gesture of gratitude and scampered away, dumping his empty tray in the big hopper.

More slowly, Kennedy followed him, and abstractedly let the plastic tray slide down into the washer's maw. *I have no illusions,* he told himself firmly. *I'm not a fanatic agency man like Haugen. I think some of the things we do are rotten. I think this contract's rotten. But there just isn't any percentage in standing up and saying so. The guy who stands up only gets slapped down twice as hard and twice as fast.*

He felt a sudden deep surge of pity for Dave Spalding. You had to pity a man whose conscience wouldn't let him rest. This was no world for a man with a conscience, Kennedy thought morbidly, as he headed back toward his desk to begin sketching out the Ganymede campaign.

5

MAY MOVED ALONG through its second week, and the Steward and Dinoli organization effortlessly made the transition from its previous batch of contracts to the one all-encompassing job they were now committed to. A bright-eyed fourth-level kid named Furman relieved Kennedy of the Federated Bauxite portfolio, and from that moment on he was a full-time member of the Ganymede project.

Watsinski was his immediate superior—the idea-coordinator of the project. Each of the other three second-level men had his own special responsibility in the affair—Kauderer handling space purchasing; McDermott, governmental liaison and United Nations lobbying; Poggioli, opinion sampling and trend-testing. But these were essentially subsidiary enterprises; the central ideological flow was channeled through Watsinski, Dinoli's heir apparent and the reigning boss of the second-level men. Watsinski's team consisted of nine: Kennedy, Haugen, Spalding, Presslie, Cameron, Richardson, Fleischman, Lund, and Whitman. These were the men who would sell Ganymede to the people of Earth.

No one, not even Watsinski, seemed in any great

hurry to get the project rolling. They spent the first few days just doodling ideas and filing them without even bringing them up for discussion. It was a curiously low-pressure beginning for a Steward and Dinoli project.

There were several target dates to be kept in mind. Kennedy scribbled them all carefully in his personal notebook as soon as they filtered down from above.

May 21, 2044—*first big publicity push*

July 8—*beginning of transition in public feeling; prepare for unsympathetic depiction of Ganymedeans*

September 17—*intensification of program; building toward climax of operation*

September 22—*Corporation will begin to ask U.N. to consider giving it aid in case necessary; underscore through S and D*

October 11—*Climactic incident will send Corporation before U.N. with a plea for help*

October 17 (optimum desired time)—*United Nations decision to occupy Ganymede to safeguard the rights of Corporation*

Kennedy refrained from letting Marge see the timetable; it was just too neat, too well planned, and he knew what her immediate reaction would be.

It would be pretty much that of Dave Spalding the day the memorandum had been sent around. Spalding's desk had been moved out of the fourth-level quarters, and now he worked near Haugen and Kennedy. He looked up when the sealed envelope was deposited on the corner of his desk, ripped it open, skimmed through it.

"Well, here it is. The blueprint for conquest."

Alf Haugen dropped his memorandum to the shining surface of his desk and glanced at Spalding, a troubled look on his heavy face.

"What the hell do you mean by that?"

Trouble bristled a moment in the office; smoothly Kennedy said, "Always the cynic, eh, Dave? You'd think the Ganymedeans were going to get trampled into the dust."

"Well, we—"

"You have to hand it to Dinoli," Kennedy continued. "He can work out a timetable six months in advance and judge every trend so well we don't need to amend the schedule as much as twenty-four hours."

"It's a trick of the trade," Haugen said. "Dinoli's a shark. A real shark. God damn, but I respect that man! And I don't even care whether he's listening or not!"

"You really think the third-level office is wired?" Spalding asked anxiously.

Haugen shrugged amiably. "Probably is. Dinoli likes to have a loyal staff around him. There are ways of finding out who's loyal. But I don't care. Hell, *I'm* loyal; if old Lou wants to tune in on what I'm saying, I've got nothing to worry about."

Kennedy folded the memorandum and tucked it away; then he left his desk and crossed the floor to Spalding's. Leaning down with both hands on the other's desk, he put his face close to Spalding's and said, "Dave, do you have a free minute? I'm going to Library Deck for a pickup and I need a hand carrying the stuff."

"Why don't you ring for a porter?"

The tip of Spaulding's shoe protruded from under his desk. Kennedy found it with his own foot and pressed down hard. "I don't trust those boys. I'd like you to help me out."

Spalding looked puzzled, but he shrugged and nodded. When they were out of the third-level area and in the corridor, Kennedy gripped him tightly by the arm and said in a low voice, "That 'blueprint for conquest' gag was a little out of place, Dave. It wasn't called for."

"Wasn't it?"

"That's neither here nor there. You're not expected to make anti-agency cracks in the third-level area. If Haugen had reported you he'd have been within his rights."

A cold smile crossed Spalding's face. "Is it against the law to speak out against a nasty business deal?"

"Yes," Kennedy said. "Either you stick with it and keep your mouth shut or you get out. One or the other. What happened to your ambitions of a couple of days ago—becoming a writer, and all that?"

Spalding smiled apologetically. "I decided to swallow my qualms and stick with it."

"That's a sensible move, Dave. I figured you'd outgrow that adolescent mood of rebellion. I'm glad to hear you talk this way."

"The devil with you, Ted. I haven't outgrown anything. I'm sticking here because I need the money. I'm drawing third-level pay now, and that's good cabbage. A few more months of Papa Dinoli's shekels and I'll have enough of a nest egg to quit and do what I want to do. What I *really* want to do." Spalding's eyes glittered. "Fight cynicism with cynicism. It's the only way."

Kennedy blinked. He said nothing.

"Now," Spalding went on. "That library pickup.

Is it legit, or did you just cook it up so you could give me a word of advice?"

"I just cooked it up," Kennedy admitted.

"I thought so. Mind if I get back to work, then?" Spalding smiled and ducked past him. "You louse," Kennedy said quietly to himself, at Spalding's retreating back. "You cold-blooded louse."

Kennedy remained in the hall for a moment; then, realizing he was standing frozen with a stupefied expression on his face, he snapped out of it and walked back to his desk.

It wasn't any secret that Dave Spalding regarded the Ganymede contract with loathing. Kennedy had already written that off to Spalding's fuzzy-minded idealism; idealists always had a way of being fuzzy-minded.

But the sudden sharp revelation just now had shown Kennedy a very unfuzzy-minded Spalding, who was cold-bloodedly extracting enough money from the Ganymede contract to let himself get quit of the whole enterprise. That cast a new light on things, Kennedy thought. He felt a faint quiver of doubt. Somehow he couldn't laugh off Spalding's opinion of the contract any more.

Haugen was at the water cooler as Kennedy returned to the third-level area, and Kennedy joined him. The beefy executive was sipping his drink with obvious enjoyment. Spalding was bent studiously over his notes.

"What time's the meeting?" Kennedy asked.

He knew what time it was. But Haugen said, "Watsinski wants us in his office in half an hour. Got any sharp ideas?"

"A few," Kennedy admitted cautiously. "Couple

of notions. Maybe Ernie'll take them. Alf?"

"Hey?"

"Tell me something—straight. What do you think of this whole business about Ganymede?"

As soon as he said it, he knew it was a mistake. Haugen turned, peered at him full-face, frowned in puzzlement. "What do I think—huh? About what?"

"The contract. Whether it's right." Kennedy began to sweat. He wished he had kept quiet.

"*Right?* Right?" Haugen repeated incredulously. He shrugged. "Is that what you were worrying about? Caught something from Spalding, maybe?"

"Not exactly. Marge worries a lot. She's socially oriented. She keeps bringing the thing up."

Haugen smiled warmly. He was forty, and knew by now he'd never advance beyond third-level; he was serene in the knowledge that his competence would keep him where he was, and that there was no danger of his slipping back or any chance of his moving forward. "Ted, I'm surprised to hear you talk this way. You've got a fine home, a splendid wife, luxury living. You're a third-level exec. You're pulling down thirty thousand a year plus bonuses, and you're bucking for second-level. You'll get there, too —you've got the stuff. I can tell."

Kennedy felt his face going red. "Soft-soap won't answer my questions, Alf."

"This isn't soft-soap. It's fact, plain hard fact. You have all these things. Lots of people don't. Okay. Now you get called in by Dinoli, and he tells you to let the public think thus-and-so about the planet Ganymede, or moon Ganymede, or whatever the blazes it is. Do you stand around asking yourself if this is right?" Haugen chuckled richly. "The hell you do! For thirty thousand a year, *who cares?*"

Kennedy took a sip of water. "Yeah. Yeah."

"You see?"

Kennedy nodded. "I think so," he said.

Half an hour later Kennedy was at his place around the table in Ernie Watsinski's office, sitting next to Haugen and across the table from Spalding. Watsinski sat perfectly quiet, a lanky uncouth figure draped over a chair, waiting for the group to assemble. Richardson was the last man to arrive; he slipped in quietly, hoping no one would notice his tardiness, and in that moment Watsinski came to life.

"Today, gentlemen, is the eleventh of May," he began, in his thin voice. "It's precisely one week since we last met in this room. It's also—I take it you've all seen the time sheet that was circulated this morning; if you haven't, please raise hands—ah, good. As I say, it's also precisely ten days till the beginning of the public phase of our campaign. A lot of work is going into this project, gentlemen—a hell of a lot of work. If you knew how Joe Kauderer is running around lining up media breaks for us—well, you'll know soon enough, when Joe makes his report to you at the big meeting with Dinoli. But the thing is really moving. Really moving.

"Now I've given you this week to think things out, to look at the big picture and fit yourself into it. You know we at S and D regard public relations work as an artistic creation. You're shaping an esthetic whole. The beauty of a fully-developed opinion pattern is like the beauty of the Mona Lisa or a Rembrandt or a Beethoven symphony. If any of you men don't *feel* this Ganymede thing with all you've got, I'd appreciate it if you'd let me know right here and now, or else later in privacy. This has to be real. It has to be *sincere*, gentlemen."

Watsinski seemed to have worked up genuine passion over his rhapsody. His eyes were glossy with the beginnings of tears. Kennedy glanced over at Spalding, but the young man sat tight-jawed without revealing a bit of the emotion he might have been feeling.

"Okay, gentlemen, let's get to work," Watsinski said suddenly, in an entirely different tone of voice. He had descended from empyreal heights with marvelous rapidity. "At our last meeting we decided on our general pattern of approach—it was Lloyd Presslie's suggestion, since taken up with Dinoli and in essence approved, that we take into account the distinct possibility of strong reaction on Ganymede and therefore build the Ganymedeans up as unsympathetic types. I guess you've all been thinking about ways and means of doing this. Richardson, start talking."

All eyes swiveled to the back of the room. This was Watsinski's way of indicating his displeasure at Richardson's tardiness; there would be no other formal reprimand.

Richardson was a thin-lipped professorial type with a dry, pedantic manner. He ran his hands through his thinning hair and said, "I've been thinking of three or four separate multilevel approaches to this thing, Ernie. But I won't throw them all out on the floor right now. The basic handle is a kiddie-approach. Kiddies and women. Men don't form their own opinions, anyway. I propose that we assault this thing by filtering anti-Ganymede stuff into the kiddie shows and the afternoon women-slanted videocasts. I've drawn up a brief on how to go about it, listing fifteen selected shows and the angle of leverage on each one. Some of the writers are former S and D stablemen. You want to go through the brief now, or file it afterwards?"

Watsinski stirred restlessly. "Better save it for later, Claude. We're still searching for the broad patterns. Detailed implementation comes later." Kennedy could see that the second-level man was inwardly displeased that Richardson had come through; Watsinski liked nothing better than to see a staffman squirm and admit he was unprepared. But if you were third-level you just didn't come unprepared to a meeting with Watsinski.

They went around the table. Haugen had developed a slippery idea for feeding pro-Ganymedean stuff into overseas video shows and newspapers, carefully picking the countries, selecting the ones least in favor in the United States at the moment. Then, via a simple contrast-switch, local opinion could be pyramided on the basic proposition, *If they're for it, we're gonna be agin it!*

Watsinski liked that. Fleischman then offered his ideas: a typically Fleischmanoid product, many-layered and obscure, for grabbing public opinion simultaneously at the college and kindergarten level and letting babes and late adolescents serve as propagandists. Watsinski went for that, too.

Then it was Kennedy's turn. He tugged nervously at his collar and put his unopened briefcase before him on the table.

"I've sketched out a plan that substantially

dovetails with the ones we've just heard, Ernie. It can be used alongside any or all of them."

"Let's have it."

"In brief, it's this: we need a straw man, a dummy to set up and kick over. Something to engage local sympathies firmly and finally."

Watsinski was nodding. Kennedy moistened his lips. He said, "At the moment the only human beings on Ganymede are a couple of dozen Corporation spacemen and scientists. I don't think there's a woman or a child on the place. Where's the human interest in that? Where's the pathos when we highlight them against the Ganymedeans? Who gives much of a damn about a bunch of Corporation scientists?

"Now," Kennedy went on, "here's my suggestion. We start disseminating word of a colony of Earthmen on Ganymede. Volunteers. A couple of hundred chosen people, brave self-sacrificing men, women, and children. Naturally there isn't any colony there. The Corporation wouldn't send noncombatants into a militarily unsettled area like Ganymede. But the public doesn't have to know that. If we make the doings of the colony consistent, if we start believing in it ourselves—then the public will believe in it too. And once we've got a firm fisthold on their sympathies, we can do anything with them!"

Kennedy had hardly finished speaking when half a dozen hands were in the air. For an instant he thought they were going to laugh him down, but then he saw the way they all looked, and realized his suggestion had inspired them to new heights.

Presslie got the floor and said, "It's a natural! Why, then we can follow through by having the

Ganymedeans *wipe out* this colony. It's a sure bet for engaging sympathy in any sort of necessary police action! Innocent women and children perishing, flames, blood—why, this is the handle we need! Of course I can suggest some modifications, but those can come later."

Watsinski nodded. "Kennedy seems to have hit on a sharp idea. I'm going to suggest it to Dinoli as our basic line of approach, and build all the other plans around it. Good work, Kennedy. Lund, let's hear from you, now. I want to kick this all the way round the table."

6

LATER THAT DAY, two hours after the meeting had broken up, Kennedy was working at his desk when the phone chimed. He snatched it up and heard Watsinski's dry voice say, "Kennedy? Ernie here. Can you come over to my place for a few minutes?"

"Be right there, Ernie."

Watsinski was waiting for him when he came in. The second-level man wore a severely funereal business-suit and a glistening red wig. He smiled perfunctorily and beckoned Kennedy to a seat.

"I took up your suggestion with Dinoli," he said immediately, without preface. "The old man loved it. He thinks it's great. So did Kauderer, McDermott, and Poggioli. We had a quick vote on it just before lunch."

Stiffly Kennedy said, "I'm glad to hear it went over, Ernie."

Watsinski nodded. "It went over. Dinoli spent half of lunch talking to Bullard—he's Mr. Big over at the Corporation, you know. They were mapping out the strategy. Dinoli is using your plan as the core of the whole thing."

Kennedy felt a self-satisfied glow. Dammit, it was

good to know your voice counted for something around this place. It was always so easy to think you were just a puppet being pushed around by the top-level men with the same ease that you pushed the vast inchoate public mind around.

"I hit a good one, huh, Ernie?"

"You did." Watsinski leaned back and permitted some warmth to enter his face. "I've always liked you, Ted. I think you've got the stuff for second-level. You know what it takes—dogged persistence plus off-beat ingenuity. That isn't an everyday combination of traits. We've got guys who come up with off-beat ideas—Lund, for instance, or Whitman, or sometimes that kid Spalding. But they don't have the push to implement their notions. And then we get the kind like Haugen, the solid pluggers who never make mistakes but who never come up with anything new or fresh either. Well, we need both types down on third-level. But second-level takes something else. I've got it. So do Poggioli and McDermott and Kauderer. I think you have it too, Ted."

"It's good to hear you say that, Ernie. I know you don't go soaping people up."

Watsinski inclined his reg wig forward. "This is strictly off the record, Ted. But Frank Poggioli is talking about pulling out of S and D and taking a big network job in video. I know he and Dinoli hashed it out, and Dinoli's willing to let him go."

"The Chief always likes to have his graduates high up in the networks," Kennedy said.

"Sure. Well, in case Poggioli goes, someone'll have to be kicked up to second-level to fill the vacancy. Dinoli also took that up with me this morning. It's between Haugen and Presslie and you. But Presslie's fresh out of fourth-level and I know McDermott's afraid to move anybody up too fast; and they think Haugen's too stodgy. I'm putting my support back of you. That business this morning helped me make up my mind."

"Thanks, Ernie. Thanks." Kennedy wondered why Watsinski was bothering to tell him all this.

Watsinski let his eyes droop quietly closed, and when he opened them again they seemed to be veiled. "Okay. Enough if-talk, Ted. I just wanted you to know where you stand in the agency. I hate to see a man feel insecure when he's in a good position." Watsinski frowned. "You know, there are guys in this agency who don't have the right spirit, and I wish we could root them the hell out of here. Guys who aren't loyal. Guys who don't have the right ideas. Guys whose minds are full of cockeyed garbage served up by antisocial creeps. You know these guys better than I do; you see them through clearer focus. As a prospective second-level man you ought to start thinking about these guys and how we can weed them out. You ought to let me know if you spot any thinking of a negative type. Okay, Ted?"

Kennedy felt a sudden chill. *So that's what he wants*, he thought. *He wants me to spy for him and finger the Spaldings who have qualms about the contract.*

"I guess I see what you mean, Ernie. Well, I'll think about it."

"Sure. Don't rush it or you'll crush it. But I know definitely there are some antisocial elements on our team, and I want to clean them out. So does Dinoli."

The office phone chimed. Watsinski picked it up, listened for a long moment, finally said, "He's here right now, Lou. I'm filling him in. Okay, Chief."

He hung up.

"That was Dinoli. Well, let me get to the main pitch, Ted: we're using the plan you threw out this morning. We're going to invent a colony on Ganymede and in October we're going to have the Ganymedeans launch a savage attack on that colony, and then the Corporation will ask the U.N. to step in and save it. Dinoli wants you to be in charge of developing material on this colony. You'll have sole charge. In essence you'll be doing second-level work. You can name your own staff; pick out anybody you like from third- or fourth-level as your assistant."

"Right now?"

"It would help," Watsinski said.

Kennedy was silent a moment. He pulled a cigarette from an ignitopak, waited for it to glow into life, and with calm deliberation sucked smoke into his lungs. He thought about Watsinski's proposition.

They were setting him up in a big way. On the surface, it was a heartwarming vote of confidence in his abilities—but Kennedy knew enough about the workings of Steward and Dinoli to realize that the upper levels never operated merely on the surface alone. They always played a deep game.

They were putting him into a big post in exchange for something—information, no doubt. They knew the Ganymede contract was a hot item, and they wanted to avoid any leaks by weeding out possible defectors like Spalding. Possibly they had their eye on Spalding already and were simply waiting for Kennedy to confirm their suspicions.

Well, Kennedy thought, *I won't play their game.*

He thought about possible assistants for a moment more. Haugen, Lund, Whitman—

No. There was one man qualified uniquely for the job. One man who would much rather be writing books than handling the Ganymede contract.

Kennedy stared bluntly at Watsinski's thin, shrewd face. "Okay. I've picked my man."

"Who?"

"Dave Spalding," Kennedy said.

For just a fraction of a second Watsinski looked as if Kennedy had kicked him in the teeth. Then control reasserted itself and Watsinski said, in a mellow, even tone, "Okay, Ted, I'll see what I can do to expedite your request. That'll be all for now. Keep up the good work."

That night when Marge asked him how things had gone during the day, he said shortly, "Pretty fair. Watsinski called me in and said I have a good shot at second-level. They gave me some special work to do."

She was wearing a translucent skylon dress with peekaboo front. As she poured him his drink she said, "I guess you don't want to talk about what you'll be doing."

"I'd rather not, Marge."

"I won't push, dear." She dropped a pale white onion into the cocktail, kissed him, and handed him the drink. He took it and said, "Dave Spalding's going to be working directly with me. And we're actually going to be handling the core of the whole project."

It seemed for a moment that Marge looked surprised. Then she said, "I hope you and Dave will get along better now. It would be too bad if you couldn't cooperate on your work."

Kennedy smiled. "I think we will. I picked him as my assistant myself." He took a deep sip of the drink and got it out of the way just in time as the cat bounded into his lap and curled himself up.

He felt relaxed and happy. This was the way life ought to be: a good job, a good drink, good music playing, your good wife fixing a good supper inside. And after supper some good company, an evening of relaxation, and then a good night in bed. He closed his eyes, listening to the jubilant trumpets of the Purcell Ode on the sound system, and stroked the cat gently with his free hand.

Spalding had taken the news pretty well, he thought. Kennedy had met with him at 2 o'clock, shortly after confirmation of the new arrangement had come through from Watsinski, and Spalding had seemed interested and almost enthusiastic about the fictional Ganymedean colony they were about to create. There had been no coldness between them, no raising of knotty moral issues, for which Kennedy was thankful in the extreme.

Instead, Spalding had immediately begun producing a wealth of ideas, characters, incidents, jumping at the work with boyish vigor. Kennedy realized that the four years was a considerable gap; Spalding was still just a kid. He hadn't had time to learn the poised manners of a mature individual. But it would be good for both of them to work together on this project.

Kennedy himself felt a sudden welling of enthusiastic interest. He knew what Watsinski had been talking about when he referred to the esthetic nature of public relations work. It could be a work of art. He and Spalding would give life to a colony of people, endow them with talents and hopes and strivings, interest the people of the world in their hardships and privations and courage.

The music swelled to a climax. Kennedy thought of old Purcell, back there in seventeenth-century England, hearing this glorious music inside his head and painstakingly jotting it onto a sheet of grimy paper—and then of the artists who performed it, the engineers who recorded it, the whole host of participants in the esthetic act. There it was, he thought: an artistic creation. Something that hadn't existed the morning before Purcell inked in his first clef, and something that now belonged to the world.

It was almost the same way with this Ganymede colony he and Spalding would design. Men and women would be able to enter into the life of that colony just as he entered into the life of the musical composition being played. It was almost in a mood of exaltation that Kennedy walked into the dining room at Marge's call.

She smiled at him. "I must have made that cocktail too strong," she said.

"Three-and-a-half to one, or I'm no judge of proportions. Wasn't it?"

"I thought so—but you look so different! Warm and relaxed, Ted."

"And therefore I must be drunk. Because I couldn't possibly be happy and relaxed when I'm sober. Well, I hate to disappoint you, Marge, but I *am* sober. And happy."

"Of course you are, darling. I—"

"And the reason I'm happy," Kennedy continued inexorably, "is only partly because Watsinski said I stood a good chance of making second-level when

Poggioli pulls out. That's a minor thing. I'm happy because I have a chance to participate in something real and vital and exciting, and Dave along with me. You know what I'll be doing?"

She smiled. "I didn't want to ask. You're usually so touchy about your work when I ask things."

"Well, I'll tell you." The glow he felt was even stronger. "Dave and I are going to invent a colony on Ganymede, with people and everything."

He went on to explain in detail what the colony would be like, how he had come to think of the idea, how Watsinski and the others had reacted when he put it forth. He concluded by letting her in on what was really classified material: he told her of Presslie's concluding suggestion, that the colony would be "destroyed" to serve as provocation for the intended United Nations occupation.

"There," he finished. "Isn't that neat? Complete, well rounded, carefully built up. It—"

He stopped. The glow of happiness winked out in an instant. Marge was staring at him with an expression that he could only interpret as one of horror.

"You're serious about this, aren't you?" she asked.

"Of course I am. What's wrong?"

"This whole terrible charade—this fake slush—being used to grab the sympathies of the world. What a gigantic, grisly hoax! And you're *proud* of it!"

"Marge, I—"

"You what?" she asked quietly. "You were sitting there *radiating* content and happiness. How could you?"

"Just take it on its own terms," he said tightly. "As a creative effort. Don't drag moral confusions into it. You always have to cobweb things up by dragging in morality and preachery."

"You *can't* take anything on its own terms, Ted. That's your mistake. You have to look at it in context, and in context I can only say that this thing stinks from top to bottom inside and out."

He slammed his fork to the table. *"Marge!"*

She stared steadily at him. "I guess I spoke out of line, Ted. I'm sorry, darling. I didn't mean to preach." The muscles of her jaws were tightening in convulsive little clumps, and Kennedy saw she was fighting hard to keep back another big emotional outburst. He reached out and gripped her hand.

"Don't get worked up over this thing," he told her. "From now on let me leave my job at 2:30 and forget it until the next morning. Otherwise we'll be at each other's throats all the time."

"You're right, dear. We'd better do that."

He turned his attention back to his meal. But the food seemed dead and tasteless now, and he was totally unable to recapture the euphoric mood of just a few moments before.

A vast gulf was opening between himself and his wife, and it was getting wider day by day. He thought back over that glow of contentment and wondered how he could ever have attained it. What he and Spalding would be doing was a pretty soulless enterprise, he admitted to himself. There was nothing nice about it. And yet he had worked himself up into a fine esthetic frenzy over it, until Marge's few harsh words had opened his eyes.

And I was proud of it, he thought. My God, don't I ever *think* at all?

7

JUNE 31, 2044—Leap Year World Holiday, by the Permanent Calendar. The extra day, intercalated in the otherwise changeless calendar every four years to take up the slack of the six hours and some minutes the Permanent Calendar was forced to ignore.

A day of revelry, Kennedy thought. A day between the days, a day that was neither Monday, Tuesday, Wednesday nor Thursday, nor Friday, Saturday or even Sunday. A timeless day on which no one worked except for holiday double-pay, on which even the rules of civilization went into the discard heap for twenty-four hours. It fell between Saturday, June thirtieth and Sunday, July first and since this was a leap year there would be two nameless days instead of the usual one at the end of the year.

The Kennedys chose to spend their day at Joyland Amusement Park on the Floating Island in Long Island Sound. Privately, Kennedy detested the hustle and bustle of the World Holidays; but they were family customs, deeply embedded in his way of life, and he never dared to speak out against them.

The road was crowded. Bumper to bumper, deflector plate to deflector plate, the little enameled beetles clung together on the Thruway. Kennedy sweated behind the wheel. The air-conditioners labored mightily. At his side Marge looked fresh and gay in her light summer clothes, red halter and light blue briefs. Her legs glistened; she wore the newest aluminum sprayons.

"The Egyptians had a better slant on this leap year business," he said. "Every year they saved up the fragment of a day that was left over, and let them pile up in the back room of the temple. Then every one thousand four hundred and sixty years all those quarter-days amounted to one full year, and there they were with a whole year that they didn't figure into the calendars. The Sothic year. Of course, the seasons got pretty loused up while waiting for the Sothic year to come around, but that was okay. They held big festivals all that year. An eagle with painted wings was burned alive in a nest of palm branches to celebrate the event. And then the seasons came right again. Origin of the Phoenix legend."

Marge giggled. Up ahead a car stalled in the furious heat and the radar eye of Kennedy's automatic brake picked up the impulse and throttled the turbos; he and Marge rocked slightly forward as the car slowed to thirty.

"It was a fine system," he went on. "And Egypt lasted long enough to celebrate two or three Sothic years. Emperor Augustus killed the Phoenix in 30 B.C. when he stabilized the Egyptian calendar. No more years of festival. We're lucky to get a day once every four years."

The car's air-conditioners whined sourly as the vehicle came to a complete halt. Marge said, "One thousand four hundred and sixty years ago America belonged to the Indians. Our ancestors were painting themselves blue and worshipping Druids in wicker baskets. And in the same amount of years hence we'll all be forgotten. Sothic years won't work nowadays; by the time the next one comes around nobody'll remember to insert it in the calendar."

"Sure they will. Otherwise you'll have winter coming in May and summer in November and—" The congestion cleared ahead and he whisked the car on. The inside-outside thermometer read sixty-nine inside the car, ninety-seven outside. The compass told him they were heading westward along the Thruway toward the Sound. Not a bad car at all, he thought, my battered old '42 Frontenac. Hardly in the class with Haugen's new Chevvy-Caddy, of course, but ample for my purposes.

They reached another snag in the traffic pattern. Kennedy let go of the wheel and let his hand rest lightly on his wife's cool knee.

"Ted?"

"Eh?"

"Let's try to have a good time together today. Relaxed. Calm. Just having fun."

"Sure, Marge. Today's World Holiday. No ulcers today." He flopped back against the cushion as the car started moving violently. *"Damn!* These holiday drivers!"

It had been a rough month. Rough, but exciting. He and Spalding had thrown themselves full force into the pseudo-colony on Ganymede. Endless reams of paper covered with biographical sketches of people who weren't, thick dossiers on Ganymedean weather and the rigors of life in a dome and a million other things. It was like writing a story of space adventure,

Kennedy thought, with one minor wrinkle: this wasn't for the fantasy mags. It was going out over the newstapes and the fax sheets and people were gobbling it up.

It went like this:

"Ganymede, 23 May 2044—Another day passed in relative comfort for the Extraterrestrial Development and Exploration Corporation's experimental volunteer station on the tiny world of Ganymede, after the heavy snowfall of yesterday. Lester Brookman, Colony Director, commented, 'Except for the usual hazards of life on an alien world, we're doing fine.'

"The colony's one invalid was reported in good health. She is Mrs. Helene Davenant, thirty-one, wife of an atmospheric engineer, who suffered an appendicitis attack early yesterday morning. Colony Surgeon David Hornsfall operated immediately. Dr. Hornsfall said after the operation, 'Mrs. Davenant is in good shape and there is no danger of complications. The low gravity will aid in her quick recovery and I hope to have her back at work in the hydroponics shed in a few days.' The news eased fears of millions on Earth who were thrown into alarm by a premature report of peritonitis."

And so it went, Kennedy thought. Emotional involvement. Soap opera on a cosmic scale. It was now a little over a month since the Kennedy-Spalding pseudo-colony had received its official unveiling, and in that month life with Marge had grown increasingly difficult.

It was nothing overt, of course. She never spoke of Kennedy's work. But there were the silences in the evening where once there had been enthusiastic chatter, the slight stiffness of the jaws and lips, the faint aloofness. They were not close any more, and even their banter had a strained, artificial character.

Well, he thought, maybe she'd get over it. Dinoli and Watsinski and the others were excited about the things he was doing with the project; he was making big strides upward in the agency, and that had to be taken into account. And today being a holiday, he hoped he might be able to effect some sort of rapprochement between Marge and himself. He banked the car sharply and sent it rocketing up the arching ramp that took it to the Joyland Bridge.

Joyland covered forty sprawling acres on the Floating Island in the Sound—built at the turn of the century for the Peace Fair of 2000–2001. The island did not float now, of course; it was solidly anchored to the floor of the Sound. Once it had floated, though, at the time of the Fair, and the only way to get there was to take a ferry that would chase the island as it moved rapidly around the Sound on its peregrinations. But the upkeep of the giant engines that powered the island had been too great; thirty years ago they had been ripped out and the island anchored a mile off shore, but the old name still clung.

The bridge to the island was a shimmering thread painfully bright in the noonday sun. Kennedy paused at the toll bridge and watched the hundreds of cars creeping one after the other across the span. The under-level of the bridge was empty; by nightfall it would be packed with returning cars. He dropped his dollar in the tollkeep's hands and spurred the car ahead, onto the bridge.

Crossing took fifteen minutes; parking the car, another fifteen. Finally he was free of routine, with a

parking check in his pocket and a fun-hat on his
head. Marge wore one too: a huge orange thing with
myriad quivering paper snakes that gave her a
Medusa-like appearance. His was more somber, a
black and gray mortician's topper. Elsewhere he saw
Roman helmets and horned Viking domes. The
place was crowded with fun-seekers in various
degrees of nudity; custom prevented any indecencies,
but in their attempts to evade the heat most people
had stripped down to a minimum, except for those
few bundled-up unfortunates who still feared overex-
posure to the sun.

A girl in her twenties wandered by, hatless, dishev-
eled, wearing only a pair of briefs; she clutched her
halter in one hand, a drink flask in the other. Marge
pointed to her and Kennedy nodded. She started to
reel forward; a moment later she would have fallen
and perhaps been trampled underfoot, but a smiling
guard in Joyland's green uniform appeared from nowhere to catch her and gently drag her away into the
shade. *This is World Holiday,* Kennedy thought. *When
we step outside ourselves and leave our ulcers home.*

"Where do we begin?" Marge asked. It was the
old problem: there was much to see, so many things
to do. A gleaming sign advertised the next firing of
the big rocket. There was a barren area on the west
shore of the island where passenger rockets were
fired; they traveled sixty or seventy miles up, gave the
passengers a good squint at the spinning orb of
Earth, and plunged back down to make a neat landing on the field. There hadn't been a major accident
since 2039, when a hundred people died through a
slight miscalculation and cast a shadow over a gay
Sunday afternoon. Price was ten dollars a head, but

Kennedy had no desire to ride the rocket.

Elsewhere there were roller coasters, drink parlors, fun houses, side shows, a swimming pool, a waxworks. One building in the center of the gaming area specialized in a more private sort of fun; for three dollars a pleasure-seeker and his companion could rent a small air-conditioned room with a bed for an hour. For three dollars more, a girl could sometimes be supplied. This was World Holiday, and fun was unlimited.

They bought tickets for the roller coaster and strapped themselves in tight. The car was jet-powered; it took off with a lurching thrust and kept going down the track, up and around, nightmarishly twisting and plunging. There was always the added uncertainty of catching up with the car before yours; there was a shield, but it wasn't very substantial, and you might just get a jet-blast from the preceding car. It didn't happen often, of course.

At the end of the ride, dizzy, exhausted, they clung to each other and laughed. Arm in arm, they staggered across to a drink parlor and ordered double Scotches at the outside window. In the dimness within, Kennedy saw a man in his fifties plunging wildly around in an alcoholic dance; he leaped up in a final frenzy, started to fall toward the floor, and an ever-present Joyland guard appeared and scooped him up in mid-fall. Kennedy sipped his drink and smiled at Marge. She smiled back with what seemed like sincere warmth. He wondered.

They headed down the main concourse, past the cheap booths that in other years they had always ignored. But this time Marge stopped and tugged at his arm.

"Look at that one!"

"Come on, Marge—you know these things are all rigged. I want to go to the fun house."

"No—hold it, Ted. Look."

He looked. There was a new booth, one that he had never seen before. The flashy sign winked at them: *Send A Letter To Granymede*.

A toothy, bare-chested carny man leaned forward over the counter, smiling jovially and inviting trade. Next to him a woman in yellow briefs and bandeau frowned in concentration as she filled out what seemed to be a telegram form.

"Come on, friends! Send your best wishes to the brave folks on Ganymede! Only one dollar for a ten-word message! Let them know how you feel about their valiant work!"

"See it, Ted?"

Kennedy nodded. "Let's go over. I want to find out a few things."

The carny man grinned at them. "Care to send a letter to Ganymede, friends? Only a dollar." He shoved a yellow blank and a pencil at them.

The woman finished her message and handed it back. Kennedy caught only the heading at the top. It was addressed to Mrs. Helen Davenant, the appendicitis victim. A get-well message, he thought.

Quietly he said, "This is a new booth, isn't it?"

"The newest in the place! Just put it up last week. And doing very well, too. Would you like—"

"Just a minute," Kennedy said. "Whose idea was it? Do you know a Mr. Watsinski? Or Poggioli?"

"What are you, a detective? Come on, there are people waiting. Step right up, friends! Don't go away, lady—the brave pioneers on Ganymede want to hear from you!"

At his left a fat, middle-aged woman was writing a letter that began, *Dear Dr. Hornsfall—*

"Let's go, Ted," Marge said suddenly.

"No. Just a second." He yanked a dollar out of his wallet, slapped it down, and picked up a pencil. With quick sloppy strokes he wrote: *Dear Director Brookman, Hope all is well with colony; too bad you're just a publicity man's soap bubble. Sincerely, Jasper Greeblefizz.*

He handed over the filled-in sheet and said, "Here, make sure this gets delivered. Come on away from here, Marge."

As he stepped out onto the main concourse again he heard the booth-tender's raucous voice: "Hey, mister, you got too many words in this message! You only allowed ten words and you got fifteen!"

Kennedy ignored him. He grasped Marge tightly by the hand and walked on at a rapid clip.

"You think my letter will get there?" he asked tightly. "You think Director Brookman will answer it?"

She looked at him strangely. Sweat was running down her face and shoulders. "I don't know why you're so upset, Ted. It's all part of the general picture, isn't it? This is a very clever gimmick."

"Yeah," he said. He looked back and saw a line of people waiting to send letters to the brave pioneers on Ganymede. A very clever gimmick. Very clever.

A woman in her late thirties came running by, face frozen in a horrified smile. She wore bright blue lipstick that was smeared all over her face, and she was clutching her tattered halter together with one hand.

In hot pursuit came a much younger man with the bright fierce eyes of a satyr. He was yelling, "Come back, Libby, we still got half an hour paid for!"

Kennedy smiled crookedly. World Holiday. Step outside yourself and leave your ulcers behind. Girls who were the epitome of prudishness thought nothing of whipping off their halters and letting the breeze cool their breasts until the park police intervened. Sober second-level men could ease their tensions in a frenzied alcoholic jig.

But World Holiday was no holiday for him. There was no escaping Ganymede even out here. He was worse off than the carny men who had to work on World Holiday, he thought; at least they drew double pay.

Marge squeezed his hand. "You look funny. You're all right, aren't you, Ted?"

"Sure. Sure. The heat, that's all. I'd be cooked without this hat."

Somehow he pretended gaiety. They had another drink, and another. They looped the loop and rode the caterpillars and goggled at the sweating freaks in the sideshow, and had more drinks. They met Mike Cameron and his wife; the third-level man looked drunk and so did his blond wife. Jerrie Cameron brushed up against Kennedy in open invitation, but he ignored it. The Camerons reeled on toward the rocket. Kennedy and Marge had another drink.

Sometime later they bought tickets for the swimming pool, the one place in Joyland where nudity went unquestioned, and spent an hour bobbing in the warm, chlorinated water. Toward evening they watched the fireworks display and wandered down to the rocket-field to see the big missile come in for a landing.

Kennedy felt dizzy and when he looked at Marge she was smiling crookedly. They wearily retraced their steps to the exit. The *Send A Letter To Ganymede* booth was doing land-office business. The program was a success, Kennedy realized dimly; even Joyland recognized the impact of his Ganymede colony on the nation.

At the parking lot the attendant was dispensing sober-tabs for all drivers; you couldn't get your car until you took one. Kennedy swallowed the tasteless little pellet and felt his mind clearing. His stomach began to knot again. He paused by his car, watching the purple and aureate brilliance of the fireworks in the dust-hung sky, listening to the big swoosh of the departing rocket.

The fun would go on all night. There was always Sunday for recuperating. But he felt no more desire for amusement, and drove home slowly and cautiously, with his hand grimly gripping the wheel. Marge was exhausted; she curled up into a fetal ball on the back seat and slept. Kennedy wondered about the Camerons, and if Jerrie had found the partner she so obviously was searching for.

Happy World Holiday to me, he thought tiredly. *Happy, happy, happy.*

8

SUNDAY WAS a gloom-shrouded botch of a day. Kennedy slept late, dreaming of the harsh hues of Joyland, and woke with his mind still clouded by bitterness and his head aching. He spent an awkward, uncomfortable day in and around the house with Marge. The 'fax-sheet gave the rundown on the World Holiday damage: a thousand lives lost in the Appalachia district alone, much carnage, property destruction, theft. A good day's fun.

It was his turn to operate the car-pool come Monday, the second of July, as 2044 swung into its second half. When he reached the office he found a crisp little note waiting for him on his desk:

> *Floor Nine*
> *6:57 A.M.*

> *Ted:*
> *Would you stop off at my office at 8:30 this morning?*
> *We're having an important visitor.*
> *LD:lk*   *Lou*

Curious, he arrived at Dinoli's office a little ahead of time and cooled his heels in the big man's oak-paneled foyer for a while until a white-toothed secretary ushered him through the maze into the first-level suite.

There was quite a turnout in Dinoli's office. Dinoli himself faced the door, keen-eyed and wide awake, hunched over with his gnarled hands locked. Kennedy smiled hello. Standing around Dinoli were four men: Watsinski, looking bored; McDermott, the tough little gamecock of a second-level man who was handling governmental liaison on the Ganymede Contract; Executive Hubbel of the Corporation. There was also a fourth man, thick-necked and coarse-featured, with a broad, genial smile and a delicate network of broken capillaries spread out over his face.

Dinoli said, "Mr. Bullard, I'd like you to meet Theodore Kennedy, Executive Third-Level of Steward and Dinoli."

Bullard swung forward. He was a bull of a man, six four or more in height, with the biggest hands Kennedy had ever seen. He proffered one, mangled Kennedy's hand momentarily in greeting, and boomed, "Very pleased to meet you, Mr. Kennedy. I've heard wonderful things about your work from Mr. Dinoli here."

"Thank you, sir."

Kennedy looked around. Despite himself he felt a little wobbly-kneed; this was *very* big brass. Two first-level men in the same room.

"Did you enjoy your holiday?" Dinoli asked, in his dark vast voice.

"Yes, sir. It was very good, sir."

"Glad to hear it. You know, of course, that Mr. Bullard here is head of the Corporation?"

Kennedy nodded. Bullard swung himself up on the corner of Dinoli's conference table, crossed his long legs, took out an ignitopak and offered Kennedy a cigarette. He took it. To refuse would have been a mortal insult in such a meeting.

Smiling, Bullard said, "I understand you're the man who's responsible for development of the—ah— colony on Ganymede. I want to tell you that it's a brilliant concept. Brilliant."

Kennedy was silent. He was tired of saying, *Thank you, sir.*

Bullard went on. "The whole nation—the whole world—is enraptured by the struggles of the unfortunate souls you've invented. And I understand you and you alone have charge of the project."

"I have an assistant, sir. A man named Spalding. He's been a great help."

He saw Watsinski pale; Dinoli seemed to scowl. A little taken aback, Bullard said, "Ah, yes. But the main responsibility is yours. And that's why I've come over here this morning to make this offer to you."

"Offer, sir?"

"A very fine one. You've succeeded in capturing the feel of the Ganymede terrain beautifully, considering the second-hand nature of your data. But Mr. Dinoli and I believe that you'd do an even finer job if you had a little actual experience with living conditions on Ganymede. It would give your project that extra touch of reality that would insure the success of the campaign."

Kennedy blinked. Dinoli was beaming.

Bullard said, "There's a supply ship leaving shortly for the Ganymede outpost. There is room for one

passenger aboard that ship. I've spoken to Mr.
Dinoli and we've agreed to offer you a chance to be
that passenger. You can spend three weeks on
Ganymede at Corporation expense. How would you
like that?"

Kennedy felt steamrollered. He took a fumbling
step backward and grabbed a chair. "Sir, I—"

"You want time to think about it. I understand
how it is. You're in the midst of a difficult work program. You have certain personal commitments.
Well, the ship departs on Thursday. If you care to be
on it, all you need to do is say the word."

Kennedy looked at Dinoli, at Watsinski, at
McDermott. Their faces gave no hint of feeling. They
wanted him to go. They wanted him to drop everything and race off to a cold little iceball in space and
live there for three weeks in utter privation so the
campaign could be more realistic.

It was impossible to come right out and say no,
right here. He would have to stall. "I'll have to take
the matter up with my wife, of course. This is so sudden. This great opportunity—"

"Of course," Bullard said. "Well, notify Mr.
Dinoli on Wednesday. He'll contact me and make
the final arrangements for transporting you."

Signed, sealed, and delivered, Kennedy thought. "Yes,
sir," he said hoarsely. "Thank you, sir." To Dinoli
he said: "Is there anything else, Mr. Dinoli?"

"No, Ted. That'll be all. Just wanted to let you
know the good news, son."

"Thank you, sir," Kennedy mouthed uncertainly.
A secretary showed him out.

He returned numbly to his office on Eleven, the
office he now shared with Dave Spalding. Trip to

Ganymede, he thought. I'll tell them Marge won't let me go. That we're expecting a baby. Anything.

It wouldn't look good, his refusing. But he was damned if he was going to spend three weeks living under the conditions he'd been writing about.

"You look as if you've been guillotined," Spalding said, as Kennedy came in. "They didn't fire you!"

"No such luck. I've got a great big opportunity. The Corporation's offering me a three-week trip to Ganymede to get the feel of things."

A sudden flicker of eagerness came into Spalding's lean face. It was an ugly look, as if Spalding had realized that *he* would be in charge, doing second-level work, all the time Kennedy was gone. "You're accepting, of course?"

Kennedy grimaced. "If I'm buffaloed into it. But I'm sure Marge will howl. She hates to be left alone even for *one* night. And three weeks—"

"She can't go with you?"

"There's just one passage available. I'd be leaving on Thursday if I accept. But that would leave you in charge of the project, wouldn't it?"

"I can handle it."

"I know you can. But suppose you pick the time I'm gone to have another attack of ethics? Suppose you walk out while I'm up in outer space, and leave the project flat? What's Watsinski going to do—say all communications with Ganymede have been suddenly cut off, and wait for me to get back to patch up the damage?"

Spalding's lips tightened. "I told you I didn't plan any walkouts. I can't afford to quit yet. I haven't shown any signs of it in the last five weeks, have I? I've been working like a dog on this project."

"I'm sorry, Dave. I had a rough weekend. I didn't mean to come down on you like that. Let's get to work."

He pulled down one of the big loose-leaf volumes they had made up. They had written out detailed biographies of each of the three hundred and thirteen colonists with whom they had populated Ganymede, and each morning they picked a different one to feature in the newsbreaks.

"I think it's time to get Mary Walls pregnant," Kennedy said. "We haven't had a pregnancy on Ganymede yet. You have the medical background Rollins dug up?"

Spalding produced a slim portfolio bound in black leather—a doctor's report on possible medical problems in the colony. Childbirth under low gravity, pressure diseases, things like that.

Spalding typed out a press release about the first pregnancy on Ganymede, with quotes from the happy mother-to-be, the stunned prospective father ("Gosh, this is great news! I know my Ma back in Texas will jump up and clack her heels when she finds out about Mary!") and, of course, from the ever-talkative Director Brookman.

While he worked, Kennedy checked the photo file for a snapshot of Mary Walls—agency technicians had prepared a phony composograph of every member of the colony—and readied it for release with Spalding's newsbreak. He added the day's news to the Colony Chronicle he was writing—excerpts were being printed daily in the tabloids—and wrote a note to himself to remember that a maternity outfit would need to be ordered before Thursday for Mrs. Walls, to be shipped up on the next supply ship.

Thought of the supply ship brought him back to his own predicament. *Dammit,* he thought, *I don't want to go to Ganymede!*

It had gotten to the point where he believed in his colony up there. He could picture slab-jawed Director Brookman, an outwardly fierce, inwardly sentimental man, could picture rosy-cheeked Mary Walls being told by mustachioed Dr. Hornsfall that she was going to be blessed with a child—

And it was all phony. The outpost on Ganymede consisted of a couple of dozen foul-smelling bearded spacemen, period. He didn't want to go there.

He realized that Spalding could handle the project perfectly well without him. It was running smoothly, now; the news sources were open and well oiled, the populace was hooked, the three hundred and thirteen colonists had assumed three dimensions not only in his mind but in Spalding's and in the rest of the world's. The colony had a life of its own now. Spalding would merely have to extend its activities day by day in his absence.

They phoned in the pregnancy story before noon, and got busy sketching out the next day's work. Spalding was writing Director Brookman's autobiography, to be serialized in some big weekly—they were still pondering bids—while Kennedy blocked in succeeding events in Mary Walls' pregnancy. He toyed momentarily with the idea of having her suffer a miscarriage in about two months' time, but rejected it; it would be good for a moment's pathos, but quickly forgotten. Having her stay pregnant would be more effective.

Near closing time the reaction hit him, as it did every day toward the finish. He sat back and stared at his trembling hands.

My God, he thought, *this is the biggest hoax humanity has ever known. And I originated it.*

He estimated that perhaps fifty people were in on the hoax now. That was too many. What if one of them cracked up and spilled it all? Would they all be lynched?

They would not, he answered himself. The thing was too firmly embedded in reality by now. He had done his job too well. If someone—anyone—stood up and yelled that it was all a fake, that there was no colony on Ganymede, it would be a simple matter to laugh it down as crackpottery and go ahead manufacturing the next day's set of press releases.

But still the enormity of it chilled him. He looked at Spalding, busily clacking out copy, and shuddered. By now the afternoon telefax sheets were spewing forth the joyous news that Mary Walls—petite little Mary Walls, twenty-five, red-haired, a colony dietician, married two years to lanky Mike Walls, twenty-nine, of Houston, Texas—was about to bear young.

He clenched his fists. Where did it stop, he wondered? Was anything real?

Was he, he wondered, just part of a fictitious press release dreamed up by some glib public relations man elsewhere? Did Mary Walls, up there on Ganymede, know that she was a cardboard figure being manipulated by a harrowed-looking man in New York, that her pregnancy had been brought about not by her loving husband's caress but by a divine gesture on the part of one Theodore Kennedy?

He wiped away sweat. A heavy fist thundered on their glassite cubicle and he looked up to see Alf Haugen grinning at him.

"Come on, geniuses. It's closing time and I want to get out of here!"

They locked away their books and the car-pool people assembled. Kennedy dropped them each off at their destinations, and finally swung his car into his own garage.

Marge had his afternoon cocktail ready for him. He told her about Bullard's visit, about Dinoli's offer. "So they want to send me to Ganymede for three weeks, and I'd be leaving Thursday? How d'you like that!"

She smiled. "I think it's wonderful! I'll miss you, of course, but—"

His mouth sagged open. "You think I'm going to accept this crazy deal?"

"Aren't you?"

"But I thought—" He closed his eyes a moment. "You *want* me to go, Marge?"

"It's a grand opportunity for you, dear. You may never get another chance to see space. And it's safe, isn't it? They say space travel is safer than riding in a car." She laughed. It was a brittle laugh that told Kennedy a great many things he did not want to know.

She wants me to go, he thought. *She wants to get rid of me for three weeks.*

He took a deep, calm sip. "As a matter of fact, I have until Wednesday to make up my mind," he said. "I told them I'd have to discuss the matter with you before I could agree to anything. But I guess it's okay with you."

Her voice cracked a little as she said, "I certainly wouldn't object. Have I ever stood in the way of your advancement, Ted?"

9

THE SHIP left at 1100 sharp on Thursday, July 5, 2044, and Ted Kennedy was aboard it.

The departure went smoothly and on schedule. The ship was nameless, bearing only the number GC-1073; the captain was a gruff man named Hills who did not seem pleased at the prospect of ferrying a groundlubber long with him to Ganymede. Blast-off was held at Spacefield Seven, a wide jet-blasted area in the flatlands of New Jersey that served as the sole spaceport for the eastern half of the United States.

A small group of friends and well-wishers rode out with Kennedy in the jetcab to see him off. Marge came, and Dave Spalding, and Mike Cameron, and Ernie Watsinski. Kennedy sat moodily in the corner of the cab, staring downward at the smoke-stained sky of industrialized New Jersey, saying nothing, thinking dark thoughts.

He was not looking forward to the trip at all.

Space travel, to him, was still something new and risky. There had been plenty of flights; space travel was forty years old and far from being in the pioneering stage. There had been flights to Mars and Venus, and there was a thriving colony of engineers living in a dome on Luna. Captain Hills had made the Ganymede run a dozen times in the past year. But still Kennedy was nervous.

He was being railroaded. They were all conspiring, he thought, all the smiling false friends who gathered around him. They wanted to send him off to the airless ball of ice halfway across the sky.

The ship was a thin needle standing on its tail, very much alone in the middle of the vast, grassless field. Little trucks had rolled up around it; one was feeding fuel into the reaction-mass hold, one was laden down with supplies for the men of the outpost, another carried mail—*real* mail, not the carnival-inspired fakery Kennedy had seen on World Holiday—for the men up there.

The ship would carry a crew of six, plus cargo. The invoices listed Kennedy as part of the cargo.

He stood nervously at the edge of the field, watching the ship being loaded and half-listening to the chatter of his farewell committee. A tall gaunt-looking man in a baggy gray uniform came up to them and without waiting for silence said, "Which one of you is Kennedy?"

"I am." It was almost a croak.

"Glad to know you. I'm Charley Sizer, ship's medic. Come on with me."

Kennedy looked at his watch. "But it's an hour till blastoff time."

Sizer grinned. "Indeed it is. I want to get you loaded up with gravanol so acceleration doesn't catch you by surprise. When that big fist comes down you won't like it. Let's go, now—you're holding up the works."

Kennedy glanced around at the suddenly solemn little group and said, "Well, I guess this is it. See you all three weeks from now. Ernie, make sure my paychecks get sent home on time." He waited a couple of seconds more. "Marge?" he said finally. "Can I get a kiss good-bye?"

"I'm sorry, Ted." She pecked at his lips and stepped back. He grinned lopsidedly and let Sizer lead him away.

He clambered up the catwalk into the ship. It was hardly an appealing interior. The ship was poorly lit and narrow; the companionways were strictly utilitarian. This was no shiny passenger ship. Racks of spacesuits hung to one side; far to the front he saw two men peering at a vastly complex control panel.

"Here's where you'll stay," Sizer said, indicating a sort of hammock swung between two girders. "Suppose you climb in now and I'll let you have the gravanol pill."

Kennedy climbed in. There was a viewplate just to the left of his head, and he glanced out and saw Marge and Watsinski and the others standing far away, at the edge of the field, watching the ship. Sizer bustled efficiently around him, strapping a safety-webbing over him. The gaunt medic vanished and returned a few minutes later with a water flask and a small bluish pill.

"This stuff will take all the fret out of blast-off," Sizer explained. "We could hit ten or fifteen g's and you wouldn't even know it. You'll sleep like a babe." He handed the pill to Kennedy, who swallowed it, finding it tasteless, and gulped water. Kennedy felt no internal changes that would make him resistant to gravity.

He rolled his eyes toward the right. "Say—what happens if there's an accident? I mean, where's my spacesuit? I ought to know where it is, in case—"

Sizer chuckled. "It takes about a month of training to learn how to live inside a spacesuit, brother. There just isn't any sense in giving you one. But there aren't going to be any accidents. Haven't they told you space flight's safer than driving a car?"

"Yes, but—"

"But nothing. The ship's in perfect order. Nothing can go wrong. You've got Newton's laws of physics working on your side all the way from here to Ganymede and back, and no crazy Holiday drivers coming toward you in your own lane. Just lie back and relax. You'll doze off soon. Next thing you know, we'll be past the Moon and Ganymede-bound."

Kennedy started to protest that he wasn't sleepy, that he was much too tense to be able to fall asleep. But even as he started to protest, he felt a wave of fatigue sweep over him. He yawned.

Grinning, Sizer said, "Don't worry, now. See you later, friend." He threaded his way forward.

Kennedy lay back. He was securely webbed down in the acceleration hammock; he could hardly move. Drowsiness was getting him now. He saw his watch dimly and made out the time as 1045. Fifteen minutes to blast-off. Through the port he saw the little trucks rolling away.

Sleep blurred his vision as the time crawled on toward 1100. He wanted to be awake at the moment of blast-off, to feel the impact, to see Earth leap away from them with sudden ferocity. But he was getting tired. *I'll just close my eyes a second,* he thought. *Just catch forty winks or so before we lift.*

He let his eyelids drop.

A few minutes later he heard the sound of chuckling. Someone touched his arm. He blinked his eyes open and saw Medic Sizer and Captain Hills standing next to his hammock, looking intently at him.

"There something wrong?" he asked in alarm.

"We just wanted to find out how you were doing," Hills said. "Everything okay?"

"Couldn't be better. I'm loose and relaxed. But isn't it almost time for blast-off?"

Hills laughed shortly. "Yeh. That's a good one. Look out that port, Mr. Kennedy."

Numbly Kennedy swiveled to the left and looked out. He saw darkness, broken by bright hard little dots of painful light. At the bottom of the viewplate, just barely visible, hung a small green ball with the outlines of Europe and Asia still visible. It looked like a geographical globe. At some distance away hung a smaller pockmarked ball.

Everything seemed frozen and terribly silent, like a Christmas-card scene.

In a hushed voice Kennedy said, "Are we in space?"

"We sure are. You slept through the whole thing, it seems. Blast-off and null-g and everything. We're a half-day out from Earth. From here till Ganymede it's all a pretty placid downhill coast, Mr. Kennedy."

"Is it safe to get out of this cradle?" he asked.

Hills shrugged. "Why not?"

"I won't float, or anything?"

"Three hours ago we imparted spin along the longitudinal axis, Mr. Kennedy. The gravity in here is precisely one g Earth-norm. If you're hungry, food's on in the galley up front."

He ate. Ship food—packaged synthetics, nourishing and healthfully balanced and about as tasty as straw briquettes. He ate silently and alone, serving himself; the rest of the men had already had their midday meal.

Four of them were playing cards in the fore cubicle that looked out onto the stars. Kennedy was both shocked and amused when he stopped through the unlocked door and saw the four of them, grimy and bearded, dressed in filthy fatigue uniforms, squatting around an empty fuel drum playing poker with savage intensity, while five feet away from them all the splendor of the skies lay unveiled.

He had no desire to break into the game, and they ignored him so throughly that it was clear he was not invited. He turned away, smiling. No doubt after you made enough trips, he thought, the naked wonder of space turned dull on you, and poker remained eternally fascinating. The sight of an infinity of blazing suns was finite in its appeal, Kennedy decided. But he himself stared long and hard at the sharp blackness outside, broken by the stream of stars and by the distant redness of what he supposed was Mars.

Mars receded. Kennedy thought he caught sight of ringed Saturn later in the day. Hours passed. He ate again, slept, read.

Two days went by, or maybe three. To the six men of the crew, he was just a piece of cargo—ambulatory, perhaps, but still cargo. He read several books. He let his beard grow until the stubbly shoots began to itch fiercely, and then he shaved it off. Once he started to write a letter to Marge, but he never finished it. He wished bitterly he had brought

Watsinski or Dinoli or Bullard along to live on this cramped ship and see Ganymede at first hand.

Even he grew tired of the splendor of the skies. He remembered a time in his boyhood when an uncle had given him a cheap microscope, and he had gone to a nearby park and scooped up a flask of stagnant water. For days he had stared in open-mouthed awe at paramecia and fledgling snails and a host of ciliated creatures, and then the universe in the drop of water had merely given him eyestrain and, bored with his host of creatures, he had impatiently flushed them down the drain.

It was much the same here. The stars were glorious, but even sheer glory palls at length. He could meditate only so long on the magnitude of space, on the multiplicity of suns, on the strange races that might circle red Antares or bright Capella. The vastness of space held a sheerly emotional kind of wonder for him, rather than intellectual, and so it easily became exhausting and finally commonplace. He turned away from the port and returned to his books.

Until finally great Jupiter blotted out the sky, and Sizer came by to tell him that the icy crescent silver he saw faintly against the mighty planet's bulk was their destination, Ganymede.

Again he was strapped into the cradle—the deceleration cradle, now; a mild semantic difference. A second time he took a pill, and a second time he slept. When he woke, some time later, there was whiteness outside the port—the endless eye-numbing whiteness of the snowfields of Ganymede.

It was day—"day" being a ghostly sort of half-dusk, at this distance from the sun. Kennedy knew enough about the mechanics of Ganymede from his pseudo-colony work of the past month to be aware that a Ganymedean day lasted slightly more than seven Earth days, the length of time it took Ganymede to revolve once about Jupiter—for Ganymede, like Earth's Moon, kept the same face toward its primary at all times.

Jupiter now was a gibbous splinter from dayside, a vast chip of a planet that seemed to be falling toward Ganymede's bleak surface like a celestial spear. Visible against the big planet's bulk was the lesser splinter of one of the other Galilean moons—Io, most likely, Kennedy thought.

No doubt the dome was on the other side of the ship. From his port, nothing was visible but the ugly teeth of broken mountains, bare, tufted with layers of frozen ammonia, misted by swirling methane clouds.

The ship's audio system barked. "All hands in suits! Mr. Kennedy, come forward, on the double. We've arrived on Ganymede."

Kennedy wondered how they were going to transport him without a suit. His question was answered before it could be asked; Sizer and one of the crewmen came toward him, swinging the hollow bulk of a spacesuit between them like an eviscerated corpse.

They helped him into it, clamped down the helmet, and switched on his breathing unit and his audio.

Sizer said, "You won't be in this thing long. Don't touch any of the gadgets and try not to sneeze. If you feel your breathing supply going bad, yell and yell *fast*. Everything clear?"

"Yes," Kennedy said. He felt warm and humid in the suit; they hadn't bothered to switch on his air-conditioners, or perhaps there weren't any. He saw men starting down the catwalk in their suits, and he advanced toward the yawning airlock, moving in a stiff, awkward robot-shuffle until he discovered the suit was flexible enough to allow him to walk normally.

He lowered himself through the lock and with great care descended the catwalk. He saw a sprawling low dome to his right, housing several slipshod prefabricated buildings. A truck had popped through an airlock in the side of the dome and was heading toward them. He saw a few figures inside the dome peering curiously outward at the newly arrived spaceship.

A sharp wind whistled about him; paradoxically, he was sweating inside his suit, but he also sensed the numbing cold that was just a fraction of an inch away from his skin. In the wan daylight he could see the cold outlines of stars bridging the blue-black sky. He realized that he had never actually visualized Ganymede despite all his press releases and publicity breaks.

It was a hard bitter place where the wind mumbled obscenities in his spacesuit's audio pickup and the stars glimmered in the daylight. He looked into the distance, wondering if any of the natives were on hand to witness the new arrival, but as far as he could see the landscape was barren and empty.

The truck arrived. Within its sealed pressurized cab rode a red-bearded man who signaled for them to climb into the back. They did, Kennedy going up next to last and needing a boost from the man behind him to make it. He felt helpless and ashamed of himself.

The truck turned and headed toward the opening airlock of the Ganymede dome.

10

He felt penned in, inside the dome. He met the sixteen men who lived there, who had lived there ever since Corporation money and Corporation skill and Corporation spaceships had let man reach Ganymede. He shifted uneasily from foot to foot, breathing the sharp, faintly acrid synthetic atmosphere of the dome, feeling mildly queasy-stomached at the lessened pull of gravity. Ganymede exerted only eighty-one percent of Earth's pull on him. He weighed just about one hundred forty-two pounds here.

He half expected to see the big figure of Colony Director Lester Brookman come striding out of the dimness to shake his hand and welcome him to Ganymede, but Brookman was just a myth he had invented one rainy May afternoon. The real head of the Ganymede outpost was a stubby little man with a bushy, gray-flecked beard. His name was Gunther. He was a third-level man in the Corporation, but up here all such titles went by the board.

He eyed Kennedy stolidly after Kennedy had dis-
encumbered himself of his spacesuit. Finally he said,
"You're Kennedy?"

"That's right."

"Papers say you'll be here until the ship returns to
Earth. That's three Gannydays from now, a little
over three weeks. You'll be living in Barracks B on
the second level; one of the men will show you where
your bunk is. There's to be no smoking anywhere in
the dome at any time. If you have any questions con-
cerning operations here, you're to ask me. If you're
told by any member of this base that a given area is
restricted, you're not to enter it under any circum-
stance. Clear?"

"Clear," Kennedy said. He resented the brusque-
ness of Gunther's manner, but perhaps that was
what six months or a year of life on a frozen waste of
a world did to a man.

"Do you know how to use a spacesuit?"

"No."

"As expected. You'll receive instruction starting at
0900 tomorrow. You'll undergo a daily drill in spacesuit technique until you've mastered its functions.
We never know when the dome's going to crack."

He said it flatly and quietly, as if he might be
saying, *We never know when it may start to rain*. Kennedy
nodded without commenting.

"You'll be taken on a tour of the area as soon as
you request it, provided there's a man free to accompany you. Under no circumstances are you to leave
the dome alone. This is definite."

"When will I get a chance to meet some of the
aliens?" Kennedy asked.

Gunther seemed to look away. "You'll be allowed

to meet the Gannys at such time as we see fit, Mr. Kennedy. Are there any further questions?"

There were, but Kennedy didn't feel like asking them. He shook his head instead, and Gunther signaled to another member of the outpost to show him to his room.

It turned out to be a crude little box with a window opening out onto the little courtyard between the three buildings of the dome; it had a hard cot covered with a single sheet, a washstand, a baggage rack. It looked like nothing so much as a cheap hotel room in a rundown section of an old city. It was very Earthlike, and there was nothing alien about it except the view that could be had by peering around the facing barracks-building at the bleak snowfields.

The three outpost buildings had been prefabricated, of course; building materials did not lie around on Ganymede waiting for visiting spacemen to shape them into neat cottages. A central ventilator system kept the dome and all the rooms within it reasonably fresh. A central power system supplied light and heat; the plumbing in the dome was crude but effective.

The entire project now attained reality for the first time for Kennedy. Despite the movies, despite research, despite everything, Ganymede had just been a name. Now it was a real place. The campaign acquired an extra dimension. This was a little planet, inhabited by intelligent beings, rich in radioactive ores, desired by a vast Corporation. He could grasp each concrete clause firmly now.

This was the place he had been selling to the world. Up here lived Lester Brookman and David Hornsfall and all his other imaginary colonists. They were myths; but Ganymede was real.

A spaceman named Jaeckel drilled him in the use
of a spacesuit, showed him how to manipulate the
controls that blew his nose and wiped his forehead
and ventilated the suit. At the end of the first hour he
had a fair idea of how to run the suit, though he was
still vague on what to do when the powerpak ran dry,
and how to send long-distance S O S signals through
his helmet amplifier.

Once he had mastered the suit, they let him go
outside the dome, always in the company of an off-
duty outpost man. The snow was thick and firmly
packed into ice; bare patches of rock thrust snouts up
here and there. A paraffin lake was located half a
mile west of the dome—a broad, dull-looking body of
dark liquid. Kennedy stood at its shore and peered
downward.

"Does anything live in it?"

"Snails and toads and things. The Ganymedean
equivalent, of course. Methane breathers, you know.
We see them come hopping up on shore during the
big storms."

"How about fish equivalents?" Kennedy asked.

"We don't know. We don't have any boats and we
don't have any fishing tackle. Radar says there's a
few shapes moving down at the bottom but we
haven't had time to find them yet."

Kennedy leaned forward, hoping to catch sight of
a methane-breathing fish snouting through the
depths, but all he saw was his own reflected image,
shown dimly by the faint light, a bulky, grotesque,
spacesuited figure with a domed head.

He was taken out to see the vegetation, too: the

"forests" of scraggly waxen bushes, geared to the ammonia-methane respiratory cycle. They were inches high, with thick rigid leaves spread flat to catch as much of the sunlight as they could, and even the strongest winds failed to disturb them where they grew along a snow-banked hillside.

Inside the dome, Kennedy had little to do. After he had seen the compact turbines that powered the outpost, after he had inspected the kitchen and the game room and the little library, there was not much else for him to see. On the third day he asked Gunther when he'd be allowed to see the inhabitants of Ganymede, and Gunther had irritably responded, "Soon!"

Kennedy became suspicious. He wondered whether the Ganymedeans were not hoaxes too, along with Dr. Hornsfall and Director Brookman.

He spoke with an angular, faded-looking man named Engel, who was a linguist in Corporation employ. Engel was working on the Ganymedean language.

"It's fairly simple," he told Kennedy. "The Gannys haven't ever developed a written culture, and a language limited to oral transmission doesn't usually get to be very complex. It starts off as a series of agreed-upon grunts and it generally stays that way. The Gannys we've met have a vocabulary of perhaps a thousand words and a residual vocabulary no bigger than three or four thousand. The language agglutinates—that is, the words pile up. There's one word for *man;* but instead of having a separate word, like *warrior*, for the concept *man-with-spear*, their word for *warrior* is simply *manwithspear*. And the grammar's ridiculously simple too—no inflections or

declensions, no variation in terms of gender or case.
The Gannys are lucky; they aren't saddled with the
confused remnants of the old Indo-Aryan pro-
tolanguage the way we are. It's a terribly simple language."

"Meaning that they're terribly simple people?"
Kennedy asked.

Engel laughed. "It's not quite a one-to-one cor-
relation. Matter of fact, they're damned quick
thinkers, and they get along pretty well despite the
handicap of such a limited language. It's a limited
world. You don't need many words on a planet
where there's hardly any seasonal change and where
living conditions remain uniform century after century. Uniformly miserable, I mean."

Kennedy nodded. Engel showed him a mim-
eographed pamphlet he had prepared, labelled *Notes
Toward A Ganny Etymology and Philology*.

"Mind if I look this over?" Kennedy asked.

Engel shrugged and said, "I guess it's all right. It
can't do any harm to let you read it."

Kennedy studied the pamphlet alone in his room
that night, for lack of any better recreation. He fell
asleep with the light on and the book still open, after
a couple of hours of mumbling disjointed Ganny
phrases which he hoped followed Engel's phonetic
system; he didn't even notice it when the room-light
cut off, as it did every night at 0100 camp-time.

On the fourth day a tremendous storm swept in
and engulfed the area. Kennedy stood in the yard
near the arching curve of the dome, staring out in
awe at the fierce torrent of precipitated ammonia
that poured down on the plain, giving way finally to
feathery clouds of ammonia-crystal snow and then,

at last, to silence. The plain was covered with a fresh fall, now, and after it came the irascible wind, sculpturing the new fall into fantastic spires and eddies. Snow dunes heaped high against the side of the dome, and a trio of men in spacesuits went outside to clear them away. In the distance he saw the spaceship still upright, its landing vanes concealed by fresh snow, its dark prow tipped with mounds of white.

And on the fifth day he was again alone in his room when a tattoo of knocks sounded. He slipped Engel's linguistics pamphlet under his soggy pillow and opened the door.

Spaceman Jaeckel stood there. "Gunther sent me to get you, Kennedy. Some aliens are here. They're waiting outside the dome if you want to meet them."

Hastily he ran downstairs, found the spacesuit rack, and donned his. Gunther was already in his, looking small and round and agile.

"On the double, if you want to see them, Kennedy! They aren't going to wait out there forever!"

Four of them went through the lock—Gunther, Engel, Kennedy, and a spaceman named Palmer. Kennedy felt a strange tingle of excitement. These were the beings the Steward and Dinoli agency was training mankind to hate; these were the beings Alf Haugen was gradually building up as enemies of humanity, and he was going to meet them now.

There were three of them, standing in a little group ten feet from the airlock entrance. Naked except for their cloth girdles, noseless, eyes hooded, they looked to Kennedy like aborigines of some bizarre South Sea Island as seen in a dream. Their skin, pale white, had a waxy sheen to it. Their mouths were glum, sagging semicircles, lipless. At first Kennedy was surprised that they could bear the murderous cold, standing in calm nudity with no sign of discomfort.

But why the hell shouldn't they, he thought. *This is their world. They breathe its foul, corrosive air and they brush their teeth, if they have teeth, with the high-octane stuff that flows in their lakes and rivers. They probably can't understand how we can possibly survive in the blazing heat of Earth, and drink that poisonous hydrogen-oxygen compound we're so fond of.*

"These three are from the closest tribe," Gunther said. "They live eleven miles to the east and come here every seventh Earth-day to talk to us."

And indeed they *were* talking; one of them began speaking in a low monotone, addressing his words to Gunther. Fascinated, Kennedy listened.

He could only pick out a word here and there; his few hours spent with Engel's booklet had not made him a master of the language. But the words he picked out interested him greatly.

For the alien seemed to be saying, ". . . once again . . . leave us . . . hatecarryingbeings . . . interfere . . . when you go . . . soon . . ."

Gunther replied with a rapid-fire string of syllables spoken with such machine-gun intensity that Kennedy could scarcely catch the meaning of a single word. He did pick up one, though; it was the Ganny word for total negation, absolute refusal.

The alien replied, ". . . sadness . . . pain . . . until go . . . sacrilege . . ."

"Mind if I ask what the conversation's all about?" Kennedy said.

Engel blinked. Gunther tightened his lips, then

said, "We're arranging for transportation of supplies to the alien village in exchange for a bit of negotiation for mining rights with the village chief. He's telling us the best time of day to make the delivery."

Kennedy tried to hide his surprise. Either Gunther had just reeled off a flat lie, or else Kennedy had been completely wrong in his translation of the conversation. It had seemed to him that the aliens had been demanding an Earth evacuation, and that Gunther had been refusing. But perhaps he had been wrong; not even the simplest of languages could be learned in a matter of days.

The aliens were stirring restlessly. The spokesman repeated his original statement twice, then tipped his head back in a kind of ceremonial gesture, leaned forward, and exhaled a white cloud. Ammonia crystals formed briefly on the face-plate of Gunther's breathing-helmet. The Corporation man replied with a sentence too terse for Kennedy to be able to translate.

Then the aliens nodded their heads and uttered the short disyllable that meant farewell; Kennedy caught it clearly. Automatically the response-word floated up from his memory, and he said it: "Ah-*yah*." The other three Earthmen spoke the word at the same time. The aliens turned and gravely stalked away into the whirling wind.

A moment later Gunther whirled and seized Kennedy's arm tightly with his spacegloved hand. Through the breathing mask Gunther's face assumed an almost demonic intensity as he glared at Kennedy.

"What did you say?" he demanded. "What did you just say? Did I just hear you say a word to that

Ganny in his own language? *Where did you learn it? Who authorized you to learn Ganny?* I could have you shot for this, Kennedy—agency pull or no agency pull!"

11

FOR A moment Kennedy stood frozen, listening to the fierce wind swirl around him, not knowing what to say. By revealing his knowledge of Ganymedean he had committed a major blunder.

"Well?" Gunther demanded. "How come you speak Ganny?"

"I—"

He stopped. Engel came to his rescue.

"That's the only word he knows," the tall linguist said. "Couple of days ago he was visiting me and when he left I said good-bye to him in Ganny. He wanted to know what I had just said, and I told him. There's no harm in that, Gunther."

Uncertainly the outpost chief released his grip on Kennedy's arm. Kennedy realized Engel was saving his own skin as well as his by the lie; evidently it was out of bounds for him to speak the native tongue.

But he saw his advantage. "Look here, Gunther— I'm not a Corporation man and I'm only technically under your command. Where do you come off threatening to shoot me for saying good-bye to a Ganny in his own language? I could let Bullard know and he'd bounce you down to tenth-level for a stunt like that."

In a short sharp sentence Gunther expressed his opinion of Corporation Executive Bullard. Then he said, "Let's go back into the dome. This is no place to stand around having a chat."

Without waiting for further discussion he signaled to have the lock opened. Kennedy was more than happy to turn his back on the bleakness of the open Ganymedean field.

They stripped off their spacesuits in silence, and racked them. Gunther said, "Suppose we go to my quarters, Kennedy. We can talk about things there."

"Should I come too?" Engel asked.

"No, you get about your business. And watch out how much classified info you teach to visitors next time, Mr. Engel. Clear?"

"Clear," Engel muttered, and turned away.

Gunther's quarters proved to be considerably more auspicious than the other rooms under the dome. A wide window gave unrestricted view of the entire area, but could be opaqued at the touch of a button; the cot was general issue and ascetic, but extra ventilator controls and brighter room lights indicated to Kennedy that Gunther was no subscriber to the theory that a commanding officer should share every privation of his men.

He opened a closet and took out a half-empty bottle of liquor. The label had been removed and a new one substituted, reading *Property of Robert Gunther*.

"Care for a drink?"

Kennedy did not, but he nodded deliberately. "Sure. Don't mind if I do. Straight?"

"There's ice," Gunther said. He fixed the drink, handed it to Kennedy, and said, "I'm sorry I blew up over such a little thing out there. You have to understand what life's like here, Kennedy. It's not easy on the nerves. Not at all. I try to maintain discipline over myself as well as the others, but there are times when my nerves just pop. I'm sorry it had to happen to you, that's all."

Kennedy smiled. "You practically ordered me off to the firing squad because I knew a word of Ganny. How come the language's so top-secret?"

It was a telling question. Gunther shifted uneasily and said, "It isn't, really. It's merely that we want to make sure all Earth-Ganymede negotiations take place through the Corporation. We wouldn't want another outfit to set up shop here and try to cut in."

"Meaning, presumably, that you suspect I'm going to learn the language, compile a dictionary of Ganny when I get back to Earth, and sell it for a fabulous sum to some as-yet-nonexistent competitor of the Extraterrestrial Development and Exploration Corporation, Ganymede Division? I assure you I've got no such sinister intentions. I'm just a hapless public relations man sent up here by his boss to get the feel of the territory."

"I haven't accused you of anything, Kennedy. But we have to take certain security precautions."

"I understand that."

"Good. In case you're filing a report, I'd greatly appreciate it if you'd omit any mention of this incident. As a favor to me."

"I guess I can manage that little thing," Kennedy said lightly.

He left Gunther soon after, feeling greatly perplexed. The outpost chief's real motivation seemed utterly transparent. Gunther was not fearing the advent of a rival corporation; it took years of legal work and billions in capital to build an organization the size of ED & E. No wildcat operation was going to send a ship to Ganymede to whisk mining rights out from under Gunther's sharp nose, making use of a Ganny dictionary prepared for them by Kennedy.

No, there could be only one possible reason why Gunther had reacted so violently when Kennedy had displayed a seeming understanding of Ganny. Gunther was afraid that Kennedy would overhear something the Corporation was trying to keep secret.

And that something, Kennedy suspected, was the fact that the Ganymedeans were hostile to the idea of having Earthmen settle on their world, and far from being willing to negotiate for mining rights were anxiously demanding that Gunther and his men get off.

That had seemed to be the drift of the conversation Kennedy had witnessed. And if that was the case, he thought, then the only way the Corporation was going to get what it wanted on Ganymede would be by a virtual extermination of the Gannys. No mere United Nations "police action," as Kennedy and the other agency men had been led to believe, but a full-scale bitter war of oppression.

Sure, they would rationalize it. The Gannys were a non-technological people who owned a vast horde of valuable radioactive ores and had no intentions of using them; for the public good of the solar system, then, these ores should be taken from them.

A cold thought struck him: any rationalization would come through the agency. Once it became apparent that the Gannys would have to be forcibly hurled to the side, his job would be to sell the people of Earth on the proposition that this was a necessary and cosmically wise action.

It was a nasty business, and he had been drawn into it deeper than he suspected. Oh, he had never thought it was a lily-white enterprise, but despite Marge's quiet opposition and Spalding's bitter outbursts he had gone along with the agency unthinkingly. The agency mask had been his defense: the unthinking reservation of judgment that allowed him to enter into a contract with little concern for the questions of values tangential to it.

Well, now he was seeing it clearly and first-hand. He returned to his room, planning to study the Ganny dictionary more intently. Next week when the aliens returned he *had* to know more of the true position of things.

But his door was ajar when he reached his room, and the light was on. There were no locks on the doors, but he had hardly expected someone to just walk in. He pushed open the door.

Engel was sitting on the edge of his bed waiting for him.

Kennedy waved cheerily to him. "I guess I owe you thanks. That could have been a nasty business with Gunther out there if you hadn't said what you did."

"Yes. Look here, Kennedy—I have to have that booklet back. Immediately. Where is it?"

"Back? Why?"

"Gunther would have me flayed if he knew I gave it to you. It was really unpardonable on my part—but you seemed so interested, and I was so anxious to have you see my work and be impressed by it." The linguist flushed and looked at his shoes. "Where is it now?"

Kennedy circled behind Engel and drew the dog-eared pamphlet out from under the pillow. Engel reached for it, but Kennedy snatched it quickly away.

"Give that to me! Kennedy, don't you understand that Gunther absolutely would execute me if he knew you had that? It's classified!"

"Why?"

"That doesn't matter. Give it to me."

Kennedy tucked it under his arm. "I don't intend to. I want to study it some more. It's a very ingenious work, Engel. I *am* impressed."

"If you don't give that to me," Engel said slowly, "I'll tell Gunther that you entered my quarters when I wasn't there and *stole* it from me. I know how many copies there are supposed to be. But I don't want to have to do that, so hand it over, will you? The linguist nibbled at his lip and flicked a globule of sweat from his forehead.

The room was very quiet a moment. Kennedy tightened his grip on the booklet under his arm. Staring levelly at Engel, he said, "You don't want to do that. I'll make a deal with you: you let me keep the dictionary, and I'll make sure Gunther never has occasion to find out you gave it to me. And I'll return it when I leave Ganymede. Otherwise, you try to tell Gunther I stole the dictionary and I'll tell him you gave it to me of your own free will, and then lied to him outside the dome just now to keep your own nose clean. It'll be my word against yours, but you'll be in a tough way trying to explain just why you took my part out there."

Engel knotted his hands nervously together. "It won't work. Gunther trusts me—"

"Like hell he does. Gunther doesn't even trust

himself. Let me keep the dictionary or I'll go to Gunther right now and tell him the whole story."

Scowling, Engel said, "Okay. The dictionary's yours—but keep your mouth shut the next time you're around any Gannys. If you stop to ask a local chief the time of day, Gunther'll roast us both."

"I'll keep quiet next time," Kennedy promised.

But as it developed, "next time" did not look like too probable an event.

Three days slipped by, in Kennedy's second week on Ganymede. He spent much of his time studying Engel's little handbook of the Ganny language, and repeated phrases and sentences to himself each night in a muttered whisper that once had his next-door neighbor banging on the partition and telling him to shut up and go to sleep.

He went on jeep trips over the Ganymedean terrain; it was nighttime on Ganymede now, and would be for four more Earth-days; Jupiter hung broodingly massive in the sky, blotting out the stars. Kennedy noticed that he instinctively avoided looking up at the great swollen planet in the sky; it was too sickeningly big, too awesome, for easy viewing.

Moons danced in the sky, swimming in and out of sight with dizzy unpredictability; now Io, now Europa, now far-off Callisto came whirling by, and their orbits were a computer's nightmare. Kennedy was impressed.

The terrain was monotonous, though—endless bluish ice-fields unbroken by sign of life. Once Kennedy asked his companion if they could visit a Ganny village for a change, instead of merely rolling on over icy wastes.

"You'll have to ask Gunther about that. I don't

have authority to take you there."

Kennedy asked Gunther. Gunther scowled and said, "I'm afraid not. The Ganny villages are restricted areas for visitors to the outpost."

"Why?"

"You don't ask why around here, Kennedy. You've been very cooperative up to now. Don't spoil it."

With a brusque gesture Gunther dismissed him. Kennedy turned away, his mind full of unanswered questions.

He studied his handbook. He waited impatiently for the Gannys to pay their next visit to the outpost; he wanted to listen to the conversation again, to find out exactly what the relationship was between Earthman and alien on this little world.

He asked questions of the other men—carefully guarded questions. He asked a mining engineer to take him to the main radioactives deposits. "I understand the Corporation expects to find transuranic elements in their natural state here on Ganymede," he said.

The mining engineer scratched his heavy-bearded chin and laughed. "Where'd you hear a crazy thing like that? Transuranics on Ganny? Maybe on Jupiter, but not here unless everything we know about planetary cores is cockeyed."

"But the data sheets we got implied it," Kennedy persisted. "Part of the general abundance of radioactive ores on Ganymede may be due to the presence of natural transuranics."

"You better check those data sheets again, Mister. There isn't any general abundance of hot stuff on Ganny. You can track that snow for days with your gamma detector and not get a peep."

That was interesting, Kennedy thought. Because if Ganymede was not as rich in radioactives as the Corporation publicity puffs had intimated, and if the natives were bluntly opposed to Terran operations on Ganymede, then the whole agency-nurtured maneuver was nothing more or less than a naked power grab on the part of the Corporation, a set-up maneuver that would drag the U.N. in to conquer Ganymede at no expense to the Corporation and then hand the little world over to Bullard and Company on a chrome-plated platter.

But he had to have more proof. He had to speak to the natives first-hand, preferably without any of Gunther's men around.

The day before the expected visit of the Gannys, Kennedy happened to mention to Gunther that he was looking forward to seeing the aliens again.

"Oh? You haven't heard? The visit's been called off. It's some sort of holy season in the village and they've decided not to see any Earthmen till it's over."

"And when will that be?"

"Five Ganny days from now. A little more than a month, Earth-time."

That was interesting too, Kennedy thought. Because that meant he would have no further opportunity at all for seeing or listening to the Gannys. And this "some sort of holy season" sounded too slick, too patently contrived to be convincing.

No. Gunther simply did not want him to penetrate Corporation activities on Ganymede any deeper than he already had. Evidently Dinoli and Bullard had misjudged Kennedy, thinking he was much less observant than he actually was, or they would never have let him go to Ganymede and possibly discover all manner of uncomfortable things.

There was only a week left to his stay now. He knew he would have to move quickly and efficiently in his remaining time, if he were to discover the underlying facts of the Ganymede operation.

He disliked blackmail. But in this case there was no help for it. He went to see Engel.

12

THE LINGUIST was not happy to see him. He greeted him unsmilingly and said, "What do you want, Kennedy?"

With elaborate care Kennedy shut the door and took a seat facing Engel. "The first thing I want is absolute silence on your part. If a word of what I tell you now gets back to Gunther or anyone else, I'll kill you."

Just like that. And at the moment, Kennedy believed he would, too.

Engel said, "Go ahead. Talk."

"I want you to do me a favor. I want you to get me one of those jeeps and fix things so I can go out alone during sleep-time tonight."

"Kennedy, this is preposterous. I—"

"You nothing. Either I get the jeep or I tell Gunther you're a subversive who deliberately gave me the Ganny dictionary and who tipped me off on a few of the lesser-known gambits the Corporation's engaging in. I can lie damn persuasively, Engel; it's my business."

Engel said nothing. Kennedy noticed that the man's fingernails had been bitten ragged. He felt sorry for the unfortunate linguist, but this was no time for pity; the Corporation showed none, and neither could he.

"Do I get the jeep?"

Engel remained silent.

Finally he pulled in his breath in a sobbing sigh and said, "Yes, damn you."

"Without any strings?"

Engel nodded.

Kennedy rose. "Thanks, Engel. And listen: I don't want you to get hurt in this business. I'm doing what I'm doing because I need to do it, and I'm stepping on your neck because it's the only neck I can step on —but I'm sorry about the whole filthy business. If everything goes well, Gunther'll never find out about the dictionary or the jeep."

"Save the apologies," Engel said. "When do you want the jeep?"

Kennedy left after dark-out time that night; the dome was shrouded in night, and the faint illumination afforded by Io and the larger radiation that was Jupiter's light only served to cast conflicting and obscuring shadows over the outpost. He locked himself into the jeep's pressurized cab, made sure his spacesuit was in order, checked the ammunition supply for the gun he had borrowed, made sure he had remembered the dictionary. Engel led him through the lock.

"Remember now," he radioed back. "I'm going to be back here at 0600. Be damn sure you're here to let me in, and that you're alone."

"I'll be here," Engel said. "Alone, I hope."

The Ganny village was eleven miles to the east of the outpost. Kennedy knew that the aliens had a thirty-two hour sleep-wake cycle, and he hoped that his visit would find them awake; otherwise he might not have another opportunity to speak to them.

He had no difficulty operating the jeep; it was equipped with compass and distance guide, and no more than twenty minutes after he had left the Terran outpost he saw what could only be the alien village, nestling between two cruel rock fangs. It was located, logically enough, along one shore of a broad river of fast-flowing hydrocarbons. The houses were clusters of small, dome-shaped igloos put together out of bluish ice-blocks, and there were aliens moving to and fro in the settlement as he drew near. He saw them stop their work and peer suspiciously into the darkness at him.

He cut the jeep's engines a hundred yards from the edge of the river, activated his spacesuit, strapped on his gun, pocketed the dictionary, and stepped outside. He walked toward the river, where half a dozen aliens were casting nets or dangling lines.

As he approahced he saw one man yank forth his line with a catch—a thick-bodied fish-like creature with fierce red eyes and short fleshy fins. There was no look of triumph on the man's face as he waded ashore and deposited his catch on a heap of similar fish caught earlier. This was food, not sport, and there was no occasion for triumph if a catch was made—only sadness if one were not.

The aliens looked alike to Kennedy. He wondered if there were some way of finding the three who had visited the outpost the week before.

"I am a friend," he said slowly and clearly, in the Ganny tongue.

They gathered hesitantly about him, those who were not too busy with their nets and their lines. He looked from one noseless, grotesque face to the next, and hoped they were better at telling one Earthman from another than he was at discerning alien identities.

They were. One said, "You are a new one."

"I am. I come to talk with you."

"It is the food-gathering time. We must work. One will come from the village to talk with you."

Kennedy looked sharply at the ring of aliens. They were stocky beings, not quite his height, lumpy-bodied, with thick, six-fingered hands and practically no necks. They were not human. It was strange to stand here in below-zero temperature on a world whose air was poison to his lungs, and talk with unhuman creatures. Nightmarish.

Another alien was coming from the village toward him. At first glance he seemed indistinguishable from all the others, but then Kennedy saw that this one had an air of authority about him that set him apart.

"You must not disturb the fishermen," the new one said as he drew near. "Their job is sacred. Who are you?"

"I come from back there."

"I know that. But you are not like the others."

"I am not a friend of the other men who come to you," Kennedy said.

"Then they will kill you. They kill those who are not their friends."

"Have they killed any of your people?"

"No. But they say they will if we do not give them welcome here. We ask them to leave. To go back to the sky. But they say they will bring others of their kind here soon. We will not oppose this, but it grieves us."

They walked away from the busy fishermen. Kennedy struggled to catch the alien's words, and realized the Ganny was speaking with special care. The spokesman said, "Your people do not understand us. This is our land. Our tribe chose this as its dying-ground hundreds of hundred-days ago. We ask them to go, or to move to another clan-ground. But they will not go. They say they will stay, and will bring many hands of hands more of their numbers from the sky. And they will not let us teach them."

"Teach them?" Kennedy repeated. "Teach them what?"

"The way of life. Respect for existence. Understanding of the currents of beingness." The complex phrases made Kennedy frown, bewildered. "They think we are simple fishermen," said the alien. "This is correct. But we are more than fishermen. We have a civilization. We have no guns and no space-vessels; we did not need them. But we have other things."

Kennedy found himself becoming deeply interested. He squatted down on a barrel-shaped projection of ice and said, "Tell me about these things."

"We have no books, none of the fine things you Earthmen have. Our world does not allow such luxuries. But we have developed other things, compensations. A language—you find it easy to understand?"

Kennedy nodded.

"Our language is the work of many minds over many years. Its simplicity caused us much pain to achieve. Do you have much time to spend with us?"

He looked at the chronometer in the wrist of his spacesuit. The time was only 0230; he had three hours yet before it was time to return to the outpost. He told the alien that.

"Good. Our next sleep-time is when the silvery moon has set. Until the time for you to leave, we can talk. I think you will listen."

The silvery moon meant high-albedo Europa. Kennedy tried to remember the schedule. Europa would set toward "morning," some six or seven hours from now.

The alien spoke, and for the next three hours Kennedy listened in wonder. When the alien was through, Kennedy realized why Gunther had not been anxious for him to see the Gannys too closely.

They were far from being mere primitive savages. They had a culture perhaps older than Earth's. The bleak barrenness of their world had made it impossible for them to develop a technology, but in compensation they had created an incredible oral tradition of poetry and philosophy.

Kennedy received a brief sketch. The philosophy was one of resignation, of calm understanding of the inexorable absolute laws of the universe. It was inevitable that a people living under conditions such as these would develop a philosophy that counseled them to accept in gratitude whatever came to them.

They were people who knew how to wait, and how to accept defeat. People who knew how to hope, even when menacing invaders from beyond the sky came to threaten.

They had a poetry, too; Kennedy listened, and wondered. Their language was awesomely simple, with a simplicity born of centuries of polishing, and the poetry was evocative and many-leveled, so far as Kennedy could penetrate it at first hearing. Everything was oral. He had never believed that a race without a written culture could achieve such things, but he had never known a race living on such a world.

He was reluctant to leave, when the time came. But he knew there would be grave consequences otherwise, so he made his apologies, breaking the spell cast by the alien being, and headed for his jeep.

At about 0530 he began driving back westward toward the outpost. In the quiet alien night the snowfields sparkled and glittered with the reflected light of half a dozen moons; it was a lovely sight, and, inside the warm pressurized cab of the jeep, he felt none of the brutality of the conditions outside, only the silent beauty.

But there was nothing beautiful about the Corporation scheme, he thought. He wondered if he could ever purge himself of the taint of the last two months' work.

He thought of Marge's gradual withdrawal from him as he became more and more involved in the Ganymede contract, and of Spalding's cynical condemnation of the project at the same time as his continued work on it. Well, Spalding had his reasons. And at least he had seen through the plan, instead of blithely accepting it the way Kennedy had done.

The Corporation was using the U.N. as its cat's-paw. Ganymede was likely territory for exploitation —the Earth had no more simple races left, no more technologically backward areas, thanks to a century of intensive development, but there still were other worlds for fast-working promoters to conquer.

Ganymede, for instance.

The Gannys had a rich and wonderful culture—anyone could see that given an hour's contact with them. So the Corporation would have to suppress that fact, or else there would be interference with its plans. Thanks to the agency and to Kennedy's own scheme, the Gannys would be mowed down, unprotesting—for that was the essence of their philosophy—to make room for the Terran exploiters.

Unless some action were taken now.

Kennedy felt clear-headed and tranquil about the part he was going to play in the coming weeks. He would return to Earth and somehow let the world know the profound nature of the Ganymedean culture; he would prevent the slaughter before it began, as partial atonement for all he had done to foment it. Marge would understand, and would forgive him for his earlier part.

He felt bitter about the deception that had been practiced on him and which he, in turn, had helped foist on all of Earth. He had no moralizing objections to Corporation activity—but he felt strongly that a culture such as he had just been shown should be preserved, and learned from. The Gannys had much to teach to an Earth caught in endless internal turmoil. He intended to vist them every night until the time came to return to Earth.

And when he was back on Earth he could reveal the truth. It isn't everyone, he thought, who has the chance to repair damage he's helped create. But I have a glittering opportunity.

The Gannys would never fight back. Armed resistance was not part of their way. But if he could prevent the conflict from ever beginning . . .

He would have to move carefully, though. He was

taking on a mighty antagonist in the Corporation.

Engel was waiting inside the airlock as Kennedy brought the jeep up, at 0559 hours. Right on time. The linguist looked pale and tense; Kennedy wondered if there were some trap waiting for him. Gunther, maybe, with armed men.

He drew his gun. The airlock slid open and he guided the jeep through. Springing from the jeep, he made sure he had his gun out and ready.

"You can put the blunderbuss away," Engel whispered. "Everything's clear."

Kennedy looked around. "No one knows I've been gone? No one missed me?"

"They've all been sleeping like babes," Engel said. "All except me. I've been sitting in my room staring at the walls all night. Where the devil did you go, Kennedy? And why?"

"That's hardly public concern, as they say. Help me off with my suit."

Engel assisted him as he climbed out of the bulky protective suit. Kennedy turned to the linguist and stared quietly at him for a long moment.

"I went to visit the Gannys tonight," he said. "I spent three hours listening to a disquisition on Ganny philosophy and hearing some Ganny poetry. These people aren't as primitive as Gunther seems to think they are, Engel."

"I don't know what you're talking about."

"You're lying. You've spoken to the Gannys. You know that their language is a marvel of communication. You know about their philosophy and their poetry and their outlook on life. And you intend to sit back and let all these things be blotted from the universe forever."

Engel's jaw tightened. He said nothing.

"Well," Kennedy went on, *"I* don't. And I'm going to do something about it, or at least try to do something, when I get back to Earth. And while I'm here I'm going to soak up as much Ganny thinking as I possibly can. It's good for the soul, Engel. You'll help me."

"I don't want to be a party to your crazy schemes, Kennedy."

"I want you to help me. For once in your life you can do something worthwhile. More worthwhile than making lists of intransitive verbs, anyway."

13

TWO DAYS that were not days, two nights that were not nights, while the greater darkness of the Ganymedean night cloaked the outpost for the full twenty-four hours of the arbitrarily designated "day." And in that time Kennedy saw the Ganny chieftain twice.

He told Engel, "You arrange with Gunther that you get assigned to take me out on my daily tour of the snow dunes and local lakes. Only we'll go to the village instead of rubbernecking around the hills."

Engel was unwilling. Engel scowled and grimaced and tried to think of reasons why the idea was dangerous, but in the end he gave in, because he was a weak man and both he and Kennedy knew it. Kennedy had long since mastered the art of manipulating people *en masse;* now he was manipulating one single man, and succeeding at it.

He had five days left on Ganymede. He knew he had to make the most of them.

During the following day Engel came to him and told him to get ready for his daily drive. They skirted the hills and the big lake west of the camp, then swerved one hundred eighty degrees and tracked straight for the Ganny village.

They spent two hours there. The old leader explained the Ninefold Way of Righteousness to them, the essence of the Ganny moral code. Kennedy listened and memorized as much as he could—letting it soak in, because he knew it was good and workable—and occasionally glanced at Engel, and saw that the linguist was not blind to the wonders of these people.

"You see what kind of people they are?" Kennedy demanded, as they rode back to the outpost.

"Sure I see what they are," Engel grunted. "I've known it from the start."

"And yet you'll stand by while they're being wiped out by Terran forces who've been deluded into thinking they're killing hostile alien demons?"

"What can I do about it?" Engel asked sullenly. "I'm a Corporation linguist. I don't argue with what the Corporation wants to do. I just think about it, inside, and keep my mouth shut."

Of course you do, Kennedy thought. *The way we all do. But for once I can't sit by and collect my check and let this thing happen. I have to stand up and fight.*

He wondered what Gunther would say when he found out that the visiting public relations man was engaged in a highly subversive series of contacts with the Gannys. The little man would have an apoplectic fit, certainly.

Kennedy found out soon enough. He had been making notes of what he recalled of the old man's talks, scribbling down his recollections of Ganny poetry and fragments of the philosophical discussions. He kept these notes hidden in his room. But on the fourth day, when he went for them to add some notes on Ganny ideas of First Cause, he found they were missing.

For a moment he felt thundering alarm. Then he thought, in a deliberate attempt to calm himself, *Engel must have borrowed them. Sure. Engel borrowed them.*

There was a knock on the door. Kennedy opened it.

Gunther stood there. Gripped tightly in his hand was Kennedy's little sheaf of notes. His eyes were bleak and cold.

"Would you mind telling me what the hell these things are?" he demanded.

Kennedy struggled for self-control. "Those? Those are my notes. For my work, I mean. Research and comments to help me in my project."

Gunther did not smile. "I've read them. They are notes on Ganny culture, philosophy, and poetry. You've been seeing the Gannys secretly."

"And what if I have?"

"You've been violating a direct order of mine. This is a military-discipline base. We don't allow orders to be violated."

"Give me my notes," Kennedy said.

"I'm keeping them. They'll be sent back to Earth to the Corporation heads, as evidence against you. You're under arrest."

"On what charge?"

"Espionage against the Corporation," Gunther said flatly.

Two spacemen of the outpost locked him away in a brig down below, and left him in a windowless little room. He stared glumly at the metal walls. Somehow, he had expected this. He had been risking too much by visiting the Gannys. But listening to them had been like taking drugs; for the first time he had found a philosophy that gave him hope in a world that seemed to be without hope. He had wanted desperately to spend every one of his few remaining days on Ganymede in the village.

The day passed. Night came, and he was fed and the door was locked again. Gunther was taking no chances. They would pen him up in here until the time came to ship him back to Earth.

He tried to sleep. For the past few days he had been getting along on two and three hours of sleep each twenty-four hour period, stealing out each night to visit the Gannys, and he was showing it; his feet felt leaden, his eyes stung. He had been subsisting on no-sleep tabs and catching naps at odd moments when he felt he could get away with it. But now he could not sleep.

His watch said 0330 when he heard the bolt outside his door being opened. He looked up. Maybe it was Gunther coming to extract some kind of "confession."

Engel entered.

"I got put on guard duty," the linguist said. "Gunther wants you watched round the clock."

Kennedy looked at him bleakly. "Why did you come in here? To keep me company?"

"I wanted to tell you that I had nothing to do with his finding out. He's just a suspicious man. He had your room searched while you were out, and he found your notes. I'm sorry."

I'm sorry too, Kennedy thought. *Because now I'll go back to Earth under guard, and I won't ever get my chance to expose things.*

He said, "Did you ever go back to the village to explain why we didn't show up for your next session?"

"No. I was afraid to."

An idea formed in Kennedy's mind. "How about letting me out now? We can borrow a jetsled. Everyone's asleep. At least we can warn the Gannys of what's happened. You can bring me back here and lock me up again in the morning."

"It's too risky. Gunther suspects me as it is," Engel said.

But Kennedy knew his man. It took him only a few minutes more of persuasion to break down Engel's resistance. Together they donned spacesuits and headed out to the area where the outpost's jetsleds were kept. Kennedy was bursting with impatience to see the villagers once again. He realized he had violated a prime rule of the Ganny way by compelling Engel to release him, but this was no time for passive resistance. There was time to put the Ganny philosophy into operation later, when the survival of the Gannys was assured.

"Set the airlock to automatic open-close and let's get out of here," Kennedy called to Engel. "We don't have all night."

The face behind Engel's breathing-helmet was stiff and tense. Engel had never entered into any of this with full willingness, Kennedy thought; it was always partly because he thought Kennedy was right, partly because he was being blackmailed into accompanying him.

The airlock started to slide open. Kennedy made room for Engel on the sled and rested his hand lightly on the firing switch.

Floodlights suddenly burst out blindingly all over the airlock area.

Gunther stood there, looking hard and bitter in the bright light. Behind him were three other men—Jaeckel, Palmer, Latimer.

"It had to be you, Engel," Gunther said slowly. "I figured you were the one that was helping him. That's why I put you on guard duty tonight. And I guess I was right. What the hell do you think you're up to on that sled, you two?"

Engel started to say something, something shapeless that was half a moan. Kennedy nudged him viciously with his free elbow.

"Hold on tight!" he whispered. "I'm going to get the sled started!"

"No, you can't!"

"Want to join me in the brig, then?"

"Okay," Gunther called. "Get off that sled. This time I'll make sure neither of you can get loose until that ship leaves for Earth."

"You make sure of that," Kennedy said. Calmly he threw the firing switch to full and shoved the thrust-control wide open.

The jetsled bucked and crashed forward in a sudden plunging motion, tossing a spume of yellow flame behind it. Kennedy heard Gunther's angry yell as the sled passed through the open airlock perhaps fifteen seconds before the time-control was due to close it again.

There was the quick harsh chatter of gunfire coming from behind them. Kennedy did not look back. He crouched down as low as he could on the sled, praying that none of the shots would touch off the fuel tanks behind him, and guided the little flat sled into the Ganymedean darkness.

His course was already figured. He would circle

wide to the west, far out enough to mislead any pursuers, he hoped, and then head for the Ganymedean village. But after that, he had no plans.

He had bungled. And perhaps he had cost the Ganymedeans their one chance of salvation, as well as cutting his own throat, by letting Gunther find out what he was doing. He tried to regard the situation fatalistically, as a Ganny might, but could not. It was tragic, no matter how he looked at it, and it could have been avoided had he been more careful.

He forced himself not to think of what would happen to him four days hence, when the supply ship blasted off on its return trip to Earth. No doubt he and Engel would be aboard as prisoners. He had cut loose all bonds with Earth in one sudden frightful moment, and he tried not to think about it.

"I was wondering how long it would take for Gunther to get wise to what we were doing," he said after they had gone more than five miles with no sign of pursuit. "It was bound to happen eventually. But we had to do what we did, Engel. *Someone* had to do it. And it just happened that I came along and dragged you into it."

Engel did not reply. Kennedy wondered about the bitter thoughts the linguist must be thinking. He himself had reexerted the old agency mask; he was not thinking at all, not bothering to consider the inevitably drastic consequences of his wild rebellion on Ganymede.

They fled on into the night. When he thought it was safe he changed the sled's course and headed straight for the village. He was becoming an expert at traveling over the icebound plain.

"None of it would have started if you had kept

your dictionary hidden away," Kennedy said. "But you showed it to me, and I borrowed it, and I learned a couple of words of Ganny, and on a slim thread like that you're washed up with the Corporation and I'm finished with the agency. But you know something, Engel? I'm not sorry at all. Not even if they catch us and take us back to Earth and publicly disembowel us. At least we stood on our hind legs and did something we thought was *right*." He stopped to consider something. "You *did* think it was right, didn't you? I mean, you didn't help me in this thing just because I was twisting your arm? I hope you did it out of ethical reasons. It's lousy enough to throw away your career in a single week, without having done it just because some other guy with ethics came along and made you do it."

Engel still was silent. His silence began to irritate Kennedy.

"What's the matter?" he demanded. "Scared speechless? Did the fact that Gunther caught us throw you into such a blue funk you can't talk?"

Still no answer. A cold worm of panic raced around the interior of Kennedy's stomach, and he swiveled his neck to see if—

He was right.

One of Gunther's final desperate shots had ripped a neat hole in Engel's breathing-helmet. The bullet had entered on a sharp angle, puncturing the helmet just in front of the linguist's nose, grazing his left cheekbone harmlessly—it left only a thin scratch— and passing out of the helmet below Engel's left earlobe. That had been enough.

Engel's air supply must have rushed out in one moist, foaming burst. Blood had dribbled from his mouth and ears as the internal suit-pressure dropped from the 14.7 psi of the suit to the much lower external pressure. Engel's face was blotchy, puffed, swollen, eyes bulging, thin lips drawn back in a contorted, grotesque smile.

He had died in a hurry. So fast that he had not even had time to grunt an anguished last cry into his open suit-microphone. And for half an hour Kennedy had ferried a corpse across the Ganymedean wastes, talked to him and chided him, and finally lost his patience and his temper at the corpse's continued obstinate silence.

Kennedy compressed his lips into a thin, bitter scowl. Engel had been so proud of his dictionary, so anxious to show it off to the visitor from Earth. And a couple of weeks later that dictionary had worked his death, as surely as if it had been the bullet that sent his air-supply wailing out into the desolate night of Ganymede.

At least it had been a quick death, with no time for the man to languish in a prison somewhere and eternally curse the day Kennedy had come to Ganymede.

He stopped by a wide-stretching lake whose "waters" glittered in the light of three whirling moons. Only they and vast Jupiter seemed to be watching as Kennedy gently lifted Engel's oddly light body from the sled and carried it to where the dark liquid lapped the edge of the ragged shore.

He waded out a foot or two into the lake and laid Engel face-down on the surface of the water. He drifted. Kennedy touched one gauntlet to the dead man's boot and shoved, imparting enough force to send Engel floating slowly but inexorably out toward the middle of the lake.

To Kennedy's horror the body remained afloat for

some minutes, spinning in a lazy circle as the currents of the lake played games with it. Face down, arms and legs hovering on the crest of the lake, Engel looked like an effigy, a straw dummy put out to drift. But finally the methane came bubbling in through the two holes in his breathing-helmet, and the spacesuit lost its buoyancy and grew heavy, filling with liquid until Engel slowly and gravely vanished beneath the surface.

Kennedy remained there a moment in tribute. He had not known Engel at all; in the words of the Ganny poem, he was only a shadow of a man to Kennedy. The linguist had been a man without a past to him, just a face and a name and an ability to collect words and understand their meaning. Kennedy had not known how old Engel was, where he had been born or educated, whether or not he was married, where he lived when he was on Earth, what his hopes or aspirations were, his philosophy of life. And now no one of those things mattered. Engel had neither present nor future, and his past was irrelevant.

Kennedy remounted the sled and continued on. The time was 0412; he would reach the village at about 0445, and according to his schedule that was the time at which the Gannys would begin to stir into wakefulness after their last period of sleep. He rode silently on, not thinking, not making any plans.

He was still a mile from the village when he saw the Terran truck from the outpost, drawn up perhaps fifty or a hundred yards from the first houses of the village. He looked down on the scene from the row of razor-backed ridges that bordered the village on the south. When he was close enough, he could see clearly what was taking place.

The villagers were lined up outside their houses, and four dark spacesuited figures moved among them. An interrogation was under way. They were questioning the villagers about Engel and himself, hoping to find out where they were hiding.

As Kennedy watched, one of the spacesuited figures knocked a villager to the ground. The Ganny rose and stood patiently where he had stood before. Brutally the Earthman knocked him down again.

Kennedy's jaws tightened. Gunther was prepared to stop at nothing in the attempt to find him. Maybe he would move on to wholesale destruction of the village, when no information was forthcoming.

With his chin he nudged the control of his suit-microphone and said, "Gunther?"

"Who's that?"

"Kennedy. Hold your fire."

"Where are you, Kennedy?"

"On the hill overlooking you. Don't fire. I don't intend to make trouble."

He had no choice. He could not hide out on this frozen methane world for long, and the aliens, though they meant well, could not give him shelter, could not feed him. He would only be bringing pain and suffering to them if he tried to remain at large.

"What are you doing up there?" Gunther asked.

"I'm coming down. I'm surrendering. I don't want to cause any more suffering. Got that? I'm surrendering. I'll come down out of the hills with my hands up. Don't hurt the villagers any more. They aren't to blame."

He rose from the shed and slowly made his way down the side of the hill, a dark figure against the whiteness. He was no more than halfway down when

Gunther's voice said sharply, "Wait a minute! You're alone. Where's Engel? If this is some sort of trick—"

"Engel's dead. You killed him back at the airlock when we escaped, and I gave him burial in a lake back beyond the hills. I'm coming down alone. Hold your fire, Gunther."

14

THE CORPORATION spaceship had not been intended as a prison ship, and so they had no facilities for confining him. Not that Kennedy was anxious to mingle with the men of the crew; reserved, aloof, a little shocked despite himself at the magnitude of what he had done, he rarely left the hammock during the long, tense trip back to Earth. He spent much of his time reading and as much as possible sleeping, or thinking about the Ganymedean culture of which he had had such a brief, tantalizing glimpse.

He ate alone, and spoke to the other men aboard the ship only when necessary. They spoke to him not at all.

The last few days before the departure of the supply ship had been unpleasant ones. Gunther had ordered Kennedy confined to the bare little dungeon-storeroom, with a guard constantly posted outside the door and meals brought in.

Gunther had questioned him.

"You're accused on two counts. You gave weapons to the aliens and you murdered Engel. Right?"

"I decline to answer that."

"The hell with that. Confess."

"I'm not confessing to hogwash like that. And don't threaten to have me shot, Gunther. The agency knows I'm here."

"It could be an accident—a man cleaning his rifle. But I won't do it. Let the Corporation take care of you. You're not my responsibility. You go back to Earth when the ship leaves."

"As you please," Kennedy said.

"But I want a confession. Tell me why you gave guns to the Gannys!"

"I didn't. The Gannys wouldn't know how to use them. And you killed Engel yourself, when we tried to get away."

"Who'll believe that? Come on, Kennedy—confess."

Kennedy shrugged and refused. After a while, Gunther gave up.

He had to admit to himself they were taking special care of him. Another man might have killed him on the spot, as a safety measure; Gunther was too smart for that. After all, Kennedy was an agency executive. This was too big a thing for Gunther to handle, and he knew it. He was tossing it back to the Corporation, letting them judge Kennedy and decide what to do with him.

Sizer let him have a gravanol pill on the way out, which surprised him a little; it was reasonable to expect that they'd leave a traitor to cope with the agonies of blast-off acceleration as best he could, without proffering the assistance of the pain-killing drug. They gave it to him, though, silently and ungraciously, but readily enough.

He had never been a particularly thoughtful man. Intelligent, yes; quick-witted, yes; resourceful, yes.

But *thinking*—evaluation of himself in relation to the world about him, understanding of the sea of events through which he moved—thinking had never been his strong point, as Marge had so frequently let him know. But now he had plenty of time to think, as the Corporation ship left the icy ball that was Ganymede far behind and coasted on toward Earth.

They had taught him many things at Northwestern; he had responded to tutorial prodding magnificently, coming through with straight A averages for the entire four years. But no one had ever taught him where his loyalties belonged. And he had never bothered to find out.

It was a world he had never made—but one that had given him thirty thousand a year at the biggest public relations firm there was, and he'd been content. He could have left well enough alone, he thought.

The day of Earthfall came. Word passed rapidly through the ship, and Sizer, grim-faced now, with none of the cheerful affability of the earlier journey, came aft to offer Kennedy a gravanol pill. He accepted the pellet and the flask and nodded his thanks to Sizer. The spaceman left.

Kennedy looked carefully around, making sure no one was watching him. A wild plan was forming in his mind. He palmed the little pill and drained the flask of water; then he slumped back in the hammock as if drugged. He slipped the pill into his pocket.

Deceleration began.

He rode down into the atmospheric blanket fully conscious, the only man on the ship who was awake. The ship's jets thundered, stabilizing her, decelerating her. Kennedy felt as if two broad hands were squeezing him together, jamming his neck against his spine, flattening his face, distorting his mouth. He could hear the currents of blood in his body. He gasped for breath like a hooked fish. It seemed that there was a mighty knuckle pressing against his chest, expelling the air from his lungs, keeping him from drawing breath.

He drew a breath. And another.

He swung in the cradle. Waves of pain shivered through him.

He started to blank out. He fought it, clinging tightly to consciousness.

And he stayed awake.

The ship was trembling, shuddering in the last moments before landing. He did not look out the viewplate, but he knew the ground must be visible now, pitching wildly beneath the ship. He could picture the sleek vessel standing perched on a tongue of fire.

They dropped down. Kennedy wiped a trickle of blood from his upper lip. He became abruptly aware of a roaring silence, and realized that the bellow of the jets had at last ceased.

They had landed. And he had not blanked out.

Now he rolled over and looked through the port as he began to unfasten himself. He saw people out there. A welcoming committee? He looked for Marge or Watsinski or Spalding, but saw no one he recognized, no familiar face. He blinked again, realizing the field was empty. Those were just maintenance men. The ship had returned under wraps of secrecy.

What a blaster of a dream that was, he thought, and in the same moment he realized that it was no dream. He had spent three weeks on another world; he had discovered that the values he held to be true were false, and that the cause he had lent himself to was dedicated to wiping out a culture that had incredibly much to offer Earth. The Corporation did not hate the Gannys. They merely stood in the way of making profit, and so they had to go.

A voice said quietly inside him, *If you run fast enough they can't touch you. It's not too late. You didn't commit any crime by talking to the Gannys. The Corporation hasn't started making the law yet, dammit. Not yet.*

The big hatch in the wall of the ship was opening, and a catwalk was extruding itself automatically so the men in the ship could reach the ground twenty feet below. Very carefully Kennedy unlaced the webbing that held him in the deceleration cradle. He dropped one foot over the side of the hammock, then the other, and went pitching forward suddenly as the wall of the ship came sweeping up to meet him.

He thrust out his hands desperately, slapped them against the wall, steadied himself. He waited a moment until his head stopped pounding and his feet were less rubbery. He glanced fore and saw the other crewmen still slumped in their cradles, groggy from the gravanol pills. It would be a few minutes yet before they awakened. And they never would have expected their prisoner to have risked, and made, a fully conscious landing.

Kennedy smiled. Quite calmly he made his way forward to the hatch and lowered himself down the catwalk to the ground. Someone in the ship yawned; they were beginning to stir.

The sun was warm and bright. He had forgotten the day, but he knew it would have to be somewhere near the end of July. The sickly heat of midsummer hung over the flat grounds of the landing field.

A few maintenance men were moving toward the ship now, but they ignored him. Somehow he had expected welcomers, video cameras, a galaxy of flash bulbs—not an empty field. But the Corporation had probably preferred a veil of secrecy cast over the arrival.

He made his way across the field and into the area beyond. He spied a taxi passing on the road and hailed it. He felt dazed by the heat after the chill of Ganymede, and the punishment of landing had left him wobbly.

He opened the taxi and slipped into the passenger's seat. He glanced out the window and looked back at the spacefield. By now they were awake aboard the ship, and knew he was missing.

"Step on it, driver. Take me to the city."

The cab rolled away. Kennedy wondered if he would be followed. It had been so simple to slip away, in the confusion of landing. One of the Ganny maxims he had learned was that through endurance of pain comes knowledge of truth, and therefore freedom. Well, he had endured pain and he had his freedom as a result of it. The unused gravanol pill was still in his pocket.

He had slipped away from them. Like in a dream, he thought, where the figures reach out to clutch you but you slip through them like a red-hot blade through butter.

They would hunt him, of course. Escape could never be this simple; the Corporation would spare no expense to get him and put him away. But if he only had a few days of freedom to accomplish some of the things he had to do, he would be content. Otherwise his surrender would have been pointless; he might just as well have spent his days as a fugitive on Ganymede.

Where can I go? he wondered.

Home?

Home was the most obvious place. So obvious, in fact, that his pursuers might never suspect he would go there. Yes. Home was best. He gave the cabby the address and lapsed back into sullen somnolence for the rest of the trip.

The house looked unusually quiet, he thought, as the cab pulled into the Connecticut township where he and Marge had lived so long.

Maybe Gunther had radioed ahead. Maybe they had intentionally let him slip away at the spaceport, knowing that they could always pick him up at home.

He gave the driver much too big a bill and without waiting for change headed up the drive into his garden.

He found his key in his trouser pocket, pressed it into the slot, and held his right thumb against the upper thumb-plate until the front door slid back. He stepped inside.

"Marge?"

No answer. He half-expected an answering rattle of gunfire or the sudden appearance of the Corporation gendarmerie, but the house remained silent. Only the steady purr of the electronic dust-eater was audible. He went on into the living room, hoping at least to find the cat sleeping in the big armchair, but there was no cat. Everything was tidy and in its place. The windows were opaqued.

The windows were opaqued! Kennedy felt a twinge of

shock. They never opaqued the windows except when they expected to be away for long periods of time, on vacations, long shopping tours. Marge would never have left the windows opaqued in the middle of the day like that—

Suspicion began to form. He saw a piece of paper sitting on the coffee-table in the living room. He picked it up.

It was a note, in Marge's handwriting, but more shaky than usual. All it said was, *Ted, there's a tape on the recorder. Please listen to it, Marge.*

His hands trembled slightly as he switched on the sound system and activated the tape recorder. He waited a moment for the sound to begin.

"Ted, this is Marge speaking to you—for what's going to be the last time. I was going to put this in the form of a note, but I thought using the recorder would let me make things a little clearer.

"Ted, I'm leaving. It's not a hasty step. I thought about it a long time, and when this Ganymede business came up everything seemed to crystallize. We just shouldn't be living together. Oh, it was nice at times—don't get me wrong. But there's such a fundamental difference in our outlook toward things that a break had to be made—now, before it was too late to make it.

"You worked on the Ganymede thing casually, lightheartedly, and didn't even realize that I was bitterly opposed to it. Things like that. I'm not leaving because of a difference in politics, or anything else. Let's just say that the Ganymede job was a symptom, not a cause, of the trouble in our marriage. I hated the contract and what it stood for. You didn't even bother to examine the meaning of it. So today—

the day you left for space, Ted—I'm leaving.

"I'm going away with Dave Spalding. Don't jump to conclusions, though—I wasn't cheating on you with Dave. I have my code and I live by it. But we did discuss the idea of going away together, and your leaving for Ganymede has made it possible. That's why I wanted you to go. Please don't be hurt by all this—please don't smash things up and curse. Play the tape a couple of times, and *think* about things. I don't want anything that's in the house; I took what I wanted to keep, the rest is yours. After you've had time to get used to everything I'll get in touch with you about the divorce.

"So that's it, Ted. It was grand while it lasted, but I knew it couldn't *stay* grand much longer, and to spare both of us fifty or sixty years of bitterness, I've pulled out. Dave has left the agency, but we have a little money that we've both saved. Again, Ted, I'm sorry, sorry for both of us.

"I left the cat with the Camerons, and you can get him back from them when you get back from Ganymede. Nobody but you and Dave and me knows what's happened. Take care of yourself, Ted. And so long."

He let the tape run down to the end and shut it off. Then he stood numbly in the middle of the room for a long while, and after that he played the tape over once again from the beginning to end.

Marge. Dave Spalding. And the cat was with the Camerons.

"I didn't expect that, Marge," he said quietly. His throat felt very dry. His eyes ached; but he did not cry at all.

15

HE POURED himself a drink, and even that was not without its painful contingent memories, because Marge had always poured his drinks for him. Then he took off his shoes and listened to the tape a third time, with much the same frame of mind as the man who keeps hitting his head against a brick wall because it feels so good when he stops.

This time around he was able to stop hearing Marge's words and listen to the way she was saying them: straightforwardly, with little hesitation or emotional quaver. These were words she had stored within her a long time, he realized, and she seemed almost happy to relieve herself of them.

No, he thought, he hadn't expected Marge to do something like this; and that, perhaps, was why she had done it. She was mercurial, unpredictable. He saw now he had never really known her at all.

Some minutes passed, and the first rough shock ebbed away. He looked at it almost philosophically now. It had been inevitable. She had acted with great strength and wisdom. The Ted Kennedy who had been to Ganymede and had his eyes opened there respected her for it.

But he felt bitterness at the fact that he had returned from Ganymede a changed man, a man who had not only shifted his stand but who had taken positive action in his new allegiance, and Marge was not here to commend him for having seen her point of view at last. His conversion had come too late for that. There was no point chasing after her, finding her, saying, "Look, Marge, I've finally repudiated the Corporation and the agency—won't you come back now?"

No. It was too late to wave his new-found allegiance and expect Marge to forgive all his old blunders. Half the unhappiness people make for each other, he thought, is caused by men and women trying to put back together something that should remain forever smashed.

It hurt, but he forced himself to forget her.

He rose, crossed the room and snapped on the video. He searched for a newscast and finally found one on Channel Seventy-two, the Bridgeport UHF channel. He listened patiently through the usual guff about the miserable late-July weather, hot and humid despite the best efforts of the Bureau of Weather Adjustment, and to an analysis of the new cabinet crisis in Yugoslavia. Then the newscaster paused, as if turning over a sheet of script, and said, "Spacefield Seven in New Jersey was the scene several hours ago of the arrival from Ganymede of Captain Louis Hills' space ferry, which had made its last trip to Ganymede three weeks ago laden with supplies for the colony there. Captain Hills reported all well on the tiny world. In an afternoon baseball game, the Red Sox defeated the—"

Kennedy moved to shut the set off. They had decided to suppress all news of him, then—and they were still rigorously maintaining the fiction that Ganymede was populated by brave men and women from Earth. Well, that was no surprise. There would be an intensive man hunt for him as soon as the Corporation could mobilize its forces. Perhaps it was already under way.

Kennedy started to form his plans. Today was July 30. The Corporation planned to go before the United Nations and ask for armed intervention on October 11. He had until then to secure evidence that would puncture the fabric of lies he had helped erect.

But he would have to move warily. The Corporation would be looking for him, anxious to shut him up before he could damage the project. And before long they would have the U.N. Security Police on his trail too, on the hoked-up grounds that he had given arms to the Ganymedeans and murdered Engel. He would have to run, run fast, and hide well. With both Corporation goons and official world police on his trail, he would need to be agile.

The phone rang. He had no idea who it might be. Marge, maybe. It didn't matter. If he answered, he might be putting the Corporation on his trail. He forced himself to let it ring, and after a while it stopped. He stared at the chocolate-colored receiver, wondering who might have called.

Well, it didn't matter.

He knew what he had to do: get incriminating data on the Ganymede hoax from the agency files, and turn it over to the U.N. But it wasn't as simple as that. Probably the instant he set foot in the agency building he'd be grabbed and turned over to the authorities, and from then on he'd never get a chance to speak up.

Of course, maybe the agency didn't know about his changed beliefs yet. Perhaps the Corporation had not seen fit to let Gunther's report get into agency hands yet; maybe Bullard and his cohorts intended to make a full loyalty investigation of the agency they had employed before letting Dinoli know that one of his hand-picked men had turned renegade on Ganymede.

But he couldn't take that risk. He would have to get the material out of the agency files by stealth, and somehow get it to a U.N. representative.

He would have to drop out of sight for a while. There was no hurry about the exposure; he had more than two months. If he hid somewhere for those two months and raided the agency when they least expected it—

He knew where he could hide. At his brother's place in Wisconsin.

Cautiously, he depolarized the windows and peered out of each, one by one, to make sure no one lurked outside. Then he opaqued them all again. He packed a single suitcase, taking with him just one change of clothes and a few toilet articles; this was no time to be burdened by personal property. He left everything else as it was—the bar, the kitchen, the living room with Marge's picture in it. He hoped the cat would be safe with the Camerons. He had had the cat for many years; he would miss it.

The phone rang again. He ignored it.

It stopped eventually. He waited just a moment, gathering his strength, and took a last quick look at the house he and Marge had picked together eight years before, and which he might never see again.

He was leaving the past behind. Marge, the cat, his bar, his collection of records, his books. All the things he had treasured. The solid, secure life for which he had long been smugly thankful, gone overnight. *Ted Kennedy, fugitive.* All his thirty-two years had been building toward this, and it seemed strange to him that such a destiny should have been at the end of the string of years that had unrolled for him thus far.

Good-bye, agency. Good-bye, books and records and drinks and wife, and sleepy old cat and exclusive Connecticut township. *Addio.* He had few regrets. His brief contact with the Gannys had taught him to put less value on material things than he once had; he was calmer, more purposeful, since learning from them. Which was why he was giving up everything in an attempt to save the Ganymedeans.

He saw that their culture had to be preserved— and that he alone could save them.

There was a gun in his night-table drawer, a snub-nosed .38 Marge had made him buy three years before, when a night prowler had terrified the females of the area. He had never used it. Fully loaded, it had rested in the drawer.

Now he slipped it into its shoulder holster and donned it, scowling in annoyance because he would need to wear a jacket in the July heat to conceal the gun. The weapons permit was somewhere in the drawer; he rummaged for it, found it finally, and slipped it into his suitcase.

The time was 1632. Kennedy thought a moment: *they may be monitoring my phone, so it isn't safe to phone the airline from here. I'll go into town to make my reservations.*

He opened the front door and cautiously looked around. No one was in sight. Either they hadn't traced him to his home yet, or they were going to let him run a little before coming down hard.

He locked the door behind him and went around back to the garage. He put his luggage in the trunk compartment, got into the car, and drove down onto the main road without looking back.

Ten minutes later he was in town. "Town" consisted of two or three stores, a bank, a post office, a church. It probably had not changed much in the past century; small towns always resist change longer than large cities. Kennedy drove down the country road into the main square and parked near the clock, which was a big old one that had been standing in the center of the town well over a century, and of course still used the twelve-hour system. He glanced up at it, frowning a bit as he computed the time. The hands read 4:45, which he translated back into the more familiar 1645. Less than three hours had passed since his landing at Spacefield Seven.

It was an hour at which the town was quiet. The afternoon movie show still had ten or fifteen minutes to run; those who weren't at it were home waiting for dinner.

Kennedy left his parked car and stepped into Schiller's, the combined pharmacy-newsstand-luncheonette-department store that served the township. Two or three locals were sipping sodas at the fountain as he came in. Kennedy scooped change from his pocket and found he had no telephone tokens. The phone in Schiller's did not have an automatic vending machine in the booth, either.

He put a quarter on the counter and said, "Give me two phone tokens, please."

"Sure. Oh, hello there, Mr. Kennedy." Schiller looked at him speculatively a moment. He was a man in his sixties or seventies, old enough certainly to remember well back into the last century; his eyes were still clear blue, his hair only recently had gone white. He wiped his hands on his stained white smock and said, "Couple of men were in here just a minute ago asking for you. Wanted to know which road to take to get out to your place, so I had my boy show them. Must have been friends of yours."

"I'm not expecting any," Kennedy said. He took the tokens from the counter.

"Hey, there they are!" Schiller exclaimed, pointing.

Through the plate-glass front window, Kennedy saw two men in dark brown business suits and austere violet traveling cloaks coming out of the bank. They were grim, efficient-looking men. Corporation men, Kennedy thought. He started to walk quickly toward the telephone booths in the rear of the store.

"Hey, Mr. Kennedy," Schiller called. "You better go out there and see those fellers before they get into their car and go chasin' all the way out to your place."

"I don't have time to see them. I've got to get into the city on some important business."

"You want me to go out there and tell 'em that?" Schiller asked helpfully.

"No—that'll only offend them. Let them make an appointment with me next time they want to see me at home." He ducked into the telephone booth in time to cut off one of Schiller's stale monologues on the ways of the new generation, and how they charged around so fast they never had time to talk to each other.

Kennedy asked for Information, got the number of the ticket deck at Roosevelt Airport, and was told that the next flight for Milwaukee was departing at 1951 that evening, arrival time in Milwaukee 2113 Milwaukee time. That sounded fine to Kennedy.

"Make a reservation for *one,*" he said. "The name is Engel." He gave the name almost unthinkingly, automatically.

"First name, please?" came the impersonal reply.

"Ah—Victor. Victor Engel."

"Thank you, sir. Would you please pick up your reservation no later than an hour before departure time?"

"I'll do that," Kennedy said. He hung up, listened to his token click down into the depths of the phone, and left the booth.

Schiller said, "Just like I told you, Mr. Kennedy. Those friends of yours drove off toward your place while you were on the phone. Guess they're going to waste some time now."

"I guess so," Kennedy said. He grinned. "I just didn't have time to see them, though. I have to get down to the city in a hurry. My boat leaves at 1900."

"Boat?"

Kennedy nodded. "I'm going to Europe for a month on company business. Don't tell a soul, of course. I really don't want it getting around or all my friends will expect me to bring back souvenirs."

He waved genially and left. As he drove rapidly

down the Thruway toward New York, he thought about Schiller and the two bleak-faced Corporation men. They were certain to come back to town once they found his house empty; perhaps they would stop in at Schiller's again, and in that case they were certain to get drawn into conversation with the old man.

He hoped they had a nice time looking for him on the departing boats to Europe.

16

HE DROVE down into New York City, cutting left on the Thruway and taking the artery that led out along the south shore of Long Island Sound to the big new airport. Roosevelt Airport was a city in itself, practically; its rambling acres covered a great chunk of Long Island. It served as the airline capital of the world.

Kennedy reached the parking area at 1747 and turned his car over to the attendant.

"Want her shined up, sir? Refueled, overhauled?"

Kennedy shook his head. "Sorry, thanks."

"Those deflectors look like they could use—"

"No," Kennedy said. He took the parking ticket, which had the time stamped on it, and folded it away in his wallet. The attendant was going to be surprised when no one ever showed up to claim the dented '42 Frontenac.

He made his way toward the shining plastic building that housed the central ticket offices and got on a line that moved slowly toward a window labelled *Reservations For Today's Flights*.

When he reached the window he gave his name: "Victor Engel. I'm going to Milwaukee."

"Of course, Mr. Engel." The girl performed three quick motions with her hands and slid a crisp white folder under the grill toward him.

"One hundred thirteen fifty," she said.

Kennedy took two bills from his wallet, passed them over and received his change. Normally he would have paid by check—but the reservation was in Engel's name, and he would have had to sign the check that way. There would have been immediate catastrophe. It was impossible to pass a bad check when the lightning-fast receptors of the Central Clearing House in Chicago could check his signature against their files and report back within fifteen seconds.

It was too bad he had to buy round-trip tickets, too. The return half would expire in thirty days, and he had no intention of returning East so soon. But a one-way trip might arouse suspicion, and he wanted to keep Victor Engel as free of suspicion as possible.

Victor Engel. The first name had been a sudden guess. It had been a curious moment when he realized he had never known the dead linguist's first name.

He moved out of the ticket deck onto the promenade. In the distance, outlined against the setting sun, a huge plane was coming in—one of the FB-11 stratoliners, the five-hundred-passenger jet jobs that crossed the country from New York to California in just under two hours. He watched it taxi in, like a great bird returning to its nest.

He ate alone in an automatic restaurant—a light meal, protoid sandwich and milk, for he was far from hungry just now—and bought an evening 'fax-sheet at a vending stand. Quickly, he made his way past the West Coast baseball scores, past the usual item on the weather, past the latest on the Yugoslavian ministerial shake-up. He found a squib on the return of the Ganymede ship. There was no mention of the public relations man who had fled the spacefield hotly pursued by Corporation mobsters.

He crumpled the 'fax-sheet and dumped it in a disposall. Finding himself outside a bookstore, he went in, browsed for half an hour, and emerged with a couple of paperbacks.

He strolled the promenade as the heat of the day died away, waiting for departure time. At 1925 the announcement came, "Universal Airlines plane for Milwaukee, Flight 165, now loading passengers at Gate 17."

The ship was not the newest model—an FB-9, seating ninety, a fairly low-ceiling liner that never went higher than 20,000 feet on passenger flights. As he boarded it, the stewardess, a shy-looking, rosy-cheeked blonde, smiled and said, "Good evening, Mr. Engel. I hope you have a pleasant flight."

"Thank you," he said, and found a seat in the front, to the fore of the wings.

After spaceflight, airplane flying seemed odd to Kennedy—oddly clumsy and oddly unsafe. The plane took off on schedule, roaring down the runway and veering sharply upward into the sky; he looked down at the darkening streets of Brooklyn and saw tiny dots that were autos passing below, and then Brooklyn passed out of sight as the ship stabilized at its flight altitude of 20,000 feet.

At that height they were well above the clouds, which formed a solid gray-white floor stretching to the horizon, billowing up here and there in puffs that

looked like ice floes on a frozen sea. There was little
sensation of vibration or of motion, but at no time
was Kennedy deceived into believing that the plane
was not moving, as so often he had felt aboard the
spaceship.

He read for a while, but lost interest quickly and
dozed off. Sooner than he expected, they were in Milwaukee; his watch read 2213, but he jabbed the setting stud to put the hands back an hour, to conform
with local time.

The Milwaukee airport probably had been a local
wonder a century before; now, it merely looked
cheap and shabby, a weathered old edifice of green
glass and plastic. Kennedy treated himself to a cup of
synthetic caffeine drink in one of the airport restau-
rants, and considered his next several steps.

It was an hour's drive from Milwaukee to
Brockhurst, where had had been born and where his
older brother still lived. But it was late, and he felt
hesitant about barging in on them unannounced
when he knew he could not get out there much before
midnight. Steve had always been a man of regular
habits, and though he probably wouldn't say anything if his brother arrived unexpectedly near midnight, it would upset his routine.

Instead of going out there, Kennedy took a cab to
town and rented a room in the first hotel he found. In
the morning he dialed his brother's number as soon
as he was up, at 0800. Steve would be having breakfast about that time, before going out on the day's run.

He was right. A gruff deep voice said, "Kennedy
speaking. Who's this?"

"Kennedy, this is Kennedy. Of the Connecticut
Kennedys, you know."

A moment of silence. Then: "Ted?"

"None other."

Hesitantly: "What—what's on your mind?"

"I thought I'd come visit you," Kennedy said. "I got into Milwaukee last night, too late to call."

"Oh. I see."

That wasn't like his brother at all; Steve normally would have been effusively cordial. Now he sounded worried and tense.

"Look, Steve, I'll take the next bus out to your place. I'm here alone, and I can't explain everything over the phone. Can you wait till I get there? I'll—"

"No," Steve said bluntly. "Stay in Milwaukee. I'll come see you. Where are you?"

"Hotel Avon. But—"

"You stay there. I'll be there in an hour."

Puzzled, Kennedy hung up. He didn't understand. Steve always had an invitation ready for him. But now, when he needed him, Steve seemed unwilling.

Maybe, he thought, Steve was getting even. He knew he had neglected Steve for a long time, and maybe now Steve resented it. But the only thing he and Steve had ever had in common was a set of parents.

Steve was eleven years his senior, and, since their father had died when Ted was seven, had served as head of the family. Steve was the salt-of-the-earth type, the hearty middle-western sort, big-bodied and smiling, with a fondness for beer and fishing excursions. He was a faithful churchgoer. He had quarreled endlessly with his brother, until Ted, more nervous by temperament, introverted and intellectual, had left home after high school, gone to Chicago and enrolled in Northwestern.

The brothers had met just once since Kennedy's marriage to Marge—in 2039, when a vacation trip of Steve's had brought him East. It had been an awkward meeting; Steve and his plump wife Betty had been ill at ease in the modern surroundings of the Kennedy home. The music he played for them had bored them, the books had awed them, and once Betty had hit a raw nerve by asking Marge when she expected to start raising a family. Betty had had two children already, with a third on the way. Marge had blushed and tried to explain that it wasn't because they didn't *want* children that they didn't have any. Since that time, Kennedy had exchanged letters with his brother sporadically, but as the years passed they had had less and less to say to each other. It was nearly ten months since he had last written to Steve.

Now he waited, pacing tensely around the confines of the shabby Milwaukee hotel room. Shortly after 0900, Steve arrived.

He had grown gray, Kennedy noticed, but he still looked impressive, a big-muscled, thick-bodied man with deep, sad eyes that belied the essentially untroubled mind behind them. He squeezed Kennedy's right hand mercilessly. Next to his brother, Kennedy felt suddenly shamefaced; he was Easternized, high-strung, overintellectual, and probably looked a woeful figure to his healthy, happy brother.

"I want to apologize," Steve said huskily. "I couldn't let you come out to the house."

"Why not?"

Steve flicked his eyes uncertainly around the room. "Are you in some kind of trouble, Ted?"

"Not really."

"I can always tell when you lie to me. You just

lied. Ted, I was always afraid you'd get mixed up in something bad. I tried to teach you to do your day's work and leave well enough alone, but I guess it never really took, or else the people down East taught you different. What did you do, Ted?"

"I didn't do anything," Kennedy lied. "I just want to stay at the house, quietly, for a while."

"You can't do that."

Coming from Steve, that was flatly incredible. "Why?"

Steve sighed. "I got a call last night from the local Security people. They wanted to know if I was your brother. I said yes. They said you were in big trouble back East, and you were wanted by Security. They wouldn't tell me what for. Then they said I'd have to cooperate or I'd be subject to arrest as an accessory after the fact."

Kennedy felt cold despite the blistering heat. "What else did they say?"

"They said you were missing and were likely to try to come to me. That if you came out here I was to notify them immediately, or else they'd make it hard on me. Then they asked me for a list of any other relatives of ours anywhere in the country, and I guess I gave it to them. Then they hung up. Ted, what have you done?"

Kennedy gripped his brother's thick arm tightly. "I swear to you I haven't done anything wrong. I've been framed by a bunch of criminals, and I have to hide for a while. I want to stay here with you."

"That's what they said you'd want to do. Sorry, Ted. You can't."

"Can't?"

Steve shook his head. "I've got a wife and five kids,

Ted. A place in the community. I can't risk losing all that. They told me I could go to prison for twenty years if I helped you."

"It's a lie!"

"Be that as it may. You better go somewhere else." Steve fished into his pocket. "I brought you some money. I guess you need it. Don't argue; just take it."

He pushed a thousand dollars in small bills into Kennedy's nerveless fingers.

"I better go now," Steve said. "Maybe they followed me. If they catch you, don't tell 'em you saw me at all. Or spoke to me." Beads of sweat dribbled down Steve's heavy face; he looked close to tears. "I'm sorry about this, kid. But I have to think of my family first. You understand?"

"Yeah, Steve. I understand."

17

KENNEDY waited fifteen minutes after his brother left, went downstairs, and checked out. He knew the chase was on, now. They had called his brother. Probably they had called anyone in the hemisphere who knew him at all, and bullied them into refusing to give him aid.

He was on his own, now. And he would have to run.

Now that the hunt had begun, time was against him. He had to secure his evidence and present it to the U.N., and he had to do it before his pursuers found him. But how, when he was sought by the Corporation and the U.N.? He had no answer. But he knew doggedly he was going to try. He summoned up as much as he could remember of the Ganny poetry—the didactic philosophical poems on survival in a hostile environment. The Gannys knew what suffering meant. And they were tough, those peaceful, violence-hating aliens. Tougher than any Earthman.

It was dangerous for him to return to New York by any direct route. He decided to go overland, by bus perhaps, taking several weeks to do it. He let a mustache grow, and before he left Milwaukee he visited a barber; his long agency haircut gave way to a midwestern trim that left the back of his neck and his ears bare. That would make him just a little harder to recognize.

He discovered, with a little shock, that Watsinski, or whoever it was that was continuing the Ganymede colony hoax, had worked him into the framework.

He was wanted, said the telefaxes and newssheets, for having distributed arms to the Gannys. According to the 'fax he picked up in Chicago three days after leaving Milwaukee, he had been sent to Ganymede to do a series of magazine articles on the colony, but instead had treacherously murdered a member of the colony and had given ammunition to the aliens. Then, being sent back to Earth under arrest, he had escaped and was being sought for treason against humanity, with a fat reward for his capture.

He stared at the picture of himself in the telefax. It was an old shot, taken when he was twenty pounds heavier, wore his hair long, and had no mustache. The sleek, complacent face on the shiny yellow sheet bore little resemblance to his own.

He headed East, keeping himself inconspicuous and crossing streets to avoid Security men. He tried not to get into conversations with strangers. He kept to himself. He was the needle in the haystack of 225,000,000 people, and if he was lucky they might not find him.

As he moved on, he kept in touch with the news from Ganymede. The character of the bulletins had taken on a distinct new coloration.

Now there was word of sinister alien armies marching beyond the hills, of bomb detonations and the dry sound of target practice. "The aliens are becoming very resentful of our presence," wrote Colony Director Lester Brookman in the syndicated column that appeared in the nation's papers on August 11. "Undoubtedly they have been stirred up by the traitor Theodore Kennedy, who, I understand, is still at large on Earth. They object to our presence on their world and have several times made ugly threats. During the current crisis we do not permit members of the colony to leave the dome in groups of less than three."

It was proceeding according to plan, Kennedy thought. The hostile aliens were on the warpath; soon they would be hunting for scalps; then would come the massacre. After that the troops would be called in to wipe out the belligerent savages. It was an old, old pattern of colonial expansion.

He knew the schedule. By September 17 the world would know that the colony of Earthmen was in imminent danger of being wiped out by the aliens, who refused to listen to reason and enter into peaceful negotiations. Five days of artful cliff-hanging would follow, and on September 22 the Corporation would make preliminary overtures toward the United Nations, asking for a police force to be sent to Ganymede to guard Terran interests. It would not be too strong a plea, for the public would need more manipulating. From September 22 through October 10 the world would pray for the endangered Earthmen; on October 11 the aliens would sweep down from the hills and virtually wipe out the gallant colony.

And, by October 17, United Nations troops would be on their way to Ganymede to quell the disturbance and police the world to make it safe for the Corporation.

Kennedy knew he had to act before October 11. After that, no amount of proof would seem convincing to a world determined to believe that a massacre had taken place.

But how could he get the evidence he needed?

He was in Trenton, New Jersey, eating lunch in a roadhouse, when the news came blaring forth: *Ganymede Colony Attacked!* The day was Sunday, September 17.

The cook reached over and turned up the radio behind the counter.

"A surprise alien attack shortly before dawn Ganymede time left the Earth colony on Jupiter's moon in grave peril today," came the announcer's voice. "An estimated five thousand aliens, armed with clubs and native weapons, swept down on the dome that houses the colony, shouting 'Death to the Earthmen!' Colony Director Lester Brookman radioed later in the day that the assault had been beaten back, but only with the loss of three Earth lives and considerable damage to the colony.

"Names of the casualties and further developments will be brought to you as soon as they are released."

A pale, pasty-faced woman eating further up along the counter exclaimed, "How horrible! Those poor people, fighting against those savages!"

"Couple of fellows were talking today that maybe the U.N.'s going to send troops up there to keep everything peaceful," the cook said. "But they better hurry if they're going to do it, or there'll be a massacre."

Kennedy frowned tightly, saying nothing, and wolfed his food. He wanted to tell them that their fears were for nothing, that there was no colony up there, that this whole alien attack had sprung full-blown from a public relations agency's drawing board months before, and was neatly calculated to be revealed this day. That the fierce savages of Ganymede were actually wise and good and harmless people.

But he could not tell them these things.

He slipped into New York late that night and rented a room in Manhattan, in a dreary old slum of a hotel in the mid-sixties overlooking the East River. The name he gave was Victor Engel of Brockhurst, Wisconsin.

The hotel was populated by a curious sort of flotsam—desiccated leftovers from the last century, mostly, who remembered the days when Life Was Really Good. Kennedy, who had taken an intensive course in twentieth-century sociohistory as part of the requirements for his degree in Communications, smiled at the darkest era of the nerve-fraying Cold War of 1946–95, the five decades of agonizing psychological jousting that had led to the Maracaibo Pact and the lasting worldwide unity that had followed. It was as if the Depression of 1995 had wiped away their memories of childhood, taking away the threat of thermonuclear obliteration that had menaced these oldsters during their youth, leaving only a time-hazed remembrance of an Elysian era.

Well, that was their fantasy, Kennedy thought, and he would not puncture it. The Golden Age syndrome was a common accompaniment to senility, and at least they had the never-never world of their dreams to compensate for the bleakness of their declining days.

At least they had some form of happiness. *And what do I do now?* he asked himself.

He was in New York, but he was no closer to the solution of his problem than if he were still on Ganymede, or on Pluto. He had no access to the incriminating data on file at the agency. He could not simply publicly proclaim his accusations—who would believe the demented ravings of a murderer and a traitor? Time was growing short; in a few weeks, the attack would be made and the Gannys wiped out. And before long he would venture out on the street and be recognized, despite the changes he had made in his appearance.

On Wednesday he bought a newssheet and read it carefully. There was word from the beleaguered Ganymede colony, carefully fabricated by a Dinoli henchman. There was a notice to the effect that the traitor Theodore Kennedy was still at large, but that security authorities expected to apprehend him shortly.

And there was a little notice in the *Personals* column. Kennedy nearly overlooked it, but he read the column out of sheer boredom, hoping to find some diversion.

The notice said:

Dearest Ted, Will you forgive me? I realize now the mistake I made. Meet me at our home Thursday night and I will try to help you in what you are doing. Believe me, darling.

                                                            M.

He read it through five or six times. He wondered if it might be a Security trap. No; of course not. It *had* to be from Marge. She was the one person on this entire world that he could trust.

He decided to go to her.

18

THE HOUSE seemed to be sleeping; its windows were opaqued, its lawn overgrown and unkempt. Kennedy paid the cab driver and cautiously went up the walk to the door. The .38 was not far from his hand; he was ready in case Security men might be near.

He put his hand to the door, opened it, went in.

Marge was waiting in the living room for him.

She looked bad. She had aged, during the month; her face was pale and she had lost weight. Her hair looked stringy. Her lips were quivering; her face had no make-up on it, and her eyes were darting nervously around the room as Kennedy entered.

"Marge . . ."

"You saw the ad," she said in a harsh whisper. "I was praying you wouldn't. You never used to read that part of the paper."

"Praying I *wouldn't?* But—"

"Good evening, Ted," a male voice said. Dave Spalding stepped out of the kitchen. A tiny nickel-jacketed gun glinted in his hand.

"Spalding? But—"

"Please put your hands up, Ted. Marge, see if he has a gun."

Marge rose and walked unsteadily toward him. Her hands fumbled over him, quickly found the .38 in his pocket, and withdrew it. Silently she handed the gun to Spalding, who kept both of them covered during the procedure.

"I'm glad you didn't have any strange ideas about that gun, Marge," Spalding said levelly. There was just the hint of a quaver in his voice. "As I told you before, I can tell when you're getting ready to do something. You would have been dead five seconds before you pulled the trigger."

It irritated Kennedy to hear Spalding speaking this way in his own home. Leadenly he realized he had fallen into a trap with Marge as the bait.

He said, "What is this, Spalding?"

"Very simple. You're a very valuable piece of merchandise to me. I'm glad I got to you before Security did. I figured you might fall for something like this."

Kennedy looked at Marge in surprise. "I thought you two were simon-pure idealists. What's happening?"

"I left the agency shortly after your trip into space," Spalding said. "But it occurred to me recently that I might do better for myself if I returned. I phoned Dinoli and offered to find you—in exchange for a second-level position in the agency for myself."

Kennedy's eyes narrowed. "All the cynicism in the air finally made its impression on you, eh, Dave?" The callousness of the younger man's statements astonished him. "So you used Marge as bait and got me here, and now you'll sell me to Dinoli so you can get back into the agency you despised so much a few months ago. Very pretty, Dave."

Something like torment appeared on Spalding's face for a moment. Kennedy said nothing, staring at the gun in the other's hand.

He wasn't too surprised. He had always suspected that Spalding was a man of no real conviction, following the tide and struggling to find a safe port. He had found that port now. He had given up trying to swim upstream.

Spalding said, "I phoned Dinoli at home, as soon as I saw you coming into the house. Security men will be here soon. I just have to keep you here and wait for them, and I can have my second-level slot."

Kennedy glanced at Marge. "That was a splendid little speech you made on the recorder, Marge. All about how you were leaving me for Dave because Dave was true and good and virtuous, and I was just an agency scoundrel. But I guess you see—"

"Shut up!" Spalding muttered.

"You've got the gun," Kennedy said. "If you don't like what I say, shoot me."

"No," Marge said. "Ted, he's gone crazy. Don't say things like that or he will shoot. He doesn't care."

Kennedy heard the clock ticking somewhere in the kitchen. He wondered how long it would take for the Security men to arrive. They would take him away, bury him somewhere in one of their interrogation centers, and the Ganymede invasion would go off as planned.

"Marge," Spalding said. "My throat's dry. Get me a drink of water from the kitchen."

She nodded and went inside. Kennedy smiled. "I'm disappointed," he said. "Not in you but in Marge. I thought she was a better judge of character than she turned out to be. She was really sold on you, I guess."

"I quit the agency, Kennedy. I tried to free-lance. I found out what it's like not to have money. I found out that having ethics isn't enough. They beat you down; they don't let you live. I couldn't fight them, so I made up my mind to join them again."

"Using me as the passkey," Kennedy said. "You knew that Dinoli and Bullard were combing the country for me, and that you had bait you could dangle, in the form of Marge. So you bargained with them. Well, good for you. I hope you're a success on second-level."

Marge returned from the kitchen, bearing a tall glass of water filled to the very top. "Here you are, Dave. It's ice-cold. Be careful you don't spill any. *Get him, Ted!*"

She hurled the water in Spalding's eyes and in the same motion threw herself against him, knocking his gun-hand to one side. Kennedy heard a roar and a boom and the thud of a slug burying itself in the wall, as he sprang toward the drenched, momentarily blinded Spalding.

He caught Spalding by the middle and spun him around. The gun waved wildly in the air. Kennedy grabbed for the gun-hand wrist, seized it and twisted, hoping to make him let go of the weapon. Instead, there was a second explosion.

Kennedy stepped back, startled by the vehemence of the blast. He felt no pain himself, and saw Marge's pale, frightened face. Spalding was sagging to the floor, a jagged hole in his throat and a bewildered, surprised look on his face.

Then Kennedy felt Marge against him. She was

quivering, and he held her tight, trying to keep himself from quivering also. He did not look at the dead man on the floor. He said quietly, "The gun went off while we were fighting. He shot himself. I think he's dead, Marge."

Through almost hysterical tears she said, "H-he put the ad in the paper. Then we came over here to wait for you. I tried to find some way of warning you, but there wasn't any. And now—"

A shudder ran through her, and through him as well. "I guess he deserved it," she said bleakly. "He would have turned you in. Ted, I've never seen a man get so rotten so fast. I was all wrong about him."

"You thought you loved him, didn't you?"

"Does it matter now?"

He tried to smile. "I guess not."

"You won't be bitter about it?"

Kennedy remembered fragments of a Ganny aphorism: *Forgiveness is the heart and soul of existence. The past must not bind the people of the present, for they must heed the nearness of the future.*

"We can start all over," he said, and for a few moments they said nothing. Then Kennedy abruptly broke away from her.

"Spalding said he called Security. They'll be here soon. I've got to get out of here."

"Where will you go?"

"Downtown, to the agency. I have to get together some evidence."

"What kind of—"

"I'll explain everything later. Do you have a car here?"

"It belonged to Dave. It's outside."

"Good. We have to get away from here, fast. And

I have a job for you."

"Anything."

"I want you to get to see Harrison Flaherty—the chief American U.N. delegate." As he spoke, he removed the gun from Spalding's clenched hand, pocketed it, and restored his own to the shoulder holster. "I don't care how you manage it, but get in there to see him. Find out where he lives and see him at home—I know it's someplace in Manhattan. Tell him you're my wife, and that I'm coming over later to surrender myself to him in the name of the U.N."

"What—"

"Don't argue about it. Just do it. And let's get out of here now. I don't want them to catch me before I can give myself up."

They drove down into New York City, taking the Second Avenue Skyway, leaving Spalding sprawled in the living room for the Security men to find. Kennedy was wanted for one murder already; it made no difference if they tacked another to his dossier.

He drove off the Skyway at East 122nd Street and stopped in a store on the corner, where he checked the directomat and discovered that the U.N. man's residence was across town, at 89th Street overlooking the Hudson. He jotted down the address and pocketed it, and hailed a cab for Marge. The time was just before nine.

"I expect to be there in less than an hour," he told her. He slammed the cab door and it drove away. He started to walk.

The business district, at this hour of night, was utterly deserted. The wide streets were empty in a way Kennedy had never seen before. He turned up

East 123rd to Lenox, and the office building that housed Steward and Dinoli was before him. He felt a nostalgic twinge. He looked around, and, seeing no watchman on duty, entered.

He passed through the open front door and was met immediately by an inner barrier. He had a key to it, but the key would work only if his thumbprint were registered in the building's central access file, down in the basement computer banks. It was a long chance, but removing a print from the computer banks was a troublesome business, and perhaps they had neglected to take his out.

He inserted his key and touched his thumb to the plate. The lock clicked; he pushed against the door and it swung back into its niche. They had not bothered to remove his thumbprint from the file after all.

He moved silently through the ghostly building, taking the stairs rather than the elevator (there was a concealed camera in the elevator that photographed all after-hours riders). Eight, nine, ten, eleven. Good old Floor Eleven again, after all these months. Almost three months. Last time he'd been here was the day before his ill-fated Ganymede journey. And now . . .

He used his key and his thumb again and let himself into the office. The lights were off, the windows opaqued. The familiar steady hum of daytime agency activity was missing.

Quietly he made his way past the outer desk to his old cubicle. He clicked on the pocket flash he had found in the tool compartment of Spalding's car, and quickly gathered together the materials he wanted:

Dinoli's bulletin quoting the timetable for unfolding of the project.

The volume of characterizations of colonists he and Spalding had compiled.

Half a dozen damning inter-office memoranda.

His own master chart for developing crises in the day-to-day life of the Ganymede colonists.

It made a heavy little bundle. He shuffled it all together, found a big envelope and shoved it in. He had enough material here to explode the Ganymede hoax from top to bottom. The whole thing was here in all its cynical completeness.

He started to retrace his steps. He stopped; a light was on in one of the second-level offices in the back. Hastily, he shifted his burden from his left hand to the right and started to draw his gun.

A voice from behind him said, "What the hell do you think you're doing, Kennedy?"

He whirled suddenly and in the dimness he saw Ernie Watsinski, lean and stoop-shouldered, staring at him. The second-level man had evidently been working late this evening. He dodged behind a desk suddenly, and Kennedy saw that the executive had a gun.

Quickly, Kennedy flattened himself against a door and ducked into one of the fourth-level cubicles. He said crisply, "Throw down your gun, Ernie. I don't want to kill you. I've seen enough men dead on account of me."

"Suppose you throw down *your* gun," Watsinski replied. "I figured you'd come here eventually."

Kennedy leaned out as far as he dared. Watsinski was barely visible; Kennedy saw the edge of one long leg protrude from the side of a desk, then hurriedly draw back.

He heard the sound of a telephone dial being turned.

He heard Watsinski's voice: "Yes, give me Security. Hello? Ernest Watsinski speaking—of Steward and Dinoli. I'm in the S and D office now, and Ted Kennedy just attempted to break in. Eleventh floor. Yes, he's armed. So am I. We're in something of a stalemate right now. Get right over here."

The receiver dropped back into the cradle. Kennedy began to sweat. From trap to trap! He eyed the distant door and wondered if he dared make a break for it. He had no idea how good a shot Watsinski was, but he knew quite definitely that if he stayed here much longer he would be boxed in by Security.

He moistened his lips. "Ernie?"

"I'm here. Just sit tight, Kennedy. Security'll be here in a few minutes."

Calmly, Kennedy squeezed a shot out. The roar split the silence; he heard the sound of the bullet crashing harmlessly into the desk behind which Watsinski was hiding. The second-level man did not return the fire; the advantage was with him only so long as his gun held ammunition. Kennedy fired two more shots in quick succession. The first hit the wall behind Watsinski; Kennedy was hoping for a lucky ricochet. The second smashed into the lighting fixture above them.

The room went dark. Kennedy sprang to his feet and headed for the door, clutching his package desperately. He heard the sound of shots behind him, wild desperate shots fired by the angry Watsinski.

He grinned to himself as he ran down the eleven flights of stairs.

19

HE EMERGED breathless in front of the building and stopped for a moment. The drizzle that had been starting as he entered the building had developed into a full-sized autumn squall. Kennedy reflected that the Bureau of Weather Adjustment had always been better at making rain than in heading it off.

The car was parked a block away. He started to run, wrapping his package under his jacket to protect the documents from the rain. He looked back and saw a car pulling up outside the S and D building. Security men; he was getting away just in time. He accelerated his pace.

He reached the car dripping wet and half-dizzy from the running, unlocked it, climbed inside. He clicked on the ignition, waited a moment for the turbogenerator to deliver some energy, and drove off. Flaherty lived on Riverside Drive and 89th. He hoped there wasn't much crosstown traffic.

There was no sign of the Security car behind him as he drove. At least, not for the first few minutes. But he saw the car come into view as he reached East 96th Street and turned right onto the Crosstown Skyway, and knew he was being followed.

The Skyway had a minimum speed of seventy. He jammed the accelerator down hard, pushed up above seventy-five. The needle on the speedometer approached the eight and the zero. The car back of him kept pace.

He swerved off the Skyway suddenly at the Amsterdam Avenue turn-off, doubled back to Columbus, then shot down to 88th Street through the side-streets. Rain and darkness combined to make driving rough. He drove westward along 88th, made a sharp right at West End, and cruised down 89th toward Riverside Drive, conscious that he was going the wrong way on a one-way street and hoping that nobody would decide to travel eastward on 89th at that moment.

No one did. He sprang from the car and headed for the apartment building on the corner. Apparently he had lost his pursuers, at least long enough to reach Flaherty.

A shingle on the side of the building said *Harrison M. Flaherty, Ambassador Extraordinary to the United Nations from the United States of America.* Kennedy did not bother to read the small print. As soon as he saw the neat block letters that said *Harrison M. Flaherty,* he knew he had come to the right place.

Just inside the door someone in the uniform of an attendant said, "Who is it you would like to see, please?"

Kennedy caught the man staring at him strangely and was conscious that he hardly looked impressive, soaked as he was by rain and sweat. His heart was pounding so hard he could hardly talk. He managed to say, "Am—Ambassador Flaherty."

The doorman scowled imperiously at him. Kennedy felt like killing him. "Is the Ambassador expecting you?"

Kennedy nodded. "My wife's up there now. At least, I think she is. Why don't you phone upstairs and see?"

"I'll do that."

Kennedy stood to one side, keeping an eye on the front door, while the doorman picked up the house phone. "Your name, please?"

"Kennedy. Theodore Kennedy."

It seemed that the doorman's wide eyes went wider, but he said, "Will you tell Ambassador Flaherty that there's a Mr. Theodore Kennedy down here to see him." Pause. "What? It's all right? Very well. I'll send him up."

The doorman pointed. "Elevator over there. Sixteenth floor."

Kennedy smiled ironically. "Thanks for the help, friend." He rang for the elevator and punched *16*.

On the way up he leaned against the elevator wall, gasping for breath. Moisture streamed down his face. He pushed his hair out of his eyes.

The elevator stopped and Kennedy got out. He saw he was inside the foyer of one of those ultra-large apartments with private entrances. He was staring at three men in the drab uniform of the United Nations Security Police, and they were looking at him coldly, almost menacingly.

"Are you Kennedy?"

He nodded. He tried to see behind them; it seemed that some kind of party was in progress. *Did Marge get here?* he wondered.

The Security men advanced on him. He made no attempt to resist. One efficiently frisked him and re-

lieved him of both guns, his own and Spalding's,
while a second held his arms. The third relieved him
of the package he carried.

"Mr. Kennedy?" a deep, calm voice said.

Kennedy looked up. He saw a bulky, impressive,
gray-maned figure of a man, standing at the entrance
to the small foyer and regarding him with curiosity
and a faint repugnance. Next to him Kennedy saw
Marge, looking white-faced and frightened.

"I'm Kennedy," he said. "My wife—"

"Your wife succeeded in forcing her way in here
half an hour ago, and insisted on telling me a wild
and bizarre story. I was entertaining guests at the
time. I will feel most resentful if the story turns out to
be false."

"It's *true,*" Kennedy said, trying hard not to sound
like a crackpot. He took a deep breath and stared at
the frowning face of the U.N. delegate. "I don't ask
you to believe me on faith, Mr. Flaherty. Lock me
up. Put me in custody. Only"—he nodded at the
package of documents held by one of the Security
men—"read those papers. That's all I ask. Just read
them."

"I'll do that," he said. He glanced at the Security
men. "Meanwhile, suppose you three place him under guard. And watch him. He seems to be quite
elusive."

The General Assembly of the U.N. in plenary session was an impressive sight for Kennedy, especially
after his night in jail. The flags of the hundred-mem-
ber organization decked the hall, and above them all
rose the U.N. flag—the World Flag.

Ganymede was the topic of the day, Juan

Hermanos of Chile was presiding. Yesterday, it had been agreed that the Portuguese delegate would have first word at this session but after the opening gavel fell, U.S. Delegate Flaherty rose solemnly and asked for the floor.

He said, "It has been decided that Mr. Carvalho of Portugal is to speak first today. But I wish to beg that the Chair see fit to ask Mr. Carvalho to yield place to the delegation of the United States."

The parliamentary shift was accomplished; in full possession of the floor, Flaherty nodded to the assembled delegates and continued:

"The topic most frequently discussed before this organization in recent months is that of Ganymede, the moon of Jupiter, on which a colony of Earthborn men and women has been planted. This colony has been planted by the Extraterrestrial Development and Exploration Corporation, whose Mr. Bullard I see in the group before me. The work of the Corporation is well known. Applying private capital where public financing was impossible, the Corporation gave mankind the key to the stars. From among its ranks were chosen the few hundred who comprise the colony on Ganymede, the colony whose privations and dangers we all have followed with such keen interest since public announcement of its existence was made last spring.

"In short the Extraterrestrial Development and Exploration Corporation has, in the past fifty years, become virtually a supranational state, with lands of its own, police of its own, now a spacefleet of its own. This sort of private enterprise is considered commendable by current standards, since we all know the officers of the Corporation have long worked in the best interests of humanity.

"But last night a visitor came to me, a young man who has been active in the task of disseminating news of the Corporation's recent programs. He brought some rather startling papers with him to show me. I have looked through them, and I can attest they are genuine. I believe it now becomes necessary to re-evaluate our entire set of beliefs, not only in the matter of Ganymede but in the matter of Corporation activity in general. I would like to yield place, if it be so resolved by this body, to Mr. Theodore Kennedy, Executive Third-Level of the public relations firm of Steward and Dinoli of this city."

The formality took a moment; Kennedy was given the floor. He rose in his place at Flaherty's left, nudging the chair back clumsily. His throat felt dry. His hands, which rested on a considerable parcel, were trembling.

He stumbled his way through the prescribed salutation. The delegates were staring at him, some with curiosity, some in boredom. In the glare of the lights he managed to pick out the thick coarse face of Bullard, the Corporation's first-level man. Bullard was leaning forward; his eyes seemed to have attained demonic intensity.

Kennedy said, "These papers I hold here give documentary proof of the most wide-scale hoax ever perpetrated in modern history. But before I distribute photostatic copies to you and let you judge for yourselves, let me briefly state my qualifications for the task I now undertake, and a summary of the charges I intend to make against the Extraterrestrial Development and Exploration Corporation.

"I have been on Ganymede from July fifth to thirtieth of this year. I have seen the planet with my own eyes. I have also helped in the fabrication of this hoax.

"Point One: The Corporation is willfully deceiving the people of the world, making use of the Steward & Dinoli agency as its means.

"Point Two: There is not and never has been a colony of men and women on Ganymede. There is a Corporation outpost which consisted of sixteen men in Corporation employ at the time I was there.

"Point Three: The natives of Ganymede are opposed to the exploitation of their world by the Corporation or by any other Earth people, and have declared this repeatedly to the members of the outpost there.

"Point Four: The Corporation, realizing that the natives of Ganymede do not wish their continued occupation of the planet to endure, have come to the decision that a full-scale war against the intransigent Ganymedeans will be necessary in order to subdue the planet and place it fully in their control. Not even the vast resources of the Corporation are equal to the task of waging this war, nor do they want to dissipate their capital and tie up men in what quite possibly would be a guerrilla campaign of great intensity.

"Point Five: Knowing these things, the Corporation engaged the agency for which I formerly worked, charging them with the task of so manipulating and controlling the sources of news that the true nature of events on Ganymede would be concealed and that the United Nations could ultimately be induced to carry out an armed intervention in the Corporation's behalf on Ganymede. This campaign has been highly successful. I regret to confess that it was I who originated the central concept of a fictitious colony on Ganymede which would engage the sympathies of the people of Earth—a colony which is scheduled for a fraudulent annihilation on October eleventh to serve as provocation for a Corporation request for intervention by United Nations forces."

Kennedy paused. He had spoken carefully and clearly, and as he looked around he saw a triple ring of shocked and unbelieving faces. They were starting to mutter; a moment more and there might even be jeers. But he was a master of his trade, and he had timed his speech carefully.

"Perhaps you feel that these charges of mine are the nightmares of a paranoiac, despite the fact that Ambassador Flaherty has given me his seal of approval. But I have prepared photostatic copies of documents which demonstrate amply the shrewd and calculating way in which the Corporation and my agency went about the business of hoodwinking an entire world. Members of the American delegation will now pass among you distributing them."

He had waited just a moment too long. A fierce-looking delegate in bright velvet robes stood up and shouted in crisp British tones, "This is an outrage, and I protest! How can such arrant nonsense be tolerated in his hall? How can—"

Kennedy ignored him. He was staring, instead, at Bullard—Bullard, whose face had grown increasingly more contorted during his speech; Bullard, who had listened in anger to the destruction of the Corporation's plans; Bullard, who sat quivering with rage, shaking with the impact of each of Kennedy's statements—

It was too late for Kennedy to duck. He could only

stand and wait as he felt the bullet crash into his shoulder and heard an instant later the strange little *pop* of Bullard's weapon; then the force of the shot knocked him backward, and as he fell he saw Security men swarming down over the struggling Bullard and heard the loud bewildered shouts of the delegates—delegates who in that moment had had all reality snatched from them, who now confronted the naked core of lies that had been cloaked so long.

20

DIZZILY, Kennedy attempted to rise.

He lay sprawled behind his chair, ignored for a moment in the general confusion. His shoulder seemed to be burning.

He put one hand on the edge of the table and hoisted himself up. He knew Marge was in the gallery somewhere and he didn't want her to worry. Delegates milled about in confusion; Hermanos was pounding the gavel and roaring for order. A flock of Security men surrounded Bullard and were dragging the Corporation man away; Bullard was white-faced with rage. Probably rage at having missed me, Kennedy thought.

A quiet voice said, "Are you all right?" The voice belonged to Ambassador Flaherty.

"I think so," Kennedy said. His shoulder throbbed painfully. He glanced at it; the jacket had a round little hole in it, singed a bit about the edges, but he did not seem to be bleeding.

But suddenly he felt weak. His wobbly legs gave way and he groped for the nearest seat and sank into it. He saw the delegation aides moving down the aisles, distributing his photostats. A hum of light conversation replaced the previous agitated buzz.

Flaherty was speaking again.

"In view of the sudden attack upon Mr. Kennedy by the Corporation executive present here, I think we cannot hesitate to take action today. The shot fired at Mr. Kennedy was a tacit admission of guilt.

"I call, therefore, for a full investigation of the relationship between the Extraterrestrial Development and Exploration Corporation and Steward and Dinoli. I ask, furthermore, that the charter of the Corporation be temporarily suspended pending full investigation, and that we consider possible ways and means of establishing direct United Nations control over space travel and interplanetary colonization, in view of the highly probable event that Mr. Kennedy's evidence will prove authentic."

Kennedy smiled despite the pain. What did a bullet in the shoulder matter, more or less, as the price for what he had done?

He turned to Flaherty and started to say something. Before he could get the first word out, though, a wave of pain rippled over him, and he struggled unsuccessfully to hold on to consciousness.

For the next few moments he heard dim voices speaking somewhere above him; then he was aware that someone was lifting him. He blanked again.

When he woke he was on a plump leatheroid couch in the inner office of Ambassador Flaherty. His jacket and his bloodstained shirt lay over the back of a nearby chair. He saw three or four people bending anxiously over him as he opened his eyes.

"Ah. He is awake." A pale man in medical uniform bent over him, nodding. "I am Dr. Marquis of the United Nations Medical Staff. The bullet has been removed, Mr. Kennedy. It caused trifling damage. A few days' rest until the soreness leaves, and you'll be all right again."

"Glad to hear it."

He craned his neck until he saw Flaherty. "Well? What did I miss?"

"Plenty. Things have been popping all day. The Security men paid a visit to agency headquarters and impounded enough evidence to send your former boss and his friends to the psych-squad. Bullard's in custody here for the attempt on your life. Security forces have taken positions around all Corporation buildings now, to head off the riots."

"Riots?"

"We broke the story to the papers right after you passed out. It caused quite a stir."

Kennedy smiled. "I'll bet it did. Let me see."

They brought him an afternoon edition of a newspaper. Splashed across the front page was the biggest headline he had ever seen:

GANYMEDE COLONY TERMED HOAX BY UNITED NATIONS!

On the inside pages was the story, capped by headlines of a size normally reserved for front-page news.

He skimmed quickly through it.

A New York public relations executive today blew the lid off the biggest and best-kept hoax in modern history. Testifying before the U.N. General Assembly, Theodore Kennedy, 32, of Steward and Dinoli, revealed to an astonished gathering that the colony supposedly planted on Ganymede was

*nothing but a public relations hoax fabricated by his agency.
Kennedy charged that the Extraterrestrial Development and
Exploration Corporation had hired Steward and Dinoli last
April to handle the project for them.*

*As a dramatic climax to the exposé, W. Richardson Bull-
ard, 53, an Executive First-Level of the Corporation, rose
from his seat in the Assembly gallery and fired point-blank at
Kennedy, wounding him in the shoulder. Bullard was taken
into police custody.*

*Also rounded up were Louis Dinoli, 66, Executive First-
Level of the public-relations firm, and the four second-level
men of the firm, as well as ranking Corporation officials.
Futher investigation—"*

Kennedy scanned the rest of the paper. There was
a marvelous shot of Dinoli, eyes blazing satanically,
being led from the S and D offices by Security men.
There was a quote from him, too: *A vile traitor has
struck us a mortal blow. He has violated the sanctity of our
organization. We nurtured a viper in our midst for eight
years.*

There was much more: pages and pages of it. Pictures of Kennedy and an amazingly accurate biography; a transcript of the entire U.N. session that
day; photographs of the Corporation leaders. A long
article covered the background of the Ganymede affair from the very first public release back in May,
quoting significant passages from the pseudo-ac-
counts of the pseudo-colony. An angry editorial
called for prompt punishment of the offenders and
more effective monitoring of the sources of news in
the future to prevent repetitions of this flagrant deception.

"Dinoli never did things in a small way," Kennedy

said, looking up. "His model was the twentieth-century German dictator, Hitler. Hitler always said it's harder to fool the people on the small things than on the big ones. You could always get them to believe that the continents on the other side of the world had been swallowed up by the ocean a lot easier than you could convince them that the price of meat would drop next week. So Dinoli set out to tell the world all about Ganymede. He nearly made it, too."

He handed back the newspapers. He felt very tired, too tired to think, too tired to evaluate what he had done. All he knew was that it was over now, and he wanted to rest and plan his next move.

"Take me home," he said to Marge.

He went home. Flaherty saw to it that there were U.N. people on hand to take care of him. The house hadn't been lived in for weeks, and Marge couldn't handle everything herself.

It had been a busy couple of days, he thought. The business of Gunther's charges had been mostly cleared up, and he had been cleared of Spalding's death as well.

He sent one of the U.N. people down the road to the Camerons to fetch the cat. He asked Marge to help him across the room to the sound system; he wanted to hear some music.

He wondered briefly about the consequences of what he had done. Certainly he had finished Steward and Dinoli; a lot of men who had been drawing fancy pay would be out scrambling for jobs tomorrow, if the psych-squads didn't get them. He tried to picture old Dinoli going through Personality Adjustment, and laughed; Dinoli would be a thorn for the adjusters, a regular bramble bush!

But the others—Haugen, Cameron, Presslie. Probably they would get off easily, pleading that they were mere employees and did not set agency policy. They might draw minor sentences. After that, though, their careers in public relations were just as dead as—

As his.

What do I do now?

His name would fade from the front pages in a few days. He knew too much about communications media to believe that his current notoriety would last.

And then?

Few jobs would be open for him. Potential employers would always be aware that he had turned against Dinoli, had broken into his own office late at night to secure damning evidence. No, he would not be a safe man to employ.

One other thing troubled him. He had been through three months of torture since being assigned to the Ganymede contract. So had Marge. It showed on both of them.

He had had his eyes opened. He had learned to *think*. His brief exposure to the Ganny philosophy had given him an entirely new outlook on existence. He had developed a conscience. But a man with a conscience was useless in his line of work, and he wasn't trained for any other profession. At thirty-two it was too late to start over. He had unemployed himself.

He looked at Marge and smiled.

"You forgive me, don't you, darling?" she asked him.

"Of course I do. It wasn't exactly all your fault, what you did." Ganny words rolled through his head

—words of forgiveness, words of love.

He realized that he longed to finish his conversation up there. He had just been beginning, just finding out that there *was* truth and wisdom somewhere in the universe . . . and he had been learning it from those strange, methane-breathing beings on snowswept Ganymede. That was what had changed him. That was what had impelled him to break faith with Dinoli and the Corporation—the higher call of Ganymede.

The U.N. man he had sent down the road to the Camerons returned. He shrugged apologetically and said, "I'm sorry, Mr. Kennedy. The Camerons weren't home, and the neighbors said they were away and wouldn't be back for a long time. I couldn't find the cat. The man in the next house says he thinks it ran away last week."

"That's all right," Kennedy said. "Thanks."

"Oh!" Marge said. "Poor old McGillicudy!"

Kennedy nodded, listening to the solemn *marcia funebre* coming from the audio speaker. Poor old cat, he thought; after a decade, nearly, of civilized life, he had to go back to the jungle. He probably had forgotten how to catch mice after all these years.

But it was just as well. The cat was part of the past, too, and the past was dropping away, sloughing off and vanishing down the river of time.

No cat, no job, no past. And fame was fast fleeting. Today he was "The Man Who Exposed The Corporation"; tomorrow he'd be just another jobless has-been, trying to coast through life on his old press clippings. He'd seen it happen to other heroes all too often.

His mind drifted back two months, to his short

stay on Ganymede. Ganymede had served as the catalyst, as it were, for the change in his life. On Ganymede . . .

Yes. He knew what he wanted.

"Marge?"

"What is it, Ted?"

"How fond are you of living on Earth?"

Her bloodshot eyes lifted slightly. "You mean—go back to—"

He nodded. He waited a moment; she smiled.

"Will you be happy there?" she asked.

"Very."

"I can't say no, can I?"

"If you don't want to go, you don't have to. But—"

She kissed his forehead lightly. "Did I say I didn't want to go?"

It had been a fine scene, a memorable one, Kennedy thought, as he relived it in his mind once again three weeks after the blast-off. It had been Saturday, December 30, 2044—the final day of the old year, and the final day on Earth for Ted and Marge Kennedy.

Spacefield Seven in New Jersey was bright with snow—the soft, fluffy, sparkling snow of Earth, not the bleak, blue-flecked, forbidding snow of Ganymede. There had been a heavy fall on Christmas Eve, and most of it still remained on the ground in the rural areas. The Bureau of Weather Adjustment had never been too good at averting snow, and Kennedy was glad of it; few things were more beautiful, he thought, than the whiteness of falling snow against the black of a winter night.

The spaceship stood tall and proud in the center of
the field. Once it had been a Corporation ship; now
it belonged to the United Nations. The crew was a
Corporation-trained crew, but they had a new loyalty now. The November trials had finished off the
Corporation.

In his mind's eye, three weeks later, Kennedy re-
created the moment. Flaherty was there, and
Secretary-General Isaacs, and most of the other
United Nations delegates, as well as representatives
from every news medium.

Kennedy stood between Flaherty and Isaacs. The
Secretary-General was saying, "Your work will be
terribly important to us all, Mr. Kennedy. And the
peoples of the world may believe this—every word
that comes to us from you will go out to humanity
exactly as it is received."

The pilots had signaled. The ship was ready. Kennedy made a neat little farewell speech and walked
across the snow-bright field toward the waiting ship.

Flash bulbs went off. Cameras ground.

He and Marge ascended the catwalk.

Now he thought back over those last minutes of his
on Earth. They had waved to him, and he had waved
back, and he had climbed aboard the ship. The
crewmen showed him to his hammock with defer-
ence.

They supplied Marge and Kennedy with gravanol
pills. He grinned, remembering his last experience
with one, and swallowed it.

Tomorrow on Earth was going to be a day without
a name, a day without a date—the Year-End World
Holiday, a day of wild and frenzied joy. As he waited
for blast-off, Kennedy's mind went back six months

to the Leap Year World Holiday—that day of black despair, half-forgotten now.

The day after tomorrow would see a new year on Earth. And for him, a new life.

Resident Administrator of the United Nations Commission to Ganymede. It was a big title, and an even bigger responsibility. In his hands would be the task of convincing the Ganymedeans that the people of Earth would treat them as brothers. That the Corporation was not representative of all Earth.

He would have to win the respect and the admiration of the Gannys. They remembered him as the man who had been different from the others; he hoped they would continue to trust him. He had asked for and received the job of teaching the Ganymedeans to forget their first bitter experiences with the invaders from Earth. Kennedy did not doubt he would succeed; the Gannys were wise, and would listen to him. There would be an exchange of knowledge—Ganny culture for Terran technology. Kennedy would help to bring all this about.

On Earth now, he thought as blast-off began, they were celebrating the coming of the new year, the birth of 2045 from the dead husk of 2044. It was something of a rebirth for him too, he thought; out of the Executive Third-Level of six months before, out of the mad world of public relations, had come a different man, one who had a real and valuable job to do and who was going to do it.

There were other worlds in space; perhaps someday man would meet a second intelligent race, and a third. The Ganymede experience would guide them in their future encounters.

The trip had been a smooth one. Now it was near-

ly over. Earth was just a hazy memory behind him.
Ahead lay Ganymede, waiting.

The ship's medic appeared. "Sir?"

"What is it, Johnson?"

"We'll be entering deceleration orbit in twelve
minutes, sir. I've brought gravanol pills for you and
your wife."

Marge took hers, grinned, and popped the pill into
her mouth. But Kennedy brushed the medic's hand
away as he offered a pill to him.

"No thanks, Johnson. I want to see the whole
thing."

"Ted!"

"I've been through it before, Marge. This time I
want to watch."

He strapped himself in, leaned back, and peered
out the port at the whiteness of Ganymede growing
nearer outside. The ship began to plunge down toward its destination; Kennedy smiled calmly to himself and waited for the landing.

TO WORLDS BEYOND

TO WORLDS BEYOND

ACKNOWLEDGMENTS

"The Old Man" first appeared in *Imagination*. Copyright 1957 by Greenleaf Publishing Company.

"New Men for Mars" first appeared in *Super-Science Fiction*. Copyright 1957 by Headline Publications, Inc.

"Collecting Team" first appeared in *Super-Science Fiction*. Copyright 1956 by Headline Publications, Inc.

"Double Dare" first appeared in *Galaxy Science Fiction*. Copyright 1956 by Galaxy Publishing Corporation.

"The Overlord's Thumb" first appeared in *Infinity Science Fiction*. Copyright 1957 by Royal Publications, Inc.

"Ozymandias" first appeared in *Infinity Science Fiction*. Copyright 1958 by Royal Publications, Inc.

"Certainty" first appeared in *Astounding Science Fiction*. Copyright 1959 by Street & Smith Publications, Inc.

"Mind for Business" first appeared in *Astounding Science Fiction*. Copyright 1956 by Street & Smith Publications, Inc.

"Misfit" first appeared in *Super-Science Fiction*. Copyright 1957 by Headline Publications, Inc.

About *ROBERT SILVERBERG*

by Isaac Asimov

If there is one thing I like to do, it is to beam condescendingly down upon bright young authors who enter my field; that is, science fiction. There is something delightful about unbending from my awesome height as established master in the genre (I am Isaac Asimov, by the way, if you haven't already guessed) to encourage some eager young person who has set his shaky foot upon the path I have myself trod so sure-footedly and so far.

I was all set to do this to young Robert Silverberg when he began to publish science fiction stories in the middle 1950's. I prepared my little speech, one that was not too awe-inspiring, of course, but yet with just a touch of necessary dignity, and was set.

And then what do you suppose the miserable ungrateful creature went and did? He zoomed upward at rocket velocities!

I was just bending down to pat him on the head when he whizzed by and nearly took the skin off my nose. When I leaned back and looked upward, there was Robert Silverberg—a first-magnitude star in the science fiction heavens. He went from mere fan to big-time writer in exactly zero time.

Inside of two months, people were saying to me, "Keep at it, Asimov, and you, too, will be a Robert Silverberg some day." (I killed them, of course, every one of them.)

But that's all right. You may think that I pass by such things, but I don't. Within me the canker of ever-aborted revenge gnaws and snarls. I shall not forget. Someday—mark my words, someday—perhaps not tomorrow, but someday—the time will come when he will want me to pat his head and say a patronizing word.

AND I WON'T!

As if this were not enough, young Robert adds to his vicious behavior by being exactly what every writer would like to be.

Consider! He is dark, handsome and slim, with somber, deep-set, burning eyes that seem to probe under skin and muscle and to bare your very soul with a skillful scalpel. I have seen girls shiver with ecstasy under that white-hot look, bestowed for but one moment though it may be, and then drawn carelessly away.

I, myself, am, of course, unaffected, but when he looks at me I hastily button my jacket.

Then, too, he is bearded; not with offensive profusion, but with neat literary flair. It gives him an almost satanic appearance. I have seen girls shiver—No, I said that already. (Of *course* I'm jealous. I am incredibly handsome, but it is a clean-cut, open-faced, honestly frank handsomeness with nothing satanic about it so that I tend to inspire very sisterly feelings in the female heart.)

And on top of that, his conversation is not frivolous. Not for him the tossed-off quip that, like a stiletto, buries itself almost unfelt in the heart. From him, rather, the stately machete of a riposte, that efficiently, and without undue haste, strips your skin from head to toe.

Surely, the cup of his iniquity is full!

Not at all. What kind of wife do you think a writer of this type ought to have? A shrew who will give him the come uppance he so richly deserves, naturally!

Well, it doesn't work that way. Barbara Silverberg is a sweet, gentle, very pretty girl who caters adoringly to Robert's every whim and who belies her appearance by being indecently brainy. She is, in point of fact, an engineer.

Naturally, I have frequently tried to get her alone in order to discuss some fine point of engineering that I need straightened out for some of my more technical writings.

You would think young Robert would understand the requirements of research. And yet, although to all outward appearances he is far too satanic and other-worldly to take note of such things, he is forever, by some odd chance, standing between Barbara and myself.

I think that is his very worst characteristic—he

simply has no tact!

It would serve him quite right if you refused to read this book—but go ahead and read it anyway. You might as well. The rat writes excellent stories.

Isaac Asimov

INTRODUCTION

We are living in the age of space. It began officially on an electrifying day in October, 1957, when the first Soviet sputnik soared into orbit. On that day, one segment of science fiction's realm was lopped away and thrust into the world of everyday fact. Today, the launching of new space satellites is a routine matter rarely deemed worth the front pages. Rockets from Earth have already landed on the Moon. Probes have gone forth to Mars and Venus. In only a handful of years men will walk through lunar dust, and in a matter of decades they will stand on the red plains of Mars.

Each new feat of our space scientists encroaches on the world of science fiction. Even so, that domain remains infinite—for science-fictioneers have all of time and space at their command. We can no longer write fiction about the launching of the first space satellites, and soon it will be impossible to envision in fiction the first manned trip to the Moon. But what of that? A man's biography does not end with his first few faltering steps. The giant strides of later years are our concern.

In science fiction, we can look beyond today's

sputtering rockets to a glittering skein of tomorrows. Men will reach the Moon, yes, and Mars and Venus too, and they will surge outward to far Pluto and then to the stars. But it will take time. Centuries may pass before other solar systems see their first visitors from Earth.

So there is still room for some creative dreaming about the remoter regions of the galaxy. The headlines of the past few years have not robbed science fiction of its scope. The universe is opening to us, but we have much of the journey yet to travel—and in the time of waiting we can divert ourselves with imagined visions of how it will be.

Here are nine stories of science fiction, then. Nine possible tomorrows, nine ventures into the unknown —nine voyages to worlds beyond.

Robert Silverberg

THE OLD MAN

In the very near future, when space flight becomes a routine job like the commercial aviation of today, a new breed of spacemen may appear. They'll be called on to perform the toughest job in the world. Unlike John Glenn, Yuri Gagarin, and the rest of our spacemen so far, tomorrow's rocket pilots will not merely be sitting passively inside a capsule while it hurtles through a fixed orbit. They'll be at the controls of vehicles moving at unimaginable speeds across vast distances in complex trajectories. It'll take a very special kind of man to pilot those ships—and such men may have certain very special problems.

The Old Man came down the ramp of the spaceship and stood at the edge of the landing field, just looking around. It was good to see Earth again. For a quarter of his lifetime, he'd seen Earth only in snatches, between space trips.

He stood there, one hand on the cold metal of the

ship's catwalk, and looked at the field. It had been a night flight in from Callisto, and the field was brightly lit, sparkling sodium lamps and glittering constellations of guide-beams to illuminate the landing strip for pilots coming down. Bright light was necessary. It was a split-second job, landing a spaceship, calling for devilishly good reflexes. The Old Man looked at his own unshaking hands, and smiled proudly.

Then he picked up his duffel and started to walk across the field.

After about four steps, a gray-clad figure stepped out from behind a dolly and grinned at him.

"Hello there, Carter!"

"Hello there," the Old Man said amiably. But the blankness on his face told the other that the Old Man did not remember him.

"I'm Selwyn—Jim Selwyn. Remember now?"

A smile crossed the Old Man's space-tanned, strain-lined face. "Sure I do—Lieutenant."

"Not any more," Selwyn said, shaking his head. "I'm retired."

"Oh," the Old Man said.

He remembered Selwyn from the far-off past of his trainee days. Lieutenant James Selwyn had been one of the big men of the Space Patrol, and he had paid a visit to the Academy to talk to the new recruits— one of whom had been the Old Man. The Old Man blushed a little for his younger self, as he remembered the blunt idol-worship with which he had approached Selwyn then.

And here was Selwyn now. Retired. A has-been.

"What are you doing these days?" the Old Man asked.

"Ground Mech. Can't get the feel of rockets out of my system, I guess. They retired me after one of my flights on the Pluto run. Guess I slowed down taking the turnover curve, or something. It's a good thing they spotted me before I had an accident."

"Yeah," the Old Man said. "Good thing. You got to have real good eyes to stay behind one of those big crates. Eyes and hands. The second your reflexes start to go, you gotta come out." Suddenly he glanced inquisitively at Selwyn. "Hey, Selwyn, tell me something."

"What?"

"You're not bitter about getting bounced—getting retired, are you? I mean, it doesn't kill you to look at the ships going out and leaving you here?"

Selwyn chuckled. "Hell, no! Not any more. I kicked like hell when I first got my notice, but it wore off. I miss it, a little—but I know my time was up when they yanked me. You remember Les Huddleston, don't you?"

The Old Man nodded grimly. Huddleston was one of the few who managed to fool them. He'd lasted past the usual retirement age, bluffed his way—until the day he was taking up the Mars ship, and didn't quite have it. He was only a fifth of a second off in his coordination, but it cost a hundred lives and fifty million dollars. They kept an eye out for the Huddlestons, now.

"Have a good trip?" Selwyn asked.

The Old Man nodded. "Pretty good. I did the Callisto run. It's all frozen and blue ice out there. Not much to see."

For some reason, Selwyn's eyes looked misty. "Yeah. Not much to see. Just blue ice."

"That's all. But I made the trip okay. I'm due to take out the Neptune run this time around. Pretty good job."

"Neptune's an interesting place," Selwyn said, leaning on the dolly. "Venus was always my favorite, though. It's got—"

Suddenly there was a crackle and the field PA system came to life. *"Flight Lieutenant Carter, please report to Administration Building at once. Flight Lieutenant Carter, please report to Administration Building at once. Thank you."*

"That's me," the Old Man said. "Guess I gotta go. They probably want to give me my new assignment, and they've got my paycheck for me. Pretty good paycheck, too."

Selwyn smiled and clapped the Old Man on the arm. "Good luck, Carter. Give 'em hell."

"Don't worry about me," the Old Man said. He picked up his duffel and started walking across the field to the big gleaming frosty white dome of the Administration Building.

He passed a couple of other pilots on the way— green kids, right out of the academy, without the knowing look and air of confidence that there was about a veteran pilot. They were running springily someplace, perhaps just working off excess energy before their next trip up—or before their first trip up.

"Hey there, Old Man!" they yelled, as they ran by. "How's things, Lieutenant?"

"Can't complain," the Old Man said, and kept walking.

He thought of Selwyn again. So that was what it was like to be washed up? You hung around the spacefield, pushing a dolly, tinkering with feedlines and hauling fuel, grateful to be allowed to smell spaceships and feel the rumble of takeoffs after your time was up. You watched the pilots who still had the eyes and the hands, and envied them.

The Old Man shook his head bitterly. It was sometimes a lousy business, running spaceships. The tests, for one thing. A test before you took off, a test when you landed. They gave him a test at Callisto, and they'd give him another one when he was ready to take out the Neptune run. They kept watch on you, all right.

"Hello, Lieutenant Carter. Have a good trip?"

It was Halvorsen, Base Medic. "Did all right, Doc. Nothing to gripe about."

"Be in to see me for a checkup soon, Lieutenant?"

"Soon enough," the Old Man said. "I'm taking the Neptune run, I hear." He grinned and kept walking.

After a few minutes more he was at the door to the Administration Building, and the plastic door swung open as he walked up to it. A crisp-looking, efficient secretary came forward and flashed a row of white teeth at him.

"Good evening, Lieutenant Carter. Commander Jacobs would like to see you as soon as possible, Lieutenant."

"Tell him I'll be right in," the Old Man said. He walked over to the water cooler, took a long slug—he couldn't risk drinking anything stronger, for fear of damaging his pilot's reflexes—and headed for the panelled door that said on it D. L. JACOBS, Base Commander.

The Old Man paused for just a moment, adjusting his flight jacket, straightening his tie, squaring his shoulders. Then he rapped on the door.

"Yes?"

"Lieutenant Carter to see you, sir."

"Come right in, Lieutenant!"

The Old Man pushed open the door and walked in. Commander Jacobs stood stiffly behind his desk, looking very military and stern. The Old Man's arm snapped up in a crisp salute, which the Commander returned.

"Have a seat, Lieutenant."

"Thank you, sir." The Old Man pulled out a chair and glanced expectantly at Jacobs. Jacobs was an old spaceman himself, the Old Man knew. He wondered how come Selwyn had become a rocket mech and Jacobs a Base Commander, and then decided neither job was worth a damn next to that of being a space pilot.

Commander Jacobs fumbled in his desk drawer, took out a long brown envelope. At the sight of his paycheck, the Old Man grinned.

"How was your trip, Lieutenant?"

"Not bad at all, sir. I'll be filing the log later. It was a good trip, though."

"They *have* to be good trips, Lieutenant. Anything less is disastrous. You know that, of course."

"Of course, sir."

The Commander scowled and handed the Old Man the pay envelope. "Here's your pay for the flight just concluded, Lieutenant."

The Old Man took the envelope, slid it into his breast pocket, and looked up. The next item on the agenda was usually the flight assignment. Those came in thick green envelopes.

But Commander Jacobs shook his head. "Please

open the pay envelope, Lieutenant. I want to make sure you read it now."

The Old Man frowned. "The pay computers haven't made a mistake yet, sir. I'd be willing to bet—"

"Open the envelope, Lieutenant."

"Yes, sir."

The Old Man ran a fingertip down the envelope, opened it, took out its contents. There was a neat blue check in there, and he put that aside. He looked at the amount briefly, then whistled.

Then he read the accompanying voucher.

"Carter, Lieutenant Raymond F.

"For Callisto tour, round-trip, at usual rates: $7,431.62.

"Severance pay, $10,000.

"Total, $17,431.62."

Numb, the Old Man looked up. *"Severance pay?"* His voice was a harsh puzzled whisper. "But that means I'm—I'm—"

Commander Jacobs nodded. "I'm afraid so. That test you took at Callisto—"

"But I passed that!"

"I know. But the indications are that you'd have failed the next one, Lieutenant. We're just avoiding an unpleasant and inevitable scene."

"So you're throwing me out?" the Old Man asked. The world seemed to spin around him. He should have expected it, but he hadn't.

"We're retiring you," Jacobs corrected.

"I still have some time left, though! Can't you let me take the one more flight to Neptune?"

"You're not a good risk," the Commander said bluntly. "Look here, Carter—you know that a pilot must be right up to peak, and nothing less than perfection will do. Well, you're not perfect any more. It happens to all of us."

"I'm still young, though."

"Young?" Jacobs smiled. "Young? Nonsense, Carter. You're a veteran. They call you the Old Man, don't they? Look at those wrinkles around your eyes! You're *ancient*, as space pilots go. You're ready for the scrapheap. And I'm afraid we have to let you go. But there'll always be room for you here, some sort of ground job."

The Old Man swallowed hard, fighting to keep back the tears. The thought of Jim Selwyn struck him, and he knew he was like all the rest. There was no place in space travel for old men. You had to be young and fresh with trigger reflexes.

"Okay—sir," he said hoarsely. "I won't fight any. I'll come around in a couple of days and talk over a ground job with you. When I'm feeling better."

"That's wise of you, Lieutenant. I'm glad you understand."

"Sure. Sure, I understand," the Old Man said. He picked up the paycheck and slid it into his pocket, saluted limply, and turned away. He walked outside, looking at the row of gleaming ships that sat there ready to spring toward the stars.

Not for me, he thought. *Not any more.*

But he admitted to himself that Jacobs was right. Those last few flights had been pretty shaky, though he tried to deny it.

There was no sense hiding the fact any more. He waved to Jim Selwyn, and started to walk toward him to tell him the news.

It was too bad, but it made sense. He was old, as

space pilots went, and couldn't expect anything else but this. It had to happen some time. He was *ancient*, in fact.

Why, he was nearly twenty.

NEW MEN FOR MARS

Men will get to Mars before the end of the present century, unless I miss my guess. They won't find it a pleasant place. The air is thin, the weather is cold, and there's not a drop of water in sight. But men will try to carve a foothold there, just as they've done in the frozen wastes of Antarctica and the dismal barrenness of the Sahara. How will they colonize Mars, though? By building self-containing pockets of earth in which men can huddle? Perhaps it'll be done by changing the men to fit the planet, instead.

The interplanetary ferry *Bernadotte* quivered in space and began the long, slow turnover motion that was bringing it inexorably closer to the cold, slumbering, oxidized wastes of Mars. Aboard the ship, UN man Michael Aherne, making his first trip to the red planet, stared anxiously through the rear viewer, searching for some sign of life.

There was none. The Dome that housed the Mars Colony was not in sight, and all Aherne could see was the bleak, barren sand. He was nervous—as, indeed, a spy whose ostensibly secret mission was known openly to everyone should be. He had been pitchforked into a nasty job, and he knew a stern test lay ahead of him.

Aherne heard a noise somewhere in the back of the cabin and whirled to see the captain of the little vessel enter—Juri Valoinen, a tall, balding, annoyingly bantersome Finn who had logged more hours in space than any other living man.

"Just another hundred minutes or so," Valoinen told him. "You ought to be able to see our Dome pretty soon—we'll be coming down right next to it, practically. I'm always afraid we're going to land right *on* it one of these days, and that'll shoot the UN budget completely to blazes."

Aherne forced himself to grin, and turned away from the viewer to walk toward the captain. Aherne was a man of middle height, stocky, sandy-haired; as Special Attaché-at-Large for the United Nations, he had been on a number of far-flung investigations, but this was about as far as he had ever been flung in the name of the UN—forty million miles, across the gulf of space—to spy on the Mars Colony. *Spy.*

Some spy, he thought bitterly.

He looked at his watch. They were right on schedule.

"They know I'm coming, don't they?" Aherne asked.

The Finn nodded, smiling knowingly. "Indeed they do. And what's more, they know *why* you're coming. I don't doubt they'll have the plush carpet rolled out for you for sure. They're going to want to make a good impression on you."

"That's what I was afraid of," said Aherne. "I'd

have preferred to go among them cold and take a look around. That way my report would be genuine."

"Who needs genuine reports?" Valoinen demanded sardonically. "My friend, it's time you learned that our organization thrives on misconception and blunder. Facts are its deadly enemies."

Instantly Aherne's face darkened. "Let's not be flippant, Valoinen. The UN is responsible for a good many things we ought to be thankful for—including the preservation of your own insignificant country," he snapped. "Not to mention the handsome salary you get for ferrying this boat back and forth between Mars and Earth."

The space captain backed off, holding up a hand to check the flow of Aherne's anger. "Take it easy, son, I think it's a wonderful organization too. But I'm old enough not to take it as seriously as all that."

"Well, maybe when you're even a little older you'll learn that the UN *has* to be taken seriously," Aherne grunted, and turned his attention back to the viewer. He narrowed his eyes, staring into the blackness at the dim coppery globe half-visible below.

After a moment he turned once again; Valoinen was still standing behind him, arms folded, thin lips twisted in a wry grin. "Well?"

"I think I see the Dome," Aherne said.

"I congratulate you."

"No, don't joke." Aherne frowned, glanced back for a moment to verify what he had seen, and scratched his head. "But—why are there *two* domes? There seems to be another one, about ten miles from the first. How come? I'm sure the UN only built one."

Valoinen showed white, even teeth in a derisive smile. "Exactly right, my friend. Only one of those is the UN dome."

"But the other?"

"You'll find out soon enough. I don't want to—ah—prejudice you. I want your report to be—ah—*genuine*." He spun on his heel and moved towards the door. "And now, if you'll excuse me, I'll have to tend to my cargo."

The bulkhead door clanged closed, and Aherne was left alone—staring out in bewilderment at the twin domes.

II

"Put the gyroscopes over there," Valoinen ordered, and three members of his crew hove to, dragging the crates to the designated spot.

"There—that finishes it," the captain said. The cargo crates were arranged in a neat semicircle outside the ship, awaiting pickup. Valoinen glanced over at Aherne, who was standing idly to one side. Aherne was feeling exceedingly uncomfortable, partly because he was bundled up in the unfamiliar bulkiness of a spacesuit and partly because he had had nothing at all to do during the unloading.

"You all right, Aherne?"

The UN man nodded, moving the helmet of his suit stiffly up and down. "Just fine," he said. The portable air generator was a dead weight hanging down his back, seemingly at the point of ripping his deltoid muscles out bodily. He felt anything but fine, though he had no intention of telling the captain that.

"They'll be here to get you any minute," said

Valoinen. "I've radioed the colony that there's a cargo pickup, and they're sending a fleet of sand-crawlers out. They said they're very anxious to meet you."

Aherne tensed. It was going to be a difficult, tricky mission. Sent here to determine if the tremendous expense necessary for continuance of the Mars Colony was justified by the results produced so far. Aherne was going to have to remain dispassionate, aloof to the very last. He was here to pass a sentence of life or death on the Colony.

The UN would rely on his report. They always did. Aherne had proved his impartiality time and again. He knew just one loyalty: to the corporate, many-headed creature known as the United Nations. A second-generation UN man, Aherne was the ideal observer.

But yet he hoped the colonists wouldn't make his task any more difficult than it already was. Aherne recognized the fact that he had a considerable natural sympathy for the Martian pioneers, a personal desire to see the Colony continue and prosper. It was part of his deepest body of beliefs that man should go out, conquer the other planets.

Still—if the Colony were inefficient, badly directed, poorly designed, it would be Aherne's duty to report it. If the Colony were barely clinging to survival, if further progress seemed completely out of the question, Aherne would have to say that too—and, so saying, kill the Colony.

He hoped the colonists would not play on his sympathies and urge him to whitewash any of their deficiencies; it would set up a painful inner conflict in him. He could not falsify his report—but he was anxious to see the Colony survive at all costs.

And a man like Aherne—monolithic, unswervingly loyal, firm in his beliefs—would fall apart completely in a situation of immediate inner stress of that sort. Aherne knew that—and, as the low-slung fleet of sandcrawlers purred along the desert toward him, he felt a tiny pulse of fear starting to thud in his chest.

He watched the steady approach of the crawlers. The air was cold and clear—his suit-thermometer, embedded in the heel of his left glove, showed a comparatively mild temperature of minus twenty-two centigrade, and the external-pressure needle was wavering at about six pounds per square inch; internal pressure, he noted reassuringly, was maintained at a comfortable sea-level fifteen pounds.

Valoinen and his men were sitting on the unpacked crates, waiting patiently. Aherne walked over to join them.

"The Dome's out that way," Valoinen told him, pointing in the direction from which the crawlers were coming. An upthrust, jagged range of dark mountains cut off vision about four miles in the distance. "Behind those hills," Valoinen said. "The Dome's right back there."

"And the other one?"

"That's a little further on," said Valoinen.

They fell silent—Aherne felt unwilling to prod for information about the second dome—and waited for the colonists to arrive. The sun, a sickly, pale green object, was high overhead, and the tailstanding *Bernadotte* cast a long, straggling shadow over the leveled, heat-fused sand of the landing clearing.

The crawlers were getting larger now, and Aherne could make them out clearly. They were long, ground-hugging vehicles with caterpillar treads spread out over a lengthwise grid, with room for a couple of passengers in a plastic bubble up front, and a cargo hold aft. There were six of them, rocking gently from side to side as they undulated through the shifting red sand.

Aherne could hear the grating, feathery sound of their treads sliding over the sand toward him. At length, the convoy breasted the final dune and pulled up in front of the *Bernadotte*.

A figure dropped lightly from the leading crawler and trotted toward them. Aherne could just barely see the man's face behind his helmet—blonde hair swept back over a high forehead, and piercing blue eyes. His body, concealed by the spacesuit, seemed long and rangy.

"I'm Sully Roberts," he announced. "Hello, skipper."

"Here's your cargo, Sully." Valoinen stretched forth his arm in an expansive gesture, holding out a sheaf of invoices.

Roberts reached out and took the invoices, carefully avoiding looking at Aherne. The colonist riffled quickly through them.

"Hmm. Well, at least the externals match. I can't guarantee that you've actually got gyros in those boxes, and not toy teddy bears, but it won't do to open 'em now, I guess."

"Don't you trust me?" Valoinen asked sharply.

"Sure I do," said Roberts. "But this is the UN's money we're spending, and we don't want to waste any of it. We have to be very careful with our appropriation, of course."

"Of course," said the captain lightly.

That was for my benefit, Aherne thought. *They're so terribly anxious to show me what good little boys they are.*

"Oh," Valoinen said. "Silly of me—I clean forgot to introduce you. Sully, this is Michael Aherne of the United Nations. He's come to stay with you for a while."

Roberts took a couple of steps forward and shook Aherne's hand. "How d'ye do! I'm Sullivan Roberts, District Overchief for the Colony. I'm very glad to meet you, Mr. Aherne, and I hope to be seeing a lot of you while you're here."

"Glad to meet you, Roberts."

Roberts waved an arm and his men dismounted from their crawlers. Assisted by Valoinen's crew, they quickly loaded the crates into the cargo holds.

"You can ride with me, Mr. Aherne," Roberts said.

"Fine." Aherne clambered up into the fore bubble of the sandcrawler, and Roberts got in beside him. Slowly, without any perceptible gradation between motionless and motion, the crawler began to move.

Aherne saw Valoinen grin and wave as he pulled out. Then, as the crawler started to surmount the hill, Valoinen climbed the catwalk of the *Bernadotte* and disappeared inside. His men followed, carrying the mail pouches from the Mars Colony, and the lock of the small ship slowly closed.

Aherne was on his own now, with no contacts with Earth. He was here, and he had a job to do.

III

The shining surface of the Dome loomed up before them like a yellow bubble extruded from the desert. Within the gleaming, high-arched curve of plastic,

Aherne could make out a dim but busy world of buildings and people. The Dome rose to a peak height of nearly five hundred feet. Within, the artificial atmosphere was warm and breathable; outside, the cold, nitrogenous air of Mars offered little to Terran lungs.

"We go in this way," Roberts said, pointing to an airlock at the base of the Dome. The lock opened at the approach of the sandcrawler, and they rode in. The other crawlers followed. The lock swung slowly shut behind the last one. Air came hissing in.

At Roberts' signal, Aherne got down from the cab of the crawler and stretched his legs. The journey across the sand had been slow and racking. The crawler had spun through the desert like a refractory camel, and Aherne found himself woozy at the end of the ride. Still, he admitted, it was the only practical way of covering that sort of terrain.

He saw busy, efficient-looking men bustling around the crawlers, unpacking the cargo holds, carrying the crates through the lock inside. Following Roberts, Aherne moved through the inner door.

Mars Colony was spread out before him.

Aherne felt a warm sensation of pride, of admiration, run through him, but he squelched it. It was a forbidden emotion; much as he admired the hardy men and women who had erected this dome and built a city on inhospitable Mars, he was here as their judge now and would have to put those feelings aside.

"There's a committee waiting to see you," Roberts said. "We've been looking forward to your visit ever since we found out you were coming."

"Lead on," Aherne told him.

* * *

The committee was assembled in a squat, unfancy corrugated-steel hut located at a crossroad near the center of the Colony. Most of the buildings, Aherne noticed, were constructed of this cheap, unattractive material. The accent was on economy in Mars Colony, not esthetic appeal.

The committee consisted of six. Sully Roberts introduced them hurriedly.

There were three District Overchiefs present, Roberts, being the fourth. Aherne shook hands with them in turn—Martelli from the North Quadrant, Richardson from the East, Fournier from the West. Roberts represented the Southern sector of the Colony. Judging from their names and physical appearances, Aherne concluded that they each represented, not only a geographical district of the Colony, but one of the major population blocs as well. For the Colony, despite all talk of assimilation, was very much the product of a group of loosely federated nations, rather than a unified world. Each country, clinging to the last remnants of its sovereignty, had insisted on representation in the Colony, and so Mars was populated by a curious racial hodgepodge which only the passage of time and the succession of generations would efface.

If, Aherne thought, there *were* any succeeding generations on Mars.

The fifth member of the committee was Dr. Raymond Carter, General Coordinator of the Colony—a forty-ish, bespectacled man whose name had been in the headlines often before the Colony had actually been planted, five years before. He had been the guiding spirit in the long crusade to build the Colony on Mars.

The sixth was Katherine Greer, introduced as a delegate-at-large, chosen by popular vote of the colonists to serve on the welcoming committee. She was a young, slender girl in her middle twenties.

"Well, Mr. Aherne," Carter said—and the tone of his voice was unmistakable—"what do you think of the progress we've made?"

Aherne paced edgily up and back in the little room, darting nervous glances at the six colonists who hung, poised, on every word.

"I'd prefer to reserve judgment on such a sweeping statement, Dr. Carter. After all, it's to determine the extent of your progress that I'm here—and I'd rather not be required to state my final conclusions ten minutes after my arrival."

"Of course not," Carter said hastily. "I didn't mean to imply—"

"Don't worry about it." Aherne was surprised and relieved to find that these people were, if possible, even more tense than he. They were desperately anxious to make a good impression on him.

"We've arranged for your quarters to be set up in my district," said Richardson, the East District Overchief. Richardson was a slim, little Negro whose precise British accent hinted at an African ancestry.

"Fine," Aherne said.

"I suppose you'd like to rest for a while now," Dr. Carter continued. "You must have had a long, trying trip."

"Excellent idea. I am pretty beat."

"Mr. Richardson will conduct you to your quarters, and your meals will be taken care of. We've made considerable strides in developing synthetics—until the Martian soil is sufficiently re-nitrogenized to be capable of harboring vegetables, of course."

"Of course," Aherne said wearily. He foresaw several weeks of uneasy verbal fencing, and decided that the eagerness of these colonists to impress him was going to become tiring.

"After you've rested," Carter said, "we've scheduled a tour of the Colony for you. Miss Greer has been assigned to you as your guide."

At the mention of her name, the girl smiled slightly, and Aherne couldn't resist a grin. These colonists weren't missing an opportunity. What better way to make a favorable impression than to see to it that a nubile young wench served as his guide? Score another point for Carter and company.

He glanced at Miss Greer. She was dressed in the utilitarian, unattractive singleton tunic that all the colonists seemed to adopt, but her face was bright-eyed and interesting, and beneath the shapeless garment Aherne's critical eye detected what probably was a much more than passable figure.

He felt himself relax. This survey trip wasn't going to be as much of an ordeal for his conscience as he had been expecting.

His room was comfortable, if hardly luxurious, and he made himself at home immediately. He noticed several Colony tunics hanging in the clothes closet, and he stripped his rumpled business suit off and slid easily into one of the soft, clinging uniforms.

And then, just as he was beginning to loosen, to wriggle out of the tensions that had gripped him since the Security Council had given him the assignment, he remembered the other dome.

What was it? Who had built it? Everyone connected with the Colony here carefully avoided all mention of it, as if it were something shameful, something to hide from sight.

Aherne knew that he'd have to find out all the details before he committed himself on any final decision about Mars Colony. No matter how promising the Colony seemed, and no matter how many Miss Greers they threw in his way, he'd have to be in control of every information-factor before he could allow himself to file his report.

The colonists had given him a pleasant room, with a soft-looking bed and attractive furnishings. There was a bookcase, in which half a dozen scarlet-bound volumes leaned at an angle against one wall, and when he drew the first out he saw it was a novel by a colonist, published there in the Colony.

They don't miss a bet, he thought, feeling another forbidden tingle of pride go through him. It wouldn't be hard to recommend continuation of a colony that showed such enterprise and such drive—provided everything else held up. So far, so good.

Aherne slept soundly that night for the first time in weeks.

IV

He expected the guided tour first thing in the morning—in fact, was positively looking forward to it. And so, when he heard a soft, gentle rapping at his door the next morning, he rolled out of bed and tried to look wide awake. He was almost positive that it was Miss Greer at the door.

He was wrong. He threw the door open and was confronted by a small, swarthy, almost copper-colored man, with deep-set eyes and jet-black hair.

"Good morning, *señor*," the stranger said blandly.

"Good morning," Aherne replied, somewhat taken aback.

"I have been sent to get you," the small man said. Aherne noticed, as the other stepped into the room, that he had an enormous barrel of a chest—the chest of a six-footer, not a man barely five-two in height. He spoke with a distinct Spanish accent.

"To get me?"

"*Si*. Please come quickly."

Too puzzled to protest, Aherne washed up, dressed—the colonial plumbing, he noted, was none too good—and followed the small man out onto the street. It was still early in the morning and few of the colonists were to be seen.

"Where are we going?" Aherne asked.

"With me," the other said noncommittally.

Aherne wondered vaguely just where he was being taken, but decided to follow without argument. It was just possible that he might find out something about the Colony that he might not learn from the official guided tour. He patted the cold butt of the Webley blaster, nestling safely in its shoulder-holster. He could hold his own with that, in case of trouble.

The little man seemed to be in a considerable hurry. He led Aherne speedily through the streets toward the outer edge of the Dome—toward the airlock.

Several of the colonists he passed on his way smiled at him, but no one seemed to want to stop him, to find out where he was going. It was just as well, Aherne thought.

They came to the airlock. Aherne saw a sandcrawler parked outside. The little man had not said a word during the entire walk. Now he indicated a rack of spacesuits hanging invitingly at the entrance to the airlock. "Take one," he said. "Put it on."

Aherne obeyed. His strange guide climbed into one of the smaller suits. Together, they passed through the airlock and outside the Dome.

"We go in this," the other grunted, and got into the sandcrawler. Aherne followed. The vehicle rocked smoothly to life and started to undulate away.

The crawler slid through a gap in the hills and pursued a twisting, sharply banked sand path in the desert. An hour later, they arrived at their destination—the second dome.

It seemed to be constructed along the lines of the other. Aherne stared around curiously as he and his silent companion went through the by-now familiar process of passing through the airlocks. At last, he was out of his suit and within the second dome. It looked much like the first, inside and out.

But after a few steps, Aherne found himself panting for breath, and a few more and he could sense his pulse quickening. There *was* a difference: the air-pressure here was considerably lower than Earth-normal. He felt his body gasping to take in the quantity of oxygen to which it was accustomed, and he swallowed hard to relieve the pressure on his eardrums.

As he stood there, reeling slightly from the change in pressure, he saw a second small, swarthy, Spanish-looking man approaching. But this time it was a face that Aherne knew well.

"You'll get used to the low pressure soon, Aherne," the newcomer said as he drew near. "We maintain it here for the benefit of our colonists." He extended a box of tablets. "Here," he said. "Aspirin. It'll relieve the reaction a little bit."

Aherne took the box, fumbled out one of the white tablets, and swallowed it dry. In a moment the pounding in his head subsided a little.

"What are *you* doing here, Echavarra?" Aherne said.

"You haven't missed me, Aherne? You haven't noticed that I've not been expounding my crackpot ideas at the United Nations these past three years?"

"No," Aherne said slowly. "Ever since the defeat of your proposal, I'd assumed you were off doing private research somewhere."

The man addressed as Echavarra grinned broadly. "Exactly right. I have been doing private research." He put an arm around Aherne's shoulder. "Come," he said. "Let us go to my home. The pressure is easier to take there."

As they walked into the heart of the colony, Aherne discovered that it appeared to be populated almost exclusively by the small, swarthy men, none of whom seemed at all bothered by the low pressure. The picture was starting to take shape.

José Echavarra had been a storm-center at the United Nations Headquarters during the days of the hot debate over who should build the Mars Colony, and how. Echavarra, a Peruvian geneticist, had bitterly opposed the American, Carter, who seemed to have the inside track on the coveted UN appropriation.

Carter had favored building pressurized domes on Mars, in which Earthmen could live in comparative comfort. Echavarra, raging, had declared that this was the wrong way to go about it—that man should adapt himself to fit the planet, not adapt the planet to fit himself.

He put forth as an example Andean miners who had been studied by Peruvian scientists. These miners lived all their lives at altitudes of 10,000 to 15,000 feet above sea-level, where the air was thin and the air-pressure low—and they had *adapted*. They were capable of existing comfortably with a pressure of only eight pounds per square inch. Echavarra had proposed to establish a colony composed of these hardy Peruvians, and gradually to breed them further along the lines they were already following, until they were suited to living comfortably in the thin air of Mars.

Aherne remembered clearly what had happened. The volatile Dr. Echavarra had spent long hours explaining his plan, and then it had been turned down flat. After all, one delegate remarked, the Echavarra plan meant that only one nation—Peru—could send men to Mars. Other peoples, raised on the customary fifteen-pounds-per-square-inch air pressure, would be incapable of surviving.

That ended the discussion. Echavarra was rejected firmly, and Raymond Carter had been chosen to head the pioneer expedition that would build the pressure-dome and establish the UN Colony, with the colonists, of course, to be chosen from all nations.

Echavarra had disappeared from sight. Now, here he was—complete with his colony of Peruvians after all. And the air pressure was low, all right. Aherne, weakening, dragged one leg after the other painfully as he followed Echavarra through the streets.

* * *

' "In here," the Peruvian said. Aherne stumbled
ahead as he was told, and entered a small, austerely
furnished room whose warm, rich atmosphere struck
his lungs with jarring force.

"I keep one room at normal pressure," Echavarra
explained. "I'm still not completely used to the stuff
these Andeans breathe myself, and I like to relax in
here from time to time."

Aherne flung himself down on a hammock
stretched tautly from wall to wall, and waited for his
metabolism to return to normal.

"Whew!" he managed to say after a moment.
"I'm not built for these pressure changes."

"You're suffering from anoxia," Echavarra said.
"Lack of oxygen. The decreased pressure in this
dome makes it harder for your lungs to get oxygen,
and the quantity of red cells in your blood increases
to compensate. It's rough for a while, but you'll ad-
just."

Aherne nodded. "I'll say it's rough."

"I'd guess you'd passed into the second threshold
of anoxia," the Peruvian commented, bustling
around nervously. "Which is about what I expected
would happen."

"What do you mean?"

"We grade the levels of oxygen need on three
thresholds," Echavarra explained. "The first is the
reaction threshold. On Earth, it's generally encountered
above 6,000 feet altitude. Pulse quickens; capillaries
relax, allowing more blood to reach the cells. Some
dizziness. And then comes stage two, as you go a little higher—*disturbance threshold*. You were just passing
over that level when I got you in here. Characteristics

are fuzziness of sight, dulling of the senses, slowness of muscle reaction. You know what it's like. It's unpleasant, but not dangerous."

"I see," said Aherne. He was still recovering his strength, and lay there unmoving. "Is there a third stage?"

"There is," Echavarra said. "*Critical threshold*. It's encountered when the pressure gets down to about one-half atmosphere. Loss of vision, pounding of heart, nosebleed, loss of muscular coordination, blackout of consciousness. Possibly convulsions. The ultimate crisis is death. Men just aren't built to take low pressure. Mars is a critical-threshold area at all times; on Earth, it's generally encountered only above 16,000 feet—such as in the Peruvian Andes," Echavarra concluded pointedly.

Aherne was feeling much better now. He swung himself to a sitting position and glared sharply at the Peruvian, who was toying with his stiff black mustache.

"All very interesting, Echavarra, though I suspect you didn't smuggle me out here just to lecture me on high altitude conditions. How about the information I want to hear?"

Echavarra smiled urbanely. "Just what would you like to know?"

"First: what are you doing here? Who financed you?"

The small man's countenance darkened. "It is a sad story. After my unhappy rejection at the hands of the General Assembly, I traveled from country to country, seeking backers for my project. Finally I raised the necessary minimum, with the generous help of my own countrymen. Naturally we could not work on the scale Dr. Carter did, but we did manage to get together enough cash to transport several hundred Andean families here and build a fair-sized dome."

"Why?"

The other smiled. "I disagreed with the basic premise of Carter's project, and I wanted a chance to try it my way. My men are already acclimated to one-half atmosphere. They work and play happily in an environment that would kill a normal man. They've been living that way for generations. Genetically, they've been bred to survive in thin-air conditions.

"I'm reducing the pressure in this dome, ever so gradually. They don't notice it—but their bodies adapt to the slight changes. Eventually I hope to get it down to where it approximates that of Mars. I won't be here to see it. It won't be with these people, nor with their children—but somewhere along the line it'll happen. And then—poof! No more domes!"

"Interesting," said Aherne coldly. "Just why did you pull this little trick this morning and spirit me away, then?"

The Peruvian spread his dark-skinned hands. "You're here to decide on the fate of the Carter colony, are you not?"

Aherne nodded. "What if I am?"

Echavarra brought his bright-eyed, eager face close. Aherne noticed that it was lined with a fine purple network of exploded capillaries. "I brought you here to show you how I'm succeeding with my genetics program. I want you to vote against Carter—and transfer the appropriation to me!"

Aherne recoiled instantly. "Impossible! The UN

has already voted to support Carter. I can't see any reason to countermand their decision. Your work has some curiosity value, I suppose, but we can hardly give serious—"

"Not so fast," Echavarra said. "Don't leap off so blindly. You're here for a while. Take your time; consider the relative merits of the two colonies. See for yourself which one is fitter to work and live on Mars."

Aherne shook his head. "I'm willing to abide by the decision of the General Assembly," he said. "Thanks for the offer, but I think I'd better get back to the UN Colony now, Echavarra."

"Stay a little longer," the Peruvian urged.

Aherne started to say no, but suddenly there was the sound of scuffling outside, and loud, angry shouting. And then the door burst open, and Sully Roberts, wearing a plastic oxygen-mask, strode into the room, half a dozen men behind him.

V

"You'll pay for this, Echavarra!" Roberts snapped angrily. His men formed a ring around Aherne; in the background, Aherne could see two or three puzzled-looking Peruvians standing on tiptoe trying to peer into the room.

"What do you mean, Mr. Roberts?"

"I mean you've kidnapped this man!" Roberts turned solicitously to Aherne. "They haven't harmed you at all, have they?"

"There seems to be some misunderstanding," Echavarra said mildly. "Mr. Aherne was not *kidnapped*. He came here voluntarily, earlier this morning, to inspect our colony. Is this not correct, Mr. Aherne?"

The UN man saw the faces of the six men from Carter's colony go tense. They were worried now; perhaps Echavarra had succeeded in seducing him over to his side? Aherne decided to remain noncommittal for the moment.

"I wouldn't say I was kidnapped," he replied, smiling. "I did, indeed, come here voluntarily."

"You see?" Echavarra said.

Robert's face was a mask of anguish and turmoil "But—"

"I want to assure you that Mr. Aherne has not been harmed," Echavarra said. "And now, if you'll excuse us while we finish our discussion—"

"We're expecting him to take part in some functions at our Dome," Roberts said. "We'd be very disappointed if he remained here with you."

Careful use of the third person in speaking about me, Aherne noted. *They're afraid of seeming to be controlling me.*

"I think they're right, Señor Echavarra," Aherne said. "I do have a responsibility to the Carter colony at the moment."

"I hope you'll give careful consideration to the matter I mentioned, Mr. Aherne."

"I'll think about it," Aherne promised. It was the diplomatic thing to say. "But as of now, I intend to rely on the earlier decision of the Assembly."

"Very well," Echavarra said, half-frowning and bowing politely. "But I do hope to see you again before you leave Mars—and perhaps you'll have changed your mind."

"Perhaps," Aherne said. He turned to Roberts. "I think it's time to go back now."

When they were outside, walking briskly through

the thin air of the Peruvian colony on their way to the
airlock, Roberts allowed some of his anxiety to escape.

"We were sure worried there, Mr. Aherne. As
soon as we found out you'd been seen leaving the
colony in the company of one of these little Indians,
we lit out after you."

"What were you afraid of?" Aherne asked as they
reached the airlock.

"Well, sir, you didn't leave any message, and we
were sure you were kidnapped. Of course, we didn't
know you had decided to visit the Peruvians without
telling us," Roberts said.

Implied in that, thought Aherne, *is veiled criticism.
What he's hinting at is that I had no business running off like
that—or that perhaps I really was kidnapped, and won't admit it.*

"Echavarra and I are old acquaintances," Aherne
said. "I had a good deal of contact with him in the
days before his project was turned down by the UN."

"He's a crackpot, of course," Roberts asserted
quickly. The big man boosted Aherne lightly up into
the sandcrawler and followed him in. "This idea of
breeding people to breathe Martian air can't possibly work, can it?"

"I'm not so sure of that." Aherne saw the immediate expression of despair reflected on Roberts'
open face, and rejoiced just a little in his own wick-
edness. He was baiting Roberts, taking advantage of
the colonist's desperate desire to win Aherne's approval, and while he knew it was unfair it was also a
little enjoyable.

After a long silence, during which both men had
kept eyes fixed firmly and uncomfortably on the

trackless wastes ahead, Roberts said, "You don't mean you'll consider giving them our appropriation, do you?"

Aherne considered possible answers for a moment or two—and then, seeing no real justification for allowing Roberts to worry over the possibility of an outcome that Aherne himself had already rejected, said, "No, of course not. The UN's already voted to support the Carter colony, and I don't see any reason for bringing Echavarra back into the picture."

Anxious faces greeted him as he clambered through the airlock of the UN Dome and re-entered the Colony. He spotted the remaining members of the committee of six, and a handful of other very worried-looking colonists.

Dr. Raymond Carter was the first to come up to him. But before anything could be said, Roberts interposed himself and explained where Aherne had been, and why.

"Visiting Echavarra, eh?" Carter said. "That crank? Did he have anything interesting to say? Last I heard, he was working on some plan for making those Indians of his survive on Jupiter—or was it the photosphere of the sun?"

Aherne smiled at the exaggeration, but ignored the comment. "I'm sorry for the delay," he said. "I felt it was necessary to examine the Peruvian colony as well as yours—as a sort of control to use in judging your own Dome."

Carter eyed him uneasily. "You weren't taken in by Echavarra, were you?"

"No," Aherne said. "At least, I see no reason to reverse the decision of the General Assembly in regard to the appropriation." He saw Carter relax visibly, and immediately added, "I do, of course, want to examine your own colony in detail before reaching any decision on your progress and future potentialities."

"Naturally," Carter said uneasily. "You can proceed with your tour of the Colony at once, if you wish. Miss Greer will be happy to accompany you wherever you would like to go."

Carter appeared almost absurdly grateful that Aherne had not deserted to the camp of the Peruvian geneticist. As he walked away toward the heart of the Colony with the voluble Miss Greer, Aherne found himself wishing he could be in a position to be honest with these people—to tell them how much he admired their accomplishments, to tell them how badly he was hoping to be able to put through a positive recommendation for continuation of the Colony.

But he had to be sure, first. An emotional identification with these pioneers was dangerous, threatening to undermine his judgment. Aherne knew his appraisal would have to be cold, rational, and remorseless. The outcome was still in doubt, so far as Special Attaché Michael Aherne was concerned.

VI

Miss Greer was tall, slim, attractive, and ready to do almost anything to win Aherne's approval. Aherne wondered, in a detached sort of way, just how far that attitude could be carried.

"You're unmarried?" Aherne asked, wondering why such a handsome girl would have felt any urge to uproot herself from Earth and join the Colony.

She lowered her eyes. "My husband's dead," she

said. "I've resumed my maiden name. It's the custom here."

"Oh. Sorry to hear that," Aherne said lamely. They turned down the long row of low-lying little houses that were situated between the airlock and the school building, which was their first stop.

"He was killed during the building of the Dome," she said. "There were eleven casualties during the time we cast it. He was one of them. I came here because of him—but I'm staying now for myself. I feel I belong here; I have work to do. Doing something important—not just for myself, but for the world."

Aherne grunted something unintelligible; he wanted to keep the discussion away from sentiment, pinned down on a level of fact. "How did they die?" he asked.

"A section fell on them. It's the only major accident we've had."

"The Colony has a low hospital record, then?"

"Fairly low. We've had plenty of minor troubles, though. Before we started posting guards at the airlock, we'd have children wandering through and outside the Dome—but we stopped that quick enough. And then we had a spell of ptomaine last year; no deaths, but we were all pretty sick for a while. And there's been a lot of gravity sickness—that's our biggest problem."

"How so?" Aherne asked.

"Well, of course you know the gravity here's only about 40 per cent of Earth's and it takes a little while to get adjusted to it. Some people had digestion problems—the food wouldn't go down properly. And one problem we haven't licked yet is pregnancy. Women just aren't built to deliver children in less than one-half grav. The muscles can't manage it."

That was one factor Aherne hadn't considered. "But children are born here, aren't they?"

"Oh, yes!" Miss Greer said, her face brightening. "Wait till you see our schoolroom! But it's risky, of course. We've built a small grav chamber in which all our deliveries are made. The problem is keeping a close check on all expectant mothers, and making sure they're within reach of the grav chamber when labor begins. Occasionally someone will premature, and there's no time to get her to the chamber. It's very complicated then."

Aherne nodded. He was noting all these things carefully. Miss Greer, he reflected, was an ideal guide. Not only was she attractive to be with, she was neither as self-conscious nor as tight-lipped as the men seemed to be, and she was revealing all sorts of facts about the Colony that Aherne might never have found out otherwise.

Facts which needed to be evaluated, to be fitted into the problem: *Is the Mars Colony promising enough to be worth continuing?*

The schoolroom was a delight. Aherne saw two dozen scrubbed, sprightly youngsters go through drills in arithmetic and spelling with about as much accuracy as could be expected, and then, at dismissal, go tumbling out of the classroom with an appealingly coltish agility. There didn't seem to be an unhappy child in the lot, nor a self-conscious one, nor a homely one. The psychologists who had chosen the colonists for the trip had chosen well.

The children ranged from three to ten years in age,

with a big gap in the five-to-seven group. That was easily explainable, of course; the colony had been planted five years ago, and no pregnant women nor children under two had been allowed to go. So there was a definite hiatus in the procession of age; children who had gone on the original ship were now eight and above, while those born in the colony were no older than four.

The youngsters moved with more assurance and poise than their parents, Aherne noticed. It made sense; they had been bred in the Martian gravity; their muscles were not previously trained by a lifetime spent on Earth, and so they were able to cope with Mars light pull more easily. *They are adapting,* Aherne thought.

He moved on, from the schoolroom to the local library, from the library to the print shop where Mars' one daily newssheet was turned out. There, he was shown with pride the unfinished, unbound copy of Dr. Carter's history of the Mars Colony, from its inception right through to the conclusion of its fifth year of activity. Aherne, looking at the contents page, noticed that the book was hopefully inscribed, *Volume One*.

Miss Greer was a pleasant and affable companion, and she never failed to be a source of diverting and informative conversation. She showed him the central telephone switchboard, the building that housed the atmosphere-generator, and then the small theater in which a band of amateurs were rehearsing a performance of *Twelfth Night* to be given that evening.

Shakespeare on Mars? Why not, Aherne thought, watching the rehearsal unfold. The colonists were capturing the Bard's smoothly flowing poetry with rare skill and insight. Aherne sat entranced in the small, cushionless-seated theater for over an hour, and asked to meet the director afterward.

It turned out that the director was also the tall, deep-voiced man who had played Malvolio. His name was Patchford. Aherne complimented him both on his performance and on his directing.

"Thank you, sir," the colonist said. "You're planning to attend our performance, aren't you?"

"Certainly," Aherne said. "Have you been doing much Shakespeare?"

"No, unfortunately," Patchford said sadly. "Our Complete Shakespeare was destroyed somehow in transit, and we haven't been able to get a replacement from Earth yet. It was sheer luck that I had appeared in a small stock-company that was doing *Twelfth Night*, not long before I left Earth. I copied all the parts from memory, and that's the version we're doing."

"It sounded accurate enough to me."

"I hope so," said Patchford, grinning. "Until the UN gets around to microfilming another Shakespeare for us, it's the best we can offer."

"I'll be looking forward to seeing it tonight," Aherne said sincerely, and he and Miss Greer moved on.

The next stop was the town hall, a rugged-looking, half-finished auditorium. From there, it was over to the hydroponics plant, where Aherne talked learnedly with a couple of the boys working there. He saw that his 'ponics-talk made a tremendous impression on Miss Greer, and he didn't care to disturb her belief in his omniscience by telling her that he had been a hydroponics technician himself for a while before entering UN service.

Aherne noted that the 'ponics plant was admirably set up, and he sampled some of its products—radishes, which seemed just a little bit tasteless, and tomatoes, which tasted fine.

And then, at last, Miss Greer decided that Aherne had seen enough of the colony for one day. She accompanied him to Carter's house, where they were scheduled to eat dinner, with a visit to Patchford's Shakespeare production slated for later in the evening. Aherne felt tired, excited, pleased, and very much less in doubt about his eventual decision.

VII

Busy days followed, as Aherne, always the center of interest, was given a thoroughgoing look at the life in the Colony. The colonists were all unfailingly polite and helpful; they were aware that they were on trial, and they were trying to live up to whatever standards Aherne could possibly set for them.

Life under the low gravity was awkward, at times, and the artificial atmosphere's faint staleness made Aherne long for the fresh air of Earth. But otherwise, the technical end of the Colony seemed to be well under control.

They were far from being self-sufficient, of course; food shipments from Earth were still of vital importance, supplementing the diets turned out by the hydroponics and the budding synthetics factory. The plan was to convert Mars' arid land into fertile soil once again, but that would take years, perhaps centuries.

Psychologically, the Colony seemed beautifully balanced. The men who had chosen the colonists had chosen wisely, despite the handicap of having to follow a prearranged nationalistic plan of choice. The eleven hundred inhabitants of the UN Dome were as sane an assortment of people as Aherne had ever seen gathered together in one place.

The Colony had, in general, lived up to expectations. And, on the morning when José Echavarra came to visit him, Aherne had just about made up his mind about the sort of report he was going to turn in.

The little Peruvian appeared suddenly, unexpectedly. Aherne, enjoying a moment of relaxation, was reading a reasonably good novel written by Roy Clellan, a colonist, and published at the Colony print shop. He looked up in surprise as Echavarra entered.

"Hello, Aherne."

"Echavarra! How'd you get past the airlock guard?"

The geneticist shrugged. "There is no law against my coming here, is there? Besides, I told the guard outside that if he didn't let me through, I'd simply radio over from my dome and tell you that I'd been turned away. He was in a cleft stick, and all he could do was let me in."

"So here you are," Aherne said. "What do you want?"

Echavarra took a seat on the edge of Aherne's bed, and folded his thin, dark fingers into a complex pattern. "You remember our earlier conversation?"

"I do," Aherne said. "What of it?"

"Are you still of your former opinion?"

"If what you mean is, do I intend to squash Carter's colony and turn the appropriation over to you, the answer is no."

Echavarra frowned. "Still no, eh? That means you must have been impressed with this little colony here."

"I was," said Aherne. "Very highly."

The small man scowled expressively. "You still do not understand. These people here—they are only guests on Mars! They are temporary visitors, staying here by sufferance of their dome. But they will always be outsiders, always dependent on artificial atmosphere!"

"I told you I don't care to discuss it," Aherne said stiffly. "These people have set up a truly wonderful social organization. Can you say the same of your high-altitude Andeans?"

"No," the other replied. "Not yet. But we will be able to breathe the air of Mars, one day. The social organization can come later, once the physical handicaps are overcome."

"I don't agree. You've taken men acclimated to high altitudes, low air pressure—but what kind of men are they? Do they represent the best of humanity? No. They're just ignorant, primitive people who happen to have developed a certain kind of physical endurance. You can't build a world with them."

"You can't build a world with people who must hide beneath a dome," Echavarra retorted. "But I see I will get nowhere with you. I trust you'll have the kindness to inform the United Nations of my whereabouts, though, and of the success of my project?"

"I'll do that," Aherne said. "For what it's worth."

Echavarra dropped a thick sheaf of papers on the bed. "Here's my report. I've analyzed the tolerance of my men to low pressure, discussed the integrated adaptations that will be necessary to produce a fully

Marsworthy race, and included some details of the biochemical analyses of muscular tissues that my associates have been making. One of them has been studying myoglobin, a form of hemoglobin which is particularly useful in governing the rate of oxygen-unloading in—but there's no point in telling this to you, is there? If you see fit, turn these papers over to the interested parties."

"I'll do that," Aherne said. "Look, Echavarra— I'm not trying to be deliberately cruel about this. I'm not here to decide whether your setup is more worthy of development than Carter's; so far as I'm concerned, that's been decided long ago. All I wanted to do was to see if the Carter colony is working. And it is. I'm satisfied."

"You're filing the report, then?"

"I am," Aherne said. It was the first time he had voiced the decision aloud, and now he was more certain than ever that it was right.

"Very good," Echavarra snapped. "I won't attempt to persuade you any further."

"It won't help," Aherne said. He felt genuinely sympathetic toward Echavarra, but as things stood there was nothing he could do. Carter's colony deserved support. Even discounting the fact that they were probably putting on a special demonstration for Aherne's benefit, the Colony seemed to be the first true example of cooperation between human beings on every level Aherne had ever seen.

Aherne picked up Echavarra's papers and tidied them into a neat stack. "I'll take care of these," he said.

"Thank you," the Peruvian said simply. He stared searchingly at Aherne for a moment. Then he turned and left.

* * *

Aherne made his decision known publicly later that day. In a short, tersely worded statement which he handed silently to Dr. Carter, he told of his great delight in seeing how the Colony functioned, and stated definitely that he planned to support continuation of the appropriation on an indefinite basis.

Carter read the statement through and looked up at Aherne. "Thanks," he said bluntly.

"Don't thank me. It's your own hard work that's done this. I'm one hundred percent sold on your colony here, Dr. Carter."

"I'm glad to hear that," the graying leader said. "For a while at the beginning, you seemed very dubious about the way things were doing here."

"It was just a pose," Aherne confessed.

"That was obvious. I could tell how much you really liked the things you were seeing. Miss Greer reported that you were just bubbling with enthusiasm."

"I was," said Aherne, privately annoyed that he had not managed to conceal his feelings better. "I'm firmly convinced that you're on the right track here."

"I'll go announce this to the Colony at large," Carter said. "They'll be glad to know our life's been extended a while longer."

My work is done, Aherne thought. It would be good to get back to Earth, to the UN, now that the pressure of decision was ended. He felt relieved that he had been able to square his decision with his conscience. It was a good feeling.

He turned to his desk, and began to make some tentative notes toward the final report he would have to file. He started sketching out a preliminary outline of Colony life.

After two sentences, he halted, disturbed. Echavarra's harsh words were echoing in his head, seeming to mock him and stamp him for a fool. *"These people—they are only guests on Mars!"* he heard once again. And: *"You can't build a world with people who must hide beneath a dome."*

The Peruvian's dry, incisive voice needled into his brain, and refused to be forgotten. Aherne chewed the end of his stylo reflectively for a moment or two. The tenor of his mind swayed. He pictured Echavarra, punctuating each word with a jab of his forefinger against the air—the artificial air of the Dome.

Am I right? Who knows? Aherne asked himself, and slowly with not as much inner conviction as he had felt a moment before, he began to fill out his report.

VIII

Deep in the cold, frozen ground, a long, fine line cut through the desert—a fault-line, far below the surface. A dark slit that indicated the end of one geological formation and the beginning of the next.

Along the fault-line was exerted the pressure of the tons of sand and mountain above. Gradually, slowly, over a period of centuries, that fault began to slip. One side depressed; the other inexorably raised. The process continued imperceptibly, until the day when the ground shivered, the final barriers broke, and a pit yawned where no pit had been before.

An entire geological formation—a block of granite some hundreds of miles square—went rearing up like a singed stallion. The broken desert shuddered. And catastrophe struck the unsuspecting domes planted square athwart the fault-line.

Aherne had been planning to leave that day.

Valoinen and his ship were scheduled to make their regular appearance the following morning, and Aherne was in the process of saying his goodbyes when it happened. The ground seemed to scream in pain, and then everything tipped sideways. The moorings of the Dome broke loose from the land, stresses that had not been planned for rippled across the dome, and a jagged split ran through the gleaming plastic from end to end.

Aherne felt the cold come rushing in. The atmosphere, so carefully generated, fled in an instant, and the harsh, nitrogen-laden air of Mars came swooping down.

"Spacesuits!" someone screamed, and the panic was on. Eleven hundred people dashing for spacesuits at the same moment. Children underfoot, screaming adults, frightened women.

Aherne gasped for breath; his head spun, and his eyes bugged wide. What had the Peruvian said? This was *critical threshold*—this was the moment from which there was no escape. The faint glimmer of the sun drifted mockingly through the rent Dome. This was it, now: the air of Mars. The unbreathable, cold, biting air of Mars. Critical threshold.

Somehow he found a spacesuit, and somehow he made his leaden fingers go through the motions that would get him inside the suit. He could barely see; his cold-nipped hands would not respond. But finally he was inside it, with air—real air—surging up around him.

Aherne leaned against the cold, corrugated-steel wall of a building for a moment, dazed, unable to understand what had happened. One moment he had been chatting amiably with Kate Greer and Sully Roberts; a moment later the sky had split, and he was fumbling to safety in the dark.

He sucked in air, gulped it down and let it warm his lungs, while his body slowly returned to normal. And then he looked around.

The scene was frightful. Wherever he looked, there were colonists. Most had managed to find spacesuits; those who hadn't, and that included a handful of children, were huddled in unconsciousness on the ground, blue-faced from oxygen loss.

Sully Roberts was next to him, folded up in a heap along the wall near the open chest where the emergency spacesuits were stored. Roberts had managed to get himself inside a suit in time, but passing the critical threshold of anoxia had been too much for him; the big man was unconscious.

"Sully! Sully!"

After a moment, Roberts looked up. He struggled to his feet, shook his head tentatively, and clawed for his balance. Aherne steadied him.

It was like moving in a nightmare world.

Roberts pointed to a body lying a hundred yards away. A colonist who hadn't made it.

"Let's get going," Roberts said hoarsely. "Maybe we can save some of them."

Later, when everything was calm and a measure of order had been restored, the shattered colony tried to take stock. A general meeting was ordered in the central auditorium, and slowly the dazed, spacesuited figures filtered in.

Aherne took his seat at the side. It was only now that the reaction was starting to hit him. He felt overwhelming bitterness, anger at this cosmic joke—for now they knew that the Marsquake had wrecked the

Dome. The report was written, the future of the Colony assured—and now, this.

He heard Carter's voice dully calling the roll.

"Anderson, David and Joan."

"Here."

"Antonelli, Leo, Marie, and Helen."

"Here."

And then the dead silence after a name, and the repetition, and then the checkmark made on the long sheet that told of the dead. The toll-taking continued through the day until finally the extent of the damage was known.

There were sixty-three dead, Carter announced, and fifty-seven in critical condition. The backlash of the quake had shattered the Dome beyond repair. Otherwise, the colony had not been harmed badly— but it would have to start from the beginning, now. If there was to be any starting over at all.

Sully Roberts was dispatched to the Peruvian dome to find out how things were there. Aherne watched the big man go, out through the useless air lock and into his sandcrawler.

It was a tragic situation, Aherne thought. And then, slowly, he came to see that it was not. The quake could have happened at any time—but, as if some Power were guiding it, it had burst at the very moment of Aherne's decision. It had waited until the returns were in, and then had unleashed its fury to show Aherne the fatal weakness in the entire dome setup.

They had planned and planned—and yet had not figured on an upheaval of the ground a hundred miles away. They could never have planned on it.

Now, and only now, was Aherne sure of what had to be done.

They remained in the meeting hall, sitting quietly, waiting for Roberts to return. Aherne studied the faces of the men near him—faces that reflected the dream that had turned into a nightmare in a sudden single unforeseen moment.

Abruptly the door opened and Sully Roberts burst in, hardly ten minutes after he had left.

"What's the matter, Sully?" Carter called from the dais. "Didn't get there?"

"No need to," Roberts said. "I met the whole batch of them on the way. Their dome was smashed too, but they got things under control quicker than we did and the whole Peruvian colony set out *en masse* to see if we needed help."

Roberts stepped to one side and Echavarra entered the hall, clad in a brightly colored spacesuit that looked oddly out of place in the drab assembly. Behind him, Aherne could see a swarm of small, spacesuited figures—the Andeans.

"We've come to see what we could do," Echavarra said. "The quake got our dome too—but naturally my people didn't feel the effects of the sudden change in air as much as yours did, since we were conditioned to something almost as bad."

Of course, Aherne thought. The Peruvians would simply have moved in a leisurely fashion toward the nearest spacesuits. No panic, no casualties.

Aherne stood up. "Dr. Carter?"

"Yes, Mr. Aherne?"

"Would you mind calling a recess of the meeting for a while? I'd like to speak to you and Dr. Echavarra privately."

* * *

Aherne felt as if he held the future of Mars in his hands as he looked across the table, flicking anxious glances from sad-eyed Carter to Echavarra and back.

"I'll put it bluntly," Aherne said to Carter. "I'm going to have to rescind my earlier report. Your colony is definitely not suited for continuation."

Carter went white. "But we can rebuild the Dome! You said—"

"I know what I said," Aherne cut in smoothly. "But it's all been voided by this quake. Dr. Echavarra put it very nicely for me during one of our meetings: you and your colony are only guests here. You're subject to the whims of the landscape for survival. It can't work on any long-range basis. You can't pin all your hopes on a fragile dome, and expect to build a lasting colony."

Carter seemed to shrink in on himself. He bowed his head. "Then I was wrong," he said. "The quake proved it."

Echavarra's beady eyes lit up. "Does that mean you're shifting to my side, Mr. Aherne?"

"Not quite," Aherne said. "You have part of the right answer: your men were adapted enough to be able to ride with the blow when the dome was destroyed, and in a couple of generations they won't even need the dome. But they're not material for building a new world with. They're ignorant, primitive men with low cultural possibilities, who happen to have high survival quotients."

He turned to face Carter, sensing now that the situation was completely in his grasp for the first time since he'd left Earth. Now he understood the entire picture, and now he knew what his report would say.

"Dr. Carter, you've got the other side of the coin.

High cultural level, low survival factor. Everything about your colony was marvelous—except the fact that it would fold up like a paper bag at the first crack in the dome."

Carter nodded grimly. "So we've discovered."

Aherne leaned forward. "Now—does what I've just said suggest a solution?"

"Could we—build one big dome for both colonies?" Carter asked hesitantly.

"Exactly. One dome. Assimilate. Mingle. Combine the hardiness of your Peruvians, Dr. Echavarra, with the all-round ability of your men, Dr. Carter. Breed a new race from the two stocks," Aherne said triumphantly. "A new race—capable of living on Mars and *belonging* there!"

"The pressure—" Echavarra said.

"Keep it at ten pounds for a while. It'll be uncomfortable for both groups, but not for long. Eventually Dr. Carter's group will develop the same kind of strength Dr. Echavarra's men have. It may take a couple of generations, but it'll work—eventually!"

The two leaders were glowing. "You'll recommend this to the UN?" Carter asked.

"If you're both agreed," said Aherne.

They nodded as one.

"Let's go back inside and announce the decision, then," Aherne said. "Because you'll have to get right to work building the new Dome. You can't live in spacesuits for long, you know."

"Right," Carter said. He rose and led the way back to the meeting hall, where the colonists were waiting impatiently for word on what was happening.

Aherne took his seat at the side again. This was

strictly Carter's and Echavarra's show, and he intended to remain completely detached.

As Carter began to speak, outlining the new plan, Aherne let his eyes wander around the auditorium. It was crowded—crowded with the tense-faced UN Colonists, and with the Peruvian men as well, garbed in their bright-colored spacesuits.

Aherne saw his report taking shape now—the memo that would set the pattern for man's future conquest of the planets. Thankful that he had seen the right way in time, he sat back, relaxing at last, and listened to Carter's enthusiastic voice as it rolled out majestically.

Then he looked down. Almost as his feet, he saw a Peruvian boy of about nine, round and awkward in his lemon-yellow spacesuit, and one of the UN colonist children, a pretty blonde girl of four. They were staring shyly at each other in mutual curiosity.

Aherne watched them. They were the forerunners, the founders of the race of the future, the new men.

No. Not men, Aherne thought. Men are creatures who belong on Earth. Not men.

Martians.

COLLECTING TEAM

A time will come when men will get past the confines of our solar system and begin to explore the galaxy at large. There are millions of suns out there, and the chances are good that many of them have planets, and that at least some of those planets are inhabited.

Survey teams will go forth to examine and classify and record the strange forms of life found on those distant worlds. Some of the explorers, no doubt, will find themselves in unearthly dilemmas as a result.

From fifty thousand miles up, the situation looked promising. It was a middle-sized, brown-and-green, inviting-looking planet, with no sign of cities or any other such complications. Just a pleasant sort of place, the very sort we were looking for to redeem what had been a pretty futile expedition.

I turned to Clyde Holdreth, who was staring reflectively at the thermocouple.

"Well? What do you think?"

"Looks fine to me. Temperature's about seventy down there—nice and warm, and plenty of air. I think it's worth a try."

Lee Davison came strolling out from the storage hold, smelling of animals, as usual. He was holding one of the blue monkeys we picked up on Alpheraz, and the little beast was crawling up his arm. "Have we found something, gentlemen?"

"We've found a planet," I said. "How's the storage space in the hold?"

"Don't worry about that. We've got room for a whole zoo-full more, before we get filled up. It hasn't been a very fruitful trip."

"No," I agreed. "It hasn't. Well? Shall we go down and see what's to be seen?"

"Might as well," Holdreth said. "We can't go back to Earth with just a couple of blue monkeys and some anteaters, you know."

"I'm in favor of a landing too," said Davison. "You?"

I nodded. "I'll set up the charts, and you get your animals comfortable for deceleration."

Davison disappeared back into the storage hold, while Holdreth scribbled furiously in the logbook, writing down the coordinates of the planet below, its general description, and so forth. Aside from being a collecting team for the zoological department of the Bureau of Interstellar Affairs, we also double as a survey ship, and the planet down below was listed as *unexplored* on our charts.

I glanced out at the mottled brown-and-green ball spinning slowly in the viewport, and felt the warning twinge of gloom that came to me every time we made a landing on a new and strange world. Repressing it, I started to figure out a landing orbit. From behind me came the furious chatter of the blue monkeys as Davison strapped them into their acceleration cradles, and under that the deep, unmusical honking of the Rigelian anteaters, noisily bleating their displeasure.

The planet was inhabited, all right. We hadn't had the ship on the ground more than a minute before the local fauna began to congregate. We stood at the viewport and looked out in wonder.

"This is one of those things you dream about," Davison said, stroking his little beard nervously. "Look at them! There must be a thousand different species out there."

"I've never seen anything like it," said Holdreth.

I computed how much storage space we had left and how many of the thronging creatures outside we would be able to bring back with us. "How are we going to decide what to take and what to leave behind?"

"Does it matter?" Holdreth said gaily. "This is what you call an embarrassment of riches, I guess. We just grab the dozen most bizarre creatures and blast off—and save the rest for another trip. It's too bad we wasted all that time wandering around near Rigel."

"We *did* get the anteaters," Davison pointed out. They were his finds, and he was proud of them.

I smiled sourly. "Yeah. We got the anteaters there." The anteaters honked at that moment, loud and clear. "You know, that's one set of beasts I think I could do without."

"Bad attitude," Holdreth said. "Unprofessional."

"Whoever said I was a zoologist, anyway? I'm just a spaceship pilot, remember. And if I don't like the way those anteaters talk—and—smell—I see no reason why I—"

"Say, look at that one," Davison said suddenly.

I glanced out the viewport and saw a new beast emerging from the thick-packed vegetation in the background. I've seen some fairly strange creatures since I was assigned to the zoological department, but this one took the grand prize.

It was about the size of a giraffe, moving on long, wobbly legs and with a tiny head up at the end of a preposterous neck. Only it had six legs and a bunch of writhing snakelike tentacles as well, and its eyes, great violet globes, stood out nakedly on the ends of two thick stalks. It must have been twenty feet high. It moved with exaggerated grace through the swarm of beasts surrounding our ship, pushed its way smoothly toward the vessel, and peered gravely in at the viewport. One purple eye stared directly at me, the other at Davison. Oddly, it seemed to me as if it were trying to tell us something.

"Big one, isn't it?" Davison said finally.

"I'll bet you'd like to bring one back, too."

"Maybe we can fit a young one aboard," Davison said. "If we can find a young one." He turned to Holdreth. "How's that air analysis coming? I'd like to get out there and start collecting. God, that's a crazy-looking beast!"

The animal outside had apparently finished its inspection of us, for it pulled its head away and, gathering its legs under itself, squatted near the ship. A small doglike creature with stiff spines running along its back began to bark at the big creature, which took no notice. The other animals, which came in all shapes and sizes, continued to mill around the ship, evidently very curious about the newcomer to their world. I could see Davison's eyes thirsty with the desire to take the whole kit and caboodle back to Earth with him. I knew what was running through his mind. He was dreaming of the umpteen thousand species of extraterrestrial wildlife roaming around out there, and to each one he was attaching a neat little tag: *Something-or-other davisoni.*

"The air's fine," Holdreth announced abruptly, looking up from his test-tubes. "Get your butterfly nets and let's see what we can catch."

There was something I didn't like about the place. It was just too good to be true, and I learned long ago that nothing ever is. There's always a catch someplace.

Only this seemed to be on the level. The planet was a bonanza for zoologists, and Davison and Holdreth were having the time of their lives, hipdeep in obliging specimens.

"I've never seen anything like it," Davison said for at least the fiftieth time, as he scooped up a small purplish squirrel-like creature and examined it curiously. The squirrel stared back, examining Davison just as curiously.

"Let's take some of these," Davison said. "I like them."

"Carry 'em on in, then," I said, shrugging. I didn't care which specimens they chose, so long as they filled up the storage hold quickly and let me blast off on schedule. I watched as Davison grabbed a pair of the squirrels and brought them into the ship.

Holdreth came over to me. He was carrying a sort of a dog with insect-faceted eyes and gleaming furless skin. "How's this one, Gus?"

"Fine," I said bleakly. "Wonderful."

He put the animal down—it didn't scamper away,

just sat there smiling at us—and looked at me. He ran a hand through his fast-vanishing hair. "Listen, Gus, you've been gloomy all day. What's eating you?"

"I don't like this place," I said.

"Why? Just on general principles?"

"It's too *easy*, Clyde. Much too easy. These animals just flock around here waiting to be picked up."

Holdreth chuckled. "And you're used to a struggle, aren't you? You're just angry at us because we have it so simple here!"

"When I think of the trouble we went through just to get a pair of miserable vile-smelling anteaters, and—"

"Come off it, Gus. We'll load up in a hurry, if you like. But this place is a zoological gold mine!"

I shook my head. "I don't like it, Clyde. Not at all."

Holdreth laughed again and picked up his faceted-eyed dog. "Say, know where I can find another of these, Gus?"

"Right over there," I said, pointing. "By that tree. With its tongue hanging out. It's just waiting to be carried away."

Holdreth looked and smiled. "What do you know about that!" He snared his specimen and carried both of them inside.

I walked away to survey the grounds. The planet was too flatly incredible for me to accept on face value, without at least a look-see, despite the blithe way my two companions were snapping up specimens.

For one thing, animals just don't exist this way—in big miscellaneous quantities, living all together happily. I hadn't noticed more than a few of each kind, and there must have been five hundred different species, each one stranger-looking than the next. Nature doesn't work that way.

For another, they all seemed to be on friendly terms with one another, though they acknowledged the unofficial leadership of the giraffe-like creature. Nature doesn't work *that* way, either. I hadn't seen one quarrel between the animals yet. That argued that they were all herbivores, which didn't make sense ecologically.

I shrugged my shoulders and walked on.

Half an hour later, I knew a little more about the geography of our bonanza. We were on either an immense island or a peninsula of some sort, because I could see a huge body of water bordering the land some ten miles off. Our vicinity was fairly flat, except for a good-sized hill from which I could see the terrain.

There was a thick, heavily-wooded jungle not too far from the ship. The forest spread out all the way toward the water in one direction, but ended abruptly in the other. We had brought the ship down right at the edge of the clearing. Apparently most of the animals we saw lived in the jungle.

On the other side of our clearing was a low, broad plain that seemed to trail away into a desert in the distance; I could see an uninviting stretch of barren sand that contrasted strangely with the fertile jungle to my left. There was a small lake to the side. It was, I saw, the sort of country likely to attract a varied fauna, since there seemed to be every sort of habitat within a small area.

And the fauna! Although I'm a zoologist only by osmosis, picking up both my interest and my knowledge second-hand from Holdreth and Davison, I couldn't help but be astonished by the wealth of strange animals. They came in all different shapes and sizes, colors and odors, and the only thing they all had in common was their friendliness. During the course of my afternoon's wanderings a hundred animals must have come marching boldly right up to me, given me the once-over, and walked away. This included half a dozen kinds that I hadn't seen before, plus one of the eye-stalked, intellgent-looking giraffes and a furless dog. Again, I had the feeling that the giraffe seemed to be trying to communicate.

I didn't like it. I didn't like it at all.

I returned to our clearing, and saw Holdreth and Davison still buzzing madly around, trying to cram as many animals as they could into our hold.

"How's it going?" I asked.

"Hold's all full," Davison said. "We're busy making our alternate selections now." I saw him carrying out Holdreth's two furless dogs and picking up instead a pair of eight-legged penguinish things that uncomplainingly allowed themselves to be carried in. Holdreth was frowning unhappily.

"What do you want *those* for, Lee? Those dog-like ones seem much more interesting, don't you think?"

"No," Davison said. "I'd rather bring along these two. They're curious beasts, aren't they? Look at the muscular network that connects the—"

"Hold it, fellows," I said. I peered at the animal in Davison's hands and glanced up. "This *is* a curious beast," I said. "It's got eight legs."

"You becoming a zoologist?" Holdreth asked, amused.

"No—but I am getting puzzled. Why should this one have eight legs, some of the others here six, and some of the others only four?"

They looked at me blankly, with the scorn of professionals.

"I mean, there ought to be some sort of logic to evolution here, shouldn't there? On Earth we've developed a four-legged pattern of animal life; on Venus, they usually run to six legs. But have you ever seen an evolutionary hodgepodge like this place before?"

"There are stranger setups," Holdreth said. "The symbiotes on Sirius Three, the burrowers of Mizar— but you're right, Gus. This *is* a peculiar evolutionary dispersal. I think we ought to stay and investigate it fully."

Instantly I knew from the bright expression on Davison's face that I had blundered, had made things worse than ever. I decided to take a new tack.

"I don't agree," I said. "I think we ought to leave with what we've got, and come back with a larger expedition later."

Davison chuckled. "Come on, Gus, don't be silly! This is a chance of a lifetime for us—why should we call in the whole zoological department on it?"

I didn't want to tell them I was afraid of staying longer. I crossed my arms. "Lee, I'm the pilot of this ship, and you'll have to listen to me. The schedule calls for a brief stopover here, and we have to leave. Don't tell me I'm being silly."

"But you are, man! You're standing blindly in the path of scientific investigation, of—"

"Listen to me, Lee. Our food is calculated on a pretty narrow margin, to allow you fellows more room for storage. And this is strictly a collecting team. There's no provision for extended stays on any one planet. Unless you want to wind up eating your own specimens, I suggest you allow us to get out of here."

They were silent for a moment. Then Holdreth said, "I guess we can't argue with that, Lee. Let's listen to Gus and go back now. There's plenty of time to investigate this place later when we can take longer."

"But—oh, all right," Davison said reluctantly. He picked up the eight-legged penguins. "Let me stash these things in the hold, and we can leave." He looked strangely at me, as if I had done something criminal.

As he started into the ship, I called to him.

"What is it, Gus?"

"Look here, Lee. I don't *want* to pull you away from here. It's simply a matter of food," I lied, masking my nebulous suspicions.

"I know how it is, Gus." He turned and entered the ship.

I stood there thinking about nothing at all for a moment, then went inside myself to begin setting up the blastoff orbit.

I got as far as calculating the fuel expenditure when I noticed something. Feedwires were dangling crazily down from the control cabinet. Somebody had wrecked our drive mechanism, but thoroughly.

For a long moment, I stared stiffly at the sabotaged drive. Then I turned and headed into the storage hold.

"Davison?"

"What is it, Gus?"

"Come out here a second, will you?"

I waited, and a few minutes later he appeared, frowning impatiently. "What do you want, Gus? I'm busy and I—" His mouth dropped open. *"Look at the drive!"*

"You look at it," I snapped. "I'm sick. Go get Holdreth, on the double."

While he was gone I tinkered with the shattered mechanism. Once I had the cabinet panel off and could see the inside, I felt a little better; the drive wasn't damaged beyond repair, though it had been pretty well scrambled. Three or four days of hard work with a screwdriver and solderbeam might get the ship back into functioning order.

But that didn't make me any less angry. I heard Holdreth and Davison entering behind me, and I whirled to face them.

"All right, you idiots. Which one of you did this?"

They opened their mouths in protesting squawks at the same instant. I listened to them for a while, then said, "One at a time!"

"If you're implying that one of us deliberately sabotaged the ship," Holdreth said, "I want you to know—"

"I'm not implying anything. But the way it looks to me, you two decided you'd like to stay here a while longer to continue your investigations, and figured the easiest way of getting me to agree was to wreck the drive." I glared hotly at them. "Well, I've got news for you. I can fix this, and I can fix it in a couple of days. So go on—get about your business! Get all the zoologizing you can in, while you still have time. I—"

Davison laid a hand gently on my arm. "Gus," he said quietly, "*We didn't do it*. Neither of us."

Suddenly all the anger drained out of me and was replaced by raw fear. I could see that Davison meant it.

"If you didn't do it, and Holdreth didn't do it, and *I* didn't do it—then who did?"

Davison shrugged.

"Maybe it's one of us who doesn't know he's doing it," I suggested. "Maybe—" I stopped. "Oh, that's nonsense. Hand me that tool-kit, will you, Lee?"

They left to tend to the animals, and I set to work on the repair job, dismissing all further speculations and suspicions from my mind, concentrating solely on joining Lead A to Input A and Transistor F to Potentiometer K, as indicated. It was slow, nerve-harrowing work, and by mealtime I had accomplished only the barest preliminaries. My fingers were starting to quiver from the strain of small-scale work, and I decided to give up the job for the day and get back to it tomorrow.

I slept uneasily, my nightmares punctuated by the moaning of the accursed anteaters and the occasional squeals, chuckles, bleats, and hisses of the various other creatures in the hold. It must have been four in the morning before I dropped off into a really sound sleep, and what was left of the night passed swiftly. The next thing I knew, hands were shaking me and I was looking up into the pale, tense faces of Holdreth and Davison.

I pushed my sleep-stuck eyes open and blinked. "Huh? What's going on?"

Holdreth leaned down and shook me savagely. "Get up, Gus!"

I struggled to my feet slowly. "Hell of a thing to

do, wake a fellow up in the middle of the—"

I found myself being propelled from my cabin and led down the corridor to the control room. Blearily, I followed where Holdreth pointed, and then I woke up in hurry.

The drive was battered again. Someone—or *something*—had completely undone my repair job of the night before.

If there had been bickering among us, it stopped. This was past the category of a joke now; it couldn't be laughed off, and we found ourselves working together as a tight unit again, trying desperately to solve the puzzle before it was too late.

"Let's review the situation," Holdreth said, pacing nervously up and down the control cabin. "The drive has been sabotaged twice. None of us knows who did it, and on a conscious level each of us is convinced *he* didn't do it."

He paused. "That leaves us with two possibilities. Either, as Gus suggested, one of us is doing it unaware of it even himself, or someone else is doing it while we're not looking. Neither possibility is a very cheerful one."

"We can stay on guard, though," I said. "Here's what I propose; first, have one of us awake at all times—sleep in shifts, that is, with somebody guarding the drive until I get it fixed. Two—jettison all the animals aboard ship."

"*What?*"

"He's right," Davison said. "We don't know what we may have brought aboard. They don't seem to be intelligent, but we can't be sure. That purple-eyed baby giraffe, for instance—suppose he's been hypnotizing us into damaging the drive ourselves? How can we tell?"

"Oh, but—" Holdreth started to protest, then stopped and frowned soberly. "I suppose we'll have to admit the possibility," he said, obviously unhappy about the prospect of freeing our captives. "We'll empty out the hold, and you see if you can get the drive fixed. Maybe later we'll recapture them all, if nothing further develops."

We agreed to that, and Holdreth and Davison cleared the ship of its animal cargo while I set to work determinedly at the drive mechanism. By nightfall, I had managed to accomplish as much as I had the day before.

I sat up as watch the first shift, aboard the strangely quiet ship. I paced around the drive cabin, fighting the great temptation to doze off, and managed to last through until the time Holdreth arrived to relieve me.

Only—when he showed up, he gasped and pointed at the drive. It had been ripped apart a third time.

Now we had no excuse, no explanation. The expedition had turned into a nightmare.

I could only protest that I had remained awake my entire spell on duty, and that I had seen no one and no thing approach the drive panel. But that was hardly a satisfactory explanation, since it either cast guilt on me as the saboteur or implied that some unseen external power was repeatedly wrecking the drive. Neither hypothesis made sense, at least to me.

By now we had spent four days on the planet, and food was getting to be a major problem. My carefully budgeted flight schedule called for us to be two days out on our return journey to Earth by now. But we still were no closer to departure than we had been four days ago.

The animals continued to wander around outside, nosing up against the ship, examining it, almost fondling it, with those damned pseudo-giraffes staring soulfully at us always. The beasts were as friendly as ever, little knowing how the tension was growing within the hull. The three of us walked around like zombies, eyes bright and lips clamped. We were scared—all of us.

Something was keeping us from fixing the drive.

Something didn't want us to leave this planet.

I looked at the bland face of the purple-eyed giraffe staring through the viewport, and it stared mildly back at me. Around it was grouped the rest of the local fauna, the same incredible hodgepodge of improbable genera and species.

That night, the three of us stood guard in the control-room together. The drive was smashed anyway. The wires were soldered in so many places by now that the control panel was a mass of shining alloy, and I knew that a few more such sabotagings and it would be impossible to patch it together any more —if it wasn't so already.

The next night, I just didn't knock off. I continued soldering right on after dinner (and a pretty skimpy dinner it was, now that we were on close rations) and far on into the night.

By morning, it was as if I hadn't done a thing.

"I give up," I announced, surveying the damage. "I don't see any sense in ruining my nerves trying to fix a thing that won't stay fixed."

Holdreth nodded. He looked terribly pale. "We'll have to find some new approach."

"Yeah. Some new approach."

I yanked open the food closet and examined our stock. Even figuring in the synthetics we would have fed to the animals if we hadn't released them, we were low on food. We had overstayed even the safety margin. It would be a hungry trip back—if we ever did get back.

I clambered through the hatch and sprawled down on a big rock near the ship. One of the furless dogs came over and nuzzled in my shirt. Davison stepped to the hatch and called down to me.

"What are you doing out there, Gus?"

"Just getting a little fresh air. I'm sick of living aboard that ship." I scratched the dog behind his pointed ears, and looked around.

The animals had lost most of their curiosity about us, and didn't congregate the way they used to. They were meandering all over the plain, nibbling at little desposits of a white doughy substance. It precipitated every night. "Manna," we called it. All the animals seemed to live on it.

I folded my arms and leaned back.

We were getting to look awfully lean by the eighth day. I wasn't even trying to fix the ship any more; the hunger was starting to get me. But I saw Davison puttering around with my solderbeam.

"What are you doing?"

"I'm going to repair the drive," he said. "You don't want to, but we can't just sit around, you know." His nose was deep in my repair guide, and he was fumbling with the release on the solderbeam.

I shrugged. "Go ahead, if you want to." I didn't care what he did. All I cared about was the gaping emptiness in my stomach, and about the dimly grasped fact that somehow we were stuck here for good.

"Gus?"

"Yeah?"

"I think it's time I told you something. I've been eating the manna for four days. It's good. It's nourishing stuff."

"You've been eating—the manna? Something that grows on an alien world? You crazy?"

"What else can we do? Starve?"

I smiled feebly, admitting that he was right. From somewhere in the back of the ship came the sounds of Holdreth moving around. Holdreth had taken this thing worse than any of us. He had a family back on Earth, and he was beginning to realize that he wasn't ever going to see them again.

"Why don't you get Holdreth?" Davison suggested. "Go out there and stuff yourselves with the manna. You've got to eat something."

"Yeah. What can I lose?" Moving like a mechanical man, I headed towards Holdreth's cabin. We would go out and eat the manna and cease being hungry, one way or another.

"Clyde?" I called. "Clyde?"

I entered his cabin. He was sitting at his desk, shaking convulsively, staring at the two streams of blood that trickled in red spurts from his slashed wrists.

"Clyde!"

He made no protest as I dragged him toward the infirmary cabin and got tourniquets around his arms, cutting off the bleeding. He just stared dully ahead, sobbing.

I slapped him and he came around. He shook his

head dizzily, as if he didn't know where he was.

"I—I—"

"Easy, Clyde. Everything's all right."

"It's *not* all right," he said hollowly. "I'm still alive. Why didn't you let me die? Why didn't you—"

Davison entered the cabin. "What's been happening, Gus?"

"It's Clyde. The pressure's getting him. He tried to kill himself, but I think he's all right now. Get him something to eat, will you?"

We had Holdreth straightened around by evening. Davison gathered as much of the manna as he could find, and we held a feast.

"I wish we had nerve enough to kill some of the local fauna," Davison said. "Then we'd have a feast —steaks and everything!"

"The bacteria," Holdreth pointed out quietly. "We don't dare."

"I know. But it's a thought."

"No more thoughts," I said sharply. "Tomorrow morning we start work on the drive panel again. Maybe with some food in our bellies we'll be able to keep awake and see what's happening here."

Holdreth smiled. "Good. I can't wait to get out of this ship and back to a normal existence. God, I just can't wait!"

"Let's get some sleep," I said. "Tomorrow we'll give it another try. We'll get back," I said with a confidence I didn't feel.

The following morning I rose early and got my tool-kit. My head was clear, and I was trying to put the pieces together without much luck. I started toward the control cabin.

And stopped.

And looked out the viewport.

I went back and awoke Holdreth and Davison. "Take a look out the port," I said hoarsely.

They looked. They gaped.

"It looks just like my house," Holdreth said. "My house on Earth."

"With all the comforts of home inside, I'll bet." I walked forward uneasily and lowered myself through the hatch. "Let's go look at it."

We approached it, while the animals frolicked around us. The big giraffe came near and shook its head gravely. The house stood in the middle of the clearing, small and neat and freshly-painted.

I saw it now. During the night, invisible hands had put it there. Had assembled and built a cozy little Earth-type house and dropped it next to our ship for us to live in.

"Just like my house," Holdreth repeated in wonderment.

"It should be," I said. "They grabbed the model from your mind, as soon as they found out we couldn't live on the ship indefinitely."

Holdreth and Davison asked as one, "What do you mean?"

"You mean you haven't figured this place out yet?" I licked my lips, getting myself used to the fact that I was going to spend the rest of my life here. "You mean you don't realize what this house is intended to be?"

They shook their head, baffled. I glanced around, from the house to the useless ship to the jungle to the plain to the little pond. It all made sense now.

"They want to keep us happy," I said. "They

knew we weren't thriving aboard the ship, so they—they built us something a little more like home."

"*They?* The giraffes?"

"Forget the giraffes. They tried to warn us, but it's too late. They're intelligent beings, but they're prisoners just like us. I'm talking about the ones who run this place. The super-aliens who make us sabotage our own ship and not even know we're doing it, who stand someplace up there and gape at us. The ones who dredged together this motley assortment of beasts from all over the galaxy. Now we've been collected too. This whole damned place is just a zoo—a zoo for aliens so far ahead of us we don't dare dream what they're like."

I looked up at the shimmering blue-green sky, where invisible bars seemed to restrain us, and sank down dismally on the porch of our new home. I was resigned. There wasn't any sense in struggling against *them*.

I could see the neat little placard now:

EARTHMEN. Native Habitat, Sol III.

DOUBLE DARE

*Other planets may be inhabited by beings more like
ourselves. Though their skins may be of strange colors, their
biology altogether alien, and their appearance unusual, their
minds may tick in a remarkably human way. Which can
create complications for Earthmen who go among the aliens
and find themselves enmeshed in delicate interstellar politics.*

By the time the spaceship had finished juggling
and actually stood firmly on Domerangi soil, Justin
Marner was beginning to doubt his sanity.

"We must be crazy," he said softly. "We *must* be."

The other Earthman, who had been gazing out the
viewplate at the green-and-gold alien vista, glanced
around suddenly at Marner's remark. "Huh?"

"There are limits to which one goes in proving a
point," Marner said. He indicated the scene outside.
"This little journey exceeds the limits. Now that
we're here, Kemridge, I'm sure of it. *Nobody* does
things like this."

Kemridge glared sourly. "Don't be silly, Justin.

You know why we're here, and you know how come we're here. This isn't any time to—"

"All right," Marner said. "I take it all back." He stared for a moment at his delicate, tapering fingers —the fingers that could have belonged to a surgeon, were they not the property of a top-rank technical engineer. "Don't pay any attention to whatever I just said. It's the strain that's getting me."

The doorbell of the cabin chimed melodiously.

"Come in," said Marner.

The door slid open and a Domerangi, clad in a bright yellow sash, gray-green buskins, and a glittering diadem of precious gems, stepped heavily into the cabin. He extended two of his five leathery tentacles in welcome.

"Hello, gentlemen, I see you've come through the trip in fine shape."

"What's going on now, Plorvash?" Marner asked.

"The ship has landed at a spaceport just outside the city," the alien said. "I've come to take you to your quarters. We're giving you two of the finest accommodations our planet can offer. We want your working conditions to be of the best."

"Glad to hear it," Marner said. He flicked a glance at his companion. "They're most considerate, aren't they, Dave?"

The taller of the two Earthmen nodded gravely. "Definitely."

Plorvash grinned and said, "Suppose you come with me now. You want to be well rested before you undertake your task. After all, you want to be at your best, since planetary pride is at stake."

"Of course," Marner said.

The alien grinned once again. "The test will begin

as soon as you wish. May I offer you good luck?"

"We won't need it," Kemridge said grimly. "It's not a matter of luck at all. It's brains—brains and sweat."

"Very well," Plorvash said. "This is what you're here to prove. It ought to be amusing, in any event."

Statisticians have no records on the subject, but it is an observed phenomenon that the most serious differences of opinion generally originate in bars. It had been in a bar at Forty-sixth and Sixth that Justin Marner had ill-advisedly had words with a visiting Domerangi, a month before, and it had been in the same bar that the train of events which had brought the two Earthmen to Domerang V had originated.

It had been a simple altercation, at first. Marner had been reflectively sipping a whiskey sour, and Kemridge, seated to his left with his long legs uncomfortably scrunched up, had been toying with a double Scotch. The Domerangi had entered the bar with a characteristically ponderous stride.

Marner and Kemridge had glanced up in some surprise. Even though contact with Domerang V had been made more than a century before, Domerangi were still rare sights in New York. They recognized this one, though—he was attached to the Domerangi Consulate on Sixty-sixth and Third, and they had had dealings with him in the matter of some circuit alignments for the building's lighting system. Domerangi, with their extraordinary peripheral vision, prefer subdued, indirect lighting, and Marner and Kemridge had designed the lighting-plot for the Consulate.

The Domerangi spotted them immediately, and eased its bulk onto the stool next to them. "Ah, the two clever engineers," the alien rumbled. "You remember me, of course?"

"Yes," Marner said quickly. "We did a lighting job for you last year. How's it working out?"

"As well as could be expected," the Domerangi said. He waved toward the bartender. "Barkeep! Two beers, please."

"What do you mean by that?" Kemridge demanded, as the beers arrived.

"Just one moment, please," said the alien. He curled two tentacles gently around the beers and poured one into each of the two feeding-mouths at the sides of his face. He belched his satisfaction. "Marvelous liquid, your beer. The one point where Earth is clearly superior to Domerang is in brewing."

"To get back to the lights,—" Kemridge prodded.

"Oh, yes," the alien said. "The lights. Well, they're a pretty fair job—as good as we could have hoped for, from a second-rate technology."

"Now hold on a minute!" Marner said hotly, and that was how it started.

"I wish we'd kept our mouths shut," Marner said glumly, after a few moments of introspection. He stared balefully at the spotless ceiling of the hotel room in which the Domerangi had installed them.

Kemridge whirled savagely and glared down at the smaller man. "Listen, Justin; we're here, and we're going to show them up and go home rich and famous. Got that?"

"Okay," Marner said. He ran a finger along his thin lower lip. "I'm sorry I keep popping off like this. But it does seem screwy to have gone to this extent just to prove a point that came up in a barroom debate."

"I know," Kemridge said lightly. "But we wouldn't have come here if the State Department hadn't heard about the argument and thought it needed settling. The Domerangi have been acting lordly about their technology as long as we've known them. I think it's a marvelous idea to send a couple of honest-to-christmas Terran engineers up here to show them once and for all who's got more where it counts."

"But suppose we *don't* show them?"

"We will! Between the two of us, we can match anything they throw at us—can't we? Can't we?"

Marner smiled gloomily. "Sure we can," he said without conviction. "I haven't doubted it for one minute."

"Good," Kemridge said. He walked to the door, and with a swift searching motion of his fingers found the plate that covered the door-mechanism. He unclipped it. "Look in here, for example," he said, after a moment's scrutiny. "Simple cybernetic mechanism. I don't quite figure the way this green ceramic relay down here controls the power flow, but it's nothing we couldn't dope out given a screwdriver and a half hour or so of spare time."

Marner stood on tip-toes and peered in. "Perfectly understandable gadget," he commented. "Not nearly as efficient as our kind, either."

"That's just the point," Kemridge said. "These Domerangi aren't half the sharks they think they are! Look Justin; we stipulated that we could duplicate anything they gave us, right? With our natural savvy and a little perspiration, we ought to be able to match the best gadget they test us with. If we follow through up here and those two Domerangi engineers on Earth mess up their half of the test, then we've done it. The State Department's counting on our versatility. That's all we need, Justin—cleverness!''

Marner's eyes lit up. "There nothing to it, Dave. I'm sorry I was so pigheaded a minute ago. We'll give them the business, all right!''

He stood up a little higher, and gingerly extended a hand into the gaping servomechanism in the wall.

"What are you doing?" Kemridge asked.

"Never mind. Get on the phone and tell Plorvash that we'll be ready to get to work tomorrow. While you're doing that, I want to fool with this relay. Might as well get some practice now!" He was radiant with new-found enthusiasm.

When Plorvash arrived the following morning, the mood was still on them. They were clear-eyed, wide awake, and firmly convinced they could master any problem.

Plorvash's knock sounded heavily on the door.

"Who's there?" Marner asked loudly.

"Me," the Domerangi said. "Plorvash."

Instantly the door flew open, and the dumfounded chargé d'affaires was confronted with the sight of the two Earthmen still snug in their beds. He peered behind the door and in the clothes closet.

"Who opened the door?" he asked suspiciously.

Marner sat up in bed and grinned. "Try it again. Go outside and call out 'Plorvash' the way you just did."

The alien lumbered out, pulling the door shut behind him. When he was outside, he muttered his name again, and the door opened immediately. He thundered across the threshold and looked from

Marner to Kemridge. "What did you do?"

"We were experimenting with the door-opener last night," Kemridge said. "And before we put it back together, we decided it might be fun to rig up a modified vocoder circuit that would open the door automatically at the sound of the syllables 'Plorvash' directed at it from outside. It works very nicely."

The alien scowled. "Ah—yes," he said unhappily. "Very clever. Now, as to the terms of this test you two are to engage in; we've prepared a fully-equipped laboratory for you in Central Sqorvik— that's a suburb not far from here—and we've set up two preliminary problems for you, as agreed. When you've dealt with those—*if* you've dealt with those, we'll give you a third."

"And if we *don't* deal with them successfully?"

"Why, then you'll have failed to demonstrate your ability, of course. We'll consider failure on the preliminary tasks as an immediate conclusion to the project."

"Reasonable enough," Marner said. "But just when do we *win* this thing? Do you go on giving us projects till we miss?"

"That would be the ultimate proof of your ability, wouldn't it?" Plorvash asked. "But you'll be relieved to know that we have no such plans. According to the terms of the agreement between ourselves and your government, the test-groups on each planet will be required to carry out no more than three projects." The alien's rugose lips smiled unpleasantly. "We'll consider successful completion of all three projects as ample proof of your ability."

"I don't like the way you say that," Kemridge said. "What's up your sleeve?"

"My sleeve? My sleeve? I don't believe I grasp the idiom," Plorvash said.

"Never mind. Just a curious Terran expression," said Kemridge.

There was a car waiting for them outside the hotel —a long, low job with a pulsating flexible hood that undulated in distressing fashion.

Plorvash slid the back door open and gestured at Marner. "Get in," he said. "I'll take you to the lab to get started."

Marner looked at the alien, then at Kemridge. Kemridge nodded.

"How about one for the road?" Marner suggested.

"Eh?"

"Another idiom," he said. "I mean a *drink*. Alcoholic beverage. Stimulant of some kind. You catch?"

The alient grinned nastily. "I understand," he said. "Well enough. There's a dispensary on the next street. We don't want to rush you on this thing, anyway." He pointed to the moving roadway. "Get aboard, and we'll take a quick one."

They followed the Domerangi onto the moving strip, and a moment later found themselves in front of a curious domed structure planted just off the roadway. A gleaming sign in Domerangi proclaimed the place's nature.

"It doesn't look very cozy," Kemridge commented, as they entered. A pungent odor of ether hit their nostrils. Half a dozen Domerangi were lying on the floor, holding jointed metal tubes. As they watched, Plorvash clambered down and sprawled out on his back.

"Come, join me," he urged. "Have a drink." He

reached for a tube that slithered across the floor towards him, and fitted it into his left feeding mouth.

"This is a bar?" Kemridge asked quietly. "It looks more like the emergency ward of a hospital."

Plorvash finished drinking and stood up, wiping a few drops of green liquid from his jaw. "Good," he said. "It's not beer, but it's good stuff. I thought you two wanted to drink?"

Marner sniffed the ether-laden air in dismay and shook his head. "We're—not—thirsty," he said slowly. "It takes time to get used to alien customs, I suppose."

"I suppose so," Plorvash agreed. "Very well, then. Let's go to the lab, shall we?"

The laboratory was, indeed, a sumptuous place. The two Earthmen stood at the entrance to the monstrous room and marveled visibly.

"We're impressed," Marner said finally to the Domerangi.

"We want to give you every opportunity to succeed," Plorvash said. "This is just as important for us as it is for you."

Marner took two or three steps into the lab and glanced around. To the left, an enormous oscilloscope wiggled greenly at him; the right-hand wall was bristling with elaborate servo-mechanisms of all descriptions. The far wall was a gigantic toolchest, and workbenches were spotted here and there. The lighting—indirect, of course—was bright and eye-easing. It was the sort of research setup a sane engineer rarely bothers even to dream of.

"You're making it too easy for us," said Kemridge. "It can't be hard to pull off miracles in a lab like this."

"We are honest people," Plorvash said sententiously. "If you can meet our tests, we'll allow that you're better than we are. *If* you can, that is. If you fail, it can't be blamed on poor working conditions."

"Fair enough," Kemridge said. "When are you ready to start?"

"Immediately." He reached into the bagging folds of his sash and withdrew a small plastic bubble, about four inches long, containing a creamy-white fluid. He held it out so they could both see it.

"This is a depilator," Plorvash said. He squeezed a few drops out of the bubble into the spoon-like end of one tentacle and rubbed the liquid over the thick, heavy red beard that sprouted on his lower jaw. A streak of beard came away as he rubbed. "It is very useful," said the Domerangi. He handed the bubble to Marner. "Duplicate it."

"But we're engineers, not chemists," Marner protested.

"Never mind, Justin." Kemridge turned to the alien. "Very well, that's the first problem. Suppose you give us the second one at the same time, just to make things more convenient. That way we'll each have one to work on."

The alien frowned. "You want to work on two projects at once? All right." He turned, strode out, and returned a few moments later, carrying something that looked like a large mousetrap inside a cage. He handed it to Kemridge.

"We use this to catch small housepests," Plorvash explained. "It's a self-baiting trap. Most of our housepests are color-sensitive, and this trap flashes colors as a lure. For example, it does this to trap vorks"—he depressed a lever in the back, and the trap glowed a lambent green—"and this to catch flaibs." Another lever went down, and the trap radiated warm purple. An unmistakable odor of rotting vegetation emanated from it as well.

"It is, as you see, most versatile," the alien went on. "We've supplied you with an ample number of vermin of different sorts—they're at the back of the lab, in those cages—and you ought to be able to rig a trap to duplicate this one. At least, I hope you can."

"Is this all?" Kemridge asked.

Plorvash nodded. "You can have all the time you need. That was the agreement."

"Exactly," Kemridge said. "We'll let you know when we've gotten somewhere."

"Fine," said Plorvash.

After he had left, Marner squeezed a couple of drops of the depilatory out onto the palm of his hand. It stung, and he immediately shook it off.

"Better not fool with that till we've run an analysis," Kemridge suggested. "If it's potent enough to remove Domerangi beards, it'll probably be good skin-dissolver for Earthmen. Those babies have tough hides."

Marner rubbed his hand clean hastily. "What do you think of the deal in general?"

"Pretty soft," Kemridge said. "It shouldn't take more than a week to knock off both these things, barring complications. Seems to me they could pick tougher projects than these."

"Wait till the final one," said Marner. "These are just warmups."

Four days later, when the two projects had been completed, Marner called Plorvash from the lab.

The alien's bulky form filled the screen. "Hello," the Domerangi said mildly. "What's new?"

"We've finished the job," Marner said.

"Both of them?"

"Both," the Earthman said.

"I'll be right over."

Plorvash strode into the lab about fifteen minutes later, and the two Earthmen, who were busy with the animal-cages at the back of the lab, waved in greeting.

"Stay right where you are," Kemridge called loudly. He reached up, pressed a switch, and thirty cages clanged open at once.

As a horde of Domerangi vermin came bounding, slithering, crawling, and rolling across the floor toward Plorvash, the alien leaped back in dismay. "What kind of trick is this?"

"Don't worry," Marner said, from the remotest corner of the lab. "It'll all be over in a second."

The animals ignored Plorvash, and to his surprise they made a bee-line for a complex, humming arrangement of gears and levers behind the door. As they approached, it began flashing a series of colors, emanating strange odors, and making curious clicking noises. When the horde drew closer, jointed arms suddenly sprang out and scooped them wholesale into a hopper that gaped open at floor level. Within a moment, they were all safely inside.

Marner came across the lab, followed by Kemridge. "We've improved on your model," he explained. "We've built a better flaib-trap. It catches the whole mess at once. Your version can deal with only one species at a time."

Plorvash gulped resoundingly. "Very nice," he

said. "Quite remarkable, in fact."

"We have the schematics in our room," said Kemridge. "The trap may have some commercial value on Domerang."

"Probably," Plorvash admitted. "How'd you do on the depilator?"

"That was easy," Marner said. "With the setup you gave us, chemical analysis was a snap. Only I'm afraid we've improved on the original model there too."

"What do you mean?"

Marner rubbed the side of his face uneasily. "I tried our stuff on myself, couple of days ago, and my face is still smooth as a baby's. The effect seems to be permanent."

"You'll submit samples, of course," Plorvash said. "But I think it's fairly safe to assume that you've passed through the first two projects—ah—reasonably well. Curiously, your counterparts on Earth also did well on their preliminaries. I've been in contact with our Consul in New York—I believe you know the man—and he says the two Domerangi now being tested responded successfully to their first two projects."

"Glad to hear it," Marner lied. "But the third one tells the tale, doesn't it?"

"Exactly," Plorvash agreed. "Let's have that one now, shall we?"

Five minutes later, Marner and Kemridge found themselves staring down at a complicated nest of glittering relays and tubes which seemed to power an arrangement of pistons and rods. Plorvash had carried it in with the utmost delicacy and had ensconced it on a workbench in the middle of the lab.

"What is it?" Marner asked.

"You'll see," promised the alien. He fumbled in the back of the machine, drew forth a cord, and plugged it into a wall socket. A small tube in the heart of the machine glowed cherry red, and a moment later the pistons began to move, first slowly, then more rapidly. After a while it was humming away at an even, steady clip, pistons barreling back and forth in purposeless but inexorable motion.

Kemridge bent and peered as close to the workings of the gadget as he dared. Finally he looked up. "So?" he asked. "It's an engine. What of it?"

"It's a very special kind of engine," Plorvash said. "Suppose you take the plug out."

The Earthman worked the plug from its socket, turned, and looked at the machine for a long moment. Then the plug dropped from his limp hand and skittered to the floor.

"It—doesn't stop going, does it?" Kemridge asked quietly. "The pistons keep on moving."

"This is our power source," Plorvash said smugly. "We use them in vehicles and other such things. Can you build one? It's the third problem."

"We'll give it a try," Marner said. "We'll do it."

"I'll be most interested in the results," Plorvash said. "And now, I must bid you a good day."

"Sure," Marner said weakly. "Cheers."

They watched the broad-beamed alien waddle gravely out of the laboratory, waited till the door was closed, and glanced at the machine.

It was still moving.

Marner licked his lips and cocked an eye at Kemridge. "Dave," he said darkly, "can we build a perpetual-motion machine?"

The machine worked just as well plugged in or un-plugged, once it had tapped some power source to begin with. The pistons threaded ceaselessly up and down. The basic components of the things seemed simple enough.

"The first step to take," Marner said, "is to shut the damned thing off so we can get a look at its innards."

"How do we do that?"

"By reversing the power source, I suppose. Feed a negative pulse through that power-input, and that ought to do it. We'll have to reverse the polarity of the signal."

Half an hour's hard work with screwdriver and solder had done that. They plugged the scrambled cord into the socket, and the machine coughed twice and subsided.

"Okay," Marner said, rubbing his hands with an enthusiasm he did not quite feel. "Let's dig this baby apart and find out what makes it tick." He turned and stared meaningfully at Kemridge. "And let's adopt this as a working credo. Dave: inasmuch as the Domerangi have already built this thing, it's *not* impossible. Okay?"

"That seems to be the only basis we can approach it on," Kemridge agreed.

They huddled around the device, staring at the workings. Marner reached down and pointed at a part. "This thing is something like a tuned-plate feedback oscillator," he observed. "And I'll bet we've almost got a thyratron tube over here. Their technology's a good approximation of ours. In fact, the whole thing's within our grasp, technically."

"Hmm. And the result is a closed regenerative system with positive feedback," Kemridge said dizzily. "Infinite energy, going round and round the cycle. If you draw off a hundred watts or so—well, infinity minus a hundred is still infinity!"

"True enough," Marner admitted. He wiped a gleaming bead of perspiration from his forehead. "Dave, we're going to have to puzzle this thing out from scratch. And we don't dare fail."

He reached doggedly for a screwdriver.

"Remember our motto," he muttered. "We'll use our natural savvy and a little perspiration, and we ought to do it."

Three weeks later, they had come up with their first trial model—which wobbled along for half an hour, then gave up.

And a month after that, they had a machine that didn't give up.

Hesitantly, they sent for Plorvash.

"There it is," Marner said, pointing to the bizarre thing that stood next to the original model. Both machines were humming blithely, plugs dangling from the sockets.

"It works?" Plorvash asked, paling.

"It hasn't stopped yet," Marner said. There were heavy rings under his eyes, and his usually plump face was drawn, with the skin tight over his cheekbones. It had been two months of almost constant strain, and both Earthmen showed it.

"It works, eh?" Plorvash asked. *"How?"*

"A rather complex hyperspace function," Kemridge said. "I don't want to bother explaining it now—you'll find it all in our report—but it was quite a stunt in topology. We couldn't actually duplicate your model, but we achieved the same effect, which fulfills the terms of the agreement."

"All a matter of response to challenge," said Marner. "We didn't think we could do it, until we *had* to—so we did."

"I didn't think you could do it either," Plorvash said hoarsely. He walked over and examined the machine closely. "It works, you say? Honestly, now?" His voice was strained.

"Of course," Marner said indignantly.

"We have just one question," said Kemridge. He pointed to a small black rectangular box buried deep in a maze of circuitry in the original model. "That thing down there—it nearly threw us. We couldn't get it open to examine it, and so we had to bypass it and substitute a new system for it. What in blazes is it?"

Plorvash wheeled solidly around to face them. "That," he said, in a strangled voice, "is the power source. It's a miniature photoelectric amplifier that should keep the model running for—oh, another two weeks or so. Then the jig would have been up."

"How's that?" Marner asked, startled.

"It's time to explain something to you," the alien said wearily. *"We don't have any perpetual-motion machines.* You've been cruelly hoaxed into inventing one for us. It's dastardly, but we didn't really think you were going to do it. It took some of our best minds to rig up the model we gave you, you know."

Marner drew up a lab stool and sat down limply, white-faced. Kemridge remained standing, his features blank with disbelief. Finally Marner said, "You mean we invented the thing—and you didn't—you—"

Plorvash nodded. "I'm just as astonished as you are," he said. He reached for a lab stool himself and sat down. It groaned under his weight.

Kemridge recovered first. "Well," he said after a moment of silence, "now that it's over, we'll take our machine and go back to Earth. This invalidates the contest, of course."

"I'm afraid you can't do that," Plorvash said. "By a statute enacted some seven hundred years ago, any research done in a Domerangi government lab is automatically government property. Which means, of course, that we'll have to confiscate your—ahem—project."

"That's out of the question!" Marner said hotly.

"And, furthermore," Plorvash said smoothly, "we intend to confiscate *you*, too. We'd like you to stay and show us how to build our machines."

"This is cause for war," Kemridge said. "Earth won't let you get away with this—this kidnapping!"

"Possibly not," Plorvash said. "But, in view of the way things have turned out, it's the sanest thing we can do. And I *don't* think Earth will go to war over you."

"We demand to see our Consul," said Marner.

"Very well," Plorvash agreed. "It's within your rights, I suppose."

The Earth Consul was a white-haired, sturdy gentleman named Culbertson, who arrived on the scene later that day.

"This is very embarrassing for all of us," the Consul said when he was apprised of the situation. He ran his hands nervously down his traditional pin-striped trousers, adjusting the crease.

"You can get us out of it, of course," Marner said.

"That machine is our property, and they have no right to keep us prisoners here to operate it, do they?"

"No, of course not," Culbertson agreed. "Not by all human laws. But the fact remains, unfortunately, that according to *their* laws, they have every right to your invention. And by the treaty of—ah—2716, waiving extra-territorial sovereignty, Earthmen on Domerang are subject to Domerangi laws, and vice versa." He spread his hands in a gesture of frustration.

"You mean we're stuck here," Marner said bluntly. He shut his eyes, remembering the nightmare that was the Domerangi equivalent of a bar, thinking of the morbid prospect of spending the rest of his life on this unappetizing planet, all because of some insane dare. "Go on—tell us the truth."

The Consul put the palms of his hands together delicately. "We intend to make every effort to get you off, of course—naturally so, since we owe a very great debt to you two. You realize that you've upheld Earth's pride throughout the universe."

"Lot of good it did us," Marner said.

"Nevertheless," said the Consul, "we feel anxious to make amends for the whole unhappy incident. I can assure you that we'll do everything in our power to make your stay here as pleasant and as restful as—"

"Listen, Culbertson," Kemridge said grimly, "we don't want a vacation here, not even with dancing-girls twenty-four hours a day and soft violins in the background. *We don't like it here.* We want to go home. You people got us into this—now get us out."

The Consul grew even more unhappy-looking. "I

wish you wouldn't put it that way," he said. "We'll do all we can." He paused for a moment, deep in thought, and said, "There's one factor in the case that we haven't explored."

"What's that?" Marner asked uneasily.

"Remember the two Domerangi engineers who went to Earth on the other leg of this hookup?" The Consul glanced around the lab. "Is this place wired anywhere?"

"I don't think so," Kemridge said. "You can speak freely. What do they have to do with us?"

"There's a slim chance for you," the Consul said, lowering his voice. "I've been in touch with authorities on Earth, and they've been keeping me informed of the progress of the two Domerangi. As you know, they got through their first two projects as easily as you did."

The two Earthmen nodded impatiently.

The old diplomat smiled his apologies. "I hate to admit this, but it seems the people at the Earth end of this deal had much the same idea the Domerangi did."

"Perpetual motion, you mean?"

"Not quite," Culbertson said. "They rigged up a phony antigravity machine, and told the Domerangi to duplicate it. Just as was done here. Our psychologies must be similar."

"And what happened?" Marner asked.

"Nothing, yet," the Consul said sadly. "But they're still working on it, I'm told. If they're as clever as they say they are, they ought to hit it sooner or later. You'll just have to be patient and sweat it out. We'll see to it that you're well taken care of in the meantime, of course, and—"

"I don't get it. What does that have to do with us?" Marner demanded.

"If they keep at it," said the Consul, "they'll invent it eventually. And then, I think, we can try to arrange a sort of even-up exchange."

Marner scowled. "That may take years. It may take forever. They may *never* discover a workable antigrav! Then what about us?"

The Consul shrugged mildly.

A curious gleam twinkled in Kemridge's eye. He turned to Marner and said, "Justin—do you know anything about tensor applications and gravitational fields?"

"What are you driving at?" Marner asked.

"We've got an ideal lab setup here. And I'm sure those two Domerangi down there wouldn't mind taking the credit for someone else's antigrav, if they were approached properly—eh?"

"You mean," said the Consul, "you'd build the machine, and smuggle it to Earth so we could slip it to the Domerangi and use that as a talking-point for a trade and—"

He stopped, seeing that no one was listening to him, and looked around. Marner and Kemridge were at the far end of the lab, scribbling equations feverishly.

ting up with the others was part of the mask Devall
imposed on himself. He donned the light summer
uniform, slapped depilator hastily on his tanned face,
hooked on his formal blaster and belt, and signaled
to his orderly that he was awake and ready.

The Terran enclave covered ten acres, half an
hour's drive from one of the largest Markin villages.
An idling jeep waited outside Devall's small private
dome, and he climbed in, nodding curtly at the orderly.

"Morning, Harris."

"Good morning, sir. Sleep well?"

It was a ritual by now. "Very well," Devall responded automatically, as the jeep's turbos
thrummed once and sent the little car humming
across the compound to the mess hall. Clipped to the
seat next to Devall was his daily morning program-
sheet, prepared for him by the staffman-of-the-day
while he slept. This morning's sheet was signed by
Dudley, a major of formidable efficiency—Space Service through and through, a Military Wing career
man and nothing else. Devall scanned the assignments for the morning, neatly written out in
Dudley's crabbed hand.

*Kelly, Dorfman, Mellors, Steber on Linguistic Detail, as
usual. Same assignment as yesterday, in town.*

Haskell on medic duty. Blood samples; urinalysis.

Matsuoko to maintenance staff (through Wednesday).

Jolli on zoo detail.

*Leonards, Meyer, Rodriguez on assigned botanical field
trip, two days. Extra jeep assigned for specimen collection.*

Devall scanned the rest of the list, but, as expected,
Dudley had done a perfect job of deploying the men
where they would be most useful and most happy.

Devall thought briefly about Leonards, on the
botanical field trip. A two-day trip might take him
through the dangerous rain-forest to the south; Devall felt a faint flicker of worry. The boy was his
nephew, his sister's son—a reasonably competent
journeyman botanist with the gold bar still un-
tarnished on his shoulder. This was the boy's first
commission; he had been assigned to Devall's unit at
random, as a new man. Devall had concealed his relationship with Leonards from the other men, knowing it might make things awkward for the boy, but he
still felt a protective urge.

Hell, the kid can take care of himself, Devall thought,
and scribbled his initials at the bottom of the sheet
and slipped it back in place; it would be posted now,
while the men were cleaning their quarters and the
officers ate, and by 0900 everyone would be out on
his day's assignment. There was so much to do, Devall thought, and so little time to do it. There were so
many worlds—

He quitted the jeep and entered the mess hall. Officers' mess was a small well-lit alcove to the left of
the main hall; as Devall entered he saw seven men
standing stiffly at attention, waiting for him.

He knew they hadn't been standing that way all
morning; they had snapped to attention only when
their lookout—probably Second Lieutenant
Leonards, the youngest—had warned them he was
coming.

Well, he thought, it doesn't matter much. As long
as appearance is preserved. The form.

"Good morning, gentlemen," he said crisply, and
took his place at the head of the table.

* * *

For a while it looked as if it were going to turn out a pretty good day. The sun rose in a cloudless sky, and the thermometer tacked to the enclave flagstaff registered 93 degrees. When Markin got hot, it got *hot*. By noon, Devall knew by now, they could expect something like 110 in the shade—and then, a slow, steady decline into the low eighties by midnight.

The botanical crew departed on time, rumbling out of camp in its two jeeps, and Devall stood for a moment on the mess hall steps watching them go, watching the other men head to their assigned posts. Stubble-faced Sergeant Jolli saluted him as he trotted across the compound to the zoo, where he would tend the little menagerie of Markin wildlife the expedition would bring back to Earth at termination. Wiry little Matsuoko passed by, dragging a carpenter's kit. The linguistic team climbed into its jeep and drove off toward town, where it would continue its studies in the Markin tongue.

They were all busy. The expedition had been on Markin just four months; eight months were left of their time. Unless an extension of stay came through, they'd pack up and return to Earth for six months of furlough-cum-report-session, and then it would be on to some other world for another year of residence.

Devall was not looking forward to leaving Markin. It was a pleasant world, if a little on the hot side, and there was no way of knowing what the *next* world would be like. A frigid ball of frozen methane, perhaps, where they would spend their year bundled into Valdez breathing-suits and trying to make contact with some species of intelligent ammonia-breathing molluscs. Better the devil we know, Devall felt.

But he had to keep moving on. This was his eleventh world, and there would be more to come. Earth had barely enough qualified survey teams to cover ten thousand worlds half-adequately, and life abounded on ten *million*. He would retain whichever members of the current team satisfied him by their performance, replace those who didn't fit in, and would go off to his next job eight months from now.

He turned on the office fan and took down the logbook; unfastening the binder, he slipped the first blank sheet into the autotype. For once he avoided his standard blunder; he cleared his throat *before* switching on the autotype, thereby sparing the machine its customary difficulties in finding a verbal equivalent for his *Br-ghhumph!*

The guidelight glowed a soft red. Devall said, "Fourth April, two-seven-ought-five. Colonel John F. Devall recording. One hundred nineteenth day of our stay on Markin, World 7 of System 1106-sub-a.

"Temperature, 93 at 0900; wind gentle, southerly—"

He went on at considerable length, as he did each morning. Finishing off the required details, he gathered up the sheaf of specialty-reports that had been left at his door the night before, and began to read abstracts into the log; the autotype clattered merrily, and a machine somewhere in the basement of the towering E-T Affairs Building in Rio de Janeiro was reproducing his words as the subradio hookup transmitted them.

It was dull work; Devall often wondered whether he might have been ultimately happier doing simple group, which also included Sergeants Meyer and Rodriguez."

He paused. "We—we accomplished little in the first half hour; this immediate area had already been thoroughly covered by us anyway. But about 0945 Meyer noticed a heavily wooded area not far to the left of the main road, and called it to my attention. I suggested we stop and investigate. It was impossible to penetrate the wooded area in our jeeps, so we proceeded on foot. I left Rodriguez to keep watch over our gear while we were gone.

"We made our way through a close-packed stand of deciduous angiosperm trees of a species we had already studied, and found ourselves in a secluded area of natural growth, including several species which we would see were previously uncatalogued. We found one in particular—a shrub consisting of a single thick, succulent green stalk perhaps four feet high, topped by a huge gold and green composite flower head. We filmed it in detail, took scent samples, pollen prints, and removed several leaves."

Devall broke in suddenly. "You didn't pick the flower itself? Devall speaking."

"Of course not. It was the only specimen in the vicinity, and it's not our practice to destroy single specimens for the sake of collecting. But I did remove several leaves from the stalk. And the moment I did that, a native sprang at me from behind a thick clump of ferns.

"He was armed with one of those notched spears. Meyer saw him first and yelled, and I jumped back just as the alien came charging forward with his spear. I managed to deflect the spear with the outside of my arm and was not hurt. The alien fell back a few feet and shouted something at me in his language, which I don't understand too well as yet. Then he raised his spear and menaced me with it. I was carrying the standard-issue radial blaster. I drew it and ordered him in his own language to lower his spear, that we meant no harm. He ignored me and charged a second time. I fired in self-defense, trying to destroy the spear or at worst wound his arm, but he spun round to take the full force of the charge, and died instantly." Leonards shrugged. "That's about it, sir. We came back here at once."

"Umm. Devall speaking. Sergeant Meyer, would you say this account is substantially true?"

Meyer was a thin-faced, dark-haired man who was usually smiling, but he wasn't smiling now. "This is Sergeant Meyer. I'd say that Lieutenant Leonards told the story substantially as it occurred. Except that the alien didn't seem overly fierce despite his actions, in my opinion. I myself thought he was bluffing both times he charged, and I was a little surprised when Lieutenant Leonards shot him. That's all, sir."

Frowning, the Colonel said, "Devall speaking. This has been testimony in the matter of the alien killed by Lieutenant Leonards." He snapped off the autotype, stood up, and leaned forward across the desk, staring sternly at the trio of young botanists facing him.

"Sergeant Rodriguez, since you weren't present at the actual incident I'll consider you relieved of all responsibility in this matter, and your testimony won't be required. Report to Major Dudley for reassignment for the remainder of the week."

"Thank you, sir." Rodriguez saluted, grinned gratefully, and was gone.

"As for you two, though," Devall said heavily, "you'll both have to be confined to base pending the outcome of the affair. I don't need to tell you how serious this can be, whether the killing was in self-defense or not. Plenty of peoples don't understand the concept of self-defense." He moistened his suddenly dry lips. "I don't anticipate too many complications growing out of this. But these are alien people on an alien world, and their behavior is never certain."

He glanced at Leonards. "Lieutenant, I'll have to ask for your own safety that you remain in your quarters until further notice."

"Yes, sir. Is this to be considered arrest?"

"Not yet," Devall said. "Meyer, attach yourself to the maintenance platoon for the remainder of the day. We'll probably need your testimony again before this business is finished. Dismissed, both of you."

When they were gone, Devall sank back limply in his web-foam chair and stared at his fingertips. His hands were quivering as if they had a life of their own.

John F. Devall, PhD. Anthropology Columbia '82, commissioned Space Service Military Wing '87, and now you're in trouble for the first time.

How are you going to handle it, Jack? he asked himself. *Can you prove that that silver eagle really belongs on your shoulder?*

He was sweating. He felt very tired. He shut his eyes for a moment, opened them, and said into the intercom, "Send in the Marks."

Five of them entered, made ceremonial bows, and ranged themselves nervously along the far wall as if they were firing-squad candidates. Accompanying them came Steber of the linguistics team, hastily recalled from town to serve as an interpreter for Devall. The Colonel's knowledge of Markin was adequate but sketchy; he wanted Steber around in case any fine points had to be dealt with in detail.

The Marks were humanoid in structure, simian in ancestry, which should have made them close kin to the Terrans in general physiological structure. They weren't. Their skin was a rough, coarse, pebble-grained affair, dark-toned, running to muddy browns and occasional deep purples. Their jaws had somehow acquired a reptilian hinge in the course of evolution, which left them practically chinless but capable of swallowing food in huge lumps that would strangle an Earthman. Their eyes, liquid gold in color, were set wide in their heads, allowing enormous peripheral vision; their noses were flat buttons, in some cases barely perceptible bumps above the nostrils.

Devall saw two younger men, obviously warriors; they had left their weapons outside, but their jaws jutted belligerently and the darker of the pair had virtually dislocated his jaw in rage. The woman looked like all the Mark women, shapeless and weary behind her shabby cloak of furs. The remaining pair were priests, one old, one *very* old. It was this ancient to whom Devall addressed his first remarks.

"I'm sorry that our meeting this afternoon has to be one of sorrow. I had been looking forward to a pleasant talk. But it's not always possible to predict what lies ahead."

"Death lay ahead for him who was killed," the old priest said in the dry, high-pitched tone of voice that Devall knew implied anger and scorn.

The woman let out a sudden wild ululation, half a dozen wailing words jammed together so rapidly Devall could not translate them. "What did she say?" he asked Steber.

The interpreter flattened his palms together thoughtfully. "She's the woman of the man who was killed. She was—demanding revenge," he said in English.

Apparently the two young warriors were friends of the dead man. Devall's eyes scanned the five hostile alien faces. "This is a highly regrettable incident," he said in Markin. "But I trust it won't affect the warm relationship between Earthman and Markin that has prevailed so far. This misunderstanding—"

"Blood must be atoned," said the smaller and less impressively garbed of the two priests. He was probably the local priest, Devall thought, and he was probably happy to have his superior on hand to back him up.

The Colonel flicked the sweat from his forehead. "The young man who committed the act will certainly be disciplined. Of course you realize that a killing in self-defense cannot be regarded as murder, but I admit the young man did act unwisely and will suffer the consequences." It didn't sound too satisfying to Devall, and, indeed, the aliens hardly seemed impressed.

The high priest uttered two short, sharp syllables. They were not words in Devall's vocabulary, and he looked over at Steber in appeal.

"He said Leonards was trespassing on sacred ground. He said the crime they're angry about is not murder but blasphemy."

Despite the heat, Devall felt a sudden chill. *Not . . .*

murder? This is going to be complicated, he realized gloomily.

To the priest he said, "Does this change the essential nature of the case? He'll still be punished by us for his action, which can't be condoned."

"You may punish him for murder, if you so choose," the high priest said, speaking very slowly, so Devall would understand each word. The widow emitted some highly terrestrial-sounding sobs: the young men glowered stolidly. "Murder is not our concern," the high priest went on. "He has taken life; life belongs to Them, and They withdraw it whenever They see fit, by whatever means They care to employ. But he has also desecrated a sacred flower on sacred ground. These are serious crimes, to us. Added to this he has shed the blood of a Guardian, on sacred ground. We ask you to turn him over to us for trial by a priestly court on this double charge of blasphemy. Afterwards, perhaps, you may try him by your own laws, for whichever one of them he has broken."

For an instant all Devall saw was the old priest's implacable leathery face; then he turned and caught the expression of white-faced astonishment and dismay Steber displayed.

It took several seconds for the high priest's words to sink in, and several more before Devall came to stunned realization of the implications. *They want to try an Earthman,* he thought numbly. *By their own law. In their own court. And mete out their own punishment.*

This had abruptly ceased being a mere local incident, an affair to clean up, note in the log, and forget. It was no longer a matter of simple reparations for the accidental killing of an alien.

Now, thought Deval dully, it was a matter of galactic importance. And he was the man who had to make all the decisions.

He visited Leonards that evening, after the meal. By that time everyone in the camp knew what had happened, though Devall had ordered Steber to keep quiet about the alien demand to try Leonards themselves.

The boy looked up as Devall entered his room, and managed a soggy salute.

"At ease, Lieutenant." Devall sat on the edge of Leonards' bed and squinted up at him. "Son, you're in very hot water now."

"Sir, I—"

"I know. You didn't mean to pluck leaves off the sacred bramble-bush, and you couldn't help shooting down the native who attacked you. And if this business were as simple as all that, I'd reprimand you for hotheadedness and let it go at that. But—"

"But what, sir?"

Devall scowled and forced himself to face the boy squarely. "But the aliens want to try you themselves. They aren't so much concerned with the murder as they are with your double act of blasphemy. That withered old high priest wants to take you before an ecclesiastical court."

"You won't allow *that*, of course, will you, Colonel?" Leonards seemed confident that such an unthinkable thing could never happen.

"I'm not so sure, Paul," Devall said quietly, deliberately using the boy's first name.

"*What*, sir?"

"This is evidently something very serious you've

committed. That high priest is calling a priestly convocation to deal with you. They'll be back here to get you tomorrow at noon, he said."

"But you wouldn't turn me over to them, sir! After all, I was on duty; I had no knowledge of the offense I was committing. Why, it's none of their business!"

"Make *them* see that," Devall said flatly. "They're aliens. They don't understand Terran legal codes. They don't *want* to hear about our laws; by *theirs*, you've blasphemed, and blasphemers must be punished. This is a law-abiding race on Markin. They're an ethically advanced society, regardless of the fact that they're not technologically advanced. Ethically they're on the same plane we are."

Leonards looked terribly pale. "You'll turn me over to them?"

Devall shrugged. "I didn't say that. But look at it from my position. I'm leader of a cultural and military mission. Our purpose is to live among these people, learn their ways, guide them as much as we can in our limited time here. We at least *try* to make a pretense of respecting their rights as individuals and as a species, you know.

"Well, now it's squarely on the line. Are we friends living among them and helping them, or are we overlords grinding them under our thumbs?"

"Sir, I'd say that was an oversimplification," Leonards remarked hesitantly.

"Maybe so. But the issue's clear enough. If we turn them down, it means we're setting up a gulf of superiority between Earth and these aliens, despite the big show we made about being brothers. And word will spread to other planets. We try to sound like friends, but our actions in the celebrated

Leonards case reveal our true colors. We're arrogant, imperialistic, patronizing, and—well, do you see?"

"So you're going to turn me over to them for trial, then," the boy said quietly.

Devall shook his head. "I don't know. I haven't made up my mind yet. If I turn you over, it'll certainly set a dangerous precedent. And if I don't—I'm not sure what will happen." He shrugged. "I'm going to refer the case back to Earth. It isn't my decision to make."

But it *was* his decision to make, he thought, as he left the boys' quarters and headed stiff-legged toward the Communications shack. He was on the spot, and only he could judge the complex factors that controlled the case. Earth would almost certainly pass the buck back to him.

He was grateful for one thing, though: at least Leonards hadn't made an appeal to him on family grounds. That was cause for pride, and some relief. The fact that the boy was his nephew was something he'd have to blot rigorously from his mind until all this was over.

The signalman was busy in the back of the shack, bent over a crowded worktable. Devall waited a moment, cleared his throat gently, and said, "Mr. Rory?"

Rory turned. "Yes, Colonel?"

"Put through a subradio to Earth for me, immediately. To Director Thornton at the E-T Department. And yell for me when you've made contact."

It took twenty minutes for the subspace impulse to leap out across the light-years and find a receiver on Earth, ten minutes more for it to pass through the relay point and on to Rio. Devall returned to the shack to find the lambent green solido field in tune and waiting for him. He stepped through and discovered himself standing a few feet before the desk of the E-T Department's head. Thornton's image was sharp, but the desk seemed to waver at the edges. Solid non-organic objects always came through poorly.

Quickly Devall reviewed the situation. Thornton sat patiently, unmoving, till the end of it; hands knotted rigidly, lean face set, he might have been a statue. Finally he commented, "unpleasant business."

"Quite."

"The alien is returning the next day, you say? I'm afraid that doesn't give us much time to hold a staff meeting and explore the problem, Colonel Devall."

"I could probably delay him a few days."

Thornton's thin lips formed a tight bloodless line. After an instant he said, "No. Take whatever action you deem necessary, Colonel. If the psychological pattern of the race is such that unfortunate consequences would result if you refused to allow them to try your man, then you must certainly turn him over. If the step can be avoided, of course, avoid it. The man must be punished in any case."

The Director smiled bleakly. "You're one of our best men, Colonel. I'm confident you'll arrive at an ultimately satisfactory resolution to this incident."

"Thank you, sir." Devall said, in a dry, uncertain voice. He nodded and stepped back out of field range. Thornton's image seemed to flicker; Devall caught one last dismissing sentence, "Report back to me when the matter is settled," and then the field died.

He stood alone in the shabby Communications shack, blinking in the sudden darkness that rolled in over him after the solidophone's intense light, and after a moment began to pick his way over the heaps of equipment and out into the compound.

It was as he had expected. Thornton was a good man, but he was a civilian appointee, subject to government control. He disliked making top-level decisions—particularly when a Colonel a few hundred light years away could be forced into making them for him.

Devall called a meeting of his top staff men for 0915 the following morning. Work at the base had all but suspended; the linguistics team was confined to the area, and Devall had ordered guards posted at all exits. Violence could rise unexpectedly among even the most placid of alien peoples; it was impossible to predict the moment when a racial circuit-breaker would cease to function and fierce hatred burst forth.

They listened in silence to the tapes of Leonards' statements, Meyer's comments, and the brief interview Devall had had with the five aliens. Devall punched the cutoff stud and glanced rapidly round the table at his men: two majors, a captain, and a quartet of lieutenants comprised his high staff, and one of the lieutenants was confined to quarters.

"That's the picture. The old high priest is showing up here about noon for my answer. I thought I'd toss the thing open for staff discussion first."

Major Dudley asked for the floor.

He was a short, stocky man with dark flashing eyes, and on several occasions in the past had been known to disagree violently with Devall on matters of procedure. Devall had picked him for four successive trips, despite this; the Colonel believed in diversity of opinion, and Dudley was a tremendously efficient organizer as well.

"Major?"

"Sir, it doesn't seem to me that there's any question of what action to take. It's impossible to hand Leonards over to them for trial. It's—inhuman, or—unEarthlike!"

Devall frowned. "Would you elaborate, Major?"

"Simple enough. We're the race who developed the spacedrive—therefore, we're the galaxy's most advanced race. I think that goes without saying."

"It does not," Devall commented. "But go ahead."

Scowling, Dudley said, "Regardless of your opinions, *sir*—the aliens we've encountered so far have all regarded us as their obvious superiors. I don't think that can be denied—and I think it can only be attributed to the fact that we *are* their superiors. Well, if we give up Leonards for trial, it cheapens our position. It makes us look weak, spineless. We—"

"You're suggesting, then," Devall broke in, "that we hold the position of overlords in the galaxy—and by yielding to our serfs, we may lose all control over them. Is this your belief, Major?" Devall glared at him.

Dudley met the Colonel's angry gaze calmly. "Basically, yes. Dammit, sir, I've tried to make you see this ever since the Hegath expedition. We're not out here in the stars to collect butterflies and squirrels! We—"

"Out of order," Devall snapped coldly. "This is a cultural mission as well as a military one, Major—and so long as I'm in command it remains primarily cultural." He felt on the verge of losing his temper. He glanced away from Dudley and said, "Major Grey, could I hear from you?"

Grey was the ship's astrogator; on land his functions were to supervise stockade-construction and mapmaking. He was a wiry, unsmiling little man with razor-like cheekbones and ruddy skin. "I feel we have to be cautious, sir. Handing Leonards over would result in a tremendous loss of Terran prestige."

"*Loss?*" Dudley burst in. "It would cripple us! We'd never be able to hold our heads up honestly in the galaxy again if—"

Calmly Devall said, "Major Dudley, you've been ruled out of order. Leave this meeting, Major. I'll discuss a downward revision of your status with you later." Turning back to Grey without a further glance at Dudley he said, "You don't believe, Major, that such an action would have a correspondingly *favorable* effect on our prestige in the eyes of those worlds inclined to regard Earth uneasily?"

"That's an extremely difficult thing to determine in advance, sir."

"Very well, then." Devall rose. "Pursuant to regulations, I've brought this matter to the attention of authorities on Earth, and have also offered it for open discussion among my officers. Thanks for your time, gentlemen."

Captain Marechal said uncertainly, "Sir, won't there be any vote on our intended course of action?"

Devall grinned coldly. "As commanding officer of this base, I'll take the sole responsibility upon myself for the decision in this particular matter. It may make things easier for all of us in the consequent event of a court-martial inquiry."

It was the only way, he thought, as he waited tensely in his office for the high priest to arrive. The officers seemed firmly set against any conciliatory action, in the name of Terra's prestige. It was hardly fair for him to make them take responsibility for a decision that might be repugnant to them.

Too bad about Dudley, Devall mused. But insubordination of that sort was insufferable; Dudley would have to be dropped from the unit on their next trip out. If there is any next trip out for me, he added.

The intercom glowed gently. "Yes?"

"Alien delegation is here, sir," said the orderly.

"Don't send them in until I signal."

He strode to the window and looked out. The compound, at first glance, seemed full of aliens. Actually there were only a dozen, he realized, but they were clad in full panoply, bright red and harsh green robes, carrying spears and ornamental swords. Half a dozen enlisted men were watching them nervously from a distance, their hands ready to fly to blasters instantly if necessary.

He weighed the choices one last time.

If he handed Leonards over, the temporary anger of the aliens would be appeased—but perhaps at a long-range cost to Earth's prestige. Devall had long regarded himself as an essentially weak man with a superb instinct for camouflage—but would his yielding to the aliens imply to the universe that all Earth was weak?

On the other hand, he thought, suppose he refused to release Leonards to the aliens. Then, he would be, in essence, bringing down the overlord's thumb, letting the universe know that Earthmen were responsible only to themselves and not to the peoples of the worlds they visited.

Either way, he realized, the standing of Earthmen in the galaxy's estimation would suffer. One way, they would look like appeasing weaklings; the other, like tyrants. He remembered a definition he had once read: *melodrama is the conflict of right and wrong, tragedy the conflict of right and right.* Both sides were right here. Whichever way he turned, there would be difficulties.

And there was an additional factor: the boy. What if they executed him? Family considerations seemed absurdly picayune at this moment, but still, to hand his own nephew over for possible execution at the hands of an alien people—

He took a deep breath, straightened his shoulders, sharpened the hard gaze of his eyes. A glance at the mirror over the bookcase told him he looked every inch the commanding officer; not a hint of the inner conflict showed through.

He depressed the intercom stud. "Send in the high priest. Let the rest of them wait outside."

The priest looked impossibly tiny and wrinkled, a gnome of a man whose skin was fantastically gullied and mazed by extreme age. He wore a green turban over his hairless head—a mark of deep mourning, Devall knew.

The little alien bowed low, extending his pipestem arms behind his back at a sharp angle, indicating respect. When he straightened, his head craned back sharply, his small round eyes peering directly into Devall's.

"The jury has been selected; the trial is ready to begin. Where is the boy?"

Devall wished fleetingly he could have had the services of an interpreter for this last interview. But that was impossible; this was something he had to face alone, without help.

"The accused man is in his quarters," Devall said slowly. "First I want to ask some questions, old one."

"Ask."

"If I give you the boy to try, will there be any chance of his receiving the death penalty?"

"It is conceivable."

Devall scowled. "Can't you be a little more definite than that?"

"How can we know the verdict before the trial takes place?"

"Let that pass," Devall said, seeing he would get no concrete reply. "Where would you try him?"

"Not far from here."

"Could I be present at the trial?"

"No."

Devall had learned enough of Markin grammar by now to realize that the form of the negative the priest had employed meant literally, I-say-*no*-and-mean-what-I-say. Moistening his lips, he said, "Suppose I should refuse to turn Lieutenant Leonards over to you for trial? How could I expect you people to react?"

There was a long silence. Finally the old priest said, "Would you do such a thing?"

"I'm speaking hypothetically." (Literally, the form was, I-speak-on-a-cloud.)

"It would be very bad. We would be unable to purify the sacred garden for many months. Also—"

he added a sentence of unfamiliar words. Devall puzzled unsuccessfully over their meaning for nearly a minute.

"What does that mean?" he asked at length. "Phrase it in different words."

"It is the name of a ritual. *I* would have to stand trial in the Earthman's place—and I would die," the priest said simply. "Then my successor would ask you all to go away."

The office seemed very quiet; the only sounds Devall heard were the harsh breathing of the old priest and the off-key chirruping of the cricket-like insects that infested the grassplot outside the window.

Appeasement, he wondered? *Or the overlord's thumb?*

Suddenly there seemed no doubt at all in his mind of what he should do, and he wondered how he could have hesitated indecisively so long.

"I hear and respect your wishes, old one," he said, in a ritual formula of renunciation Steber had taught him. "The boy is yours. But can I ask a favor?"

"Ask."

"He didn't know he was offending your laws. He meant well; he's sincerely sorry for what he did. He's in your hands, now—but I want to ask mercy on his behalf. He had no way of knowing he was offending."

"This will be seen at the trial," the old priest said coldly. "If there is to be mercy, mercy will be shown him. I make no promises."

"Very well," Devall said. He reached for a pad and scrawled an order remanding Lieutenant Paul Leonards to the aliens for trial, and signed it with his full name and title. "Here. Give this to the Earthman who let you in. He'll see to it that the boy is turned over to you."

"You are wise," the priest said. He bowed elaborately and made for the door.

"Just one moment," Devall said desperately, as the alien opened the door. "Another question."

"Ask," the priest said.

"You told me you'd take his place if I refused to let you have him. Well, how about another substitute? Suppose—"

"*You* are not acceptable to us," the priest said as if reading Devall's mind, and left.

Five minutes later the Colonel glanced out his window and saw the solemn procession of aliens passing through the exit-posts and out of the compounds. In their midst, unprotesting, was Leonards. He didn't look back, and Devall was glad of it.

The Colonel stared at the row of books a long time, the frayed spools that had followed him around from world to world, from gray Danelon to stormy Lurrin to bone-dry Korvel, and on to Hegath and M'Qualt and the others, and now to warm blue-skied Markin. Shaking his head, he turned away and dropped heavily into the foam cradle behind his desk.

He snapped on the autotype with a savage gesture and dictated a full account of his actions, from the very start until his climactic decision, and smiled bitterly; there would be a certain time-lag, but before long the autotype facsimile machine in the E-T Department's basement would start clacking, there in Rio, and Thornton would know what Devall had done.

And Thornton would be stuck with it, as Department policy henceforth.

Devall switched on the intercom and said, "I'm

not to be disturbed under any circumstances. If there's anything urgent, have it sent to Major Grey; he's acting head of the base until I countermand. And if any messages come from Earth let Grey have them too."

He wondered if they'd relieve him of his command immediately, or wait until he got back to Earth. The latter, more likely; Thornton had some subtlety, if not much. But there was certain to be an inquiry, and someone's head would have to roll.

Devall shrugged and stretched back. *I did what was right,* he told himself firmly. *That's the one thing I can be sure of.*

But I hope I don't ever have to face my sister again.

He dozed, after a while, eyes half-open and slipping rapidly closed. Sleep came to him, and he welcomed it, for he was terribly tired.

He was awakened suddenly by a loud outcry. A jubilant shout from a dozen throats at once, splitting the afternoon calm. Devall felt a moment's disorientation; then, awakening rapidly, he sprang to the window and peered out.

A figure—alone and on foot—was coming through the open gateway. He wore regulation uniform, but it was dripping wet and torn in several places. His blond hair was plastered to his scalp as if he had been swimming; he looked fatigued.

Leonards.

The Colonel was nearly halfway out the front door before he realized that his uniform was in improper order. He forced himself back, tidied his clothing, and with steely dignity strode out the door a second time.

Leonards stood surrounded by a smiling knot of

men, enlisted men and officers alike. The boy was grinning wearily.

"Attention!" Devall barked, and immediately the area fell silent. He stepped forward.

Leonards raised one arm in an exhausted salute. There were some ugly bruises on him, Devall noticed.

"I'm back, Colonel."

"I'm aware of that. You understand that I'll have to return you to the Marks for trial anyway, despite your no doubt daring escape?"

The boy smiled and shook his head. "No, sir. You don't follow, sir. The trial's over. I've been tried and acquitted."

"What's that?"

"It was trial by ordeal, Colonel. They prayed for half an hour or so, and then they dumped me in the lake down the road. The dead man's two brothers came after me and tried to drown me, but I outswam them and came up safely on the other side."

He shook his hair like a drenched cat, scattering a spray of water several feet in the air. "They nearly had me, once. But as soon as I got across the lake alive and undrowned, it proved to them I couldn't have meant any harm. So they declared me innocent, apologized, and turned me loose. They were still praying when I left them."

There seemed to be no bitterness in Leonards' attitude; apparently, Devall thought, he had understood the reason for the decision to hand him over and would not hold it against him now. That was gratifying.

"You'd better get to your quarters and dry off, Lieutenant. And then come to my office. I'd like to talk to you there."

"Yes, sir."

Devall spun sharply and headed back across the clearing to his office. He slammed the door behind him and switched on the autotype. The report to Earth would have to be amended now.

A moment or two after he had finished, the intercom glowed. He turned it on and heard Steber's voice saying, "Sir, the old priest is here. He wants to apologize to you for everything. He's wearing clothing of celebration, and he brought a peace-offering for us."

"Tell him I'll be right out," Devall said. "And call all the men together. Including Dudley. *Especially* Dudley. I want him to see this."

He slipped off his sweat-stained jacket and took a new one out. Surveying himself in the mirror, he nodded approvingly.

Well, well, he thought. *So the boy came through it safely. That's good.*

But he knew that the fate of Paul Leonards had been irrelevant all along, except on the sheerly personal level. It was the larger issue that counted.

For the first time, Earth had made a concrete demonstration of the equality-of-intelligent-life doctrine it had been preaching so long. He had shown that he respected the Markin laws in terms of what they were *to the Marks*, and he had won the affection of a race as a result. Having the boy return unharmed was in the nature of an unbegged bonus.

But the precedent had been set. And the next time, perhaps, on some other world, the outcome might not be so pleasant. Some cultures had pretty nasty ways of putting criminals to death.

He realized that the burden the Earth exploration teams carried now had become many times heavier

—that now, Earthmen would be subject to the laws of the planets who hosted them, and no more unwitting botanical excursions into sacred gardens could be tolerated. But it was for the ultimate good, he thought. *We've shown them that we're not overlords, and that most of us don't want to be overlords. And now the thumb comes down on us.*

He opened the door and stepped out. The men had gathered, and the old priest knelt abjectly at the foot of the steps, bearing some sort of enameled box as his offering. Devall smiled and returned the bow, and lifted the old alien gently to his feet.

We'll have to be on our best behavior from now on, he thought. *We'll really have to watch our steps. But it'll be worth it.*

OZYMANDIAS

And some of the worlds of the galaxy will not be inhabited by living creatures at all. When the men of Earth reach them, they will find only the signs of dead civilizations—the Pompeiis and Chichén Itzás of other planets. Such worlds will be the concern not of zoologists nor of diplomats nor of military men, but of archaeologists. And in their probing, the archaeologists may uncover something of grave and shattering consequence for the worlds of living beings.

The planet had been dead about a million years. That was our first impression, as our ship orbited down to its sere brown surface, and as it happened our first impression turned out to be right. There had been a civilization here *once*—but Earth had swung around Sol ten-to-the-sixth times since the last living being of this world had drawn breath.

"A dead planet," Colonel Mattern exclaimed bitterly. "Nothing here that's of any use. We might as well pack up and move on."

It was hardly surprising that Mattern would feel

that way. In urging a quick departure and an immediate removal to some world of greater utilitarian value, Mattern was, after all, only serving the best interests of his employers. His employers were the General Staff of the Armed Forces of the United States of America. They expected Mattern and his half of the crew to produce results, and by way of results they meant new weapons and military alliances. They hadn't tossed in 70 per cent of the budget for this trip just to sponsor a lot of archaeological putterings.

But luckily for *our* half of the outfit—the archaeological putterers' half—Mattern did not have an absolute voice in the affairs of the outfit. Perhaps the General Staff had kicked in for 70 per cent of our budget, but the cautious men of the military's Public Liaison branch had seen to it that *we* had at least some rights.

Dr. Leopold, head of the non-military segment of the expedition, said brusquely, "Sorry, Mattern, but I'll have to apply the limiting clause here."

Mattern started to sputter. "But—"

"But nothing, Mattern. We're here. We've spent a good chunk of American cash in getting here. I insist that we spend the minimum time allotted for scientific research, as long as we *are* here."

Mattern scowled, looking down at the table, supporting his chin on his thumbs and digging the rest of his fingers in hard back of his jawbone. He was annoyed, but he was smart enough to know he didn't have much of a case to make against Leopold.

The rest of us—four archaeologists and seven military men; they outnumbered us a trifle—watched eagerly as our superiors battled. My eyes strayed through the porthole and I looked at the dry wind-blown plain, marked here and there with the stumps of what might have been massive monuments millennia ago.

Mattern said bleakly, "The world is of utterly no strategic consequence. Why, it's so old that even the vestiges of civilization have turned to dust!"

"Nevertheless, I reserve the right granted to me to explore any world we land on, for a period of at least one hundred sixty-eight hours," Leopold returned implacably.

Exasperated, Mattern burst out, "Dammit, *why?* Just to spite me? Just to prove the innate intellectual superiority of the scientist to the man of war?"

"Mattern, I'm not injecting personalities into this."

"I'd like to know what you *are* doing, then? Here we are on a world that's obviously useless to me and probably just as useless to you. Yet you stick me on a technicality and force me to waste a week here. Why, if not out of spite?"

"We've made only the most superficial reconnaissance so far," Leopold said. "For all we know this place may be the answer to many questions of galactic history. It may even be a treasure-trove of superbombs, for all—"

"Pretty damned likely!" Mattern exploded. He glared around the conference room, fixing each of the scientific members of the committee with a baleful stare. He was making it quite clear that he was trapped into a wasteful expense of time by our foggy-eyed desire for Knowledge.

Useless knowledge. Not good hard practical knowledge of the kind *he* valued.

"All right," he said finally. "I've protested and I've lost, Leopold. You're within your rights in insisting on remaining here one week. But you'd damned well better be ready to blast off when your time's up!"

It had been foregone all along, of course. The charter of our expedition was explicit on the matter. We had been sent out to comb a stretch of worlds near the Galactic Rim that had already been brushed over hastily by a survey mission.

The surveyors had been looking simply for signs of life, and, finding none, they had moved on. We were entrusted with the task of investigating in detail. Some of the planets in the group had been inhabited once, the surveyors had reported. None bore present life.

Our job was to comb through the assigned worlds with diligence. Leopold, leading our group, had the task of doing pure archaeological research on the dead civilizations; Mattern and his men had the more immediately practical job of looking for fissionable material, leftover alien weapons, possible sources of lithium or tritium for fusion, and other militarily useful things. You could argue that in a strictly pragmatic sense our segment of the group was just dead weight, carted along for the ride at great expense, and you would be right.

But the public temper over the last few hundred years in America has frowned on purely military expeditions. And so, as a sop to the nation's conscience, five archaeologists, of little empirical consequence so far as national security mattered, were tacked onto the expedition.

Us.

Mattern made it quite clear at the outset that *his* boys were the Really Important members of the expedition, and that we were simply ballast. In a way, we had to agree. Tension was mounting once again on our sadly disunited planet; there was no telling when the Other Hemisphere would rouse from its quiescence of a hundred years and decide to plunge once more into space. If anything of military value lay out here, we knew we had to find it before They did.

The good old armaments race. Hi-ho! The old space stories used to talk about expeditions from Earth. Well, we *were* from Earth, abstractly speaking —but in actuality we were from America, period. Global unity was as much of a pipedream as it had been three hundred years earlier, in the remote and primitive chemical-rocket era of space travel. Amen. End of sermon. We got to work.

The planet had no name, and we didn't give it one; a special commission of what was laughably termed the United Nations Organization was working on the problem of assigning names to the hundreds of worlds of the galaxy, using the old idea of borrowing from ancient Terran mythologies in analogy to the Mercury-Venus-Mars nomenclature of our own system.

Probably they would end up saddling this world with something like Thoth or Bel-Marduk or perhaps Avalokitesvara. We knew it simply as Planet Four of the system belonging to a yellow-white F5 IV Procyonoid sun, Revised HD Catalog 170861.

It was roughly Earthtype, with a diameter of 6100 miles, a gravity index of .93, a mean temperature of

45 degrees F. with a daily fluctuation range of about ten degrees, and a thin, nasty atmosphere composed mostly of carbon dioxide with wisps of helium and hydrogen and the barest smidgeon of oxygen. Quite possibly the air had been breathable by humanoid life millions of years ago—but that was—millions of years ago. We took good care to practice our breathing-mask drills before we ventured out of the ship.

The sun, as noted, was an F5 IV and fairly hot, but Planet Four was a hundred eighty-five million miles away from it at perihelion, and a good deal further when it was at the other swing of its rather eccentric orbit; the good old Keplerian ellipse took quite a bit of punishment in this system. Planet Four reminded me in many ways of Mars—except that Mars, of course, had never known intelligent life of any kind, at least none that had troubled to leave a hint of its existence, while this planet had obviously had a flourishing civilization at a time when Pithecanthropus was Earth's noblest being.

In any event, once we had thrashed out the matter of whether or not we were going to stay here or pull up and head for the next planet on our schedule, the five of us set to work. We knew we had only a week —Mattern would never grant us an extension unless we came up with something good enough to change his mind, which was improbable—and we wanted to get as much done in that week as possible. With the sky as full of worlds as it is, this planet might never be visited by Earth scientists again.

Mattern and his men served notice right away that they were going to help us, but reluctantly and minimally. We unlimbered the three small halftracks carried aboard ship and got them into functioning order. We stowed our gear—cameras, picks and shovels, camel's-hair brushes—and donned our breathing-masks, and Mattern's men helped us get the halftracks out of the ship and pointed in the right direction.

Then they stood back and waited for us to shove off.

"Don't any of you plan to accompany us?" Leopold asked. The halftracks each held up to four men.

Mattern shook his head. "You fellows go out by yourselves today and let us know what you find. We can make better use of the time filing and catching up on back log entries."

I saw Leopold start to scowl. Mattern was being openly contemptuous; the least he could do was have his men make a token search for fissionable or fusionable matter! But Leopold swallowed down his anger.

"Okay," he said. "You do that. If we come across any raw veins of plutonium I'll radio back."

"Sure," Mattern said. "Thanks for the favor. Let me know if you find a brass mine, too." He laughed harshly. "Raw plutonium! I half believe you're serious!"

We had worked out a rough sketch of the area, and we split up into three units. Leopold, alone, headed straight due west, toward the dry riverbed we had spotted from the air. He intended to check alluvial deposits, I guess.

Marshall and Webster, sharing one halftrack, struck out to the hilly country southeast of our landing point. A substantial city appeared to be buried under the sand there. Gerhardt and I, in the other vehicle, made off to the north, where we hoped to find remnants of yet another city. It was a bleak, windy day; the endless sand that covered this world mounted into little dunes before us, and the wind picked up handfuls and tossed it against the plastite dome that covered our truck. Underneath the steel cleats of our tractor-belt, there was a steady crunch-crunch of metal coming down on sand that hadn't been disturbed in millennia.

Neither of us spoke for a while. Then Gerhardt said, "I hope the ship's still there when we get back to the base."

Frowning, I turned to look at him as I drove. Gerhardt had always been an enigma: a small scrunchy guy with untidy brown hair flapping in his eyes, eyes that were set a little too close together. He had a degree from the University of Kansas and had put in some time on their field staff with distinction, or so his references said.

I said, "What the hell do you mean?"

"I don't trust Mattern. He hates us."

"He doesn't. Mattern's no villain—just a fellow who wants to do his job and go home. But what do you mean, the ship not being there?"

"He'll blast off without us. You see the way he sent us all out into the desert and kept his own men back. I tell you, he'll strand us here!"

I snorted. "Don't be a paranoid. Mattern won't do anything of the sort."

"He thinks we're dead weight on the expedition," Gerhardt insisted. "What better way to get rid of us?"

The halftrack breasted a hump in the desert. I kept

wishing a vulture would squeal somewhere, but there was not even that. Life had left this world ages ago. I said, "Mattern doesn't have much use for *us*, sure. But would he blast off and leave three perfectly good halftracks behind? Would he?"

It was a good point. Gerhardt grunted agreement after a while. Mattern would *never* toss equipment away, though he might not have such scruples about five surplus archaeologists.

We rode along silently for a while longer. By now we had covered twenty miles through this utterly barren land. As far as I could see, we might just as well have stayed at the ship. At least there we had a surface lie of building foundations.

But another ten miles and we came across our city. It seemed to be of linear form, no more than half a mile wide and stretching out as far as we could see— maybe six or seven hundred miles; if we had time, we would check the dimensions from the air.

Of course it wasn't much of a city. The sand had pretty well covered everything, but we could see foundations jutting up here and there, weathered lumps of structural concrete and reinforced metal. We got out and unpacked the power-shovel.

An hour later, we were sticky with sweat under our thin spacesuits and we had succeeded in transferring a few thousand cubic yards of soil from the ground to an area a dozen yards away. We had dug one devil of a big hole in the ground.

And we had nothing.

Nothing. Not an artifact, not a skull, not a yellowed tooth. No spoons, no knives, no baby-rattles.

Nothing.

The foundations of some of the buildings had endured, though whittled down to stumps by a million years of sand and wind and rain. But nothing else of this civilization had survived. Mattern, in his scorn, had been right, I admitted ruefully: this planet was as useless to us as it was to them. Weathered foundations could tell us little except that there had once been a civilization here. An imaginative paleontologist can reconstruct a dinosaur from a fragment of a thighbone, can sketch out a presentable saurian with only a fossilized ischium to guide him. But could we extrapolate a culture, a code of laws, a technology, a philosophy, from bare weathered building foundations?

Not very likely.

We moved on and dug somewhere else half a mile away, hoping at least to unearth one tangible remnant of the civilization that had been. But time had done its work; we were lucky to have the building foundations. All else was gone.

"*Boundless and bare, the lone and level sands stretch far away,*" I muttered.

Gerhardt looked up from his digging. "Eh? What's that?" he demanded.

"Shelley," I told him.

"Oh. Him."

He went back to digging.

Late in the afternoon we finally decided to call it quits and head back to the base. We had been in the field for seven hours and had nothing to show for it except a few hundred feet of tridim films of building foundations.

The sun was beginning to set; Planet Four had a thirty-five hour day, and it was coming to its end.

The sky, always somber, was darkening now. There was no moon. Planet Four had no satellites. It seemed a bit unfair; Three and Five of the system each had four moons, while around the massive gas giant that was Eight a cluster of thirteen moonlets whirled.

We wheeled round and headed back, taking an alternate route three miles east of the one we had used on the way out, in case we might spot something. It was a forlorn hope, though.

Six miles along our journey, the truck radio came to life. The dry, testy voice of Dr. Leopold reached us:

"Calling Trucks Two and Three. Two and Three, do you read me? Come in, Two and Three."

Gerhardt was driving. I reached across his knee to key in the response channel and said, "Anderson and Gerhardt in Number Three, sir. We read you."

A moment later, somewhat more faintly, came the sound of Number Two keying into the three-way channel, and I heard Marshall saying, "Marshall and Webster in Two, Dr. Leopold. Is something wrong?"

"I've found something," Leopold said.

From the way Marshall exclaimed *"Really!"* I knew that Truck Number Two had had no better luck than we. I said, "That makes one of us, then."

"You've had no luck, Anderson?"

"Not a scrap. Not a potsherd."

"How about you, Marshall?"

"Check. Scattered signs of a city, but nothing of archaeological value, sir."

I heard Leopold chuckle before he said, "Well, *I've* found something. It's a little too heavy for me to manage by myself. I want both outfits to come out here and take a look at it."

"What is it, sir?" Marshall and I asked simultaneously, in just about the same words.

But Leopold was fond of playing the Man of Mystery. He said, "You'll see when you get here. Take down my coordinates and get a move on. I want to be back at the base by nightfall."

Shrugging, we changed course to head for Leopold's location. He was about seventeen miles southwest of us, it seemed. Marshall and Webster had an equally long trip to make; they were sharply southeast of Leopold's position.

The sky was fairly dark when we arrived at what Leopold had computed as his coordinates. The headlamps of the halftrack lit up the desert for nearly a mile, and at first there was no sign of anyone or anything. Then I spotted Leopold's halftrack parked off to the east, and from the south Gerhardt saw the lights of the third truck rolling toward us.

We reached Leopold at about the same time. He was not alone. There was an—object—with him.

"Greetings, gentlemen." He had a smug grin on his whiskery face. "I seem to have made a find."

He stepped back and, as if drawing an imaginary curtain, let us take a peek at his find. I frowned in surprise and puzzlement. Standing in the sand behind Leopold's halftrack was something that looked very much like a robot.

It was tall, seven feet or more, and vaguely humanoid; that is, it had arms extended from its shoulders, a head on those shoulders, and legs. The head was furnished with receptor plates where eyes, ears, and mouth would be on humans. There were no other openings. The robot's body was massive and squarish, with sloping shoulders, and its dark metal skin was pitted and corroded as by the workings of the elements over uncountable centuries.

It was buried up to its knees in sand. Leopold, still grinning smugly (and understandably proud of his find) said, "Say something to us, robot."

From the mouth-receptors came a clanking sound, the gnashing of—what? Gears?—and a voice came forth, oddly high-pitched but audible. The words were alien and were spoken in a slippery sing-song kind of inflection. I felt a chill go quivering down my back.

"It understands what you say?" Gerhardt questioned.

"I don't think so," Leopold said. "Not yet, anyway. But when I address it directly, it starts spouting. I think it's a kind of—well, guide to the ruins, so to speak. Built by the ancients to provide information to passersby; only it seems to have survived the ancients and their monuments as well."

I studied the thing. It *did* look incredibly old—and sturdy; it was so massively solid that it might indeed have outlasted every other vestige of civilization on this planet. It had stopped talking, now, and was simply staring ahead. Suddenly it wheeled ponderously on its base, swung an arm up to take in the landscape nearby, and started speaking again.

I could almost put the words in its mouth: "*—and over here we have the ruins of the Parthenon, chief temple of Athena on the Acropolis. Completed in the year 438* B.C., *it was partially destroyed by an explosion in 1687 while in use as a powder magazine by the Turks—*"

"It *does* seem to be a sort of a guide," Webster remarked. "I get the definite feeling that we're being given an historical narration now, all about the wondrous monuments that must have been on this site once."

"If only we could understand what it's saying!" Marshall exclaimed.

"We can try to decipher the language somehow," Leopold said. "Anyway, it's a magnificent find, isn't it? And—"

I began to laugh suddenly. Leopold, offended, glared at me and said, "May I ask what's so funny, Dr. Anderson?"

"Ozymandias!" I said, when I had subsided a bit. "It's a natural! Ozymandias!"

"I'm afraid I don't—"

"Listen to him," I said. "It's as if he was built and put here for those who follow after, to explain to us the glories of the race that built the cities. Only the cities are gone, and the robot is still here! Doesn't he seem to be saying, *'Look on my works, ye Mighty, and despair'*?"

" *'Nothing beside remains.'* " Webster quoted. "It's apt. Builders and cities all gone, but the poor robot doesn't know it, and delivers his spiel nonetheless. Yes. We ought to call him Ozymandias!"

Gerhardt said, "What shall we do with it?"

"You say you couldn't budge it?" Webster asked Leopold.

"It weighs five or six hundred pounds. It can move of its own volition, but I couldn't move it myself."

"Maybe the five of us—" Webster suggested.

"No," Leopold said. An odd smile crossed his face. "We will leave it here."

"What?"

"Only temporarily," he added. "We'll save it—as a sort of surprise for Mattern. We'll spring it on him the final day, letting him think all along that this planet was worthless. He can rib us all he wants—but when it's time to go, we'll produce our prize!"

"You think it's safe to leave it out here?" Gerhardt asked.

"Nobody's going to steal it," Marshall said.

"And it won't melt in the rain," Webster added.

"But—suppose it walks away?" Gerhardt demanded. "It can do that, can't it?"

Leopold said, "Of course. But where would it go? It will remain where it is, I think. If it moves, we can always trace it with the radar. Back to the base, now; it grows late."

We climbed back into our halftracks. The robot, silent once again, planted knee-deep in the sand, outlined against the darkening sky, swiveled to face us and lifted one thick arm in a kind of salute.

"Remember," Leopold warned us as we left. "Not one word about this to Mattern!"

At the base that night, Colonel Mattern and his seven aides were remarkably curious about our day's activities. They tried to make it seem as if they were taking a sincere interest in our work, but it was perfectly obvious to us that they were simply goading us into telling them what they had anticipated—that we had found absolutely nothing. This was the response they got, since Leopold forbade mentioning Ozymandias. Aside from the robot, the truth was that we *had* found nothing, and when they learned of this they smiled knowingly, as if saying that had we listened to them in the first place we would all be back on Earth seven days earlier, with no loss.

The following morning after breakfast Mattern announced that he was sending out a squad to look for fissionable materials, unless we objected.

"We'll only need one of the halftracks," he said. "That leaves two for you. You don't mind, do you?"

"We can get along with two," Leopold replied a little sourly. "Just so you keep out of our territory."

"Which is?"

Instead of telling him, Leopold merely said, "We've adequately examined the area to the southeast of here, and found nothing of note. It won't matter to us if your geological equipment chews the place up."

Mattern nodded, eyeing Leopold curiously as if the obvious concealment of our place of operations had aroused suspicions. I wondered whether it was wise to conceal information from Mattern. Well, Leopold wanted to play his little game, I thought; and one way to keep Mattern from seeing Ozymandias was not to tell him where we would be working.

"I thought you said this planet was useless from your viewpoint, Colonel," I remarked.

Mattern stared at me. "I'm sure of it. But it would be idiotic of me not to have a look, wouldn't it—as long as we're spending the time here anyway?"

I had to admit that he was right. "Do you expect to find anything, though?"

He shrugged. "No fissionables, certainly. It's a safe bet that everything radioactive on *this* planet has long since decomposed. But there's always the possibility of lithium, you know."

"Or pure tritium," Leopold said acidly. Mattern merely laughed, and made no reply.

Half an hour later we were bound westward again to the point where we had left Ozymandias. Gerhardt, Webster, and I rode together in one half-track, and Leopold and Marshall occupied the other. The third, with two of Mattern's men and the prospecting equipment, ventured off to the southeast toward the area Marshall and Webster had fruitlessly combed the day before.

Ozymandias was where we had left him, with the sun coming up behind him and glowing round his sides. I wondered how many sunrises he had seen. Billions, perhaps.

We parked the halftracks not far from the robot and approached, Webster filming him in the bright light of morning. A wind was whistling down from the north, kicking up eddies in the sand.

"Ozymandias have remain here," the robot said as we drew near.

In English.

For a moment we didn't realize what had happened, but what followed afterward was a five-man quadruple take. While we gabbled in confusion the robot said, "Ozymandias decipher the language somehow. Seem to be a sort of guide."

"Why—he's parroting fragments from our conversation yesterday," Marshall said.

"I don't think he's parroting," I said. "The words form coherent concepts. He's *talking* to us!"

"Built by the ancients to provide information to passersby," Ozymandias said.

"Ozymandias!" Leopold said. "Do you speak English?"

The response was a clicking noise, followed moments later by, "Ozymandias understand. Not have words enough. Talk more."

The five of us trembled with common excitement. It was apparent now what had happened, and the happening was nothing short of incredible. Ozymandias had listened patiently to everything we had said the night before; then, after we had gone, he had applied his million-year-old mind to the problem of organizing our sounds into sense, and somehow had succeeded. Now it was merely a matter of feeding vocabulary to the creature and letting him assimilate the new words. We had a walking and talking Rosetta Stone!

Two hours flew by so rapidly we hardly noticed their passing. We tossed words at Ozymandias as fast as we could, defining them when possible to aid him in relating them to the others already engraved on his mind.

By the end of that time he could hold a passable conversation with us. He ripped his legs free of the sand that had bound them for centuries—and, serving the function for which he had been built millennia ago, he took us on a guided tour of the civilization that had been and had built him.

Ozymandias was a fabulous storehouse of archaeological data. We could mine him for years.

His people, he told us, had called themselves the Thaiquens (or so it sounded)—had lived and thrived for three hundred thousand local years, and in the declining days of their history had built him, as indestructible guide to their indestructible cities. But the cities had crumbled, and Ozymandias alone remained—bearing with him memories of what had been.

"This was the city of Durab. In its day it held eight

million people. Where I stand now was the Temple of Decamon, sixteen hundred feet of your measurement high. It faced the Street of the Winds—"

"The Eleventh Dynasty was begun by the accession to the Presidium of Chonnigar IV, in the eighteen thousandth year of the city. It was in the reign of this dynasty that the neighboring planets first were reached—"

"The Library of Durab was on this spot. It boasted fourteen million volumes. None exist today. Long after the builders had gone, I spent time reading the books of the Library and they are memorized within me—"

"The Plague struck down nine thousand a day for more than a year, in that time—"

It went on and on, a cyclopean newsreel, growing in detail as Ozymandias absorbed our comments and added new words to his vocabulary. We followed the robot as he wheeled his way through the desert, our recorders gobbling in each word, our minds numbed and dazed by the magnitude of our find. In this single robot lay waiting to be tapped the totality of a culture that had lasted three hundred thousand years! We could mine Ozymandias the rest of our lives, and still not exhaust the fund of data implanted in his all-encompassing mind.

When, finally, we ripped ourselves away and, leaving Ozymandias in the desert, returned to the base, we were full to bursting. Never in the history of our science had such a find been vouchsafed: a complete record, accessible and translated for us.

We agreed to conceal our find from Mattern once again. But, like small boys newly given a toy of great value, we found it hard to hide our feelings. Although we said nothing explicit, our overexcited manner certainly must have hinted to Mattern that we had not had as fruitless a day as we had claimed.

That, and Leopold's refusal to tell him exactly where we had been working during the day, must have aroused Mattern's suspicions. In any event, during the night as we lay in bed I heard the sound of halftracks rumbling off into the desert; and the following morning, when we entered the messhall for breakfast, Mattern and his men, unshaven and untidy, turned to look at us with peculiar vindictive gleams in their eyes.

Matterns said, "Good morning, gentlemen. We've been waiting for some time for you to arise."

"It's no later than usual, is it?" Leopold asked.

"Not at all. But my men and I have been up all night. We—ah—did a bit of archaeological prospecting while you slept." The Colonel leaned forward, fingering his rumpled lapels, and said, "Dr. Leopold, for what reason did you choose to conceal from me the fact that you had discovered an object of extreme strategic importance?"

"What do you mean?" Leopold demanded—with a quiver taking the authority out of his voice.

"I mean," said Mattern quietly, "the robot you named Ozymandias. Just why did you decide not to tell me about it?"

"I had every intention of doing so before our departure," Leopold said.

Mattern shrugged. "Be that as it may. You concealed the existence of your find. But your manner last night led us to investigate the area—and since the detectors showed a metal object some twenty miles to the west, we headed that way. Ozymandias was quite surprised to learn that there were other Earthmen here."

There was a moment of crackling silence. Then Leopold said, "I'll have to ask you not to meddle with that robot, Colonel Mattern. I apologize for having neglected to tell you of it—I didn't think you were quite so interested in our work—but now I must insist you and your men keep away from it."

"Oh?" Mattern said crisply. "Why?"

"Because it's an archaeological treasure-trove, Colonel. I can't begin to stress its value to us. Your men might perform some casual experiment with it and shortcircuit its memory channels, or something like that. And so I'll have to assert the rights of the archaeological group of this expedition. I'll have to declare Ozymandias part of our preserve, and off bounds for you."

Mattern's voice suddenly hardened. "Sorry, Dr. Leopold. You can't invoke that now."

"Why not?"

"Because Ozymandias is part of *our* preserve. And off bounds for you, Doctor."

I thought Leopold would have an apoplectic fit right there in the messhall. He stiffened and went white and strode awkwardly across the room toward Mattern. He choked out a question, inaudible to me.

Mattern replied, "Security, Doctor. Ozymandias is of military use. Accordingly we've brought him to the ship and placed him in sealed quarters, under top-level wraps. With the power entrusted to me for such emergencies, I'm declaring this expedition ended. We return to Earth at once with Ozymandias."

Leopold's eyes bugged. He looked at us for support, but we said nothing. Finally, incredulously, he said, "He's—of military use?"

"Of course. He's a storehouse of data on the ancient Thaiquen weapons. We've already learned things from him that are unbelievable in their scope. Why do you think this planet is bare of life, Dr. Leopold? Not even a blade of grass? A million years won't do that. But a superweapon *will*. The Thaiquens developed that weapon. And others, too. Weapons that can make your hair curl. And Ozymandias knows every detail of them. Do you think we can waste time letting you people fool with that robot, when he's loaded with military information that can make America totally impregnable? Sorry, Doctor. Ozymandias is your find, but he belongs to us. And we're taking him back to Earth."

Again the room was silent. Leopold looked at me, at Webster, at Marshall, at Gerhardt. There was nothing that could be said.

This was basically a militaristic mission. Sure, a few archaeologists had been tacked onto the crew, but fundamentally it was Mattern's men and not Leopold's who were important. We weren't out here so much to increase the fund of general knowledge as to find new weapons and new sources of strategic materials for possible use against the Other Hemisphere.

And new weapons had been found. New, undreamed-of weapons, product of a science that had endured for three hundred thousand years. All locked up in Ozymandias' imperishable skull.

In a harsh voice Leopold said, "Very well, Colonel. I can't stop you, I suppose."

He turned and shuffled out without touching his

food, a broken, beaten, suddenly very old man.

I felt sick.

Mattern had insisted the planet was useless and that stopping here was a waste of time; Leopold had disagreed, and Leopold had turned out to be right. We had found something of great value.

We had found a machine that could spew forth new and awesome recipes for death. We held in our hands the sum and essence of the Thaiquen science —the science that had culminated in magnificent weapons, weapons so superb they had succeeded in destroying all life on this world. And now we had access to those weapons. Dead by their own hand, the Thaiquens had thoughtfully left us a heritage of death.

Gray-faced, I rose from the table and went to my cabin. I wasn't hungry now.

"We'll be blasting off in an hour," Mattern said behind me as I left. "Get your things in order."

I hardly heard him. I was thinking of the deadly cargo we carried, the robot so eager to disgorge its fund of data. I was thinking what would happen when our scientists back on Earth began learning from Ozymandias.

The works of the Thaiquens now were ours. I thought of the poet's lines: *"Look on my works, ye Mighty—and despair."*

CERTAINTY

The alien beings Colonel Devall had to deal with in "The Overlord's Thumb" were relatively primitive folk, still living in a ritual-and-taboo kind of culture, much like many that still exist on Earth. But another possibility worth exploring is that our men in the stars may encounter strangers of greater complexity, strangers with quite unearthly powers of persuasion—

Colonel Dean Wharton gripped the solido firmly between finger and thumb and stared into its glossy depths. Color began to rise slowly in his face. The solido showed a spaceship of unmistakably alien design descending, in a landing orbit, toward the surface of the uninhabited planet known in Terran charts as Bartlett V. Bartlett V was a Terran observation outpost. An alien landing on it was an infringement of Terran sovereignty. Colonel Wharton scowled.

Glaring straight into the pale, uneasy face of Lieutenant Crosley, Wharton said, "How long ago was this picture taken?"

"About an hour, sir. But you were in Deepsleep, and we didn't think—"

"No, you didn't think," Wharton said acidly. "Okay, let's have the rest of the story. You sent warnings to the ship, I hope."

Crosley nodded. "We beamed them wide-channel in Terran, General Galactic, Dormirani, Leesor, and Fawd. We sent the same message in each language: telling them that this is a Terran observation outpost, that they can't land here without prior permission, that they would have to depart at once. By this time they had completed their landing. We estimate their position at about 120 miles northeast of here, on the Creston Plateau."

"And did you get an answer?"

"A few minutes ago. It was in what Breckenridge says is a Fawdese dialect. They said, in effect, that they didn't recognize Terran sovereignty over this planet, for one thing, and for another they had come here to make certain scientific observations. They said they'd leave here in a week or two, after they've completed their observations."

"To which you made what reply?" Wharton said.

Crosley shook his head. "None, sir. I got word that you were coming out of Deepsleep, and so—"

"—and so you passed the buck to me. All right, Lieutenant. In your position I'd have done the same thing. Get me Breckenridge."

"Yes, sir."

Lieutenant Crosley performed a smart little salute and about-faced. Alone, Wharton shook his big, shaggy head sadly. This was what came of a century of unbroken Galactic peace. Youngsters like Crosley didn't even know what war meant. And a bunch of aliens thought it could put down on a Terran outpost planet without as much as a by-your-leave. Wharton sighed, feeling his age, admitting to himself that he had hoped to serve out his last few years without incident. He was getting close to the hundred-twenty-five-year mark; mandatory retirement came at age 130. And only an hour and a half of Deepsleep every day kept him going now. Well, there was going to be an incident, now, whether he liked it or not. Colonel Wharton straightened his shoulders.

Captain Breckenridge entered the room. The linguistics man was short and stocky, with choppy, irregular features and stubby red hair. "Sir?"

"Breckenridge, you say this alien ship spoke to you in Fawdese?"

"A Fawdese dialect, sir."

"That's what I'm getting after. Where is that ship from? The Fawd Confederacy knows better than to plonk a ship down on Terran property. Unless the Fawds are looking to provoke a war, that is."

Breckenridge said, "Oh, these aren't Fawds, sir. They simply speak a Fawdese dialect. Plenty of peoples in the Fawdese sector speak Fawdese without belonging to the Confederacy."

"You're stating the obvious," Wharton said irritably. "I want to know where these people are from."

"The best I can give is an educated guess."

"Well?"

"They come from the western tip of the Fawdese lingual sector. That's plain from their shifted vowels. There are three Fawdese-speaking races out that way: the Cyross, the Halivanu, and the Dortmuni." Breckenridge ticked them off on his fingers. "The

Cyross aren't a technological people. They wouldn't be sending ships this far for centuries. The Dortmuni are passive-resistance non-belligerents. *They* wouldn't be looking for trouble either. That leaves the Halivanu as the likely senders of that ship up on the plateau. You know, of course, the legends about the Halivanu—"

"Just legends. That's all they are."

"They've been documented pretty well. It's been proven that—"

"*Nothing's* been proven, Breckenridge! Hear me? Nothing has been proven about the Halivanu." Wharton rose, gripping the edges of his desk. He realized that his legs were quivering. Just to hammer the point across, he said, "I'm not interested in hearing about any strange powers the Halivanu may be thought to have. I'm interested only in getting them off this planet, and getting them off fast. Come on across to the signal room with me. I'll send these Halivanu packing right now."

There *were* all sorts of legends about the Halivanu, Wharton admitted dourly to himself as he and Breckenridge crossed the clearing and entered the outpost's communications room. Spacemen venturing into the Fawdese sector had brought back stories about mental vampires that could suck a man's mind dry, and similar gory tales. But nothing had ever been proven. The Halivanu were introverted humanoids who had little to do with the rest of the universe, keeping to themselves and seeking no outside contacts. Eerie legends always sprang up about recluses, Wharton thought. He shrugged away his uneasiness. His job was to protect the integrity of the boundaries of the Terran sphere, boundaries which these Hali-

vanu—if they *were* Halivanu—were clearly trans-
gressing.

"Set up contact with that ship," Wharton ordered.
Signalman Marshall acknowledged and began
turning dials. After a few moments he looked up and
said, "I can't get them to recognize me, sir."

"That's all right. They'll be listening, never worry.
Breckenridge, you're better at this dialect business
than I'd be. Pick up the mike and tell them that
they're trespassing on Terran ground, and that they
have exactly—ah, make it three hours—three hours
to blast off. Otherwise we'll be compelled to treat
their landing as an act of war."

Nodding, Breckenridge began to speak. Wharton
found that he could understand most of what was
being said; he knew the basic Fawd tongue, of
course, since it was one of the five great root-lan-
guages of the galaxy, and the Halivanu language dif-
fered from Fawd only in a broadening of the vowels,
minor grammatical simplifications, and inevitable
vocabulary shifts.

There was silence for a full minute after Breckenridge had finished.

"Repeat it," Wharton said.

Breckenridge recited the ultimatum a second time.
Again, the only response was silence. Nearly two
minutes ticked by; fidgeting, Wharton was on the
verge of ordering yet another repeat when the speaker sputtered and emitted, in a dry, rasping tone, the
word, "Eritomor—"

It was the Fawdese for *"Earthmen."* A moment
later came more Fawdese words, spoken slowly and
carefully. Wharton's face went steely as he listened.
The Halivanu spokesman was explaining politely

hat since the Free World of Halivanth did not recog-
ize the Terran claim to this uninhabited world,
here was no reason why the Halivanu ship should
eave. However, the Halivanu had no desire to claim
he planet for themselves, but they simply wished to
arry out certain solar observations over a period of
ome nine or ten Galactic Standard days, after which
ime they would be glad to depart.

At the conclusion of the statement, Breckenridge
aid, "They declare that they don't recognize our
laim and—"

Wharton shut him up with an impatient gesture.
"I understood the message, Lieutenant." He picked
up the microphone himself and said, in halting
Fawdese, "This is Colonel Dean Wharton speaking.
If you want to make solar observations here, you'll
 have to clear it through regular diplomatic channels.
I'm not authorized to grant any landings. And so I
have to request that you—"

He was interrupted by a voice from the speaker.
"Eritomor—vor held d'chayku kon derinilak—"

It was the same speech the Halivanu spokesman
had delivered before, repeated in the same slow, flat
tone, as though spoken to a wayward child. Annoyed, Wharton waited till the Halivanu was finished, and tried to speak again. But he got no more
than a few words out before the Halivanu reply
started for the third time.

"It's a tape," Marshall murmured. "They've got
the ends looped together and it's going to keep re-
peating indefinitely."

"Let's monitor it for a while," Wharton said.

They monitored it. After the tenth successive repetition he ordered the signalman to shut down. Noth-

ing was going to be gained through radio ul-
timatums, obviously. The Halivanu simply would
not listen. The only thing to do, clearly, was to send
an emissary over to the alien ship to explain things in
person. And if that didn't work—

Other steps would be necessary. "Sound a Red
Alert," Wharton said. "We'd better start getting this
place tightened up for battle. Just in case," he added.
"Just in case."

The thirty-seven men of the Bartlett V outpost occupied their battle stations with obvious relish. To
most of them, an alien invasion—even an invasion by
only one ship—was a pleasant diversion indeed, for
men serving a three-year hitch on an empty planet a
thousand light-years from home. The break from the
usual routine of observation and report-filing was
more than welcome.

Colonel Wharton shared none of their delight,
though. He was old enough to remember what war
was like—as a raw recruit in 2716 he had taken part
in the mop-up activities of the Terra-Dormiran conflict, just over a hundred years before. There hadn't
been war in the galaxy since. And, inasmuch as there
wasn't a man in his outfit older than ninety, none of
his men had any real idea of what a galactic war was
like. Ships splitting open in midspace like gaffed fish,
whole continents leveled in scorched-earth cam-
paigns, an entire generation of young men practically
wiped out—no, there was nothing nice about war,
from any angle. But maybe a century of peace had
caused galactic complacence. Certainly no alien ship
would have dared make a landing like this in the last
century, Wharton thought. And who could have

imagined such a reply to an ultimatum from a Terran commanding officer.

The worst part of the situation was that the responsibility was all his. The quickest subradio message to Earth would take a month to arrive; a month more would be needed for a reply. If he waited, Terra's territorial integrity could have been violated a dozen times over. So the buck ended with Colonel Wharton. If the Halivanu insisted on remaining, he could choose between blasting them off the planet and probably starting a war, or letting them stay and thereby issuing an open invitation to the entire universe to come trespass on Terran worlds. It wasn't a pretty choice. But there was no one he could go to for advice except men of his own rank on other outpost worlds, and it was senseless to do that. He would have to make his own decisions.

Breckenridge came up to him as he stood observing the conversion of the outpost to a fort. The post was amply armed, and Wharton held regular artillery drills. But he had never dreamed he would actually be ordering a Red Alert out here on this relatively nonstrategic world.

"Sir?"

"What is it, Breckenridge?"

"I'd like to volunteer for the job of going to see the Halivanu, sir. I think I'm the best fitted man for talking to them."

Wharton nodded. Breckenridge had been his choice; but the man had made matters simpler by volunteering. "Accepted, Captain. Order Smithson to break out a jetsled for you. You'll leave at once."

"Any special instructions?"

"Repeat that ultimatum to them, as a starter.

Make it clear that we're automatically bound to blast them down if they don't get off here in a couple of hours. Get the point across that we can't help ourselves, that it's our job to destroy any alien ships that make unauthorized landings, and that therefore the responsibility for starting a possible war is all theirs."

"I've got it, sir."

"Good. Don't bluster, don't threaten—just convince them that our hands are tied. Make them see the pickle we're in. Dammit, I don't *want* to shoot at them, but I will if I have to—and I'll have to if they stay here. Tell them they can make all the solar observations they want if they'll only go through the proper channels."

Breckenridge nodded. There were beads of sweat on his face. He looked troubled.

Wharton said, "You don't *have* to volunteer for this, Captain. There are other men I could send if—"

"It's my job. I'm not withdrawing."

"You're worried about those crazy stories you've heard, Breckenridge. I can almost read your mind."

"The stories are—nothing but stories, sir," Breckenridge said stolidly. "Just so much jetwash. May I leave now, sir."

Wharton smiled. "You're a good man, Breckenridge. Dismissed."

By jetsled it would take more than an hour for Breckenridge to reach the alien spaceship; allow him half an hour for parleying, Wharton thought, and an hour or so to return. Make it three hours round trip. So if Breckenridge were successful, the Halivanu ship would be blasting off about the same time that

Breckenridge returned to base. *If*, Wharton thought. He stood for nearly half an hour in front of the radar screen, staring at the white blip that represented the Halivanu ship a hundred twenty miles away, and at the tiny white bug racing northeast across the screen that was the reflected image of Breckenridge's sled.

Then he walked away and tried to busy himself in routine activities. But his mind kept going back to the Halivanu incident. He felt very tired. There was nothing he wanted to do more than crawl into the Deepsleep tank and let the cool therapeutic fluids wash over him.

Wharton reminded himself forcibly that he had already taken his Deepsleep time for the day. He rationed it strictly, one session and no more per diem. Which meant he'd have to stay on his pins unaided.

The afternoon shadows lengthened. Bartlett V was a moonless world, and night fell fast. The little sun was dipping rapidly toward the horizon, casting an orange light over the empty, barren plains. The radar screen showed that Breckenridge was now on his way back.

He returned four hours after he had departed. The screen still showed the Halivanu ship on the plateau. The linguist reported immediately to Colonel Wharton.

"Well?"

Breckenridge smiled wanly. "It's all arranged, sir. They'll be leaving next week, as soon as they've completed their observations."

Wharton sat down abruptly. "What did you say?"

"I agreed to let them stay, sir."

Wharton felt as though he'd been tomahawked. In a rigidly controlled voice he said, "You agreed to let them stay, Breckenridge? How polite of you! But I thought I sent you there to deliver an ultimatum—not to make agreements."

"Of course, sir. But I discussed it with them and we agreed it would be unreasonable to drive them away before they had finished their observations. They clearly don't mean any harm. They're not even carrying armaments, sir."

"Breckenridge, are you out of your head?" Wharton asked, aghast.

"Sir?"

"How can you stand there and talk such drivel to me? Your opinion of their harmlessness is irrelevant, and you know it. You were sent bearing an ultimatum, that is all. I wanted their reply."

"But we talked it over, sir. It can't hurt us to make a little concession like this."

"Breckenridge, did those aliens drug you? You're talking like a madman. What right did you have—"

"You said yourself that you would rather give in and let them stay than start a war, sir. And since they insisted on staying, I followed your instructions and told them it would be okay, provided they left when—"

"Followed *my* instructions?" Wharton roared. His hand drummed menacingly on the desktop. "When did you ever hear me say such a thing?"

"Why, just before I left," Breckenridge said innocently.

"Now I *know* you're out of your head. I never said a word about granting concessions to them. I told you to let them know that if they weren't off this planet by my deadline I'd be compelled to destroy them. Not a syllable about concessions. And—"

"I beg to contradict you, sir, but—"

Sighing, Wharton rang for his orderly. A moment later the man stuck his head in the door. Wharton said, "Rogers, take Captain Breckenridge to the infirmary and have him detained for a psychiatric examination. And send Smithson to me."

Smithson entered a few minutes afterward. The enlisted man stood diffidently near the door.

Wharton said, "Tell me exactly what transpired between Captain Breckenridge and the aliens."

Smithson shook his head. "Sorry, but I can't, Colonel. I didn't go into the alien ship. Captain Breckenridge wanted me to wait outside in the sled."

Keeping his voice tight, Wharton said, "Oh. In that case you can't help me, Smithson. Dismissed."

"Yes, sir."

Wharton waited until the door closed and put his head in his hands. His shoulders slumped wearily.

He hadn't given Breckenridge any instructions to parley. Yet the linguist swore up and down that he had. What would make a solid man like Breckenridge snap like that?

Wharton shook his head. They told stories about the Halivanu, vague stories of vaguer mental powers. But that stuff was—Breckenridge himself had put a name to it—jetwash. Wharton was certain of it. In his time he had seen too many legends fade like the dreams they were to be taken in by anything new. Imaginative spacemen *always* attributed mystical powers to little-known races, but such attributions had to be discounted pretty near to one hundred per cent.

Drawing in his breath sharply, Wharton jabbed down on his call-button. The orderly appeared.

"Send me Lieutenant Crosley, quick-quick."

Crosley arrived five minutes later. It was nearly night now. The Lieutenant looked even more pale, less relaxed than ever. He was a recent Academy product, not much past thirty.

Leaning forward, Wharton said, "We've got some complications, Lieutenant. Incidentally, I'm making a tape recording of this conversation."

Crosley nodded. "Complications, sir?"

"I sent Breckenridge to the aliens with an ultimatum this afternoon. I wanted him to tell them they had three hours to get off the planet, or I'd open fire. But instead he granted them permission to stay here until they finished their observations, and now he claims he said so on my authority."

"I wondered why he was taken to psych ward."

"Now you know. I don't pretend to understand why he cracked up, Crosley, but I *do* know we've got to send another man to the Halivanu right away, withdrawing Breckenridge's permission and telling them to get moving."

"Of course, sir."

"I'd like you to go, Crosley. Right now. Take one of the enlisted men with you, and make sure you both go into the Halivanu ship. Tell them that the previous messenger was unauthorized, that you're the authorized messenger, that if they don't blast off by sunrise we'll be forced to let them have it."

Crosley looked a little paler, but he remained steady. "I'll leave right away, sir."

"Before you go: repeat the message you're bearing."

Crosley repeated it.

"You won't attempt to negotiate with them, Lieutenant. Is that clear?"

"Yes, sir."

"You'll deliver the ultimatum and leave. It isn't essential that you wait around for an answer. If they're still here by morning, we'll blast them."

"Yes, sir."

"You understand what I'm saying, now? You won't tell me later that I authorized you to negotiate?"

Crosley smiled. "Of course not, sir."

"Get going, then."

The hours passed. Taps sounded, but Wharton remained awake, pacing his office uneasily. Starlight, bright in the moonless dark, filtered through his windows. Wharton clenched his fists and stared out into the night.

He pitied Breckenridge. It was a hellish thing to lose your grip on actuality. To maintain that something is true when it's flatly false. The psych tests had shown nothing; Breckenridge firmly and positively believed that he had been instructed to parley. Schizophrenia, the psych officer said. But schizophrenia wasn't something a person got suddenly, like a twisted ankle, was it? It was a slowly building pattern of action and belief. And Breckenridge had always seemed one of the most stable men of all.

Inescapably Wharton came to the conclusion that the Halivanu had done something to him. But Breckenridge said they hadn't, and the EEG tests revealed no hint of recent drugging or hypnosis. Not that the EEG was necessarily infallible—

Wharton glowered at his faint reflection in the window. He was *certain* the Halivanu had no mysterious powers. They were just another isolationist race, bent on their own destinies and aloof from the rest of the universe. That was no reason for crediting them with magical abilities.

A light glimmered outside. Wharton heard the roar of the jetsled. Crosley was returning.

Impatiently, Wharton dashed outside. The night air was clear, cold, tangy. Crosley and his driver, an enlisted man named Rodriguez, were getting out of the sled.

They saluted when they saw him. Returning the salute with a shaky arm, Wharton said, "Did you run into any trouble?"

"No, sir. But we didn't find him, either," Crosley replied. "We searched for hours, but—"

"What in the name of the cosmos are you babbling about?" Wharton demanded in a choked voice. "You didn't find *whom?*"

"Why, Breckenridge, of course," Crosley said. He exchanged a puzzled glance with Rodriguez. "We traveled in wide circles just as you said, until—"

Wharton felt dizzy. "What's this about looking for Breckenridge?"

"Didn't you send us out to look for him? He got lost in the plains coming back from his trip to the alien ship, and we were ordered to look for him. Sir? Sir, are you feeling all right?"

Cold fingers seemed to be encircling Wharton's heart. "Come inside with me, Lieutenant. You too, Rodriguez."

He led them into his office and played for them the tape he had made of his conversation with Crosley earlier. The two men listened in growing confusion.

When the tape had run its course, Wharton said,

"Do you still maintain that I sent you out to look for Breckenridge?"

"But—yes—"

"Breckenridge is asleep in the infirmary. He was never lost. He came back hours ago. I sent you out to deliver an ultimatum. Didn't you recognize your own voice, Crosley?"

"It sounded like me, yes. But—I don't remember —that is—"

Further questioning led down the same dead end. The tape transcript only bewildered Crosley. He grew paler and paler. He was certain they had merely traveled in wide circles looking for Breckenridge, and Rodriguez backed him up on that. Even when Wharton assured him that he had watched their path on the radar, and they had gone direct to the Halivanu ship and returned straightaway, they shook their heads.

"We never went near that ship, sir. Our orders—"

"All right, Lieutenant. Go to bed. You too, Rodriguez. Maybe in the morning you'll have better memories."

Wharton could not sleep. First Breckenridge, then Crosley and Rodriguez, all of them coming back from the Halivanu ship with insane stories. The first cracks began to appear in Wharton's self-confidence. Maybe there *was* something in those spacehounds' tales of the Halivanu.

No. Beyond belief.

But how else to explain what had happened to his men? Schizophrenia wasn't contagious, was it? It was hard to swallow the fact that three men had gone

out to the aliens and three men had returned . . .
changed. That was the only word for it. And changed
retroactively. Crosley even denied the validity of the
tape he had made.

By morning, Wharton knew what his only choice
was. He was no longer concerned with protecting
Terra's sovereignty. That was important, but not as
important as finding out just what kind of hocus-
pocus the Halivanu had pulled on his men. And the
only way to find out was to go to the aliens himself.
He couldn't keep sending out men. Soon he would
run out of officers that way.

Besides, they were only green kids at best. It took
a *man*—a veteran of the Dormiran campaign—to go
in there and find out the real story.

But, of course, certain necessary precautions ought
to be taken—just in case.

When morning came he sent for Captain Lowell,
one of the senior officers—*the* senior officer, with both
Breckenridge and Crosley on the unreliable list.
"Lowell, I'm going to make a trip to the Halivanu
ship myself. You're in charge of the base till I get
back. And—listen carefully—I'm going to give the
Halivanu four hours to get off this planet. At the end
of four hours' time I want you to blast them with the
heavy-cycle guns, even if I order you not to do it. Got
that? Go against my direct order, if you have to. But
blast them when the time is up."

Lowell looked utterly befuddled. "Sir, I don't understand—"

"Don't try to understand. Just listen. I've made a
tape of this conversation. Keep it safe and play it for
me when I get back."

Leaving behind a sorely confused Lowell,

Wharton made his way out to the jetsled. Smithson, who had piloted Breckenridge, was again at the controls.

They traveled in silence, the jets boosting the sled quickly and smoothly over the flat plains. The sun rose higher as they traveled. Wharton found himself yearning for the comfort of Deepsleep. But that would have to wait a few more hours, he thought. The matter would be settled, one way or another, in a few hours. If only Lowell would have the guts to disobey him, in case he came back *changed*. Wharton smiled. He was confident he'd return in full command of his senses.

It was midmorning when the sled reached the plateau where the Halivanu had established camp. Wharton saw tents surrounding the sleek alien-looking spaceship, and half a dozen Halivanu were busily setting up instrumentation. They were tall, thin beings with coarse-grained, glossy gray-green skin. As the sled pulled up, one of them detached himself from the group and came toward Wharton.

"You Earthmen must enjoy paying us visits," the alien said in the Fawdese dialect. "By my count, you're the third."

"And the last," Wharton said. Despite himself, he felt an uneasy chill. The Halivanu had a strange, sickly-sweet odor. Wharton faced him, looking up; the creature was nearly seven feet tall.

"What is your message?" the Halivanu asked, and in the same instant Wharton felt something like a feather brushing the back of his skull.

"I—*what are you doing?*" He put his hand to the back of his head—but the feather still tickled him—

And then his panic died away.

"Well?" the alien demanded.

Wharton smiled. "I'm the Terran commander. I've come to—to tell you that it's all right—that you can stay here until you're through."

"Thank you," said the Halivanu gravely. He smiled, revealing black gums, and Wharton returned the smile. "Is that all?"

"Yes. Yes, that's all," Wharton said. He looked at Smithson. "We didn't have anything else to say, did we, Smithson?"

Smithson shrugged. "I don't think so, sir."

"Good. We might as well go back, then."

Lowell greeted him as the jetsled rumbled into the center of the compound. "Did it all go well, sir?"

"Fine," Wharton said. "Have Bailey rig up the Deepsleep tank for me, eh? Lord, I can use some rest —haven't felt this tired in days."

"The Halivanu are leaving, then?"

"Leaving?" Wharton frowned. "Why should they be leaving? They've only begun their work."

"But—Colonel—"

"Yes, what is it?" Wharton snapped testily.

"You left an order—you said that at the end of four hours we should open fire on the Halivanu if they were still here."

Wharton frowned and started to walk on. "Must have been a mistake, Lowell. Order countermanded. *Bailey!* Bailey, get the tank ready!"

Lowell ducked around and put himself in front of the Colonel. "I'm sorry, sir. You told me to proceed on schedule even against your direct order."

"Nonsense!"

"There's a tape recording in your office—"

"I don't care. The Halivanu have permission to stay here. Let's have no talk of going against my direct orders, shall we?"

Mottled blotches appeared on Lowell's jowly face. 'Colonel, I know this sounds strange, but you yourself insisted—"

"And I myself countermand the order! Do I have to make it any clearer, Captain? Please get out of my way. I say 'please' because you're an officer, but—"

Lowell stood his ground. Sweat rolled down his forehead. "The tape—"

"Will you give ground, Lowell?"

"No, sir. You definitely specified that I should not listen to any subsequent order countermanding your original one. And therefore—"

"Any commanding officer who gives a non-retractable order has to be out of his head," Wharton snapped. He signaled to two of the men nearby. "Place Captain Lowell in restrictive custody. I may be easygoing, but I won't tolerate insubordination."

Lowell, still protesting, was borne away. Wharton went on into his office. A tape was in the recorder. With a thoughtful frown he nudged the *playback* knob and listened.

"*. . . I'm going to give the Halivanu four hours to get off this planet. At the end of four hours' time I want you to blast them with the heavy-cycle guns, even if I order you not to do it. Got that? Go against my direct order. . . .*"

Wharton's shaggy eyebrows lifted questioningly. Beyond a doubt it was his own voice. But why should he have said such a thing? The Halivanu had every right to be here. Why, right here on his desk was the authorization from Terra, allowing them to stop here for a while and make solar observations. The paper was right here—he fumbled through a pile of documents without coming across it. He shrugged. It had probably been misfiled. But he knew it was here, somewhere. He had seen it with his own eyes, after all.

What about the tape, then? Colonel Wharton shook his head and decided he must be getting old, to have ever given Lowell weird orders like that. Somewhere deep in his mind a silent voice was lifted in inner protest, but the complaint, wordless, never reached conscious levels. Yawning wearily, Wharton flipped the *erase* knob on the tape recorder, waited until the message was completely obliterated, and ambled over to the infirmary for his ninety minutes of Deepsleep.

MIND FOR BUSINESS

Espionage and counter-espionage will probably remain with us, even into the era when Earthmen flit from solar system to solar system with blithe abandon. With a galaxy full of intelligent races, it's likely that the complex schemes of some future spy agencies will coil and tangle and become hopelessly snarled. Far across the universe, some Earthborn secret agent may be faced with a somber problem: how do you tell a genuine rescue party from an alien counterfeit?

Once it was clear to both of them that the little ship was permanently disabled, Connelly turned to the alien and grinned in open appreciation. "Very clever, you Nidlans. This is the neatest trap I've seen yet."

He stared at the screen, looking out at the bleak, wind-swept surface of the small, lonely planet, and then glanced back at the Nidlan. The alien was slouched comfortably in the far corner of the small cruiser, beaming with an inward glow of self-assurance.

"My people don't like it when Earthmen kidnap Chiefs of Staff," the Nidlan said. "They take steps."

Connelly nodded. "Very respectable steps, too. I was so busy hurrying away from Nidla with you that I let the trap take me. It must be a gigantic force field, set to draw in any ship that comes by without taking the right precautions. Eh?" He cocked an eye at the Nidlan. "What do you think, Lomor?"

"I have no opinion on the matter," the other said, shrugging. "All that concerns me is the fact that you've abducted me from my home world, and that I'll shortly be rescued." The Nidlan got up and crossed the cabin of the ship to the viewscreen, walking unsteadily. The ship had ploughed into the mountainside at about a forty-five-degree angle, and the gyros had unaccountably stabilized things some ten degrees out of true, which made motion difficult. The alien peered pensively out at the unappetizing view.

"Nice," Connelly said.

"Very nice," said the alien smugly. "Your little experiment in espionage didn't seem to work very well, did it, Connelly?"

"Guess not," the Earthman replied laconically. "We're stuck here—both of us—half a light-year from the Nidla system."

"Yes," said the Nidlan. "My people will be here as soon as they discover the trap's been sprung. We've anticipated attempts by Earthmen to penetrate our defenses, and we've studded the local area with these ... ah ... mousetraps. It's a fine counter-espionage system."

"Oh, yes," Connelly agreed. "A very fine system." He moved to the control board and started to press buttons. The Nidlan peered close, trying, without success, to read the unfamiliar Terran designations on the controls.

"What are you doing?" he asked finally.

"Shifting the guns around so they face front," Connelly explained. "By the time I get through, this place is going to be a fortress. With those rocks behind us and that plain out in front, you're not going to be as easy to rescue as you've been thinking, Lomor." He glanced meaningfully at the alien, who frowned.

"You Earthmen," Lomor said in annoyance. "Always making things so difficult."

Connelly smiled quietly to himself and went right on punching keys. Through the viewscreen the Nidlan saw the small but effective guns of the little cruiser rapidly lowering into the positions Connelly had set up.

The ship was backed up against a wall of stone, and armed to the teeth. The Nidlan shook his head petulantly. The Earthmen always seemed to have a trick or two left in the bag, at all times. That was how Connelly had been able to descend on Nidla in a one-man ship and blithely carry off so important a personage in the Nidlan military hierarchy as Lomor dal Govnim, and that was how Connelly had escaped from the Nidlan system so easily.

Now, true enough, Connelly was trapped—had been snared, through blind luck, by a cosmic mousetrap laid by Nidla. The traps could be avoided, as Lomor knew quite well. Only a blunder had gotten Connelly trapped, and it was refreshing to know that the Earthmen *could* blunder.

But they had an ugly way of turning their biggest blunders into their most impressive triumphs. That was the trouble with them.

"Finished?" Lomor asked.

Connelly nodded. "I think so. When your rescuers

come to fetch you, they'll have a fine fight on their hands." He ran a hand along the back of his neck. "How long did you say it would be before they'll notice the trap's been sprung?"

"Not very long," said Lomor coldly. The Nidlan was tense and abrupt; Connelly's bland confidence at all times—the very factor that had led Lomor to fall for him in the first place—was now almost unbearably annoying. Connelly had a terrifying air of serenity that made Lomor wonder whether letting the snare take him *had* been a blunder for the Earthman, or whether perhaps this was all a deliberate maneuver, part of some unknown larger plan.

"You think we've got a couple of days?" Connelly asked.

"I don't know," said Lomor.

Connelly grinned. "You're just not telling. But I don't mind. It's natural enough." He turned to the subradio and rapidly started setting up coordinates. After a moment or two, the machine began to glow and hum.

"Now what are you doing?" Lomor asked.

"I'm going to get us taken off this forsaken place," Connelly said. "By the *right* people."

The red light above the set indicated that the subradio was functioning. Connelly glanced up quickly to check it, grinned infuriatingly at the Nidlan, and cleared his throat.

Then he proceeded to dictate an S.O.S. on the widest beam that was open. He beamed to the whole universe the naked fact that he, Paul Connelly, Earthman, had been caught in a Nidlan trap on some uninhabited planet, that his ship had crashed and was useless, and that he was awaiting rescue.

He went on to add a detailed set of instructions for landing and blasting off from the planet without getting ensnared in the Nidlan trap.

Connelly repeated the message twice, then cut off the machine. He whirled on the swivel chair and met Lomor's horrified glare with a calm smile.

"How do you know how the trap operates?" Lomor demanded.

"You've just blundered, friend," Connelly told him coolly. "I might have been only bluffing with those instructions, and now you'd have confirmed my guess about the trap. Except," he added, seeing the color rise on the Nidlan's face, "that I *did* know how your trap works. After all, I fell into it."

"Why? Deliberately?"

Connelly shrugged his shoulders. "Oh, no—not at all. But let's assume it was a blunder on my part. If it was, at least I've profited by my blunder to the extent of knowing how I got caught. Let's see you do likewise."

The Nidlan shook his head angrily, and repressed a biting comment. It didn't do any good to insult the Terrans; they just grinned.

"That S.O.S.," Lomor said, "did it go on wide-beam?"

"The widest there was," said Connelly. "*Someone's* bound to pick it up."

Someone did.

The Nidlans, being closest, caught it first. The message reached the office of Drilom dal Kroosh, Lomor's first assistant—and, in Lomor's unfortunate absence, the acting head of the office—just about the same time that the news of the trap-springing did.

Drilom looked up at the young officer who had brought him both dispatches.

"They both just came in, eh?"

"Both of them," the subaltern said. "One right after the other."

Drilom chewed a worn pencil-stub. "Hm-m-m. This Earthman Connelly is proving to be an intolerable nuisance. First he was crude enough to kidnap the Chief of Staff from under our noses, for who knows what purposes of his own, and now that we've caught him he's been so crass as to send out a widebeam S.O.S. The whole galaxy will know about the Earth-Nilda friction at this rate."

"Yes, sir," the underling said.

Drilom glared at him. "Don't agree with me!"

"No, sir," said the subaltern helplessly.

Drilom ignored him. He stared down at the two dispatches for a long moment, toying with the gold braid on his uniform sleeves, while he groped for the snap decision his military culture required of him. Finally he looked up and snapped, "Get me Konno dal Progva."

"At once, sir."

Drilom's second-in-command arrived a moment later. Drilom hastily filled him in on the happenings.

"I see," Konno said sagely, when Drilom was through. Konno was a wiry, shriveled-up Nidlan with a much-respected talent for strategy. "The Earthman is holed up on our trap planet—presumably with Lomor in his custody."

"Right."

"And presumably, also, a ship from Earth has picked up the S.O.S. and is heading for the planet, there to rescue Connelly and gaily carry Lomor back to Earth—where they'll pick his brains thoroughly."

Drilom nodded grimly. "That's the picture," he said.

Konno wrinkled his sharp nose into a grimace of concentration. "If we send a Nidlan military expedition there to grab Connelly, we're liable to arrive at the same time the Earthmen do—which will touch off a quarrel and possibly catapult us into conflict with Earth before the schedule allows."

Sweat was pouring freely down Drilom's face. "I'm desperate, Konno. What am I supposed to do? If I pass the buck upstairs, it'll look bad for me, and—"

The other held up a hand. "Peace, Drilom. Look—suppose we send a decoy."

"Decoy?"

"Sure. Suppose we send a ship of Earth design—say, one of those small Terran merchant ships we trapped last month—manned by a crew of young men hand-picked for Terran appearance. Those Terran ships all look alike anyway." His beady eyes gleamed brightly. "Suppose we were to do that—pass ourselves off as merchantmen. If we got there before the Earth rescue party did, and if we could persuade Connelly that we were the true rescuers—"

Drilom dal Kroosh stared around the cabin of the stolen Earthship, transfixing first one, then another of his crew with angry, expressive glances. He hadn't expected, when he had broached the plan to his superiors, to be ordered to head the bogus rescue party himself.

But there hadn't been any way out of it, and so he had collected his crew—all strapping six-foot Nidlans, carefully chosen for the degree they approached the theoretical Terran norm of appearance —and had taken off for the little planet. He'd set up the nullifier patterns as instructed—the Earthman, he admitted wryly, had hit on exactly the proper method of circumventing the trap and had explained it accurately enough in his S.O.S., for all to hear— and had landed.

The ship was now standing in the sandy plain that faced the vaulting pile of rocks amid which Connelly's ship had crashed. Drilom, staring into the screen, thought he could make out the dim, coppery gleam of the distant Terran ship, but he wasn't sure.

He turned to the chief radioman, a spare-limbed Nidlan named Pribor. "Make contact with Connelly," he ordered brusquely, and resumed his nervous pacing up and down the cabin.

While Pribor fiddled with the dials on the Earth-built radio, struggling manfully with the unfamiliar controls, Drilom turned to Huompor dal Vornik, the tall Nidlan standing at his side.

"I'm going to be down below watching from the monitor screen. If that Earthman ever got sight of me, he'd know the game in a minute. It's all in your hands now. And be careful; you know how important it is."

Huompor saluted smartly. "Yes, sir."

"Remember," Drilom said anxiously, "you're an Earthman. The reason you got here so fast is you're the captain of a merchant vessel that plies the neutral area. Say as little else as you can—and make it quick. Once we get Connelly and Lomor aboard we can drop the masquerade and head back to Nidla. Set?"

"Set, sir," Huompor replied.

"Ready to go, sir," called the radioman.

Drilom ducked down the hatch after scowling one last time at Huompor. He made his way to the monitor-screen on the lower level, and watched the whole thing from there.

He saw Connelly's face appear on the upstairs screen. The Earthman was young and mild-looking, with a lazy way about him of blinking his eyes that irritated Drilom considerably. Connelly didn't look clever enough to have caused all the difficulties he had. Drilom hoped he'd be unwary enough to fall for the Nidlan ruse. If Connelly somehow got back to Earth with Lomor, the consequences would be most unpleasant for Nidla's territorial ambitions.

Upstairs, Huompor dal Vornik stepped into the field of the screen and gave the standard Earthman salute.

"Lieutenant Connelly?"

"That's me," the Earthman agreed amiably.

"The name is Smith," Huompor said. "Captain of a merchantman in the vicinity."

"Oh?"

"We've intercepted your S.O.S.—we were in the neutral area on a trade run. Now, about this rescue," Huompor said, a little too eagerly.

"You're going to rescue me?" Connelly asked.

"Why else would we undertake this maneuver? Now—the most efficient way to carry it out would be for you to abandon your ship and be picked up at—"

Connelly raised one hand. "Skip the rest, friend. It doesn't appeal to me." The screen abruptly went blank.

And a moment later, a golden blast of energy from Connelly's starboard guns raked across Drilom's bow, missing the ship by a comfortable margin but making things so hot inside that the cooling system overloaded and nearly short-circuited.

"Definitely hostile," Drilom said morosely. His ship was now at a safer distance from Connelly's, and he was contemplating the situation with gloomy detachment.

"What could that shot have meant?" Huompor asked. "Perhaps it was some sign of friendship among Earthmen."

Drilom nearly choked. "That shot could mean only one thing, even among Earthmen, young man: *Get away, and stay away*. I don't know what you did wrong, but he saw right through your act. Two sentences out of your mouth and he knew you were a fake."

"I don't see how," said Huompor. "It was one of my best impersonations," he said wistfully.

"Doesn't matter," Drilom said. "Connelly didn't fall for it. And Lomor's still in there."

One of the other crew members appeared at that moment, saluted, and said, "Sir, another ship's just arrived!"

"Where?"

"It's approximately four hundred meters closer to Connelly than we are. We picked it up on the radar screen about ten minutes ago. It went through the same nullifier pattern we did, and it seems to be the identical model that we're using."

Drilom frowned, unamused by the irony of the situation. "Identical? That means it must be the *real*

Earth rescue ship!" He held his head. "Now we're in for it, if they find out what we're doing here. I hope this doesn't touch off the war ahead of time!"

"What do you suggest we do, sir?" Huompor asked.

"Just sit tight," said Drilom desperately. "Sit tight, and don't do anything. Come. Let's see what happens."

He walked to the nearest screen, and with trembling fingers brought it into focus.

The small, worthless sun that lit the nameless trap planet had long since set, but by the flickering green light of the planet's one moon Drilom could see the other ship. It was, indeed, identical—the very same model light cruiser that the Nidlans had used. It was planted on end at the edge of the desert.

Drilom called down to his radio operator, "Tune in and find out if they're saying anything!"

A moment later, the signalman shouted in return, "They're a Terran merchant vessel! It's the real rescue party, all right!"

Drilom watched silently. He was waiting to see the figures of Connelly and Lomor leave the niche in the mountains and go to the Earth ship, and he wondered idly if there was any way of intercepting the pair as they crossed the desert. A minute passed, and suddenly the misty, moonlit plain was illuminated by a crimson flash of brightness.

"I'll be cursed," Drilom said in quiet wonderment. "He fired on them, too."

All kinds of possibilities presented themselves now —the possibility that Connelly was insane, the possibility that Lomor had somehow gained control of the damaged ship, the possibility, always to be considered, that Connelly and the Terran ship were playing out some elaborate ruse for Drilom's benefit.

In the midst of his feverish speculations, Pribor broke in. Drilom looked up sourly at his signalman.

"Well, what is it?"

"We've just had a call from the Terran ship, sir. Their commander would like to meet with you. He suggests that you and four of your men go outside, and he'll do the same; you can meet halfway between the two ships."

Drilom's forehead wrinkled as he considered the proposition. Earthmen were, by axiom, not to be trusted—but yet, the proposal seemed to be made in good faith. Perhaps, he thought, the Earthmen were so bewildered by Connelly's reaction that they were genuinely at a loss, and wanted to talk the thing over with someone. Perhaps they thought Drilom's ship was from Earth; perhaps they knew the truth, and Drilom stood a chance of effecting a valuable compromise that would push him up a notch or two in the Nidlan hierarchy.

There was no way of telling. But it seemed safe to give it a try. "Tell him I accept," he said.

Later in the evening, Drilom and a small party suited up and made their way across the desert to the prearranged spot. They were armed to the teeth, with natural precaution.

The other delegation was there already. Drilom saw men much like himself, though they seemed to be bigger by a little, and behind them loomed a ship identical to his own.

The other commander was a deep-voiced man who introduced himself as Ledrash. Drilom could see nothing of him except dimly glimpsed craggy features within the helmet.

"He fired on you," Drilom said. "That's what he did to us. I can't understand it at all."

"Neither can we," said Ledrash. "Here we came all the way off our trade run to get him off this lump of rock, and look at the way he greets us! Where are you from?" Ledrash asked.

"Earth," Drilom lied.

"We're both from Earth, then," Ledrash said. The two commanders stared stonily at each other. Drilom began to suspect something. Connelly had fired on the second ship as well as his own. Could it be that Ledrash and his men were non-Earthmen too, carrying on the same sort of game for motives of their own? It was an idea, he admitted.

"It doesn't seem likely that Central would approve two rescue missions," Drilom ventured. "It seems to be a waste of crew time to send two ships to do a job that calls for one."

"I was just thinking along the same lines," Ledrash said ominously. "It's improbable that we're both from Earth."

"We came in good faith," Drilom said.

"So did we," said Ledrash. He crossed his thick-muscled arms, and Drilom caught the shadow of a somber smile behind his helmet. "One of us is lying."

Drilom looked uneasily at Ledrash's four men, and back at his own. It was an explosive situation, and he was navigating blindly, on sheer bluff. "If you're really Earthmen—" Drilom started to say, and then was interrupted. A member of Ledrash's crew who had been staring fixedly back of Drilom toward the mountains suddenly pointed up.

"Another ship, sir!" he shouted.

Ledrash whirled. "Where?"

The crewman gestured ineffectually. "There . . . there . . . just like ours," he said, struggling for words in his excitement. Finally he voiced what he was trying to say. "On the other side of the mountains—blasting off!"

Ledrash ran a few yards away for a better view, with Drilom right behind. The two commanders stared out blankly at the mountains, with the long, gradually dying scarlet trail of light hanging above the jagged peaks. A third ship had been there—and had left.

Ledrash turned slowly. "Get back to the ship and tell Dorni to try Connelly on the radio," he said. "On the double."

The signalman trotted off toward Ledrash's ship, while the little group remained frozen in the desert, waiting. A few minutes later the crewman returned. "There's no answer, sir. His radio's silent."

Ledrash sat down heavily on a wind-sculptured rock. "No answer?"

"No, sir."

Drilom moistened his dry lips. "He got away."

Ledrash nodded curtly. "Suppose we go over to my ship and talk this over," he suggested.

Drilom started to suggest his own ship as a preferable alternative, and stopped. There was nothing to fear from Ledrash. Drilom felt a curious feeling of camaraderie toward the other commander starting to grow within him. He had been flummoxed, all right —but so had Ledrash, and it made Drilom feel better to know he had company. The truth was clear, now: Ledrash was no more of an Earthman than he was.

And while they held each other at arm's distance, the real Earthmen had come and gone.

They climbed the catwalk in silence and entered Ledrash's ship. It was, Drilom noted, the same model precisely as his own. They got out of their suits.

The other men, Drilom observed, were humanoids, and could pass for Earthmen or Nidlans easily. They were big, heavy-boned, dark-skinned.

Ledrash ran a hand through his hair. "We've been had," he said hoarsely. He smiled feebly at Drilom. "We've been taken—both of us."

"Let's check, first," Drilom insisted.

"How?"

"By going over to Connelly's ship," said Drilom.

Ledrash scowled, and finally pointed to two of his men. "Suit up, both of you. Take two of these"—indicating Drilom's men—"and get over there for a look-see."

Drilom nodded at two of his men. "Go with them," he ordered. "And make it fast."

An anxious few minutes passed, while the four crewmen jogged across the desert. Drilom lost sight of them as they entered the shadowy foothills of the mountains, and began to pick their way through the rocks to Connelly's ship.

Time passed, and the tension started to pull tight. Finally, after what seemed like hours, the men returned.

"Well?" Drilom demanded, knowing the answer. "Anything there?"

"Not a soul," said one of the men. "They left the air lock open. The ship's deserted."

"He got away, all right," said Ledrash.

"*Both* of them did," Drilom corrected.

"Both? I thought it was just the one Earthman."

"No," Drilom said. "Connelly had an influential Nidlan aboard as his prisoner."

"Oh." They grinned sheepishly at each other, each aware that he had made a blunder. Finally Drilom said, "You're not an Earthman, are you?"

Ledrash shook his head. "No use keeping up the pretense when the truth is obvious to both of us. I'm from Corilan. And I'll bet you're a Nidlan."

Drilom nodded. The two of them sat there in the Corilano ship, contemplating each other. It made sense, now. Corilan was a powerful planet located almost centrally between Earth and Nidla. Nidlan espionage had been aware for some time that the Corilani had formulated a series of actions which might conceivably rebound to the greater profit of Corilan, in the event of disagreements between the other two major powers of the galaxy.

So they had picked up Connelly's S.O.S., and the same plan had occurred to them as to the Nidlans. Fool Connelly, and spirit him off. Only it hadn't worked.

And his S.O.S. had also been picked up by real Earthmen.

"How come you came out here?" Drilom asked.

"We wanted the Earthman," said Ledrash. "And you?"

"The same."

"I won't probe any further," Ledrash said. "The situation's delicate enough as it is."

Drilom smiled at the big, square-hewn Corilano. "I'll say. When that Earthman gets back to his sys-

tem with Lomor—with our Chief of Staff, that is—we
won't have a military secret left worth hiding."

"How sad," the Corilano said. "How very sad for
Nidla." He stood up and walked across the cabin.
"We are aware that you plan a conflict with Earth.
This will make it hard for you."

"Don't speak of it," Drilom said. "Let's keep *some*
secrets from each other, shall we? Our planets are
theoretically rivals, you know."

"What does that matter to us?" said Ledrash. He
turned and faced the Nidlan squarely. "We are both
human beings," he said with obvious feeling. "We
have something in common that binds us together—
we have both been badly fooled by the Earthmen."

"True enough," Drilom said. He smiled and extended a hand. "Comrades in adversity," he said.

They fell silent for a while, as the sun began to rise.
It was an unimpressive sunrise; the star that lit the
trap planet was scrawny and definitely third-rate,
and it cast a sickly, yellowish morning glow. Drilom
suddenly realized that he had been up all night, and
that he was terribly tired.

"Let's go back to my ship for a while," Drilom
suggested.

The Corilano commander nodded. "Good idea."

They covered the sands in silence for a while, and
then Drilom said, "It's very strange, you know."

"What is?"

"Look: you and I came down separately, in identical ships, and went through the same nullifying pattern to avoid a trap. And he fired on both of us
almost at once."

"While the true Earthmen," Ledrash said, "did

exactly the things we did, in the very same sort of ship, looking exactly the way we do—and Connelly went with them."

"It doesn't figure," said Drilom worriedly, as they approached the catwalk of his ship. "The three ships went through identical patterns of action. Only the motives were different, not the patterns we produced. He had no way of telling that. And yet he knew the real rescuer from the phonies."

"And yet he knew," the Corilano repeated "How?"

Drilom hoisted himself into the air lock, and Ledrash followed. They stripped off their suits and Drilom took a bottle from a cabinet. He poured drinks for both of them.

"This is why I suggested we came over," he said "We need these."

As he raised the drink to his lips, Drilom heard the excited rapping of Signalman Pribor. "Come on in," he said.

Pribor burst into the room, recoiled at the sight of the burly Corilano sprawled out in a chair, and at Drilom's impatient gesture said, "I've just been checking the tapes on the monitor pickup, sir. And it seems we've recorded the conversation that took place between the third ship and Connelly."

Drilom darted a glance at Ledrash and snapped, "Play it at once!"

Pribor inserted the tape in a playback and waited In a moment, the warning hum appeared, and then voices.

"*Connelly?*" said the voice of the Earthship's commander.

"*That's right,*" they heard Connelly's familiar voice say.

"The name is Danvers. Captain, Merchant Service. We were over at Mokrin on our regular run when we got your message. Right now we're just outside landing range of this trap planet you're on. Want us to come down?"

"Sure do," said Connelly. *"I'd like to get going."*

There was a long pause. Then, finally, Captain Danvers said, *"Couple of details first, Connelly."*

"Shoot."

"This little jaunt is costing us good money. What's the chance of salvaging your ship?"

"The ship's pretty battered," Connelly said.

"Um-m-m. Maybe we'd better call the Patrol, instead, then. Unless you're sure your department can handle the charge on this thing. Our budget can't take much more fuel expenditure."

"Don't worry," Connelly said at once. *"It'll be on 'Deep Info'—You'll come out ahead."*

"Good enough," said the merchantman captain. *"We'll be right down."*

"Glad to hear it," Connelly said. *"And glad to hear the voice of a genuine Earthman again—the kind that knows how to haggle!"*

Drilom pounced on the playback and shut it off angrily. "There's our mistake," he snapped.

"Where?"

"Attitudes. We had the external pattern down fine —but not the way of thinking. That's why he saw through us. We went about negotiations the way soldiers would, brisk, efficient, to the point. A *real* merchantman would bargain. He wouldn't want to get mixed up in this except for a price."

Ledrash nodded bleakly. "What are you going to do?"

"Go back home and file a report," Drilom said in a hollow voice. "We're not ready to start trouble with these Terrans—not ready at all."

"You'll have to learn some of their tricks first," Ledrash suggested sardonically. "*Then* fight them."

Drilom shook his head. "No," he said. "It won't work. By that time, they'll have half a dozen new ones. We'll never beat them that way." He smiled suddenly. "But maybe—some day—we'll be smart enough not to *need* to beat them!"

MISFIT

An earlier story in this book considered the problem of how men will colonize planets where they are physically unfit to cope with other-worldly living conditions. One possible suggestion was that it may be necessary to adapt humans to fit the new worlds.

Take that suggestion a step further, now. In the far future, the worlds of space are populated by adapted Earthmen—and what will become of an unadapted man, our sort of man, when he finds himself on a world where he does not belong?

Foss stood outside the Colony Officer's shack, feeling the tremendous drag of the alien world's gravity tugging at his bones. He tried to keep himself from slouching, but it was hard. On an Earth-type world, his lean body carried 170 pounds; here on Sandoval IX he weighed 306. That sort of drag could do things to a man's insides fast.

A little knot of Adapted Men clustered across the wide street, grinning mockingly at him. Low-slung, broad-beamed, they weren't bothered by the 1.8 grav of Sandoval IX. They had been bred for it; they thrived here. And they were openly enjoying Foss's discomfort.

He knocked again.

Nothing but silence followed. Foss turned away from the door and glared at the watching Adaptos. "Hey—you! Where's Haldane? I want to see him."

After a pause one of them said lazily, "He's in there, Earthman. Just keep knockin'. He'll hear you sooner or later, I guess." He burst into uproarious laughter. Angrily, Foss pounded on the Colony Officer's door with both fists. Lifting his arms was agonizing; it was like raising them through a fog of molasses.

This time the door opened. Colony Officer Haldane appeared, a dark scowl on his wide leathery face. Like all of the Adapted Men on Sandoval IX, Haldane was short—no more than five-four or so— with tremendous girth through the shoulders and hips. His neck was a thick pillar; his thighs must have been immense. His type had been genetically engineered for worlds like Sandoval IX.

"Yes?" he asked, in a deep, rumbling voice. "You new here, Earthman? Don't remember seeing your face around here before."

"I just got here," Foss said. He pointed to the field behind him, where the slim golden column of his two-man ship rested. "Came in from Egri V. I'm looking for someone here. Maybe you can help me."

"That's doubtful. We don't run a lost-and-found for Earthmen here, you know."

Foss felt sweat rolling down his face. Sandoval IX was a hot world as well as a heavy one.

"All I want is some information," he said tightly. "Just information. I'm not asking for any help."

The Adapted Man shrugged easily. "You wouldn't *get* any help, whether you asked for it or not. *Earthman*."

"I said I wouldn't ask," Foss snapped.

"Okay. Come on inside and I'll hear you out, I guess."

There was a woman inside, immensely broad through the hips, big-breasted and flat-faced. To Foss she was repugnant-looking, but Adapted Men had different standards of beauty. She was ideally designed for child-bearing on a heavy-gravity planet, and, judging from the two stocky children playing on the floor, she had already made a good start.

"My wife," Haldane grunted as he led Foss past. "And my children."

Foss smiled mechanically and kept going. They turned into a small, shabby room that was probably the Adapted Man's study. Haldane dropped ponderously into a vast pneumochair and didn't bother to gesture to Foss to sit. Foss sat anyway, in a smaller chair that looked sturdy enough to hold an elephant. He took a sharp breath as the gravity-strain on his heart was suddenly eased.

"What's your name and what do you want here?" Haldane asked.

"My name is Web Foss. I'm an Earthman attached to the Civil Government on Egri V. Two weeks ago my wife . . . ran away. She came here. I want to bring her back."

"How do you know she came here?"

"I know. Don't worry about that. I thought you might be able to help me find her."

"Me?" Haldane asked with jeering mock innocence. "I'm just a mere local official. She might be anywhere at all on Sandoval IX. There are more than twenty colonies on this planet, you know."

"Twenty's not very many," Foss said. "I'll search them all if I have to."

A smile creased Haldane's bleak face. With elaborate lack of courtesy he drew a bottle from his desk, poured himself a drink, and replaced the bottle without offering it to Foss. He sipped slowly, ignoring the Earthman. At length he said, "You know, Mr. Foss, Earthmen aren't very popular on the Adapted Worlds. We don't get very good treatment when we visit the —ah—Normal Worlds. Cheap hotels, second-rate transportation, sly snickers, that sort of thing. 'Look at the Adapted Man—isn't he funny?' You know what I'm talking about?"

"I know. I can't help what ignorant people say or do. They don't understand that the Adapted Men are just as human as anyone else, that without them many planets couldn't have been settled. But—"

"Spare me the sermon," Haldane said. "The fact still remains that we were bred from Earth stock and now get treated as something not quite human. Dammit, we *are* human—and better than damned soft Earthmen who'd be dead in a year on a planet like this!"

"It's not a matter of better or worse," Foss said. "On a heavy-grav planet like this, you're better suited than we are. After all, you've been Adapted for it. On an Earth-norm world, it's the other way around. It's all relative. But my wife—"

"Your wife's here. She's not in this particular colony, but she's on Sandoval IX."

"Where?"

"That's your problem, Mr. Foss."

Foss rose, fighting the gravity every inch of the way. "You know where she is. Why won't you tell me?"

"You're an Earthman," Haldane said quietly. "A superior being. Go find her by yourself."

Without a word, Foss turned and left the Colony Officer's study, made his way through the dark cluttered hallway, past the children and their mother, out into the street. He kept stiffly erect, resisting the temptation to shuffle. That would be simpler, easier on his straining thigh-muscles, but he forced himself to walk springingly as if the gravity was Earth-norm instead of 1.8.

He hadn't expected much better treatment from Haldane. It was rare for an Adapted Man to even the score with an Earthman; usually it was a confused and bewildered Adapto on an Earth-norm world who met only laughter as he struggled to cope with a light grav pull or with an atmosphere so rich in oxygen that it left him half-drunk. Some of the Adaptos were bred to survive in an atmosphere only eight or ten per cent oxygen; when they hit the 20 per cent of an Earth-norm world, they spent their time on a continuous oxygen jag.

The shoe was on the other foot now, and the Adaptos enjoyed the feeling. An Earthman had ventured into an Adapted World, reversing the usual pattern. They weren't going to go out of their way to make things easy for him.

But Carol was here . . . somewhere. He'd find her. Somehow.

He stepped out into the street. The little cluster of Adaptos was still there. Foss crossed the street and headed toward them.

The group broke up as he got there. They melted away in six directions, as if they didn't want anything to do with the lean, hard-faced Earthman.

"Hold it," Foss said. "I want to talk to you."

They kept moving, strolling casually away.

"Hold it!"

He sprang forward and grabbed an Adapto by his open collar. He was almost a foot taller than the man. "I asked you to wait a minute. I want to talk to you."

"Let go of me, Earthman."

"I said I wanted to talk to you."

The Adapto jerked himself out of Foss's grasp and hit him. Foss saw the punch coming, lifting from the hip and heading for his jaw, but there was absolutely nothing he could do about it. His gravity-prisoned body simply would not react as it had been trained to do. He made a single ineffectual attempt at ducking, and then the Adapto's fist cracked into the side of his face.

He hit the ground with astonishing speed. Crack— *boom!* He had gone over like a skulled tenpin. After a moment he felt his jaw tentatively; it still seemed to be in one piece. He realized the Adapto had merely tapped him; an unpulled punch would probably have been fatal.

Foss got up, slowly. The Adapto stood his ground, legs spread belligerently.

"Want another?"

"One's enough," Foss said. His jaw felt numb. "I just wanted to ask you something."

The Adapto sauntered away, down the wide empty street. Foss watched him go. It had been a mistake to attempt the use of force; even the weakest of these colonists could flatten him with a slap, and Foss was no weakling himself.

This wasn't his world, though. It belonged to the Adaptos, and he was a misfit here—a man for whom walking and breathing were constant problems, not second nature. He looked up at the warm blueness of distant Sandoval, and scowled. It was hard to blame the Adaptos.

The offspring of men, they were objects of ridicule when they went among the so-called Normals. They were simply getting even, now.

He balled his fists angrily. *I'll show them*, he thought. *I'll find Carol—without their help*.

He took a couple of steps down the broad street, knowing that if he stood still long enough his muscles would tighten and become useless.

The settlement had a rough, half-finished look. It was only three generations since the Adapted Man program had got under way, and Sandoval IX had been settled less than a decade before by a pilot group tailored to withstand its heat, humidity, atmospheric makeup, and gravity. There were perhaps ten thousand Adaptos here now, in twenty colonies scattered over the planet's face. In time they would spread and populate the entire world. In time.

And a few centuries hence mankind would spread from one end of the galaxy to the other—with even the most forbidding world inhabited by beings that could be called human.

Foss took a heavy step. He was thinking of Carol—of Carol, and of that last quarrel back on Egri V. He hardly remembered how it had started, by now—but he would never forget how it had finished.

Would never forget the bright anger in Carol's eyes as she said, "I've had enough, Web. Of you and of this planet. I'm leaving tonight."

He hadn't believed her. Not until he discovered she'd withdrawn half of their joint savings account and vanished. There weren't any scheduled flights out of Egri V for three weeks, and for a while he had hoped she was still somewhere on the planet.

Until he found out she'd hired a private courier to drop her off at his next port of call. Foss had spoken to the courier.

"You took her to Sandoval IX?"

"That's right."

"But that's an Adapted World. She couldn't last long there!"

The courier shrugged. "She wanted to get off Egri V in a hurry. I told her where I was going, and she paid me. No questions asked. I dropped her off there on my supply route last week."

"Okay," Foss had said. "Thanks."

And then he had borrowed the two-man ship from the Ministry, and gone after her. Carol wasn't the pioneer type; she wouldn't have gone to Sandoval IX if she knew what sort of world it was. It had been a wild, desperate move, and one she no doubt regretted by this time.

He reached a street corner and paused. The blocky figure of an Adapto was coming toward him.

"You the Earthman who's looking for his woman?"

"That's right," Foss said.

"She's in the next settlement. Ten miles west of here, roughly. I saw her last time I made a trip over that way, four-five days ago."

Foss blinked in surprise. "You're telling me the truth, aren't you?"

The Adapto spat. "I wouldn't lie to an Earthman."

"How come you're telling me? I thought none of you meant to help me at all."

The Adapto's deep-set black eyes met his. Slowly he said, "We were just talkin' about it. We figure it's simpler to tell you where she is. That way you won't be mousin' around here botherin' us all the time. Go after your woman, friend. We don't want you here. An Earthman smells up the air. He louses up the crops."

Foss licked his lips tensely holding back his temper. "Okay," he said. "I won't inflict my presence on you any more than I have to. Ten miles west, you say?"

"Yeah."

"I'm on my way," Foss said. He thought for a moment: there wasn't much fuel left in the two-man ship, and a heavy world like Sandoval IX had a high escape velocity. He could get to the next settlement by blasting off, orbiting, and making a new landing ten miles westward, but that would consume a tremendous amount of reaction mass; quite probably he wouldn't be able to make a second blastoff later, after he'd found Carol. He would have to leave the ship here, and find some other way of covering ten miles.

He pulled out his wallet. "I'd like to rent a landcar from you, if you've got one. I won't need it more than an hour or so. Is it worth ten credits to you?"

"No."

Foss cursed silently. "Fifteen?"

"Save your breath, friend. My car isn't for rent at any price."

"A hundred," Foss said desperately.

"I said save your breath."

"If you won't rent me a car, someone else will." He stepped around the Adapto and headed down the street, moving as fast as was possible.

"You can save your energy too," the Adapto called after him. "You'll need it for the hike."

"Huh?"

He turned. The Adapto was smiling scornfully at him. "Nobody's going to rent you a car, friend. Fuel's too precious here to waste on you. It's only ten miles. Let's see you walk it, Earthman."

Only ten miles. Let's see you walk it.

Foss heard the words over and over again. He entered a bar further down the street. Ten or twelve Adaptos were there, drinking. They looked up coldly as he came through the photon-barrier.

"We don't serve Earthmen here," the bartender said. "This is a restricted bar. Locals only."

Foss glowered at him. "I didn't come in here to drink." He looked around. "I want to rent a land-car," he said loudly. "My wife's in the next settlement. I want to go get her. Who'll rent me his car for an hour?"

No response. Foss drew a hundred-credit bill from his wallet. "I'll put a hundred credits on the line for somebody's car. Any takers?"

The bartender said, "This is a drinkin' place,

Earthman, not a public square. You want to transact business, transact it outside."

Foss ignored that. "Well? A hundred credits?"

Someone at the bar chuckled. "Put your money away, Earthman. We're not goin' to rent you anything. It's only ten miles. Start walking."

Foss was silent a moment. *Only ten miles.* For an Adapto, that was an afternoon's invigorating hike. For an Earthman, it meant a day or more of weary leg-dragging. They were daring him to do it. They wanted to see him die trying.

Well, he wouldn't give them the satisfaction.

"Okay," he said softly. "I'm going to walk there, and I'm going to walk back. And tomorrow I'll be back here to show you that an Earthman can do it."

They turned away. No one was looking at him.

"I'll be back," Foss said.

He left the bar and headed across the field toward his ship. His muscles ached; his heart was throbbing wearily from the exertion needed to pump almost twice as hard. Earth-norm people weren't meant for Sandoval IX. A few weeks or maybe a month or two in this kind of grave and the tired heart would give out completely.

His throat was dry and his eyes were tearing by the time he reached the cabin of the ship. He assembled a lightweight survival kit—compass, drinkflask, food tabs, saline drops, other essentials. He strapped the pack to his back. It was a five-pound kit, the sort of burden a man would hardly notice ordinarily. Here it weighed nine pounds, and Foss knew it would seem a lot heavier than that before he was through walking.

He stopped for a moment to rest in the acceleration cradle. Then, relentlessly, he dragged himself to his feet and clambered down out of the ship, taking every step of the catwalk carefully instead of jumping as he usually did. A jump here might snap his ankles.

The afternoon sun was high overhead. *Ten miles*, he thought. How long would it take to walk ten miles? It was 1300 now; if he covered only two miles an hour, he'd be there before nightfall.

A watching group of Adaptos called something to him as he started out. He couldn't hear what it was, but he was willing to bet it wasn't any sort of encouragement.

The land spread out broad and flat before him as he walked; it was good farm-land, rolling and brown, sun-warmed, fertile. Far off in the distance rugged steep hills, not quite steep enough to be mountains, formed a backdrop. The air was warm. A brown dirt road wound through the farmland, leading on to the next settlement, where Carol was.

It was lovely country. It was too good a world to allow it to go to waste, which was why men had been Adapted to live on it. But Foss did not belong in the landscape scene, and he knew it.

He pulled himself along. Muscles designed to support a man of 170 pounds groaned under the burden of 306; ligaments complained. He felt mountainous, gross, impossibly heavy and impossibly weak. Torrents of sweat drenched his body.

After a while he stopped and cut a walking-stick from a tree at the side of the road. Pulling the living limbs from the tree required fearful effort; he was gasping and wheezing by the time he had done it. He moved on, shoving himself forward with jabs of the stick.

He had covered two and a half miles by the end of the first hour. That was little better than schedule, but the effort left him limp. He didn't do quite so well during the second hour; the pedometer he was carrying showed that he was now only four miles out, plus two hundred yards. His pace was slackening.

Six miles to go—

He shambled on mechanically, not worrying now about his posture, not worrying about anything but the sheer one-foot-after-another plodding that would bring him to his goal.

Every step will bring me nearer, he thought. He made a little chant of it: *EVry STEP will BRING me NEARer,* taking a step forward on each accented syllable. *EVry STEP will BRING me NEARer,* over and over, until it began to drag out . . . *EVry . . . STEP will . . . BRING me . . . NEARer,* with longer and longer intervals between the beat.

Finally he sank into a little heap on the side of the road and rested. His breath came short. His heart thudded so hard that he shook with each pulsation. Then he thought of the mocking Adaptos waiting somewhere behind him—possibly trailing him, waiting for the moment he dropped of exhaustion. He levered up off his walking stick and kept going.

What's 1.8 grav? he asked himself. *Hell, I stand up to five and six grav all the time in a spaceship.*

Yeah. For ten seconds at a time, he answered himself.

He checked his watch, then the pedometer. The digits swam. He was now three and a half hours out of the colony, and had covered a little better than five miles. He was falling further and further behind schedule.

EVry . . . STEP will . . . BRING me . . . NEARer. . . .

He dragged his left leg forward, planted it on the ground, swung the right one up past it, then the left, the right. . . .

He lost track of the time, of the distance, of everything. He looked at the dial every now and then, but it made no sense. From time to time, when he remembered about it, he took a tablet from his kit and swallowed it. That gave him the energy to go on a little further, and yet a little further.

The sky darkened as the sun dropped out of sight. The warmth of the day trickled off into space. Foss kept moving. *Only ten miles. Let's see you walk it.*

Houses came into sight. Streets. People.

No, not people. Adaptos, short, squat, grotesque. Foss found himself looking down at a leathery brown face. He leaned forward on the walking-stick, trying to catch his breath.

"I'm Web Foss," he said. "I'm looking for an Earthwoman. Mrs. Carol Foss. Is she here?"

For one wild dizzy moment he thought the Adapto might sneer and tell him that he'd simply traveled in a wide circle, that he was back in the same settlement from which he'd started out so long ago.

The Adapto nodded gravely. "The Earthwoman is here, with us. I'll take you to see her."

"You're not joking, now. She's really here?"

"Of course," the Adapto said impatiently. Foss noticed him staring strangely at him. "Where's your ship?" he asked.

"Ten miles the other way. I walked here."

"You—*walked?*" the Adapto said.

Foss nodded. "Take me to my wife, will you?" The fatigue of the trip seemed to wash away. For the first time in hours, he stood up straight.

They had put Carol in a dark back room of one of the settlement houses. As Foss entered, he saw her lying asleep on a crude pallet. The room was windowless; the air was stale and offensive. Three empty bottles of liquor lay on their sides near the bed: two gin, one some local brew. The room looked dismal.

He approached the bed and looked at his wife.

The gravitational pull did strange things to her face; it tightened the jaw muscles, made the lips rubbery and down-drooping, imparted an idiot sag to the eyelids. She looked as if she had lost twenty pounds; her face was harshly angular and almost skull-like.

"My God," he said out loud. "Is that what a human being looks like after two weeks here?"

She stirred. Foss turned and saw two Adaptos standing curiously behind him.

"Get out of here," he said. "Leave us alone."

"Web," she murmured. *"Web. . . ."*

She hadn't opened her eyes yet.

Foss leaned close over her and with trembling fingers touched her cheek. The skin was dry and flaky. "Wake up, Carol. Wake up."

She opened her eyes hesitantly—then, seeing him, sat half-upright in bed, sinking back again after a moment. "Web," she said.

"I got here this morning. The courier told me where you had been dropped off, and I figured I'd better come get you. This isn't the sort of world you would be likely to enjoy on a permanent basis."

She sat up again, with a resolute effort. "It's been hell. As soon as I felt the grav I knew I couldn't stay here . . . but that courier was gone, and there was no way I could get in touch. And the Adaptos weren't very helpful."

"At least they gave you a place to stay. I didn't even rate that."

"It was like a nightmare—trying to walk against that gravity." She shuddered. "I couldn't go more than ten or twenty steps without falling down. And the Adaptos—they just stood around and laughed, for the first couple of hours. Then I collapsed, and after that they were a little more decent. I had a little money; they brought me liquor, and I drank . . . it was the only way I could . . . could stop feeling the drag this place has!"

Foss held her wrist. It was almost cold.

"I guess I've been here a week or two," she went on. "I sleep most of the time, they feed me, a little. They treat me the way they would some animal that was sick. Web?"

"Eh?"

"Web, can we go home? Both of us?"

"That's why I came here, Carol."

She shook her head. "I was an idiot . . . running away like that, coming here. But I got my reward, I guess."

"We'll leave tomorrow," he said. "I have a ship." *Ten miles away*, he added silently.

She was staring at him. "Look at yourself in the mirror," she said suddenly. "Over there."

Foss rose, crossed the room, looked at his image. Even in the dim light, the sight rocked him. The face was that of a skeleton—a stubble-bearded skeleton with staring eyes, pale, gaunt cheeks, bloodless lips. That ten-mile trip had left its mark. He looked like his own ghost.

He managed to chuckle. "Pretty awful, isn't it? You're no better. But we can fatten up again when we're back on Egri V."

"Come here. Sit down next to me."

He cautiously lowered himself to the edge of the bed. He wriggled out of his kit-pack and stretched out next to her, feeling sick with fatigue. Seconds later, he was asleep.

Only ten miles. Let's see you walk it.

Ten miles there, ten miles back. And for the second ten-mile hitch he not only had to drag his own feet along, he had to support Carol.

The sun was blazingly warm when they set out, and grew warmer through the day. They talked incessantly, desperately, turning themselves into automata that marched on, on, without paying attention to the passing of the hours or the extent of road still ahead.

"We're lucky," Foss said after a while. "I put the ship down any old place. I could have landed it twenty miles away. Or two hundred. It's only ten."

"*Only* ten," Carol said.

"Only ten."

They rested frequently. Foss found himself growing oddly stronger as the day went on, as if his body were adjusting—*adapting*—itself to the increased pull of gravity, getting used to the drag exerted on it. He knew that was just illusion, of course; still, it was less of an effort than it had been on the way out.

The sun blazed down. Somewhere ahead was the colony, and in the colony was Foss's ship.

Somewhere.

It was still daytime when they got there.

A welcoming committee of Adapted Men stood by the road as they came by. "Walk straight," Foss whispered. "Don't slouch. Pretend you were just out for an afternoon's stroll, nothing more."

"I'll try. It's hard, though."

"You have to do it. Just for a few minutes—until we reach the ship."

He recognized a few faces. There was Colony Officer Haldane and his wife, and there the man who had knocked him down, and there some of the other jeerers. They were staring wordlessly at him.

"I came back," Foss said, when he was within speaking distance. "And I brought my wife."

"So I see," Haldane said coldly.

"I just thought I'd let you know I made it. I didn't want it to worry you."

"We weren't worried," Haldane said. "We didn't care."

But it was a lie, Foss knew. He could tell by the way their dark faces were scowling and their eyes glared that they *did* care.

They had sent the misfit out into the desert to die, but he had come back alive. He had beaten them. One single Earthman.

"Excuse me," Foss said. "You're in my way. I want to get back to my ship."

But three of the Adaptos stood blocking the road, staring at him. He felt Carol's hand grip his arm more tightly. *No more trouble now*, he prayed.

Not now.

"Get out of my way," Foss said sharply. "Let me get past."

There was a moment of silence. Then Haldane said, "Get out of his way."

Sullenly, the three Adaptos gave way. Foss and Carol went past, on their way to the ship. He felt very tired, but he knew now there wouldn't be any further trouble.

He walked on about twenty paces. Then he stopped and looked back. They were all staring after him.

"Thanks for everything," he said, smiling. "All the kind help. But I managed without you, didn't I?"

His eyes met Haldane's—and Haldane looked away. That was what Foss had been waiting for. An Earthman had met an Adapto on the Adapto's home grounds, and the Earthman had won. Foss could see that in Haldane's eyes.

He boosted Carol up into the ship, and followed her in. Just before he slammed the hatch shut, he peered out at the group of Adaptos outside. They were staring at him incredulously, as if they couldn't believe he had actually returned alive.

He grinned at them. The next time an Earthman came here, they'd have a little more respect for him.

"So long," he yelled. Then he slammed the hatch, dogged it shut, and went inside to begin setting up the homeward orbit.

Robert Silverberg—Bob, to his science fiction fans around the world—lives in New York City with his equally talented, and beautiful, wife (an electronics engineer) and a currently undetermined number of cats. All share a large old house.

His science fiction writing includes over twenty books, among them *Revolt on Alpha C, Lost Race of Mars, Starman's Quest, Collision Course,* as well as over a thousand short stories and novelettes.

Ace Science Fiction
Purchase Order

NAME _____

STREET _____

CITY OR TOWN_____

STATE & ZIP _____

Please send me the following:

COVER PRICE

TITLE _____

AUTHOR _____ _____

TITLE _____

AUTHOR _____ _____

TITLE _____

AUTHOR _____ _____

TITLE _____

AUTHOR _____ _____

TITLE _____

AUTHOR _____ _____

POSTAGE & HANDLING _____

TOTAL _____

Please enclose a check or money order made out to BOOK MAILING SERVICE for the total of the cover prices of the books ordered plus 50¢ per book for postage and handling. (Maximum $1.50) No postage and handling required if order is accompanied by <u>DESTINIES</u> subscription.

The Book Mailing Service policy is to fill an order for any title currently in stock upon receipt. However, delivery is usually from one to four weeks since postal transit time must be taken into account. Payments for titles not in stock will be promptly refunded.